THE SECRET OF
DRULEA COTTAGE

BETWIXT THE SEA AND SHORE
BOOK 1

THE SECRET OF DRULEA COTTAGE

BETWIXT THE SEA AND SHORE BOOK 1

CLAIRE KOHLER

Cover by MoorBooks Design

This book is a work of fiction. Names, characters, places, and incidents are either the product of the author's imagination or are used fictitiously.

ISBN: 979-8-9855674-0-3

Second Edition: 2022

To Mom:
Without your encouragement,
this book would not exist.

Thank you for believing in my dreams enough that I could
believe in them, too.

Acknowledgments

My first thank you goes to the Lord for aligning all the necessary elements to make this desire of my heart become a reality. His generosity and kindness are beyond my comprehension.

I also want to express my deep gratitude to the people who came alongside me at various points in this creative journey. My family's, and especially my husband's, support as I went through the arduous process of brainstorming, researching, writing, editing, and promoting *The Secret of Drulea Cottage* is so appreciated.

My precious launch team also deserves great praise for taking the time to read through the novel and share it with others. Thank you to Barb Besecker, Becky Briggs, Lydia Brown, Candace Carney, Patsy Case, Sydney Castro, Lois Corrigan, Isabella Deal, Missy Durham, Slavka Edelmayer, Leslie Fitzpatrick, Heather Gibbs, Elizabeth Haber, Jessica Hernandez, Kristi Horton, Brooke Hickman, Heather Isales, Amanda Keller, Connie Keller, Tina Kohler, Renee Lewis, Laura Marlowe, Sherry Marlowe, Pat Martin, Rachael Martin, Felipe Marulanda, Ashleigh Mays, Becca Miller, Jordan Moore, Kim Moore, Carmen Post, Adrianne Rathmell, Abby Rex, Sara Slagle, Aimee St. Amand, Karen Swan, Kate Tenke, Rachel West, and Haley Wright.

Prologue

A dark-haired woman hesitated at the bedside. Her mother lay so still, so peaceful. If not for her ragged breathing, she would almost look like she was already gone.

Slowly, the older woman's eyelids fluttered open to reveal strange amber eyes, identical to the ones now staring back at her.

"Come closer, peedie[1] freck.[2] Just na too close."

The younger woman's breath hitched at the term of endearment. It had been so long since her mother had called her that, so long since she had been a small child content to sit in her mother's arms.

She did as she was bidden, sitting in the chair nearest Bethany Fairborn's frail form. Now that Briony was closer, though, the beads of sweat on her mother's forehead stood out more prominently.

Bethany coughed into her hand several times, making her daughter's heart clench.

"I shall always love you, my dear bairn.[3] Remember that, no matter what happens. And you must promise me something before I go," Bethany whispered with all the strength she could muster.

"Anything, Mum," the young woman answered.

---

[1] Small.
[2] A child or animal that wants attention.
[3] A child.

"You must stay away from the water."

Briony looked down at the floor, holding back tears as she tried to get a handle on herself. She couldn't fathom why this was her mother's dying wish, why this was so important.

Is her fear o' the sea that strong? How can she hate it so much?

Briony felt the enigmatic pull she always did when she thought of the ocean. It called to her in a way she could neither explain nor understand. She had no reason to desire it as she did, for the sea had stolen her father from them years ago. At least, that was what her mother told her since Briony had no memory of the man.

She glanced out the window of the small cottage, wishing she could run to the waves at that very moment and escape the expectation lurking in her mother's eyes. No matter how Briony replied, she knew she would cause misery; the only question was who would have to bear it.

She turned back to her mother, ignoring the lump in her throat as she said, "I promise."

At hearing those words, Bethany gave Briony an earnest smile that lit up the room much more than the candles around them. Then, with a small sigh, the older woman closed her eyes and relinquished her spirit.

Briony almost felt it depart, ascending from her mother's physical form before slipping away.

And it was at that precise moment that a series of bloodcurdling howls rang through the air. The sounds rose from just beyond Everton's shores, filling the entire village with dread. The only person who didn't notice them was the young woman herself, for the cries melded with her own moans of anguish as perfectly as if they had all come from the same throat.

A Night of Reluctant Guests

Orkney Islands,[4] 1759

Briony Fairborn gaped at the ship coming up near the shore below her cottage. Her home lay on a rocky cliff overlooking the vast blue ocean. Drulea Cottage was well known to passersby, for it stood alone against the horizon as a haunting silhouette whenever someone came to the village of Everton.

On this particular evening, Briony had been sweeping some dirt from her kitchen floor when the unexpected ship caught her eye. At first glance, she could have easily mistaken it for one of the ships Everton often traded with during the warm months. The village was firmly established as a seller of furs and lumber because of the abundant forest that bordered it. It was one of the only places in Orkney that possessed several trees.

But what would a ship be doing coming in at this hour?

The village's usual trade partners knew better than to come in this late. This ship appeared to be struggling to reach the port, which was understandable with the strong winds that usually met sailors as they arrived. Although Everton

---

[4] An archipelago in the Northern Isles of Scotland.

welcomed outside trade, strangers often felt a sense of foreboding when their ships came close, almost as if nature herself was urging them to stay away.

Briony watched the ship successfully dock. Since most of the villagers were probably already in bed, she wondered if anyone else had noticed the new arrival. The passengers and crew might need a guide once they departed their vessel. Briony set down her broom and checked her reflection to make sure she was presentable.

Staring back at her was a lovely young woman with thick black hair and amber, almost yellow, eyes. Her cheekbones were prominent, and her skin was clear and pale. Her dear friend, Adaira, often told her she was quite pretty, but Briony expected Adaira was only trying to make her feel better for never getting any suitors.

Once she was ready, Briony marched down the path to the next closest home; it belonged to Mister and Mistress[5] McGuff. They wouldn't appreciate being called upon without an invitation, especially by her, but Mr. McGuff was one of the village leaders and would want to know about the strangers' arrival.

Briony slowly raised her fist to the dark wooden door and knocked. After a moment, the door opened, and there stood five-year-old Fergus, his thumb in his mouth. He smiled when he saw her and held out his arms for a hug.

Picking the boy up happily, Briony said, "Hello, Fergus. How are you this evening?"

His little brown eyes scrunched up as if he was about to cry. "My mum's mad at me, Mistress Briony. She says I should na have let Mr. Gully into sissy's bed."

"You put Mr. Gully in Hannah's bed?" Briony echoed, trying to keep the laugh out of her voice.

Fergus nodded, his lower lip quivering. "He looked cold, so I thought he would like her blanket and koad."[6]

"And you thought Hannah would want a frog in her bed?"

"Why na? Mr. Gully's na just any frog! He's—" Fergus

---

[5] A woman of high social standing, regardless of marital status. (*Miss* was not used for adult women unless referring to a prostitute.)
[6] Pillow.

2

broke off when he spotted his mother approaching the doorway.

Briony took a stabilizing breath at the sight of her. As always, Penelope McGuff looked so put together that it was almost impossible to tell that she had just woken up: brown hair back in a smooth bun, dress not ruffled in the slightest—the very picture of a proper Orcadian wife. The only thing that contradicted her neat appearance was the sleep lingering in her eyes.

But Penelope's haze of slumber departed the instant her eyes latched onto the young woman holding her son. "Briony, put him down this instant. And Fergus Matthew! You know yer supposed to be in yer room right now."

Briony knew better than to argue and put him down as quickly as she could without injuring the boy. As for Fergus, he knew the safest place for him was far from his mother, so he did as he was told without even pausing to say farewell.

"Briony Fairborn, you better have a good reason fer coming here so late," Penelope McGuff spat.

Briony scoffed. "O' course I do. Do you think I would listen to yer venom otherwise?"

Penelope's eyes flashed. "I ought to have you thrown out o' town, you—"

"And lose the best midwife in all Orkney?"

Penelope was red-faced with anger. "Bah! The only reason yer still around is because yer mother saved my Hannah's life. Got nothing to do with *yer* skills."

Briony knew Mrs. McGuff was lying—Briony came from a line of the finest midwives Scotland had ever had. In all the decades the Fairborns had been in Everton, they had rarely lost a babe or mother. Mrs. McGuff would be a fool to get rid of Briony, no matter what her personal feelings were.

Rather than continue their never-ending argument, though, Briony switched subjects. "I thought yer husband would like to know that a ship just came into port."

Penelope raised her thin eyebrows, deepening the wrinkles on her forehead. The woman was about ten years Briony's senior, though she acted like the age difference was much greater. "A ship coming in now? That's mighty peculiar. Aye,

Donal must know about this. Have you told anyone else, lass?"

"Nay, you were the first."

"Then dinna just stand around waiting fer some grand reward fer having eyes that work. Get to Adaira Stubbins and tell her so that the inn can be ready fer guests."

As soon as she'd said that, Mistress McGuff stepped back and slammed the door in Briony's face.

The young woman huffed and turned from the door. *A wee bit o' gratitude would have been nice.*

Everton Inn was about half a mile from the McGuffs' cottage, but Briony was used to the walk, so it wasn't long before she reached her destination. A drizzle fell upon her as she did, darkening her blue dress until it was almost black.

Briony suspected Adaira was still awake, so she checked the kitchen and found her taking a fresh pie from the oven. Briony wasn't surprised to find her there; though Adaira ran everything at the inn for her aging father, her favorite place was undoubtedly the kitchen. The whole village appreciated her dedication to baking, and no one could rival her delicious pastries.

"Hello, Adaira!"

Adaira jumped and almost dropped her latest masterpiece. She managed to catch her balance just in time and set the pie down to cool. She spun around to the cause of the trouble, her eyes softening at the sight of Briony.

"Briony, you gave me such a fright! What are you doing here at this time o' night?" she asked as she sat down on a stool.

"I'm sorry to trouble you, but there are newcomers at the dock, and I thought I'd give you some time to prepare lodging fer them."

Adaira frowned, bouncing up from her seat to grab towels from the linen closet. "Newcomers? How many?"

"I only saw the ship from my cottage, so I could na tell you," Briony replied, following her friend out of the kitchen.

"There better na be very many. Otherwise, I won' be able to accommodate them all."

"Would you like some help?"

"Aye, please," Adaira said as she handed Briony towels. "I

4

may need quite a bit if there are a lot o' newcomers. Especially if my current guests remain much longer. Mr. Burgess and his son, William, have been here fer twelve days, and they seem to like it so much that I would na be surprised if they decide to build themselves a house."

"Do you truly think so? William would certainly like that, given how attached he is to you."

Adaira shrugged noncommittally and looked away. The two of them walked to the first open guest room, and Adaira placed two towels on the bed.

The front door wrenched open and slammed against the wall. "Adaira," a man called.

The friends rushed to the foyer, dumping the rest of the towels on the bed as they left.

Gareth Peterson, the son of the vicar, stood at the entrance, his face frantic. His messy brown hair was soaked, and he seemed to barely have enough strength to stand. "Adaira, do you have any rooms?"

"Aye, Gareth, what is it?"

Gareth panted a few times and leaned against the door to support himself, carelessly dripping water onto the floor. "There are some strangers who just came in. One o' them is hurt! Doctor Sherwin is with him, but they have to move him inside. I had to see if you had anywhere to put him up."

"How many—" Adaira started to ask, but Gareth was already pushing himself off from the door and scrambling back outside.

Briony and Adaira hurried after him and peered out the doorway. About a quarter of a mile down the path, a man was being carried on a stretcher by Donal McGuff, Matthew Levins, and Tam McLaren. Dr. Ewan Sherwin walked nearby, keeping a close eye on the men as they moved. They came up the hill slowly, their feet digging into the saturated earth.

When they got closer, Briony examined the injured man. His blond hair was like wet straw, and his beard was neatly trimmed. Coupled with what looked to be high-quality clothing and an impressive stature, Briony surmised he would be very good-looking if his face weren't contorted in pain.

The man grunted as the villagers stumbled on the path,

turning his head in her direction. Briony drew back so that he wouldn't catch her staring, but the man's eyes never opened for the entire trip up the hill.

Briony couldn't see any blood, but he was missing his right shoe, and his exposed foot and ankle were severely swollen. *How could that have happened?*

Briony Fairborn, why would you care more about the cause o' the man's circumstances than about his well-being? Briony almost smiled at the thought of her mother's scolding voice. Bethany had always urged her daughter to be kind above all else, despite Briony's curious nature. With a twinge of guilt, Briony sent up a prayer for the man's health and watched as her drenched neighbors carried him inside.

Only after that did Briony become aware of the other two foreigners coming up the path behind them. One was a beautiful young woman in an expensive-looking dress, and the other was a heavily built, bearded man in uniform. The woman looked to be near tears, or perhaps she was already crying, but Briony couldn't be certain in such heavy rain. Her blond hair was done up in an intricate braid, the likes of which Briony had never seen before.

The man had a grim expression, and his eyes kept shifting warily among the villagers. Something about him sent a shiver down Briony's spine, though she had no idea why.

"Briony, I need that help you offered," called Adaira, who had gone into the hallway while Briony was staring.

"Aye, what would you have me do?"

Adaira zoomed back to the linen closet and jerked it open. She thrust some blankets into Briony's arms. "Put fresh blankets in all the rooms, starting with the injured man's."

Without another word, Adaira scurried off to the kitchen. Briony did as her friend wanted, shuffling into the nearest bedroom even though it was already bursting with people.

"Set him down gently now, men. We dinna want to worsen his condition," Dr. Sherwin urged.

They slowly put the man on the bed and moved back.

"Good," the doctor said. "Now, you must step out and let me do my job. I can' work with all o' you in here."

The two foreigners nodded, politely stepped around

6

Briony, and walked out in the direction of the sitting room.

Matthew Levins, on the other hand, didn't possess such manners.

"Get out o' the way, Fairborn wench! Did you na hear the doctor?" he growled. Donal McGuff and Tam McLaren stood behind him, not as vicious with their gazes but unable to leave with Matthew blocking them.

"I have blankets from Mistress Stubbins. Do you need them, Dr. Sherwin?" she asked, not budging from her place.

Dr. Sherwin looked up, only then noticing her presence. At first, he scowled, but then his countenance became pensive. "Actually, I may need you, Briony Fairborn."

"Dr. Sherwin, you can' seriously want help from her." Matthew looked at the doctor as though he was insane.

But Dr. Sherwin sent him a condescending glare. "You mean the *only* person in the whole village with a wee bit o' medical knowledge besides myself? Nay, why would I possibly want her help? I may na like the woman, but she's my only option, so unless you want to tell that distraught lass outside that this man died because we were busy arguing, I suggest you get out."

Matthew reddened and clamped his mouth shut. He and the other men bustled out, all giving Briony dirty looks, which she easily returned.

"Briony Fairborn, if yer quite done glowering at everyone, this man needs our help." The doctor gestured for her to join him at the man's bedside.

Briony turned sheepish and scurried over. "What do you need me to do?"

"The man's tibia is fractured at the ankle, so the first thing we need to do is . . ."

***

Once the man's immediate needs were met, Dr. Sherwin told Briony to bring the people waiting outside into the room.

When Briony exited, though, she found only the young blond woman; the bearded man from earlier was nowhere to be seen. Briony felt a touch of compassion at the tears she saw shining on the woman's face.

This injured fellow must be very important to her. The two of them looked close in age, so Briony's first guess was that they must be married. She didn't see a ring on the woman's hand, but perhaps they didn't wear them in the land these strangers were from.

"Mistress, you can see him now," Briony stated.

The woman started at the midwife's arrival before wiping her eyes with a handkerchief. "Is he well?"

"He's resting right now. Dr. Sherwin is waiting to talk to you," Briony said as she took the young woman down the corridor.

When they arrived at the man's room, the doctor rose from his seat. "Mistress Mendes, I set the bone in place and gave him some medicine fer the pain. He'll be all right, but healing will be slow. 'Twill be about six weeks before he recovers. I'd like fer you to remain here until then."

The woman's mouth twisted slightly before she nodded. "Thank you, Doctor. My brother and I are indebted to you. And to you as well, Mistress . . .?" She turned to the midwife.

Brother? Now that Briony thought about it, the two did have similar features.

"Fairborn, but you dinna have to thank her," Dr. Sherwin butted in.

Briony's mouth dropped open in disbelief. *I did almost as much as the doctor did, and now he's trying to take all the credit!*

But before she could call him out, Mistress Mendes placed a hand on Dr. Sherwin's arm and said, "I apologize for our eventful arrival. Everyone has been so helpful to us. I only hope we can repay that kindness during our time here."

The doctor blushed, and Briony noted how his eyes lingered on the woman's hand. "There's no need. The village o' Everton welcomes you and will continue to fer as long as you remain. Fer now, we'll leave you to sit with him. If you'd like, I can let yer other companion know o' yer brother's status."

Mistress Mendes batted her eyes and nodded before pulling her hand away. "Please do. Captain Costa had to go down to the ship to see about repairs; he'll be most relieved to hear the good news."

"Then I'll make sure he hears it. Good night, mistress."
Dr. Sherwin stepped back as the beautiful woman sank into the
chair nearest her brother's bed.

"Good night," she sighed, turning to look at her brother's
sleeping form.

The doctor backed up toward the doorway and tried to
slip out, but as he did so, he suddenly tripped over himself.

Briony snorted at the man's awkwardness, but neither he
nor Mistress Mendes paid her any mind. *I might as well na even be
here.*

With a roll of her eyes, Briony followed the doctor out, not
bothering to bid Mistress Mendes good night.

"What was that back there?" Briony asked once she'd shut
the door. "I did na think you were capable o' being nervous
around any—Hey!"

Dr. Sherwin was already walking away as if she hadn't
spoken at all.

"O' all the rude, arrogant—"

"You best be getting to Captain Costa," he called without
turning. "'Tis time fer me to be heading on to bed."

Briony marched forward. "But, Dr. Sherwin, you—"

"Oh, pardon me!" exclaimed William as he opened his
bedroom door and almost collided with the midwife. Briony
looked down at the tired eight-year-old standing there in his
nightclothes.

"'Tis quite all right, William. I better be going." She looked
back up and saw that Dr. Sherwin was gone.

"Is everything fine out here, Mistress Fairborn? I heard a
lot o' noise."

"We had some late visitors come in, but 'tis nothing to
worry about. You can rest easy." She smiled at the brown-
haired boy, thinking how sad it was that he was more
courteous than most of the men in town.

"Have a good evening, then, Mistress Fairborn."

"And you too, William."

Briony remained in the hallway for a few moments after
William had gone back inside. She had half a mind not to go
see this Captain Costa. She was tired, and in that brief moment
when she'd seen the captain, his dour expression had unnerved

9

her quite a bit.

But then she thought of Mistress Mendes and how much she cared about her brother. *If Captain Costa cares about Mr. Mendes half as much as that, 'twould be unkind o' me to just turn in fer the night without talking to him.*

With a sigh, Briony made her way back to the sitting room at the front of the inn. She peered out a window and was glad to see that the rain had abated, though the overcast sky told her it could start up again at any moment. Only then did Briony think to check the time.

She looked back at the clock on the mantel to see it was already a quarter past ten. With Midsummer's Eve fast approaching, it was almost Simmer Dim, a time in summer when the sun only went down enough to create a sort of twilight until it rose again at about four in the morning.

Briony tugged open the front door of the inn and made her way down the hill. She tried to avoid the wet areas on the path, but mud still spattered her dress and shoes as she walked. And though the rain had ceased, a fierce wind continued to blow, almost stealing her yellow headscarf several times. A few of her ebony locks escaped their binds and blew about like angry snakes, which lent a haunting look to her overall visage.

She was careful to keep her features as blank as possible when she arrived at the ship, a task she did so well that no one would have been able to tell she was anxious.

No one except me, that is.

"Hello? Captain Costa?"

Briony didn't hear an answer, so she took a step onto the ship. She noticed the words *São Nicolau* on the side and assumed that must be its name. It seemed sturdy under her feet, but Briony felt uncomfortable nonetheless. The vessel looked like it had taken quite a beating—one of the masts had completely collapsed and now lay in pieces, the sides of the hull had several holes in them, some of the deck's floorboards were missing, and many of the other floorboards were damaged. Briony knew little about ship repair, but she could tell this would take many days to fix.

"Hello?" There was still no answer, so she made her way over to the doors leading below deck.

Suddenly, a startled shout in a foreign tongue came from right behind her. Briony jumped, staunching a scream of surprise. She spun around and found a young sailor staring at her. He had brown hair and hazel eyes with a curious glint in them.

"Oh! I did na see you there. I'm looking fer Captain Costa. Have you seen him?"

"Want Costa?"

"Aye, Costa."

He replied in that same foreign language again, and her eyes widened in confusion. He waited for her to respond, but when she didn't, he marched to the door below the ship's wheel and opened it.

Briony nodded her thanks, hoping the captain would be able to understand Scots English. She wandered over and peeked inside, instantly spotting the burly man from earlier leaning over a table covered in maps.

"Captain Costa?" Briony asked.

"Yes, senhorita?[7] What do you need?" he said gruffly, turning to her as though greatly reluctant to stop his current task.

"I came to tell you that Mr. Mendes is going to be all right. He's sleeping right now and will need some time to recover before you leave—"

"How much time?" he cut in. He took a step around the table toward her, making Briony even more intimidated.

"Six weeks."

Captain Costa grumbled something Briony didn't understand but that she suspected was a curse. He returned to his previous position and looked away from her.

"Where do you hail from?" she asked.

"Portugal," he said, keeping his eyes on his maps.

"Were you intending to sail here?"

"Senhorita, I'm very busy, and you're hindering my work. Unless you have something else *worth* mentioning, please leave."

Briony was very put off by the man's unfriendliness, so she

---

[7] Portuguese title for an unmarried woman.

simply said, "Nay, that was all," and left for Drulea Cottage.

How rude! And I was trying to be kind. I did na have to come down here. . . . I hope Mr. Mendes is na like the captain. If he is, then he can' heal quickly enough.

Cold as the Sea

"Nay, Mum, come back!" Briony shrieked as she awoke in a sweat. She jerked about in panic, wondering where her mother was.

But then the cold memory of Bethany's death pierced her mind, and she realized she had only been dreaming.

Briony got out of bed slowly, still reeling from the vividness of the dream: She was standing on the beach, staring up at Drulea Cottage high on the cliff. Suddenly, her mother's voice cried out, and Briony turned to see Bethany Fairborn a ways off in the sea, struggling to stay afloat. Briony went out to her, trying to reach her before she went under. But then an immense wave broke over Bethany, and she was gone.

Briony had been plagued by nightmares like these since Bethany's death almost a year before. Her mother had died from influenza, but strangely enough, Briony's dreams tended to center around water.

As she took a few deep breaths to steady herself, Briony's nostrils filled with the flowery aromas from outside. Normally, she could dismiss the painful nightmares after a few moments, but not so on this particular morning. An uneasy knot twisted within her stomach, refusing to uncoil even as she went about her normal routine. Briony tried to ignore it as she got ready for the day, but ignoring it only seemed to make it worse.

Perhaps 'tis because the anniversary o' her death is so close. I just need to think about something else. I suppose I'll go down and ask Adaira how that Mr. Mendes is doing.

13

Briony put on a pink dress and brown headscarf and headed out. As she meandered toward the inn, she could hear the sea echoing in her ears. Many emotions billowed up within her, and try as she might, the night she wanted to forget, the night her mother had passed, came to the forefront of her mind.

It had happened just before Johnsmas, the day when all of Everton reveled in the start of summer. In the past, this had been a time of celebration and mirth, but death's cold fingers had made that impossible for the Fairborn family that year. Briony had longed to embrace her ailing mother, or even just hold her hand, but that could have spread the illness, so she'd had to keep her distance. All she could do was watch as the woman grew weaker and weaker until she could barely lift her head from her pillow.

But even at the end, Bethany Fairborn had composed herself with a dignity and strength of character that few could attain. If only it hadn't been to make Briony promise something she knew she would regret.

"You must stay away from the water. . . ."

Briony didn't recall the strange sounds or the great storm her neighbors claimed there had been that night, but those words remained crystal clear. The urgency in her mother's voice as she'd made this final request had been all too familiar, for it was the same tone she'd always taken when discussing this topic. A topic they'd been fighting over for Briony's entire life.

No matter how much Briony had begged, bartered, and shouted, Bethany had steadfastly kept Briony from entering or going near the water. Even without ever having touched it, though, Briony's heart still beat to the rhythm of the waves. Her lungs still rejoiced in the salty air. Her eyes still brightened at every beauteous sunset, whose light danced across the water like a maiden in love.

Briony shook herself back to reality and turned her eyes from the sea. *Mum was right; the ocean is a wicked temptress. Why else would I desire the very thing that killed my father?*

Before she could ruminate on thoughts like these further, though, she realized she had arrived at the inn. She went into

14

the kitchen and saw Adaira removing some muffins from the oven. Another batch already sat on the table.

"Good morneen,[8] Adaira. May I trouble you fer a spell?" Briony asked as she walked up behind her friend. Adaira started at the noise, nearly launching her muffins into the air.

"I swear you'll be the death o' me, Briony!" Adaira set the muffins down so hard they wobbled on the tray. "Or at least the death o' my baking. 'Tis too dangerous fer my pastries these days. I'm liable to give up on baking them."

"Nay, you can' do that." Briony waved her hands. "The entire village would be after me."

"Then perhaps I won' today. I'm na making any promises fer morn[9] though," she threatened, furrowing her brow. Briony did her best not to laugh, but Adaira saw right through her.

"You better take me seriously, you know!" Adaira waggled a finger at her.

Briony chuckled, giving up on holding it in. Adaira's scowl shifted instantly, and soon she was laughing with her.

"What's all this noise in here?" came an indignant shout that immediately staunched the women's happy spirits.

Terrence Stubbins hobbled into the room with his cane, and Briony held in a sigh at the sight of him. She hated that poor Adaira was saddled with such a curmudgeon. His wrinkled clothes reeked of alcohol. *No doubt he spent most o' the night in the tavern again.*

"I apologize, Father. We did na mean to wake you. Please, go back to bed," Adaira urged.

Terrence looked between the two of them, disapproval glinting in his eyes. "Causing so much ruckus! I know I did na raise you to be that way, daughter. Must be this one's influence on you. Heaven knows she's na good fer anything but trouble, just like her mother."

Briony seethed, opening her mouth to reply, but Adaira placed a hand on her arm. The contact helped Briony clamp down on her anger, for Adaira's sake.

When Terrence realized neither of the women was going to say anything else, he turned around and waddled back

---

[8] Morning.
[9] Tomorrow.

toward his bedroom, grumbling as he went.

Briony rolled her eyes.

"I'm sorry, Briony. I know 'tis hard, but if you get into an argument with him, 'twill only make things worse." Adaira removed her hand from Briony's arm.

Briony looked away. "Aye, aye, I know. But still, how can he talk like that? 'Twas na my mother's fault! She did everything she could."

Adaira's voice became pained. "I know that. And I believe he knows it too, but he's just so bitter that he wants someone to blame."

"If he had na been so caught up in superstition, maybe things would have been different."

Then maybe my mother would have known Valerie Stubbins was pregnant soon enough to prevent at least one o' the deaths.

Adaira ran a finger along the counter, a wistful expression on her face. "Or maybe they would have been just the same. We'll never know now. All we can do is try our best to move forward."

"I just wish he could do that too," Briony said with a huff.

"So do I. I thought he'd get better over time, but the longer my mum and brother are gone, the worse he gets. I'm surprised Tam still puts up with him at the tavern if he's as ill-tempered there as he is here."

"You know Tam will put up with just about anything as long as he gets paid. . . ." Briony's voice trailed off, and she stared out the window, stewing on Terrence's words.

Old wives' tales claimed fairies might harm the mother or abduct the child if knowledge of a pregnancy was widespread. Because of this, Terrence had convinced Valerie to keep her condition hidden for as long as possible. No one but the family had known, not even Bethany Fairborn, who had taken care of all expectant mothers in Everton since she had become the town midwife.

No one could have predicted the tragedy that was to come. Valerie had gone into labor three months early while Dr. Sherwin was out of town, and by the time Bethany had reached Valerie's side, it was too late. She had done everything she could, but it wasn't enough to save them.

"Anyway, why have you come so early this morneen?" Adaira asked, drawing Briony from her thoughts.

"I needed something to distract me," Briony said, not meeting her friend's eyes.

"Another nightmare?"

Briony nodded.

"My father's cruel words must have been even harder to hear, then. I'm sorry, dearie."

"I'll be all right. Did you know it has been almost a year since she died?"

"Aye, just a few weeks from now. I'm sure 'tis still very difficult to bear. Just remember that I'm here fer you." Adaira's face was full of compassion, so much so that the midwife's eyes began to well up with tears.

Briony coughed and turned away. "I wanted to see how that man who came in yesterday with the broken leg is doing . . . Mr. Mendes?"

Adaira accepted the shift in topic with a sad, understanding smile. "His sister went out to their ship a wee bit ago to talk to that other fellow who came with them. She asked if I could take her brother a few muffins if I finished baking before she returned. How about you take them instead and see fer yerself?"

"All right, though I must warn you that na as many may get down there as I take," Briony said, trying to lighten the somber mood. She grabbed four muffins and put them on a plate.

Adaira winked. "Just so long as you dinna let any o' my guests go hungry."

"Never!" Briony grinned and strode off toward the bedrooms. She knocked lightly at the foreigner's before entering.

Mr. Mendes lay in the bed with his back to her. The brown shirt he wore clung closely to him, hinting at lean muscle beneath.

The man's splinted foot rested on a pillow, reminding Briony of the strenuous process she and Dr. Sherwin had gone through the night before. The swelling in his leg and foot seemed to have gone down some, but a frightful bruise

17

stretched across the exposed skin. *I really wish I knew how that happened.*

"I'm sorry to trouble you, Mr. Mendes, but I brought you some breakfast."

The man shifted toward her, grunting as he turned. She felt bad for making him move since she could tell it was painful, but then she lost her train of thought when she met his striking eyes, pale green like the wings of the butterflies around her cottage.

"I didn't hear you come in. Are you Dr. Sherwin's wife? I apologize for not introducing myself when you were helping him—"

"You dinna need to apologize. You were in far too much pain last night fer introductions. And nay, I'm na married to Dr. Sherwin. I'm Briony Fairborn, the village midwife." She put the plate down on the small table next to his bed.

"Senhorita Fairborn, I'm in your debt. Without you and Dr. Sherwin, I don't know what I would have done."

Briony smiled. "Think nothing o' it. I was glad to help. How are you feeling this morneen?"

"Much better than yesterday, as you can tell, I'm sure. My leg still hurts quite a bit, but I expect it takes a long time to fully recover. You do think it will fully recover, right?" His voice and countenance seemed nonchalant, but Briony caught a brief glimpse of fear in his eyes.

"From what Dr. Sherwin said last night, it sounds like you will be just fine."

Mr. Mendes exhaled a heavy breath, revealing his genuine worry about the matter. "Good. And did he say how long it will take the bone to heal?"

"About six weeks. The doctor wants you to stay here until then."

The man's face darkened in disappointment for a moment, much like his sister's and the captain's had upon hearing the recovery time, but then a sparkle came into his eyes. "In that case, perhaps I'll get to see you again while I'm here. I'm much more charming when I'm not in pain, you know."

Briony flushed. *Is he flirting with me?*

"I-I'm sure you are." She internally winced at how stupid

18

she sounded.

The man smiled. "Once I'm back on my feet, I'll do my best to prove it to you."

Briony frowned even as her heart skipped a beat. *How do I respond? Do I want him flirting with me?*

Her gaze flickered back to his light-green eyes. She couldn't tell if he was being sincere or not.

Probably na, and even if he is, once he knows the truth o' my upbringing, he'll want nothing to do with me. I better na give him any false hope.

"Dinna trouble yerself, sir. You must have better things to do. *I* certainly do." She spun around without waiting for his reply and marched out.

There. I hope that was rude enough fer him. I'm sorry, Mr. Mendes, but you dinna want to get to know me. 'Tis better fer both o' us.

An Unexpected Arrangement

As Briony reached the end of the corridor, Adaira came by with some washcloths. She stopped and asked, "How is he doing?"

"I can' tell if the medicine Dr. Sherwin gave him is working extremely well or if he's simply skilled at masking his pain. Either way, he was very . . . agreeable." Briony hoped Adaira didn't notice how her voice cracked a little as she spoke.

"Agreeable? Hmm, that's good. Even if he was na, I might overlook it since he's such a handsome fellow. Perhaps he may need to stay longer than Dr. Sherwin initially thought. Broken bones do take a long time to heal," Adaira said with a smirk.

"Nay, Adaira, you can' be thinking that!" Briony shouted, just as Mr. Burgess and his son passed by. The elder one was courteous enough not to stare, but William, clearly intrigued by the women's conversation, stopped to listen.

When Mr. Burgess noticed that his son wasn't moving anymore, he turned and grabbed the boy's shoulder. "William, come along. Yer being impolite. My apologies, mistresses."

Adaira nodded at him, but Briony was too embarrassed to look Mr. Burgess's way.

William gave both the women a sheepish smile. "Sorry!"

Briony said nothing, but her face was warm as she watched the boy scurry after his redheaded father. Once the Burgesses were in their room, Briony pulled Adaira into the privacy of the kitchen.

"So what is it yer so sure I'm thinking? It must be bad fer you na to want others to hear," Adaira sneered.

"You wish to set him up with me. You can' try to be a matchmaker in my life. I know this man is na from around here, but as soon as he discovers the truth about me, he'll lose any interest he might have had. 'Tis unlikely he would be interested, anyway." The words tasted like ash in Briony's mouth even though she was only being a little dishonest.

Adaira raised her eyebrows, the smirk not leaving her face. "Why do you think I was intending him fer *you?* I was meaning to snatch him up fer myself. But since you jumped to that conclusion so readily, that must mean you find him attractive, too. Perhaps you would be a better fit fer Mr. Mendes than I. I'll have to keep that in mind."

"What! I—" Briony broke off with a frustrated growl.

Why do I make it so easy fer her? I should know better than that by now. After all, we've been friends fer years. . . . Wait a second—

The amused expression on Adaira's face told Briony she had fallen directly into her trap. "Adaira, yer such a toad. You were never intending Mr. Mendes fer yerself."

Adaira burst out giggling. As per usual, her laughter was so contagious that Briony couldn't hold back a few chuckles of her own.

"Now you've told me all I need to know, Briony. Mr. Mendes is in my sights fer you, so I'll be doing my best to give you two the chance to get to know each other better."

"Please dinna do that, Adaira. Please."

"Why na? He would be a mighty lucky man to snag you."

Briony sighed. "I may have been a wee bit rude to him earlier. I'm sure his opinion o' me is na good."

Adaira frowned. "Why were you rude? Did he say something that made you angry? You know you let that temper get the better o' you all too often."

Briony shook her head and dropped her voice to a whisper. "Nay. He was—I think he was . . . *flirting* with me."

Adaira's face lit up like the fires of Johnsmas. "Briony, that's wonderful! I told you yer a catch. 'Tis about time someone else noticed how pretty you are."

"So you say," Briony groaned.

"And I'll keep saying it until you start to believe it," Adaira declared, placing a hand on her hip. She gave Briony a sharp look, daring her to say anything else.

Briony rolled her eyes and turned to leave.

But Adaira wasn't finished. "I still dinna understand why you were rude."

How can she na get it? Briony turned back to her friend. "Because it can' go anywhere. I'm illegitimate. I have no chance at finding a husband."

"Briony, yer a great person. Yer parents' status when you were born does na change that."

"O' course it does. It changes everything! You dinna understand. Yer na like me. You did na grow up with everyone hating you fer something you had no control over."

Adaira's eyes filled with hurt. "Yer right, I'm na like you. I'm just the daughter o' the town drunk."

Shame colored Briony's cheeks. She reached out a hand to the woman's shoulder. "I'm sorry, Adaira. I know you've had to overcome yer father's reputation. And you *have*. No one resents you fer his behavior. They know yer different from him. But they can' see past what my mother did. And my grandmother. And even my great-grandmother. I have a legacy o' illegitimacy. Everyone is just waiting fer me to end up the same way they did. No man will think me worthy o' being a wife. 'Tis a hard truth, but I've come to accept it."

"Well, I will never accept that fer you. I will *always* keep hoping and praying that the right man comes along who sees you fer who you are."

Briony didn't know how she got to have such a good friend, a true sister. She released Adaira's shoulder with a smile. "Thank you. If it weren' fer you, I dinna know where I'd be. I better get going though. I need to go to the market, but I have to go back home first to get my basket. Do you need anything?"

"Nay, I'm stocked up pretty well right now. I'll see you later, then."

Briony nodded and left, humming to herself. Adaira's

words were comforting, but as she walked, her thoughts strayed back to Terrence Stubbins's comment and the village's general outlook on her family. While she understood their aversion to an extent, she also knew one misdeed didn't destroy everything good about a person.

Briony's mother had always shown kindness, despite what she had received in return. She had always been so strong. Briony wouldn't have even thought her mother was capable of tears if not for one night—

Briony paused, remembering that moment:

She was eight years old. Someone was crying in her dream, and it woke her up, but as soon as she opened her eyes, she realized the sound wasn't coming from her head; it was coming from outside. She tiptoed out the back door only to find her mother gazing at the ocean. That wasn't so strange since she often caught Bethany doing that when she thought Briony wasn't looking.

But why is she crying? She never cries.

"Mum, why are you sad?" Briony whispered.

Bethany slowly turned to her daughter. She gave Briony a small grin, despite the sorrow in her eyes.

"Come here, my peedie freck," she said as she held out her arms.

Briony eagerly got into her mother's lap, but she continued to look at Bethany expectantly.

"I was only a wee bit homesick, and I thought that if I came out here, I would na wake you. Looks like I was wrong though," Mum admitted with a yawn.

"But we are home, aren' we?" Briony asked.

This was the only home she had ever known, and Mum had always told her the cottage had been in the family since Briony's great-grandmother claimed it.

"Aye, we are, bairn. But we also have another home, an old home I sometimes think about."

Little Briony frowned in confusion. She knew for certain she had never been there. "Why do we na live there?"

"Well, Briony, I knew this would be a better place fer you. A safer place. Because no matter what, I'm going to make sure you stay safe. Do you understand?" Bethany said firmly, as though she was desperate to make sure her daughter knew it.

Briony nodded before nestling into her mother's embrace. Soon after, she fell asleep, and the subject of their "other home" was never mentioned again.

It had been such a long time since Briony last thought about that conversation that she'd almost forgotten it. Rather than feeling pain at the memory, though, Briony felt a spark of curiosity.

Why did I never ask her about it again? If Mum did live somewhere besides Drulea Cottage, what made her come back?

Briony opened the door to head to the market only to find Dr. Sherwin standing just outside. He cleared his throat upon seeing her and looked about awkwardly for a few seconds before speaking.

"Greetings, Mis . . . *tress* Fairborn."

Briony raised her eyebrow at the slip. She had long suspected no one called her "mistress" except to her face, since everyone thought she was a strumpet.[10] It didn't matter that she had never even kissed a man before.

"What do you want, Dr. Sherwin?" He was delaying her trip to the market, and every second wasted was another second she could be missing out on a great deal.

"May I come in?"

Briony groaned inwardly, but courtesy demanded she comply. She nodded and stepped back to allow him entrance.

She gestured to one of her two wooden chairs. "Have a seat."

"I shall be brief, Mistress Fairborn," he said as Briony lowered herself into the other chair. "I need you to help Mr. Mendes in his recovery. The swelling in his ankle has gone down significantly, and I believe he'll be ready fer some light exercise soon. However, he will need someone to walk with him because he's na ready to put all his weight on his ankle yet."

Briony frowned. "I have no experience in something like this. Besides, 'tis na my duty to help him. Why can his sister na do it?"

---

[10] A promiscuous woman.

25

"Mistress Fairborn, Everton must be accommodating to its guests. How would it look if we weren' even able to provide an injured visitor with proper care while he's here? Surely 'tis too much to ask Mistress Mendes to do it herself. Nay, it must be you."

Briony scoffed. *This man's obsession with appearances is too much to bear.*

"Yer his doctor, na me. Dinna you wish to look good in front o' Mistress Mendes?"

The doctor coughed and looked away. "I'm sure I dinna know what you mean, Mistress Fairborn."

"Hmm, o' course na."

"The simple fact is I have other patients besides Mr. Mendes. Surely you can spare some o' yer *abundant* time to give him the help he needs."

Briony glared at him as she remembered how he had taken all the credit for setting the man's bone. This time, she wasn't going to just go along with him. "I'm na yer servant to order around as you please. If you want it done, you do it."

Dr. Sherwin's eyes narrowed. "I'd be a wee bit more gracious fer this opportunity if I were you."

"Opportunity? What sort o' opportunity is this fer me? All I'll be doing is easing up yer workload." Briony rose from her seat, about to tell Dr. Sherwin to leave.

"Mistress Fairborn! Show some decorum, fer heaven's sake. Do you think raising yer voice is going to help you? I could easily take away yer only source o' income if I tried."

Briony gasped. "Take away my job? You could na do that."

The man sneered. "Do you truly want to test that?"

"If that's true, then why have you na already done it?"

"I may na like you, Mistress Fairborn, but I'm na cold-blooded enough to force you from yer home." He leaned back in the chair, wiping his glasses with a handkerchief as though the conversation bored him.

Briony snorted in disbelief. Then a memory washed over her, a memory of something she hadn't thought about in a very long time. Pain pounded in her temples as she tried to push it away.

"Nay, you tried to do something worse." Her voice was only a whisper, but out of the corner of her eye, Briony thought she saw Dr. Sherwin stiffen for a moment before continuing to clean his glasses.

"Perhaps yer unwillingness is because I did na offer you money."

Briony's temper flared. "What! 'Tis na about money. 'Tis about—Ugh, you would na understand. Fine, I'll do it, but fer Mr. Mendes's sake. Na fer Everton, and certainly na fer *you*."

She stomped over to the door and opened it. Regardless of manners, she was unwilling to let the man stay a moment longer.

Dr. Sherwin rose from his chair as if he was suddenly too good to sit in it. "Once you start, you'll need to come see me at four o'clock every other day to let me know his status. If anything needs to be changed to help him heal faster, I can decide then."

Briony just glowered at the doctor as he moved to the exit. He had barely stepped over the threshold when she slammed the door behind him.

The Joys of Old Men and Pregnant Women

After taking a few minutes to compose herself, Briony made her way down to the market. This was always one of her favorite places to go. There were so many sounds and smells permeating the air, and the entire space hummed with a special sort of energy. Apart from Everton Inn, the market square was the heart of the village, the place where news of the outside world spread to listening ears and rare trinkets could be attained for only a few coins. It was a tiny world of its own, one where Briony's money was just as good as everyone else's and she could pretend she wasn't the village outcast.

She wove her way past the first few merchants, who were trying to sell linens and jewelry at their stalls. They called to her charmingly, claiming they offered the latest fashions from England and Wales. She was tempted to stop, but she knew that if she did, she would spend more money than she ought to, so she marched past without a second glance at the alluring wares.

The man who normally sold her seafood was named Vincent McLaren, the second son of old Steven McLaren. Vincent was a smelly fellow with large ears and a portly belly. He had a habit of saying strange things that no one understood. Most people dismissed his words as the ravings of a lunatic, but Briony wasn't so sure. There was something about him that made her wonder if he knew more than people gave him credit for. He was also one of the only fishermen whose business wasn't completely controlled by the laird.[11]

"Fish! Come get yer fresh fish here! Hello, Mistress Fairborn, would you like to buy a lovely trout this morneen? Caught one just two hours ago, and he put up quite a fight. I'm only asking fer my usual price. No doubt he'll taste delightful." He gestured toward the fish in question while giving her a practically toothless smile.

If Briony were to make a list of her greatest weaknesses, her temper would be at the top, but sea trout was definitely in the top five. She simply couldn't refuse to purchase it anytime it was available. It was too bad for her that Vincent also knew about that weakness because every time she came to the market, he would make sure she knew about his latest catch.

"You know me too well, Mr. McLaren. I'll take it," Briony replied as she stared at the trout. It lay between several cod and a few haddock, just waiting to be cooked. She moved a hand to her pocket[12] to retrieve some money.

"Indeed, 'tis quite dangerous. Really, 'twould be too easy to guess. You should be more careful," he mumbled.

Faint alarm bells rang in her mind. "Is it such a danger?" Briony asked even though she had no idea what he was talking about.

"Truly 'tis, miss. If the others could only see the signs, they would get such a fright they might run you out o' the village." Vincent gave her a look as though she should know what he meant, but Briony was even more puzzled than before.

Signs o' what? I already give many o' them a fright, but . . . Why am I even trying to understand him? Most o' what he says does na make sense.

"Do you have any shrimp today?" she asked, hoping to change subjects. Mr. McLaren nodded and brought some into view from behind the stall. They looked fresh enough, so she said she would take them also.

---

[11] Scottish equivalent of a lord who owned a large piece of land in the community.

[12] A cloth bag women wore under their petticoats or aprons.

She was just about to move on when she heard a throat clearing behind her. "That was my fish there, lass. Hand it over." demanded a nasal voice.

Briony winced and spun around to none other than Lady Oliver, the laird's wife.

The midwife twisted her face into a hard smile as she looked the older woman in the eye. Lady Oliver's wrinkled skin hung bulbously from her face, making her sneer even more grotesque. She claimed she was only forty years of age, but Briony suspected she was at least fifty. Today she wore an elaborate green dress with jewels around her throat, but all that beauty did nothing to hide the woman's overall ugliness, both inside and out.

She may not have been an Oliver by blood, but she and her husband were well matched in their singular animosity toward the Fairborns. While most of Everton avoided Briony as much as possible, the Olivers seemed to specifically seek her out to harass her.

Just as their son, Alastair, did before he died eleven years ago.

Three of Lady Oliver's servants stood in front of her, one of them extending his hand toward the trout.

Briony leaned away from the man's hand. "'Tis the only trout Mr. McLaren has, Lady Oliver, and I have na been able to eat one in more than a fortnight."

The other woman scoffed. "Neither have I, so you best be giving it to Hamish here before you anger me."

Briony narrowed her eyes at the deceitful hag, for she had seen Hamish Dunnet buy six trout only a week before. If Lady Oliver were simply less gluttonous, Briony wouldn't have been in such a pinch. As it was, though, she was lucky if she managed to snag a single trout every couple of weeks.

And what if yer presence is already angering me? Briony opened her mouth, ready to say precisely that, but then she thought back to her conversation earlier with Dr. Sherwin. And his threat.

She sighed. *Best na to argue with too many people on the same day. Especially one who is even less reasonable than the doctor.* Taking one last look at the delectable fish, she dropped it into the servant's hand.

"Ah, so yer na completely stupid, after all. I must be going now. This place smells much too natural[13] fer my sensitivities," Lady Oliver said before sauntering away. The servants trailed after her like moths to a flame.

Briony huffed at the slight, but then she realized something else: the sneaky woman had gotten the fish without even paying for it.

"That thief! I ought to just—"

"Calm yerself, lass. That would na happen if she knew. She would na dare speak ill o' you if she knew where you came from. Oh, if only!" Vincent cackled.

"Mr. McLaren, what are you talking about?" Briony locked her eyes onto the odd man, trying to force an answer from him with her penetrating gaze.

Vincent looked away guiltily. "Best you dinna find out from me. That's na the way. Nay, 'tis na the way. You must learn fer yerself. 'Tis the only way to true knowing. True knowing is better than showing."

The man smiled madly and spun around in a circle, seemingly caught up in delirium.

Briony grimaced, tired of his riddles. "If you won' tell me, then how shall I know?"

Vincent spun back to her with a small frown. "The others dinna know, only I. And I shall never tell you. Nay, I promised. A promise must be kept."

"Others? What others?"

The man's eyes widened, and his face turned pale. "No others. Na a one. Only you, dearie."

Before Briony could ask more, Vincent turned and dashed out of the stall, his arms flying above his head. The other villagers barely glanced up; this sort of behavior was normal for Everton's "mad fisherman."

Briony stayed motionless for a few moments, mulling over the peculiar words. *She would na speak ill o' me if she knew where I'm from? That reminds me far too much o' when Mum mentioned our "other home."*

Briony shook her head to clear her thoughts. *Surely 'tis*

---

[13] Illegitimate.

32

nothing. He's mad, after all.

She took a few steps away from Mr. McLaren's stall to continue collecting the food she needed, but then another thought occurred to her. *Maybe he meant older people in the village when he said, "The others dinna know." Was he lying about how much they know? He seemed like he was trying to hide something.*

Those old goats would never tell me anything, though, so what's the point in wondering about it?

She looked down at the basket in her hand as inspiration struck. *But I know exactly whom they would tell.*

***

After a great deal of coaxing and promises, Adaira agreed to help Briony get the information she wanted. The two of them headed for Nathaniel Levins's house that afternoon. Besides the tavern, that was the usual place where the older men gathered to complain about how bad the world had gotten and reminisce over the good old days.

Typically, villagers would stop and chat with the neighbors they saw, but as Briony and Adaira walked down the street, a total of six people went by them without even saying hello. Adaira frowned at the discourtesy, but Briony was used to it.

As the women neared the tailor shop, a couple stepped out. Briony wouldn't have paid them much attention, except she glimpsed an unexpected motion.

Freda Calhoun, one hand on her pregnant belly, was waving at the two women in a manner that seemed almost friendly.

Shocked, Briony was about to wave back, but then she noticed the scowl on Mr. Calhoun's face and changed her mind. It was obvious the man had no interest in speaking to her, so she gave Freda a polite nod and tried to pull Adaira to the other side of the road.

Freda, on the other hand, was not nearly as observant and stepped directly in front of the two friends. "Briony, Adaira, where are you off to?"

The high-pitched tone of the woman's voice told Briony she was about to hear another long list of complaints, but she forced herself to smile. Normally, Briony had very little patience, but she tended to be more gracious when it came to pregnant women. Though she'd never done it herself, she knew carrying a new life for nine months was no easy task.

"Freda, yer looking well today," Adaira chirped.

Freda's gaze swept over the pretty brunette distastefully. "There must be something wrong with yer eyes, then, since this is the worst I've felt in my entire pregnancy."

Briony glimpsed Daniel clenching his jaw. He didn't seem to be in the mood for his wife's whining either, and Briony almost felt sorry for him. She, too, wished she could be somewhere else right about then, but as the town midwife, she was obligated to make sure Freda was all right. "What seems to be the problem?"

"What's na the problem? I'm tired all the time, and every part o' me *aches*. And the dreams. I never—"

"Freda! Dear, this is na the time to be discussing this. I'm sure they have things to do." Daniel gripped his wife's shoulder and pulled her back.

Freda looked at her husband like he had lost his mind. "What? Daniel, I have to talk to her *now*. She has to fix this."

Briony saw Daniel's face shift to anger, so she jumped in to keep them from getting into a full-fledged argument. "Most o' those things sound pretty normal, but if you'd like, I can discuss them with you in more detail once Adaira and I finish with our errand."

The spark in Freda's eyes faded a bit. "*Normal*, you say? Well, I'm sure that after you hear *all* the details, you shall na think everything is so normal. But fine, I'll expect you later this afternoon, then."

Daniel let out a frustrated breath, turning to follow his wife as she waddled away with as much pomp as an eight-months-pregnant woman could muster.

Adaira looked at Briony with wide eyes. "Is she always like that?"

Briony pursed her lips and nodded.

"I'm so glad I dinna have yer job. I would na be able to handle hearing that all the time."

"I barely can either. . . ." Briony's attention shifted to four men at a new merchant ship by the dock. They were swaying back and forth as they struggled to carry a large piano down the gangplank. She watched them for a moment, worried they would drop it.

There's only one person in town wasteful enough to buy a piano. I hope he's na nearby—

"Put yer backs into it, men! You'd think you were my age with how much trouble yer having."

Laird Oliver.

Despite the distance between them, Briony's gut clenched with dread. If the man saw her, he would surely find a new way to make her feel like she was lower than a worm. He was currently preoccupied, but that could change at any second, so Briony grabbed Adaira's arm to get them moving again.

Though Everton was one of the smallest settlements on the island of North Ronaldsay, it wasn't small enough to avoid having a laird. These men who owned large estates of land often served as unofficial leaders of their towns. And since Joseph Oliver was the village's only laird, he and his wife seemed to think they could make people do whatever they pleased.

If only the lairdship o' Harray was na passed on through blood, the rest o' the town would be much better off.

Briony preferred the wiser counsel of Mr. McGuff and Dr. Sherwin at the town meetings; they were far more apt to offer ideas that benefited all of Everton, not just the Olivers.

Na that anyone cares about my opinion. I could probably just na show up and no one would notice.

The smell of burning kelp hit Briony's nose as she and Adaira strode toward their destination. Laird Oliver had heard that many lairds in other towns had gotten rich selling the ash, so it hadn't taken long for him to convince many of the villagers this was the best way to preserve Everton's economy throughout the summer. Now the scent was so familiar that Briony barely even noticed it as it traveled up from the shore. Some families would spend as many as eight hours burning seaweed every day before letting it cool overnight. Then they would break the ash into lumps and send it south to be turned into soap and glass.[14]

". . . do the talking when we arrive, all right? Briony?"

"What?" Briony turned to Adaira in surprise. "Sorry, I did na realize you were speaking."

"I *said*, 'Let me do the talking.' It takes nary a minute to rile you up, and I dinna want yer temper spoiling our chances o' getting information."

"Fine," Briony muttered.

When they reached Nathaniel Levins's dilapidated house, loud voices met their ears. If it had been anyone else's home, Briony might have been concerned. However, she knew that all these men ever did was shout at each other; if they didn't, they wouldn't be able to hear well enough to carry on a conversation.

"Get the door, Angus," croaked one of the men when Adaira knocked. The door squeaked open, with old Angus Dunnet standing on the inside. His gray hair was thin and messy, matching his scatterbrained personality.

Straining her neck to see over Mr. Dunnet's shoulder, Briony barely got a glimpse of the man's companions: Nathaniel Levins, Steven McLaren, and Phillip McGuff. They were all seated around a small footlocker in the living room, apparently playing a card game.

"Hello there, Adaira. Yer interrupting us from something *very* important. What brings you here?" Mr. Dunnet asked, completely ignoring Briony.

"I've come fer information I thought you or one o' yer friends might be able to give," Adaira said.

"Do you have news from the Mainland?"[15] Steven McLaren called, his eyes still on his cards.

"Nay, I dinna have any news."

"Are those English dogs finally going to give up Scotland?"[16] Mr. Levins interjected.

Briony stepped out from behind Adaira. "She clearly just

---

[14] An Orcadian practice carried out from the early eighteenth century until the early nineteenth century.

[15] The main island of Orkney.

[16] Scotland came under English rule as part of the newly formed Great Britain in 1707.

said we dinna have any news, Mr. Levins."

The other men at the table, who hadn't even realized Briony was there, suddenly jerked back.

"Briony Fairborn! Angus, did you let that witch into my house?" Mr. Levins asked.

Adaira put her hands on her hips and glared at the old man. "She's no witch, Mr. Levins. She's my friend, and she needs yer help."

"We're quite busy, much too busy to help her. Besides, she might put a curse on us."

"Aye, yer na welcome here," shouted Steven McLaren, raising his fist.

Mr. Levins turned to his friend. "Yer na the owner o' this house, Steven. Dinna speak like you are."

"Yer only mad because yer losing, Steven," added Mr. McGuff.

"I ain't losing, McGuff!"

At that point, the conversation devolved into senseless arguing. Briony sighed in annoyance, already regretting her decision to come here.

Adaira marched up to the footlocker and slammed her hand down on it. "Anyone who can tell us what we need to know gets free dinners fer a fortnight."

Everyone stopped speaking so quickly it was like all the air had been sucked out of the room. The men glanced at each other and then at Briony.

"What sort o' information do you need?" Mr. McGuff asked.

"I need to know more about my background. Especially about where my family comes from, or if my mother ever lived somewhere besides Everton."

"Curious about yer family? Many people have been mighty curious about yer family ever since yer great-grandmother Edith came to Everton. Just a bunch o' good-fer-nothing strumpets, if you ask me," Mr. Levins said.

Briony drew in a sharp breath and stomped toward the group.

Adaira clasped her friend's shoulder to calm her down. "*Besides* that, what can you tell us?"

"Edith was always quiet, kept to herself. My parents never liked her much," chipped in Mr. McGuff. "They suspected she was a runaway."

"And then when people knew she was with child, nobody wanted to talk to her. I was only a boy at the time, but I remember all the adults warning their bairns to stay away from her. Especially the girls," added Mr. Dunnet.

"Did anyone ever speak o' where she came from?" Adaira asked.

"Aye, some people thought she came from France because o' her complexion. Others said Italy or Spain," replied Mr. Levins.

"And o' course, there were the rumors," mentioned Mr. Dunnet.

"Rumors?" Briony asked. Adaira gave her a hard look, no doubt trying to remind Briony of her promise to let Adaira do the talking.

"Surely you must know what they used to say. Yer mother must have told you," Mr. McGuff said.

Briony shook her head.

Mr. McLaren, the only one who hadn't spoken since Adaira made her offer, grunted in clear disbelief. He crossed his arms over his chest and muttered something about "filthy liars," but no one in the room paid him any mind.

"People used to say they saw her out on the beach late at night, singing to the ocean. She had the most beautiful voice. Like an angel," Mr. McGuff explained.

"Or a fairy," remarked Mr. Levins. "A few people thought she was one o' the Fair Folk and that was why she sang."

"Freaky odd, she was," grumbled Mr. McLaren.

Briony frowned as she took in their words. "What about my mother? Was she always here in Everton? Did she ever move somewhere else?"

"Na that I remember," said Mr. Levins. "Any o' the rest o' you remember a time when Bethany Fairborn left Everton?"

All the men shook their heads.

"That's it? There's nothing more you can tell me?" Briony looked from face to face, seeing nothing useful. She growled in frustration and stamped to the door. "Adaira, let's go."

"So, do we get the free meals still?" Mr. Dunnet asked.

Adaira pursed her lips. "You did na tell us very much, but I suppose I can give you one week's worth o' free dinners."

Protests immediately rose at that, but Adaira wouldn't be swayed. Briony tapped her foot impatiently, but when it became clear that the men weren't going to let Adaira leave easily, the midwife threw open the door and marched over to the Calhouns' house.

Why did I think they would be any help? Perhaps my mum's secrets are just destined to stay buried with her.

Weighty Impressions

Barking wakened Briony from her slumber. She stepped outside and gazed down at the shore below, instantly spotting the culprits: eight or nine grey seals. Two of the larger ones had a fish between their mouths, while the others stood nearby. Briony watched with amusement as they tugged it back and forth for a few minutes before one finally wrested it away. The winner snarled at the other seals, making them all waddle off in fear. Briony chuckled at how funny they looked; there could be no doubt that their bodies were made for life in the water, not life on the land.

Every year around this time, about thirty seals would show up on the beach below Drulea Cottage. Briony wondered where they came from and why they always chose to return.

Her mother had hated the seals and had kept Briony far away from them, though Briony had no idea why. From what she could tell, the only trouble the animals caused was additional competition for the fishermen, and that was only for about a month before the seals returned home.

Sometimes Briony would sit and watch them bask in the sun on the beach, enjoying one another's company without a care in the world. She would imagine herself like one of them—understood and accepted.

If only humans were so easy to get along with.

Briony looked over at the time: eight o'clock. Today was the day she had to start walking with Mr. Mendes. She wondered if the man was expecting her yet. For all she knew, Dr. Sherwin hadn't even told him she would be the one coming.

With a sigh, Briony decided to head down to Everton Inn as soon as she'd dressed and eaten. If Mr. Mendes wasn't awake by then, she would simply help Adaira with chores until he was ready. It wasn't like she had anywhere else she needed to be.

Briony trudged down the beaten path, dreading the thought of seeing the young foreigner again. She hadn't spoken to him since the single conversation they'd had in his room the day after his arrival. But as soon as Dr. Sherwin had removed the man's splint yesterday, he'd been quick to find Briony and remind her of their agreement. *Will Mr. Mendes be rude after what I said last time? Or worse . . . will he keep flirting with me?*

She thought about his pale-green eyes and groaned. They had been difficult enough to resist the first time.

Briony had almost arrived at the inn when she collided with something tall and hard. She toppled to the ground gracelessly, hearing a loud curse as she did. She looked over to see what she'd walked into and grimaced. It was Laird Oliver.

Several furs lay around him, and two of his servants stood nearby with shocked expressions. After a moment, they recovered enough to help the laird to his feet.

"Yer recklessness made me drop my furs, and now they have dirt all over them. I hope you realize you'll be the one cleaning them, you——"

It was then that Laird Oliver looked over and noticed exactly whom he had collided with. His cheeks flushed with anger. "Briony Fairborn, you ungrateful wench. How dare you knock into me. After I was generous enough to let you stay here despite yer upbringing, this is how you repay me? I always knew you meant naught but ill."

"Laird Oliver, please dinna talk so loudly," she groaned, holding her head as the world spun around her. The laird was no slim man to run into.

"You dinna tell me what to do, you——"

"Sir, pardon my interruption, but we really must be going," said one of the servants.

Laird Oliver fixed him with a murderous look. The servant trembled so much Briony almost wondered if he had been the one to run into her, for he seemed as dizzy as she was.

"And 'tis important enough fer you to interrupt me?"

"Lady Oliver, sir, if you remember?"

The laird's eyes widened in understanding. A shot of fear ran through them before he covered it up with a scowl and turned to Briony. "Yer lucky I have somewhere to be. But mark my words: you'll be hearing from me soon. I expect proper compensation fer these furs."

Briony, still recovering from the impact, said nothing. The laird must have interpreted this as acquiescence, though, because he shifted his attention back to his servants. "Let's go, men. Stop wasting time standing there."

The servants jumped at his order and quickly followed behind him as he marched off toward his house.

Briony tried to give the servant who'd spoken up a grateful smile, but the man refused to make eye contact with her.

"Thanks fer nothing, then," she shouted to his back even though she knew he couldn't hear her.

Some things never change.

Briony shakily stood after a few more seconds, noting a dull ache in her back as she did. She hobbled the rest of the way to the inn, immediately going to one of the empty chairs in the sitting room.

"Ah, Senhorita Fairborn. How lovely to see you," said a high voice.

Briony almost leaped from her seat; she'd been so eager to sit down that she hadn't noticed Mistress Mendes in the chair across the room. "Oh, I did na realize you were there."

The younger woman pressed her lips together in a way that suggested it was highly unusual for her to be overlooked. Briony could believe that, considering how beautiful she was. Her hair was like honey, gleaming in the morning light with an almost magical shine. She had smooth ivory skin and pretty brown eyes. *They dinna compare to her brother's striking green ones though—*

Briony internally winced. *It does na matter what his eyes look like.*

"Dr. Sherwin has tasked me with assisting yer brother in his recovery," she said with a trace of bitterness, though she hoped Mistress Mendes wouldn't notice. The young woman had been spending most of her time inside the inn with her brother, so Briony hadn't interacted with her much.

"Thank you. You're a gem. You've already been so helpful." The blond smiled with such sincerity that Briony felt guilty for initially refusing to help.

"'T-'Tis fine. Dinna worry about it."

"Are you sure it won't be too much for you?"

Briony hesitated, thinking of how she didn't want to see Mr. Mendes again. *Perhaps I could—Nay, I better do this. What if Dr. Sherwin's threat about my job was real?*

"'Tis nothing. Yer visitors here in Everton, and everyone in the village just wants yer stay to be a pleasant one," Briony lied.

"Well, I doubt we could have been luckier in the place our ship ended up, then."

Briony's brow furrowed. "Speaking o' that, why is yer ship here?"

Mistress Mendes's eyes, which had been glancing out the window, zoomed back to Briony's like an arrow. "We were on our way to Norway from our home in Portugal when the storm hit us. It was a business trip for my brother but a pleasure trip for me since I've never been there before. I must say it was the strangest storm I've ever seen. It appeared out of nowhere; there hadn't been a cloud in sight. Then suddenly everyone was fighting to keep the ship from flipping over, and I was trying not to be swept away. I've never been more terrified in my life."

"And was that how yer brother broke his leg?"

"Yes, one of the masts broke, and he was right underneath it. After all that happened, I'm honestly surprised he wasn't hurt worse."

"So, you were on yer way to Norway? I've never been there either. What has yer brother told you about it?"

The woman paused for a moment, and Briony thought her face seemed a little paler than before. "He—"

But then someone appeared beside them, and whatever

44

the woman had been about to say was lost.

"Good morneen, ladies. I dinna think we've been properly introduced. Mistress Fairborn, would you do the honors?" John Burgess stood by their chairs with a polite grin, looking to Briony expectantly.

Briony sprang to her feet. "O' course, Mr. Burgess. Mistress Mendes, may I present Mr. John Burgess. And Mr. Burgess, this is Mistress—"

"Lucia, please. The pleasure is all mine," she twittered.

"Charmed. I hope yer stay here is very restful and relaxing, fer both you and yer brother. My apologies fer his accident," he said, his voice full of warmth.

Briony's lips turned up at the corners. That was one of the things she liked about Mr. Burgess: he was incredibly kind. She was sure he knew of her illegitimacy, but for reasons she couldn't fathom, he didn't treat her differently for it. *'Tis too bad he'll have to go back home to Hollandstoun eventually. Everton needs more people like him.*

"Thank you, sir." Mistress Mendes's smile was so large it looked painful.

"I'll let you get back to yer discussion now. Excuse me." Mr. Burgess nodded at both of them and went on his way.

Mistress Mendes stared at him as he walked away, releasing a small sigh once he disappeared down the corridor.

She turned back around with a giggle. "We should have come here sooner. I had no idea there were such handsome men in Scotland. Tell me, is he married?"

As Briony returned to her own seat, she blinked at the other woman's boldness. *First Dr. Sherwin and now Mr. Burgess? Does she intend to flirt with every unmarried man in town?*

I suppose John Burgess is a good-looking fellow. His sky-blue eyes and flaming hair look nice together, and he's pretty muscular. But he's probably ten years older than I am, and Mistress Mendes looks even younger than me.

"He's a widower with a young son. He lives on a farm a few miles south o' here."

Briony waited for the light to fade from Mistress Mendes's eyes at the mention of a child. However, the woman's happy expression remained in place.

"Oh, is he? And he's not courting anyone now?"

"Nay, he's unspoken fer."

Her impossibly large smile grew even larger. She almost looked a little unhinged in her glee. "Thank you for telling me. Do you think you could—"

Briony stood, not wanting to hear whatever this strange woman was going to ask. If it involved matchmaking, she wasn't the person to talk to, anyway. "I better get going to help yer brother. Is he awake?"

Mistress Mendes's lips shifted into a pout, but she nodded. "Yes, he is. I suppose I'll talk with you later, then, Briony. May I call you Briony? I'd very much like to, and it would be wonderful if you called me Lucia."

"Uh, sure. Goodbye, Lucia." Briony turned and walked to Mr. Mendes's room as quickly as she could without making it obvious she was fleeing. *Are all Portuguese people so brazen? What have I signed myself up fer?*

When Briony knocked on the man's door, she heard a soft "enter" and went inside. To her surprise, another person was already in the room, a man she had no desire to see again.

I almost forgot Captain Costa is in Everton, too. His presence was just as formidable as before, perhaps even more so now that Briony could see him clearly in the morning light. He was much bulkier than Mr. Mendes, and Briony couldn't suppress a small gulp.

When the captain saw her, irritation shot across his face before he masked it behind a neutral expression. *Or perhaps that's just what I thought I saw.*

He rose from his seat and said, "Good morning, senhorita. I understand I have you to thank for helping my friend here when he first arrived. I'm most grateful for your service."

Briony frowned, unsure how to respond to such a different greeting from the one he gave the first time they met. There was a smile on his face, but Briony didn't like the look in his dark eyes.

"Dinna think anything o' it," she said after a moment. "Anyone in my place would have done likewise."

She was certain he noticed the terse quality of her tone, but Briony wasn't going to suddenly be friendly just because he told her good morning. His behavior on the ship had left a strong impression that wouldn't be smoothed away that easily.

"That may be so, but still, know that if you need anything, I'm at your disposal," he pressed.

Briony raised her eyebrows, but she didn't reply. After a few awkward seconds, Captain Costa bowed and said, "I shall leave you both, then."

He went out the door without a sound, and as soon as he was gone, Mr. Mendes fixed Briony with a probing look. "Is something wrong?"

"Nay, I'm just here to take you fer a walk. Dr. Sherwin wants me to start walking with you every day to help you recover."

Mr. Mendes didn't react to this news. He was still staring at her as though he was looking for something. "What was that between you and Captain Costa?"

"We met earlier. He just did na leave a good first impression."

A wrinkle formed on the man's forehead as he took in her words. "So, you would say first impressions are important, then?"

She shrugged. "I suppose they can be."

"Hmm. Let me ask you a question, then, to see what you would do: You want to show your gratitude to the beautiful woman who saved your life, but she has 'better things to do.' Would you persist in thanking her or honor her wishes to leave her alone?"

Briony flushed with shame. She had been so caught up thinking he was flirting with her when he had only wanted to thank her. *Stupid, stupid! O' course that was it. He would na flirt with me. . . .*

Did he call me "beautiful" just now? Briony's face reddened even more. Other than Adaira and her mother, he was the first person to describe her that way.

She looked at Mr. Mendes and tried to speak, but she found herself completely tongue-tied.

"I suppose I should just be glad fate has given me another chance to see her. And she'll be helping me again, so she must be kinder than her first impression implied."

"Um . . ." Briony wished she could be anywhere else at that moment.

Suddenly, the man smiled, making all the tension in the room dissipate. "And you're just in time. I'm not sure how it's possible, but I do believe you've saved me yet again."

"Saved you?"

"Yes, you're a real miracle worker," Mr. Mendes said with a twinkle in his eyes.

Briony felt a smile forming on her lips. "And how did I save you this time?"

"From boredom, of course! Don't tell Senhorita Stubbins, but the book she gave me is frightfully dull." He pointed to it on the nearby table.

Briony chuckled. She picked up the book and examined the cover. "What? You think it dull? 'Tis one o' my favorite stories."

Mr. Mendes placed a hand on the back of his neck and stammered, "Oh . . . Is it? Did I say dull? What I truly meant was *challenging*. Yes, the content required such . . . *deep thought* that I needed some time to . . . clear my mind before reading any more of it."

Briony snickered, extremely at ease for being around a man she barely knew. "I was only jesting, Mr. Mendes. In truth, I hate it, too. 'Tis one o' the least interesting books in town."

"Ah, you fooled me for a moment. I get very cross when someone fools me, you know," he said with a playful tone before his countenance hardened. "Anyway, if you're going to be the one helping me, there's something I have to ask you. And if you answer incorrectly, I fear I'll have to request a new walking partner."

Briony raised her eyebrows. "Oh?"

"Come closer." He beckoned with his hand.

Briony took a few steps toward the bed and bent down. Mr. Mendes leaned in as if he was telling her a secret and said, "Are you good company?"

Briony laughed again. She wasn't used to a man being so close to her, but for some reason, the proximity didn't bother her. "I'm afraid I can' answer that. You'll have to find out fer

48

yerself."

Mr. Mendes leaned back with a thoughtful expression. "Hmm, we shall see."

"Fer now, let's try to get you out o' that bed." Briony extended her arm for Mr. Mendes to grasp. He gripped it slowly, tenderly, as if he was afraid she might break.

"'Tis all right to grip my arm a little more tightly. I'm strong enough to handle it, and I know you need some extra strength right now."

Mr. Mendes looked embarrassed as he tightened his grip. A pleasant sensation shot through her where his hand touched her skin, but it also left her jittery and uncomfortable. She felt a blush appear on her cheeks, so she looked down to keep him from noticing.

Her gaze was drawn to the sturdy form of Mr. Mendes's arm. It was obvious he had a great deal of physical strength. *It must be quite a blow to his pride to need my help with something as simple as walking. 'Twould be difficult fer me to accept, too, especially if I had to rely on a stranger.*

Mr. Mendes cleared his throat.

Briony looked up at his face, and her eyes widened when she realized he'd caught her staring at his muscles.

"Try taking a step," she said, holding back a stutter.

Mr. Mendes complied, but as soon as he put weight on his injured ankle, he sucked in a sharp breath.

"Sit back down fer a moment," she urged, but Mr. Mendes waved his free hand in protest.

"It's nothing. I want to make it around the room on the first try. Just ask me something to distract me."

Briony pursed her lips, unsure if he was truly ready for walking yet.

"Please," he said with such softness Briony felt like she couldn't refuse him.

"Fine, but let me know if it becomes too painful. Why dinna you tell me what sort o' business yer in?"

Mr. Mendes took another step, but this time, he was more careful and it didn't seem to hurt as much. "I'm a merchant. Portugal exports a lot of agricultural products, like wine, salt, and dried fruits. I mainly sell salt from Setúbal and my hometown of Aveiro. I was actually on my way to Norway when the storm blew us off course."

"It must be very exciting to travel so much. I've never even been out o' Orkney before."

The man cocked his head to the side. "Truly? When there's so much world out there? Are you one of those homebodies who never want to explore the unknown? I don't see how anyone could be content to stay somewhere like this."

Briony frowned, offended at his arrogant tone. "Somewhere like this? Pray tell, what's so very wrong with it? You seem awfully quick to judge."

"Quick to judge? Just how much excitement can such a small place have? There are what, eighty people who live here?"

"One hundred and three," she snapped, "but what does it matter how many there are? If you've found somewhere that yer heart knows is home, the amount o' neighbors you have makes no difference."

Mr. Mendes opened his mouth to reply, but Briony wasn't finished. "Just because you've seen more o' the world than I have does na mean you can decide this village is na worth yer time. You've spent yer entire visit inside one room, so what inkling do you have o' what lies beyond it?"

Briony paused, stunned by her own reaction. *Why am I getting so defensive? This is Everton. Most o' my memories o' this place are far from happy.*

But all my good memories are here, too. Memories o' Adaira and Mum . . .

Or am I just worried he's going to judge me as harshly as he has my home?

Briony swallowed thickly. *Mr. Mendes and I actually had a chance o' getting along pretty well, and now I've ruined it with my quick tongue.*

The man coughed awkwardly. "I stand corrected. I apologize for my assumption."

Briony scrutinized him. *What? He's apologizing to me?*

"Perhaps there's a way I can make it up to you?" The man's green eyes sparkled with hope.

Rarely do I receive an apology, and never when my temper has gotten the best o' me. Maybe there's more to this Mr. Mendes than I thought.

She considered his words for a moment. "I have something better in mind. Once yer up fer it, how about I show you around Everton? Yer walks should include more than just the inn, and I'd love to give you the chance to see the village in a better light."

He gave her a warm smile. "I'd like that very much."

The Perils of Friendship

In no time, Briony found herself in a new routine, one she enjoyed more than she would have expected. Each day consisted of morning chores, followed by meeting Mr. Mendes at the inn at ten o'clock. It wasn't long before they were gallivanting through the village, meeting townsfolk and chatting about Everton's history.

The walking itself would last for thirty minutes at most, for Mr. Mendes could only handle so much, but the conversations usually stretched on for at least an hour, sometimes more. Briony looked forward to these talks and soon found herself wishing she didn't need an excuse to see Mr. Mendes every day. His kind and witty nature quickly endeared him to her, and she secretly hoped he liked her company as much as she did his.

The only part of the arrangement that bothered Briony was her obligation to report to Dr. Sherwin every couple of days. He intimidated many of the villagers besides her, but the first time she went to talk to him about Mr. Mendes was especially nerve-racking.

When she arrived at Dr. Sherwin's house, her nerves were so bad that her knees were like jelly. *I'm sure he's still perturbed about my outburst the last time we spoke. What if there are repercussions?*

It took several minutes for Briony to gather up enough courage to knock on the man's door. It opened with a loud creak, and Dr. Sherwin stood on the other side with a scornful expression.

"Hello, Doctor." Briony tried to give him a friendly smile, but her mouth felt stiff.

He said nothing as he turned and walked into his office. If he hadn't gestured with his hand for her to follow, she would have been too scared to move.

Briony gulped and took a seat across from him after he'd sat down at his desk.

"Write down Mr. Mendes's condition here," he said, handing her paper and a pen. Briony took them hesitantly, unsure how much detail he wanted. She opened her mouth to ask, but the man was already nose-deep in some medical papers. She wrote down a few sentences about Mr. Mendes's stride and her best judgment of his pain levels before setting the page down.

"That will be all," Dr. Sherwin said, dismissing her with his hand.

And that concluded their meeting.

The next time she went to the doctor's house, the encounter was much the same—he took Briony's notes on Mr. Mendes with barely a word spoken between them. Briony supposed that was simpler than trying to talk to him, so she came to accept the silence with a small degree of comfort. One fewer critical word was always a blessing.

One morning, Briony decided to take Mr. Mendes to Cramer's Field. It was one of the most scenic places in Everton, full of tall, vibrant grass and pretty flowers.

I hope he finds it as lovely as I do. . . . He has been to so many places though—Will it seem dull to him? Maybe 'tis just naïve o' me to think he might like it.

Nonsense! 'Tis still a good place fer him to see even if he has seen plenty o' nice fields before. With that thought in mind, Briony shoved her fear into the tiniest crevice of her heart and set off for the inn.

After she'd arrived and Mr. Mendes had invited her in, she immediately asked, "Do you like the outdoors much?"

"Indeed, I love being out in nature. It's a glorious gift to witness the Lord's creation with my own eyes," he said as he took her proffered arm.

Mr. Mendes leaned on her a bit more readily this time than

he had on the first day. Briony smiled as she noted that, in her effort to be friendlier since then, they'd also avoided any further arguments.

Briony led him outside and turned right to go up the hill. "I'm glad you think so since we're going to Cramer's Field today. 'Tis one o' the most beautiful places in all Everton. At least, I think so."

"Then I'm sure I'll agree."

After a few minutes, Briony said, "'Tis just up here," and the two of them stopped to gaze at the sight before them.

Acres of green ocean waved back and forth in the breeze. The sun was bright that morning, making the dewy grass glisten. Bees and butterflies flitted through the air about their business. Flowers were spattered sporadically through the grass, creating a brilliant array of colors. It was truly a sight to behold.

They stood there drinking it in for several minutes in a warm silence, broken only by the bees' gentle hums. Briony held Mr. Mendes's arm, bearing most of his weight so that he could remain standing.

But then Mr. Mendes drew in a quick breath. "I do believe I need to get off this leg for a bit."

"O' course. We can head back to the sitting room."

"No, let's not head back just yet. If you take me to that spot over there with the stones, I can still enjoy the view while I rest."

"If yer sure."

Once Mr. Mendes nodded, Briony helped him over to the large rocks at the edge of the field. They were a popular source of amusement for the village boys, who often jumped from the tallest ones to prove their bravery to each other.

As Briony took a seat on an adjacent stone, she asked, "When you traveled to all those far-off places, did you miss home, or was it too thrilling to get homesick?"

"Honestly, I never did suffer much from homesickness. I've never understood people's attachment to a piece of land or a particular town. I consider my ship more of a home than Aveiro."

"But what about the people you left behind—yer friends

and family?"

"Well, I always got to travel with my fri—" Mr. Mendes broke off for a moment. "I was never fortunate enough to have good friends. I . . . I'm actually a visconde back home." He rubbed the back of his neck and turned his eyes from her to the field.

"A what?"

"I believe the word in English is 'viscount.' After my parents died three years ago, I gained the title."

Briony's eyes nearly fell out of her skull. *A viscount? Actual nobility here in Everton?* Her first conversation with the man ran back through her mind, and, suddenly, she felt sick to her stomach.

"But you said you were a merchant. . . ."

Mr. Mendes nodded. "Yes, and that's true. I never felt like being a visconde was the right thing for me, and after my parents died, there were too many painful memories in my childhood home, so I bought a ship and started my own merchant business. In fact, I've been considering renouncing my title entirely."

"Why would you renounce it?"

"Because everyone who has ever tried to get close to me was only after my influence." His voice shook with emotion. "I don't even know what it means to have a true friend."

Someone hurt this man deeply. He may na be saying it directly, but his tone is practically shouting it. Briony's heart ached with sympathy.

"My parents and sister are the only ones who really cared about me. And now Lucia is all I have left."

Briony put a hand on the man's arm and said, "I'm so sorry, Mr. Mendes. I know what 'tis to be alone in the world. And I know what 'tis to lose someone you care about."

"Then you understand why I'm cautious about letting anyone else close—one way or another, it always ends in pain." Mr. Mendes gently pulled away from her touch and grasped a stray dandelion that had landed near his leg.

"I understand why you feel that way, but I dinna believe it should keep you from trusting people. Aye, death separates us from our families, and people can betray us, but na everyone is false. My friend, Adaira, is like a sister to me, but we weren' always like that. I *chose* to take a risk by letting her get close, and 'twas one o' the best decisions I've ever made. My life is so much fuller than it would have been if I'd kept her at a distance. I'd take a hundred betrayals over giving up a friend like her."

Mr. Mendes, who had been fidgeting with the dandelion in his hand, suddenly froze.

Did I anger him? I can' tell from his expression. . . .

They sat for a few seconds in awkward silence until the man said, "That's very wise, Senhorita Fairborn. I know I'm not supposed to ask this, but I have to know: What is your age? You can't be older than I, yet you seem to possess far more wisdom."

Briony felt another blush creep onto her skin. She wasn't used to anyone being so interested in her. The fact that he was an attractive young man only made things worse.

Should I even answer? Perhaps I could tell him a younger age since I'm nearly a spinster.

Briony turned to him with a lie on her tongue, but when she saw the earnest question on his face, she stopped. At that moment, Briony decided that she wanted to be honest with this man.

More honest than I've ever been with anyone. And that thought terrifies me.

"I've seen twenty winters," Briony whispered.

She stared intensely at Mr. Mendes as she waited for his reaction. Rather than judgment, though, the creases around his eyes deepened, and a grin appeared.

"In that case, I can't have you continue calling me Mr. Mendes, for I'm but a year older than you. You must call me Santiago."

Briony's heart sped up. *Does he realize how intimate that is?*

"Perhaps 'tis na such an unusual occurrence in Portugal, but here, na many people speak so informally to each other."

He frowned, and a trace of regret came into his voice as he said, "If it brings you discomfort, please ignore the request."

"Nay, 'tis just . . . It does na matter, I suppose. I should like to call you Santiago. And you must call me Briony, to be fair."

Santiago's face lit up with delight, and the radiance of it melted Briony's anxiety away.

Right now, I dinna think I even care how others may react. Na when it makes him this happy.

She returned the smile. "I thought you wanted to be careful about letting others get close to you. Dropping formalities does na seem to align with yer plan."

Santiago chuckled lightly and mumbled under his breath.

"What?" Briony asked.

"I'm beginning to feel like you see right through me."

The midwife gulped and stared at the ground in embarrassment. His candor was far too unnerving. *Would he be this open with everyone? Part o' me hopes na.*

"Is that a bad thing?" she ventured, kicking at the dirt as she spoke.

"Of course it is. I can't have you learning all my secrets," he replied jovially. "At least, not all at once."

Somehow this conversation had become a lot more personal than Briony was prepared for. She leaped up, eager to escape the strange tension in the air.

"Well, 'tis getting late. I better return you to yer room." She held out an arm without looking at him.

"I hope I've not done anything to upset you," he said as he rose to his feet.

"Nay, na at all," Briony stated, beginning to take them back. "I just have some cleaning I need to finish at home."

Santiago didn't say anything after that, neither as they entered the inn nor when they reached his room.

Briony didn't want him to think he had upset her, but she didn't know how to bid him farewell, so she simply turned to leave.

"Briony," he called, making her stop.

Her heart rate rose even more at the sound of her name on his lips. She didn't turn, couldn't turn, not when it meant having to face him.

"Thank you for listening today and for the advice. Also, do be careful, please. You're making it very hard not to consider you a friend."

Anything she might have been about to say dried up on her tongue when she heard those words. Before she knew what she was doing, her feet were flying from the room. In almost no time, she had fled down the corridor and out the main door.

She placed a hand on her chest, feeling like she'd just run five miles. *What am I doing? All he said was that he was starting to think o' me as a friend. Why did I run away?*

Adaira has been my only friend fer so long. . . . What if I can' be what he's hoping fer? 'Tis only a matter o' time before he finds out I'm illegitimate; once that happens, will he treat me the same way as my neighbors do?

Madness and Folly

The following day, it took all of Briony's courage just to knock on Santiago's door. She was so nervous that he was going to ask her why she'd run off before that she couldn't even look him in the eye when she entered.

"Good morning, Briony."

She nearly jumped when he spoke, especially since it was so strange to hear him use her first name. She looked up at him, surprised at the chipper tone in his voice. "Hello, Mr.— Santiago. Is there anywhere specific you'd like to visit today?"

Santiago smiled at her as if she was a ray of sunshine on a cloudy day. "I've been hearing from my sister about the interesting trinkets at the market. Can we go there?"

Briony found herself smiling back before she could stop herself. *Why should I bother stopping myself though? I might as well enjoy being friends with him while I can since he will probably shun me as soon as he knows about my background.*

"I think that's a splendid idea. Perhaps you'll discover something you have na seen before."

"Great! Then let's go." Santiago pushed himself up and grabbed Briony's arm.

They walked gingerly once they were outside, avoiding leftover puddles from the previous night's rain. When they arrived at the market, Briony quickly realized the whole place was abuzz with energy. Visitors were uncommon enough in Everton, but a group of forty foreigners was practically unheard of.

Many of the unmarried women flirted with the sailors as Briony and Santiago browsed the stalls. The language barrier was off-putting for some, but the most persistent ones didn't let that stop them from trying to get the men's attention. Briony watched the displays with disgust as several women practically threw themselves at the sailors. Briony suspected, though, that most of the men weren't interested in anything more than a good time, and she feared those "good times" might make a lot more work for her very soon.

"Do you know the crew members well?" Briony hazarded to ask.

Santiago turned his attention from the merchants' wares. "No, Captain Costa handpicked the crew. They're all quite excellent sailors. Why do you ask?"

"I was merely curious," she replied.

Santiago's eyes lingered on her face for a little longer than necessary before shifting back to the nearest booth, which just so happened to have a lot of fine jewelry. Briony, too, set her focus on the necklaces and bracelets, admiring their beauty. *I wish I could buy one fer myself, but I'm sure the prices are especially high right now since we have visitors.*

A particular pearl necklace caught her eye, and Briony extended a hand to it. It was one of the prettiest things she had ever seen. "Sir, how much—"

"Hello, there," came a voice, cutting Briony off.

Her stomach dropped when she recognized the speaker. *'Twas only a matter o' time before Santiago and the laird met, but I'd hoped na to be present when it happened. Especially since the last time I saw him was when we collided on the street.*

She plastered on a grin and spun around. Laird Oliver was standing a little ways off, looking like a cat that had just caught a mouse, a very nervous mouse named Briony.

"Greetings, Mr. Mendes. I am The Much Honored Joseph Oliver, Laird o' Harray. I would have come to introduce myself earlier, but my many responsibilities kept me from getting away."

Briony rolled her eyes at the man's bravado. *If "responsibilities" means stuffing yer face and mistreating yer servants, then I'd have to agree. You weren' even polite enough to ask me to introduce you to Santiago.*

The young merchant nodded as Laird Oliver continued. "I hope yer having a pleasant time here in Everton. I do wonder how well things can be going, though, with this woman as yer guide—"

"It has been going quite well, actually," Santiago cut in.

Briony's heart swelled, but the portly man's eyes widened in surprise. He frowned at the two of them for a moment before raising his eyebrows suggestively at Briony.

She looked away, embarrassed and angry. *I really hate that man. Despite all the rumors, I'm a virgin. I may have followed in my family's footsteps professionally, but that does na mean I intend to do everything my family did.*

"Still, Dr. Sherwin must have been feeling ill to have chosen her. Actually, Briony Fairborn, I've been meaning to talk to you."

The man waddled forward on his stout legs, coming to a halt right in front of her. He narrowed his eyes, and Briony mentally prepared herself for the onslaught of insults that were about to spew from his mouth.

Before he could start, though, Santiago was already speaking. "It is quite an honor to meet you, Laird Oliver. Your name has been mentioned many times in passing, and I had hoped to see you in person while here, despite your many 'responsibilities.' Now that I'm actually in your presence, it's easy to understand why everyone spoke so well of you."

Briony gaped at Santiago as she listened to the blatant flattery.

Laird Oliver, on the other hand, beamed at the praise, not seeming to suspect it was anything less than sincere. He opened his mouth to reply, but Santiago was too quick yet again.

"What is it you need to speak with *Mistress* Fairborn about?"

Briony didn't miss Santiago's emphasis on the respectful form of address, especially since the laird hadn't bothered to use it.

The laird's lips lowered into a frown. "The other day, this wench ran into me and made me drop my furs. She did na do

63

anything to help me pick them up, nor did she compensate me fer my loss. She's naught but trouble, and 'twould be wise fer you to remember that, lad. She needs to be put in her place."

Santiago's countenance turned thoughtful. "Ah, I did hear about that, senhor,[17] and I must confess I'm the one to blame. I'm deeply sorry, for she was on an important errand for me at the time. I'm more than willing to take care of the expense since it's my fault she was in such a hurry."

Briony placed her free hand on Santiago's arm. *Please, dinna do that. I dinna want you paying fer something you had nothing to do with.*

The laird's eyes homed in on the action, no doubt interpreting it as something else. "Well, if that's the case, dinna worry about it. I'm sure we can find other ways o' making up the difference. Perhaps we could come to some kind o' arrangement. I've heard yer a merchant, though I have na learned what sort."

Briony tried to say something, but Santiago grabbed her hand, shocking the words right out of her.

"Perhaps we could. Why don't you come visit me later on and we can discuss it?" the younger man said.

A greedy smile lit up the laird's face. "Aye, I shall call on you later in the afternoon, then, once I've had lunch."

Laird Oliver's cordial expression wavered when his eyes met Briony's, but he managed to keep it from slipping off completely before he turned and sauntered away.

Briony barely noticed his departure, though, since she was too busy thinking about the fact that Santiago was still holding her hand. Her stomach was tense all over, and every part of skin touching Santiago's own felt like it was up against a heated stove.

She glanced at Santiago and noticed that he wasn't even looking at her; he was peering at the spot where the laird had been standing.

Does he na realize he's still holding my hand?

She kept staring at him until he turned back to her. There was a question in his gaze, but then his eyes swept down to

---

[17] Portuguese title for a man; Mr.

their joined hands. With a jolt, Santiago released her fingers and dropped his hand to his side.

"Ah, I apologize. I wasn't paying attention. Were you saying something?"

Briony cleared her throat. "Laird Oliver is na someone you want to have many dealings with, especially na on my account."

Santiago frowned. "Why is that? Just because he's a narrow-minded fool?"

A chuckle burst from Briony's lips. "You have such a brilliantly direct way o' speaking sometimes. You've judged him correctly. He is a fool with nary a good bone in his body. But please, dinna do anything fer my sake. I've been dealing with him all my life. I can handle this."

"But you shouldn't have to, should you?"

"Nay, she definitely should na!" said a voice from behind them.

Briony and Santiago both flinched and spun around only to find Vincent McLaren, the mad fisherman.

"I did na mean to startle you, but the two o' you sure are jumpy," he cackled. His laugh turned into a wheeze as he tried to catch his breath.

Briony glowered at the man. *He keeps getting into my business lately and complicating things. I hope he does na make a habit out o' this.*

Mr. McLaren waggled a finger at her. "Now, dinna be fixing me with that look, lass. I can' help that yer na very observant. You dinna even notice things right under yer nose."

"You exaggerate, Mr. McLaren," she argued, her face hardening.

"Exaggerate? Bah! If that were so, you would na be searching fer the truth about yer mum."

"What do you mean by that? What do you know about my mum?" Briony hadn't meant to raise her voice, but by the time she'd finished speaking, she was almost shouting.

The middle-aged fisherman recoiled from her intensity. Santiago also seemed surprised, for she could feel his eyes piercing into her, but she kept her focus on Vincent McLaren. *I want a straight answer this time.*

The older man looked this way and that before he said,

"Why do you think yer mother never let you near the water? If you can figure that out, you may find the answers you seek."

"What's he talking about, Briony?" Santiago asked.

Briony turned to her companion and replied, "'Tis a very long story. You would na want all the details."

Santiago shook his head vehemently. "No, I want to hear. Please, you can trust me."

Briony, however, wanted to get more information from Mr. McLaren first, so she turned her attention back to—

An empty space. The fisherman was nowhere in sight. She couldn't even smell his distinctive odor.

"Wait, where did he go? Mr. McLaren!" she called. She twirled completely around, tugging the merchant along with her, but there was no sign of him.

"I can't see him, Briony," Santiago said.

"That man is slipperier than a seal. I dinna know how he does it. I'll probably find him later when I'm na expecting it. That's how it usually goes."

"In that case, could you tell me why he said those things?"

Briony sighed. "Maybe another time. I need to get you back to the inn."

Santiago's brow furrowed, but he didn't say anything else about it as they strolled out of the market.

Thank you fer na asking again. I'm sorry, but I'm na ready to tell you. Na yet. Maybe na ever.

After Briony left the man in his room with a short farewell, she wandered into the sitting room and took a seat.

Is there some other reason Mum never let me near the water beyond just a fear o' drowning? Could it have something to do with this connection I feel to the ocean?

If only Mum were still here so I could press her fer answers.

Then an unexpected thought crept into her mind. *I wonder what her opinion would have been o' Santiago. . . . Surely she'd like him as much as—*

"You have an awfully big smile on yer face there, my friend," Adaira commented as she walked up, feather duster in hand.

Briony touched her mouth to confirm Adaira's words. "Am I smiling? I did na even notice."

"Has Mr. Mendes been charming you with his curious accent and green eyes?"

"Adaira." She shook her head. "Nay, he has na been charming me. Besides, I'm na someone he should be charming, remember?"

Adaira gave her a knowing glance before turning to dust the mantel. "Aye, I remember what you said, but I've also been remembering something else that makes me think yer *exactly* the person he should be charming."

"And what is it you remember?" Briony asked, folding her arms.

"Back when we were kids and wanted to figure out who our future husbands would be, we buried those coals in the ground. Do you recall? The next day when we came back and dug them up, yers had two hairs in it. They were blond, just like a certain someone's hair."

"Nay, that's na how it happened. Only one o' the hairs was blond. The other was black."

Adaira paused in her dusting. "Oh . . . Perhaps the black hair came from yer head and was na fer divining a husband."

"Or perhaps 'tis childish to believe a coal can tell you what color hair yer future husband will have," Briony snapped. "I need to go see Dr. Sherwin, so please excuse me."

Adaira spun around with a hurt look. "Briony, you know I only want you to be happy."

The midwife broke eye contact and turned away so that Adaira wouldn't notice the tear streaking down her cheek. "I know, but 'tis folly to wish fer something that can never be."

A Tear within the Sea

The next morning, Briony went to apologize to Adaira before going down to Santiago's room. She found her friend in the foyer with some towels. Unfortunately, her father was already talking to her.

"I dinna know why it keeps feeling this way. That young doctor can' help me either. All he does is tell me the same thing over and over again. . . ."

Briony stopped paying attention to what the man was saying. *If I dinna step in, who knows how long Mr. Stubbins will drone on about his ailments?*

"Hello! 'Tis so good to see you both." Briony put as much cheer into her voice as she could.

Mr. Stubbins twisted around and scowled at the midwife. "I'll talk to you later, Adaira," he said without looking at his daughter, "when you have more *respectable* company."

Respectable, my foot! There's nothing respectable about being the town drunk, is there?

Briony almost said as much, but that would have ruined her whole purpose in addressing the man in the first place. Instead, she just kept a saccharine smile on her face until he was out the door.

"Yer unusually subdued this morneen. Is there something going on I should know about?" Adaira asked with a raised eyebrow.

"I just needed to talk to you alone, and that seemed like the fastest way to get rid o' yer father. Besides, I doubt you wanted to listen to his complaints anyway."

"Ah." Adaira nodded, but her countenance was a little guarded. "And what was it you wanted to say?"

Briony grabbed the woman's hand. "I'm so sorry fer being rude to you yesterday. I dinna think yer childish or foolish at all. I just . . ."

"Dinna believe you deserve love."

Briony's eyes widened. "N-Nay, that's na it. I just know what will happen when he finds out the truth, so *please* try to understand."

"O' course I understand, dearie. Maybe even a wee bit more than you do," she said, tapping Briony on the nose. "Dinna worry about me. I'm well acquainted with that temper o' yers; you might even say we're as old o' friends as you and I are."

Briony grinned, relieved that things were resolved between them. "It gladdens my heart to know yer na angry."

"Well, na everyone can be as much o' a hothead as you, you know. Now, go on, and I'll see you later." Adaira shooed Briony away with a hand, and the midwife scampered off down the hallway.

When she reached Santiago's door, she paused. *I wonder if I should wait a wee bit longer since 'tis half an hour early. Those seals just would na let me sleep any longer this morneen. I dinna recall them being this noisy in the past—*

Hushed voices on the other side of the door interrupted her thoughts. She instantly recognized one as Santiago's, but he was speaking in Portuguese, so she had no idea what he was saying. A second male voice responded in the same language, this one much deeper and harsher.

There was a pregnant silence before Briony heard the harsh voice again, this time much louder. Its owner spoke quickly, but one word he used was strangely emphasized: *morta.*

Santiago spoke again, and Briony thought she heard resignation in his tone. It gave her a sick feeling inside, and she couldn't help thinking there was something very wrong.

Suddenly, she heard movement, so she jumped away from the door and ducked down the hallway toward the back exit. Briony had just barely rounded the corner when the door opened.

She peered around to look and spotted two men in the corridor. One was the captain, and the other was the young sailor she had met when she first went aboard the *São Nicolau*.

Briony waited until they had left before she returned to her place in front of the merchant's room. *What does "morta" mean? It sounded important. Perhaps Santiago will tell me.*

She knocked on the door and entered when she heard Santiago's invitation.

"Briony, you're early. Is something wrong?" The man's expression seemed nervous.

She tilted her head, wondering how she could ask her question without revealing she'd been eavesdropping. She held out her arm for him to grasp.

"Nay, I'm fine. I do have a question though."

"Then I shall do my best to answer it." He took her arm and slowly rose for their walk.

"I was down by the dock yesterday and overheard two o' the sailors speaking. I dinna know any Portuguese, but I thought you might be able to help me translate."

Santiago's lips turned up into a smile, but the motion seemed strained. "I can certainly do that for you. What did you hear?"

This is where I must be careful.

She racked her brain for all the Portuguese words she could remember. "Ah, I only remember a few words: são, morta, pelo, mim—"

Santiago went as stiff as a board. "You heard these words *yesterday?*"

Briony's face flushed, but she didn't want to admit her lie. She nodded and attempted a casual grin.

Santiago's voice became deadly serious as he said, "I don't want you to go near the ship by yourself again. Stay away from it, all right?"

Briony frowned. "But why—"

"Promise me you won't. *Promise me.*"

What's going on? Why does he sound so desperate?

The force of the man's gaze was almost painful, but Briony held her ground. "I can' promise that when I dinna know why."

"You can't just trust me?"

She wanted to trust him, this man who told her of places she'd never been, places she could only dream of. *I dinna want to hurt him by saying nay. I can' do that to him.*

She opened her mouth, but then she stopped. She thought of the meeting she had just overheard in his room. *I want to believe he's a good man, but Santiago Mendes has secrets. And secrets are dangerous.*

"Is there something yer na telling me?" Briony whispered, barely able to force the words past her lips.

Santiago huffed. "That's entirely unfair of you to ask *me* that. Your whole life is surrounded by secrets. Is it even possible to know the real you?"

Briony's anger flared up. "What are you talking about? I've been nothing but myself around you. All you've seen is the real me."

"Yesterday, that fisherman said something about your mother. And the other man—Laird Oliver . . . He had nothing but ill intent toward you."

"And you suppose I deserve it?" She was shouting now, but she didn't care.

Santiago touched her arm gently, but then he pulled it back. "Briony, you're burning up!"

She looked down at her arm and noted the pinkish tinge on her skin. She didn't feel any warmer, though, just angry. "I'm fine. Dinna act like you care. Some friend you've turned out to be."

Something in Santiago's face broke. All visible signs of anger disappeared, leaving only sorrow behind. "I spoke too hastily when I said that before. I don't think friendship is in the cards for us."

"Well, I can agree with you on that," she sputtered, but her heart wasn't in the words.

"Please ask my sister to come here. She should be able to walk with me today."

Tears welled up in Briony's eyes, but she pushed them back. *I won' let him see that I care, especially if we're na even friends.*

Briony walked out the door with her head held high, but as

she stumbled through the hallway, the dam sprung a leak and those same tears began to trickle down her face. *I should have known this friendship was too good to be true. How could I let myself think 'twas real? And worse, I was starting to hope fer something impossible.*

"Briony, whatever is the matter?" Adaira appeared from one of the bedrooms, her brown eyes full of concern. One arm carried a basket of laundry, while her free hand pressed against her hip. She looked ready to either embrace her friend or beat up whoever had made her cry.

"I can' talk about it right now. Please, tell Mistress Mendes that her brother wants her. I have to go," she blubbered. She slipped around her friend and ran to the back door before Adaira could react.

"Dearie, will you be all right?"

"Aye, dinna worry!" Briony wrenched open the door and raced up the path. She walked briskly, not pausing to glance at the people she passed. She needed time alone, and there was one place in particular she often went to when life felt difficult.

To most, it was nothing more than an outcrop just past Drulea Cottage, but to Briony, it was a secret haven. The stones there sat in a strange formation, almost making a perfect circle.

My own barrier from the rest o' the world.

The only way in was through a single gap between two stones, a spot just barely wide enough for a grown person. It led to a large cliff that offered a beautiful view of the sea. Many people would have been nervous to be on a ledge so high up, especially since sharp rocks jutted from the water just below, but Briony liked to sit right on the cliff's edge where the wind blew freely on her face.

Almost there. Just a wee bit farther—

"Mistress Briony, I'm so glad to see you!" a high voice piped up.

Briony stopped in her tracks, just in time to keep from falling on young Fergus McGuff. She bent down to almost his level and raised an eyebrow at him, but the boy just smiled at her like she was the best part of his day.

Briony forced her lips up, hoping he wouldn't notice her

red eyes. "How are you, Fergus?"

"I've been wanting to tell you something, but I could na find you. Where have you been?"

Guilt pricked at her conscience. *I've been so focused on Santiago that I did na realize I've been neglecting poor Fergus. I'm sure his mum is happy about that, but I hate the thought that he was looking fer me and could na find me.*

"I'm so sorry. I've been busy trying to help one o' the visitors with his recovery. Have you met Mr. Mendes?"

Fergus's sullenness melted into understanding. "Oh! The one with the broken leg? He's so nice. He gave me some candy when I met him. Dinna say anything to Mum though."

Briony's grin became real as she listened to the child. He always had that effect on her. He was just so funny she couldn't help being in a good mood around him.

"But, Fergus, what did you want to tell me?"

Fergus's eyes widened. "Right! 'Tis very important, Mistress Briony." He leaned in close to her ear. "Mr. Gully is a girl!"

Briony chuckled as the boy drew back. "What? How did you find that out?"

"'Twas na me—Hannah found out. There were eggs on her . . ." Fergus trailed off and looked around at everything except Briony.

"Fergus, where were the eggs?"

The boy tapped his foot on the ground, his face as red as a tomato. "They were on Hannah's koad."

Briony burst out laughing. "Fergus, what happened when she found it?"

"She screamed, and I came in with Mum, and then Mum screamed. 'Twas so funny." Fergus's entire face lit up as he told the story.

The two of them laughed together, Fergus in remembrance and Briony at the thought of Mistress McGuff screaming.

But then Fergus's countenance darkened. "I got in a lot o' trouble. I mean, a lot. And Mum got rid o' Mr. Gully."

Briony rubbed Fergus's head in sympathy. She had to fight not to laugh again, but she held it together for the boy's sake.

Fergus suddenly glanced up the hill. "I better get going, or Mum will be mad again. I'll tell her I saw you."

Briony waved her hands back and forth. "Nay, nay! You dinna need to mention me."

Fergus looked slightly confused, but he nodded in agreement. "All right. Goodbye, Mistress Briony."

The little boy sprinted up the path toward his house, and Briony beamed as she watched him depart. She stood there for a moment, feeling much better, but then she remembered where she had been going and, more importantly, why. As soon as she did, sadness billowed up within her again and she couldn't reach the outcrop fast enough.

Once Briony got to her destination, she dangled her feet off the ledge and looked out at the vast sea. *It looks so tranquil today. If only the rest o' my life could be like that. Why did Santiago push me away? Was it truly because he thought I dinna trust him?*

Briony tossed a pebble over the side and watched it splash.

Perhaps he's right. Perhaps I've closed myself off too much fer him to truly know me. Fer anyone to know me.

Several more tears formed in her eyes. She leaned over and sighed as they, too, splashed into oblivion below. *Is that all that's in store fer me? To die and be forgotten like a tear within the sea?*

Briony rose to her feet and turned away before she could notice two black eyes peering at her from the water.

Ice and Storms

When Briony woke the following morning, a strange scent filled her nostrils, and she found herself going to the front door before she was even fully awake. She tugged it open and found a large stack of sea trout on her doorstep. There was no note to suggest who had left them there, but Briony knew they hadn't been there the night before; the smell was so strong that she was sure she would have noticed them if they were. There was no stench of decay, though, and they looked like they were freshly caught.

'Twould be foolish to eat them, but they are rather tempting. . . .

Scoffing at herself, Briony scooped up the fish and marched to the edge of the cliff behind her cottage. *'Tis truly a shame that someone wasted so much food, but 'tis too risky to eat them when I have no idea where they came from.*

Briony released the fish and watched them topple into the waves below.

Two grey seals appeared in the water nearby for a moment before dropping back out of sight. They were ecstatic to receive such an easy meal, and Briony felt a stab of jealousy that they got to enjoy her favorite food instead of her.

Dinna be ridiculous, Briony. 'Tis just a bit o' trout. I know it has been a while since you've gotten to eat any, but 'tis na worth being upset over. Besides, you shall have a feast once Johnsmas arrives. I'm sure Santiago will enjoy it—

Briony stopped as she recalled their fight and melancholy settled in. She shook it off as best she could, for she wasn't

77

ready to give up on the friendship just yet.

Na without properly fighting fer it. Though I'm sure he's keeping something from me, I know I have na been completely open with him either. Just because he has a secret does na mean he's a bad person.

Briony thought of her own secrets as she walked into the town church for the Sunday service. *I'm surprised Santiago has na already learned I was born out o' wedlock. Laird Oliver is usually eager to talk about my "many" sins.*

I never did ask Santiago if the laird stopped by after we saw him that day.

She spotted Adaira up toward the front and slid in next to her.

"Where's yer father?"

Adaira rolled her eyes. "He claimed he was 'ill.' He usually is after a night at the tavern."

Briony just patted Adaira's shoulder in sympathy. Then she took a glance around the church at all the faces, her eyes stopping when they met Santiago's. He was standing by the pew across from hers, apparently about to sit down beside his sister.

Her stomach clenched at his green gaze. It was intense in a way that made her want to look away, but she found herself unable to.

Does he regret how we left things yesterday? Please let it be so. She sent him a small smile.

Santiago's lips curved up, and he opened his mouth as if he wanted to speak, but then the vicar reached the pulpit. Briony shifted her gaze as Santiago took a seat, but she could still feel his stare as Vicar Peterson spoke.

About halfway through the sermon, Adaira leaned over. "You must tell me what's going on between you and our favorite merchant. I declare, he has been looking at you this entire time."

Briony's face warmed so much she was sure even her ears were red. "I honestly dinna know. Fer one moment, we were friends. The next, we were arguing. And now . . ."

Adaira smirked. "Even a blind person could see there's more than friendship on that man's mind."

"Adaira, be quiet!"

"Shh," Mrs. McGuff said from the row ahead of them. Briony looked in horror as the woman turned and glared daggers at her. Fergus and Hannah sat on either side of Mrs. McGuff, and Mr. McGuff sat on Fergus's other side.

"Hi, Mistress Briony," Fergus whisper-yelled, giving her a wave.

Mr. McGuff grabbed his son's hand and grumbled in his ear. Fergus grimaced and slouched down in his seat, looking at the floor.

Briony put her hand over her face, thoroughly humiliated. She tried not to notice the fact that Adaira was still smirking.

After what seemed like the longest service she had ever attended, Briony leaned over to her friend and growled, "Adaira! What if Mrs. McGuff overheard our conversation?"

"Relax, dearie. She has always been hard o' hearing."

Briony frowned. "What? I did na know that."

"Aye, that's why she sits so close to the front every week. She's much too proud to admit it, but I overheard her and Dr. Sherwin talking about it once on my way home from the market . . ."

Briony drowned out Adaira's gossip as her eyes drifted back to the blond merchant, finding that he was looking her way once more.

Something sparked in his eyes that gave her the courage to rise from her seat and step toward him. *I've never been very good at making amends, but maybe—*

"I seek Mistress Fairborn. Where may I find her?"

That voice . . . Briony spun toward the sound like a magnet. *There's something about that voice.* Briony couldn't quite put her finger on it.

A man stood off to her left with Donal McGuff. He was of average height and build with black hair and pale skin. There was a strange beauty to him that both attracted and repelled Briony as soon as she saw him. He reminded her of the ocean, screaming of danger yet also of something more. Something that Briony's soul yearned for.

His clothing was simple and a little oversized. Shoes donned his feet, unusual for natives at this time of year but normal enough for foreigners.

He hadn't seen her yet. *Which feeling should I trust, the one telling me to run away or the one telling me to talk to him?*

Deciding to follow the second instinct, Briony strode over. As she got closer, the man turned in her direction so swiftly that it was as if he already knew who was approaching. Briony drew in a quick breath of surprise when she glimpsed his black eyes. They were all too familiar, but she couldn't remember where she'd seen them before.

"Ah, here she is. Mistress Fairborn, this man has been looking fer you," Donal said and excused himself. He seemed strangely happy to leave, especially considering how cordial he tended to be with visitors.

"Hello, Mistress Fairborn. 'Tis a pleasure to see you again," the man greeted with a warm smile.

"*Again?* I dinna recall meeting you, Mr. . . .?"

"Niall Moreland, but please call me Niall. I'm most grieved that you dinna remember me. I suppose 'twas a long time ago, but the memory fer me is quite clear. We were only wee bairns then. 'Twas about this time o' year, too. Surely you recall that day, though, fer 'twas the day you saved my life."

Briony gasped as raw pain filled her mind. Memories began to emerge, overcoming her attempts to thwart them. . . .

***

While on an errand for her mother, eight-year-old Briony heard an earsplitting cry.

'Tis coming from the beach!

She scurried down to the shore to see what was happening and was horrified at what she found: a wee lad crouched against the rocks, naked but for a gray piece of clothing wrapped around his waist. Half a dozen bairns stood taunting and throwing rocks at him as he wailed. Briony recognized them all—Alastair Oliver, St. John and Gareth Peterson, Elspet Milligan, Adaira Stubbins, and Ewan Sherwin.

"Stop! Stop!" she shouted, but they couldn't hear her over the boy's cries.

Briony darted her eyes about, hoping she would see an adult who could fix this, but no one was there. She garnered up her courage and dashed toward the group.

Just as she reached them, though, a foot shot out in front of her, causing her face to collide with the hard sand.

More laughter ensued, but this time, it was directed at her. Briony pushed herself up from the ground and scowled at the other children. "Leave him alone!"

"Make us," bellowed Alastair Oliver, the one she was sure had tripped her.

She glared up at him. *He has always been rude to me, but now he's picking on a stranger? That's just too far.*

Briony shoved him, knocking the taller boy to the ground. Then she stumbled closer to the wee lad, who was trembling in fear. She grabbed his arm and ran a few steps, but the other children chased them.

There's no way to outrun them. Unless . . .

Briony stopped in front of some rocks and spun around, watching as the others drew nearer. She glanced at the young boy; he was roughly her age, but he seemed younger because of his terror.

"Can you make a run fer it while I distract them?"

The boy raised his eyes, black as night, to hers for a moment and nodded. "Aye, thank you." His voice sounded hoarse, as though he hadn't spoken in a long time.

"Stop it, all o' you! This is wrong!" Briony exclaimed as she turned her eyes back to them.

She felt the boy slipping away behind her, but she didn't dare look. She had to make sure the others kept their attention on her long enough for him to escape—

***

Briony winced as she pushed the memory back before the worst of it could resurface. She had tried so hard to forget it, but now this man was undoing her efforts.

His painfully familiar black eyes watched her carefully.

Briony let out a shallow breath as she tried to collect herself. "Ah, I remember you now. You were the wee lad that day on the beach. I never knew what happened to you. Where did you go?"

Niall's face brightened. "I'd only run a short distance before I saw my mum and da'. When I told them how you'd saved me, they rushed to make sure you were all right, but they said everyone was gone by the time they arrived. I've always regretted what happened that day. I should na have run off like that and left you. Did anything happen to you afterward?"

Something buzzed in her mind at those words, something off about them, but then the memory started to reappear—

Briony looked away from him. She had closed that door in her mind a long time ago; she refused to open it again now. "Dinna let it trouble you. 'Tis all in the past."

The man's eyes narrowed suspiciously. "Still, I should have stood up fer myself, na let a female get in harm's way because I was frightened. Perhaps I can make it up to you. To start with, would you like to have dinner with me this evening? I'm staying at Everton Inn, and I hear they have delicious food."

Briony mulled it over for a moment. *Spending time with Niall might dredge up more o' what I can' bear to remember. . . . But he looks so eager fer me to say aye. . . .*

And he is very handsome with his mysterious eyes. Briony blushed at the thought and grinned, having reached a decision.

"Aye, I'd be delighted to have dinner with you tonight. Mistress Stubbins, the one who runs the inn fer her da', is a good friend o' mine, so I spend much o' my time there anyway. The food truly is delicious."

"If you have the time, would you mind showing me around Everton some beforehand? Otherwise, I may na be able to find my way back to the inn, and dinner may be long gone."

"I suppose I could do that," she replied, the smile not leaving her face.

He smiled in return, and soon Briony found herself inexplicably captivated by the strange newcomer. They chatted as they walked through the streets, mostly about the buildings and daily life in the village. Briony introduced him to Mistress McGuff and her bairns, Matthew Levins, and the Calhouns when they passed each other. The townsfolk were all very amicable toward the newcomer, except for Fergus, who stuck out his tongue when Niall went to shake his hand.

"What is that building?" Mr. Moreland asked after they had ended their conversation with the Calhouns.

"'Tis the tavern. Mr. Tam McLaren runs it. I can take you inside if you'd like?"

She wondered if Mr. Moreland was the sort of man who spent much time drinking. *He does na look like a drunkard, but I suppose 'tis impossible to know just from his appearance.*

"Aye, perhaps there will be more people you'd like to introduce me to."

Stepping inside, Briony was surprised to see so many Portuguese sailors having beers. Captain Costa was among them, taking a long swig out of a half-full mug.

Briony grimaced. She'd been fortunate enough not to see the man in quite a while. *I wonder which captain I'll speak to this time: the curt one I met on the night he arrived or the polite one who didn't seem completely genuine. I guess I better just speak to him. How he responds is na up to me.*

"Captain Costa, sir."

The man set down his drink and looked over at the two of them. At first, his features seemed to harden, but then he grinned quite civilly. "Senhorita Fairborn, what a pleasant surprise. I don't believe I've met your companion before."

Briony walked the rest of the way over, Mr. Moreland close behind. "That's because he just came into town from . . ."

She frowned, realizing Niall had never told her where he was from. She looked to him for the answer.

Niall hesitated before clearing his throat. "The Mainland."

"Ah. If you did na know, Captain, the Mainland is Orkney's largest island. This is Mr. Moreland, an old friend o' mine."

Mr. Moreland's eyes snapped to hers when she called him a "friend," and she instantly regretted it. The word had fallen from her lips effortlessly, but now she realized it was too informal. *After all, we only met once as bairns, and that was only fer a very brief time.*

"Good to meet you, Senhor Moreland. If Senhorita Fairborn thinks highly of you, you must be a good fellow. She has the utmost respect in my eyes since she saved the life of

83

my employer. I'm Captain Andreas Costa."

Mr. Moreland's eyebrows rose. "She saved another soul besides mine? Please, do share."

"Have a seat, then," he said, gesturing to the two empty chairs in front of him.

Niall and Briony complied easily, and the captain began his rendition of the tale.

Briony knew the gist of what he was going to say, so she let her eyes wander around the room as he spoke, noticing that several sailors were staring at Mr. Moreland and mumbling in their native tongue. *How I wish I knew Portuguese.*

Mr. Moreland, on the other hand, was completely engrossed in the story, and his face lost more and more color as it went on. He never looked away from Costa and never interrupted, but by the time the captain drew to a close, the man was as white as a sheet.

"Mr. Moreland, are you well?" Briony asked.

He shook himself and gave the midwife a half smile. "Aye, Captain Costa's tale was simply so riveting. I can hardly imagine how all o' you were able to stay calm in the midst o' such peril. And, Mistress Fairborn, I had no idea you were such a skilled healer."

The sailors puffed up at the flattery, but Briony turned her attention to the floor, unused to the praise.

Almost instantly, the sailors offered Mr. Moreland and Briony drinks and began to share more stories of their adventures. Briony was careful not to overindulge, and she noted that Captain Costa kept his men from going overboard in their consumption as well. Some of the townsfolk also sat down to listen in and share tales of their own with nary a hateful glance in Briony's direction. Everyone was caught up in the merry atmosphere of the room.

All in all, it was much more pleasant than Briony had expected, and by the time she and Mr. Moreland took their leave, she was in a wonderful mood. It was the first time Briony had enjoyed herself in the tavern; she tended not to spend much time in places where people congregated since more people meant more hostility directed her way. Usually, she only came there to help Adaira retrieve her drunken father.

But today, people have been friendlier with me than I can ever remember. I've even gotten a few smiles, mostly from Mr. Moreland, but still.

"Did you meet my friend, Adaira, when you first arrived?" Briony asked as she and Niall meandered up to the inn.

"Nay, I only met an older fellow who did na seem very friendly." Mr. Moreland opened the inn door for her, and they entered the foyer.

"You must be one o' the only ones unlucky enough to have Mr. Stubbins show you to yer room instead o' his daughter. She's probably in the kitchen since dinner is usually about an hour from now. I'll go check so you can meet her, Mr. Moreland."

"Thank you; I'd love to meet her. Seeing as we're 'old friends,' though, I must insist that you call me Niall," he said with a wink.

Briony's heart quickened at the movement, and the room suddenly felt hot. Her mistake earlier had slipped from her mind, but now she wondered if it hadn't been a mistake at all. *Mr. Moreland—or rather, Niall—does na seem to mind.*

"*Niall*, was it?" a sharp, ominous voice asked.

Briony turned toward the male voice, locking in on a deep pair of eyes across the room. Hurt flashed in those green orbs for a split second as they met hers, but then they flitted over to the man beside her and hardened like a block of ice.

Guilt pierced Briony's chest, though she couldn't think of why it came. *Tis na like I've done anything wrong, save fer putting off making amends with Santiago.*

Lucia, who was standing at the hall entrance with her brother, obviously sensed the tension as well. Her hand trembled as she held Santiago's arm, and her brown eyes, usually so striking, seemed washed out. Still, she made no move to hold Santiago back as he led them over to Briony and Niall.

Briony pieced together a smile and turned to Niall, hoping this exchange would go well. "This is Mr. Santiago Mendes, the one who hurt his leg, and his sister, Lucia Mendes."

Niall's eyes, black already, seemed to darken even more as they took in the Portuguese merchant.

85

Briony gulped, but she continued to pretend everything was normal. "And this is Mr. Niall Moreland, an old . . ." Her voice petered out as she got caught up in Santiago's gaze again.

"An old what?" He raised a light eyebrow.

"*Friend.*" Niall took a step forward, a storm swirling in his eyes.

What's happening? Briony looked to Santiago desperately, mentally asking him to stop whatever was going on.

He noticed her expression and hesitated in what he'd been about to say. Something warred in his eyes for a moment, something Briony couldn't fathom, but then the animosity faded from his face.

"It's an honor to meet any friend of *Briony's.*" Santiago held out his hand to shake.

Briony noticed how Niall's eyes narrowed when Santiago used her first name and how he didn't attempt to shake the merchant's hand. "So *yer* the one Briony helped. I trust that 'twill na be very long before you recover enough to return home."

Shifting Ties

Santiago frowned and lowered his hand. When he next spoke, the icy edge had returned to his voice. "I'm still in the early stages of healing, so it will probably be weeks before I'm ready to depart. Then again, Briony has been walking with me regularly so I can regain my strength. She's very kind to those she considers friends."

"Briony has always been far too willing to give o' herself to help someone. I wonder if you might recover even faster if 'twas someone *else* helping you."

Santiago's face morphed at that moment as all pretense of courtesy fell away, leaving only aggression in its place.

Niall smirked back at him, seeming to enjoy that his words had gotten under Santiago's skin.

Why are they so angry with each other? Whatever the reason, I better get rid o' this friction quickly.

"*Santiago*, I've been meaning to talk to you." She put as much warmth into her voice as she could while saying the merchant's name.

The line of his mouth softened just the slightest, and he nodded.

"Lucia, may I exchange places with you?"

Lucia gave her a relieved look as Briony took Santiago's arm, but Niall looked hotter than a Johnsmas bonfire.

"I'll be back in a moment fer dinner, Niall. Adaira will be bringing out the food soon, so please let her know I'll be joining you."

Niall gritted his teeth, glaring at Santiago's hand on Briony's arm. Without giving a response, the dark-eyed man stomped off to the sitting room, taking the tension with him.

At least, Briony thought he did until she looked into Santiago's eyes and felt a completely different kind of tension. A shiver shot down her spine, and she broke eye contact, but she knew the flush in her face must be visible to everyone.

Lucia's brow furrowed as she looked between the two of them, but then she pursed her lips and said, "I suppose I'll go see if Mr. Burgess is around. I've been meaning to run into him again, after all." She gave Briony a final smile before sauntering away.

Briony, breathing a little easier now that everyone was gone, tugged Santiago to the door.

"Briony, why are you taking us outside? I thought you said dinner was almost ready." There was no trace of bitterness in the man's voice, only confusion, which gave Briony a thrill of hope that things could be patched up between them.

"I'd rather this be a truly private conversation. I dinna know about yer sister or Niall, but Adaira is notorious fer eavesdropping. Better to be safe."

Something akin to humor snuck onto Santiago's face for a few seconds, but then a neutral countenance replaced it. "And what sort of conversation will we be having?"

Briony didn't answer at first as they ambled out and then onto the path. They reached the same edge of Cramer's Field where they had stood before. She gestured for Santiago to sit down on the stone where they had rested last time, which he did without saying anything more.

She took a deep breath, looked straight into those shining green eyes, and said, "An honest one, I hope. I care too much about you to let one argument destroy our friendship. You may claim that we were never friends, but I dinna believe that. And I dinna know if you value our friendship as much as I do, but I want to give it another chance if yer willing. What do you say?"

The man's face, which hadn't betrayed any feeling when she'd started speaking, now shifted into a smile so large his beard couldn't conceal it.

And suddenly, everything felt right in the world again. The

beautiful warmth of sunshine after a rainstorm filled Briony's heart, and before she was even aware of it, she was smiling back.

Then Santiago turned somber. "Briony, I-I'm so sorry. I shouldn't have said those things. You don't have to tell me anything about yourself that you don't want to. Your secrets are your own, and I don't have any right to pry."

"Nay, you were right. I told you before 'tis better to risk some hurt by letting people close to you, and here I've done the exact opposite by pushing you away. I want to change that if you'll let me. Would you mind if I resumed my morning walks with you?"

Santiago clasped her hand in his. "I'd like nothing better. But, Briony, what I said before about the docks . . ." He sighed. "If you wish to see the *São Nicolau* sometime, please let me know and I'll go with you, all right?"

And here we are, back to the same place again—secrets. But maybe if I open up more, so will he.

Briony nodded and rose. "I will. Now, we better get back to the inn; otherwise, we'll miss dinner."

Santiago grinned, but this time, it didn't quite reach his eyes.

They shuffled into the dining room, but just as Briony helped Santiago to a seat, she heard a growl from the kitchen.

"Do you think I'm a fool? I know exactly who you are, and I remember *what you did.*"

Briony raced toward the sound and found Niall glaring across the room at Adaira, who looked ready to collapse from fright.

"What's going on here?" Briony asked.

Niall's terrifying stare wheeled over to the young midwife. "Briony, how could you befriend her? After she tried to—"

Briony held up a hand. "Niall, calm down."

Adaira, looking like she'd just seen a ghost, cried, "Briony, what's he talking about? I dinna know what I did to upset him so. He's talking like a madman!"

Niall roared, "Dinna tell me you've forgotten. Or was it *normal* fer you to abuse strangers as a child?"

Confusion riddled the younger woman's face.

Briony stepped between Adaira and Niall. "Adaira, this is Niall. He's the boy from the beach that day. The boy—"

"The boy you threw rocks at and laughed at till he cried," Niall finished.

Adaira gasped as recognition filled her eyes. "That was you?"

"Aye, that was me, you evil witch. I'm na such a wee bairn anymore though."

"I-I'm so sorry fer what we did to you. 'Twas so wrong—"

"Are you *truly* sorry? Do you have any idea how traumatizing that was?" He stepped forward, moving merely a few inches, but it felt like miles. His stance was bloodthirsty, wolfish, as he closed in. Briony wondered what she'd seen in the man; right then he seemed like more of a beast.

"Truly, 'twas a horrible mistake! I've regretted it ever since," Adaira whimpered. She trembled, guilt and terror fighting for dominance within her.

"Yet you did na even recognize me at first," Niall spat, full of disgust.

"Well . . . 'twas . . ." Tears began to fall onto her cheeks.

Niall took another step. Briony stood straighter to block the man's view of her friend.

Then someone cleared his throat from behind Niall. The three people in the kitchen turned to look. There stood John Burgess, raising an eyebrow. His son peeked around from behind him at Niall.

"Pardon me, but has dinner already been served? My son and I were taking a walk and lost track o' the time. I hope we're na too late," Mr. Burgess said.

Briony let out a sigh. *Mr. Burgess, I liked you before, but yer one o' my favorite people now. If you did na do that on purpose, you must have the best timing in the world. I dinna think I've ever seen Adaira look more relieved.*

Adaira wiped at her eyes and smiled. "Nay, yer just in time. Please have a seat. I'll bring it out shortly."

Mr. Burgess nodded, but he didn't sit down. Instead, he looked pointedly at Niall.

"I dinna believe I've had the . . . *pleasure* . . . o' meeting you yet. My name is John Burgess." He held out his hand, scowling as he did so.

Niall took it, shaking it twice as he sized the man up. "Niall Moreland. I've just arrived in town."

"Ah, yer here fer dinner, then?"

"Aye, Briony was—"

"He was just on his way out, and I was about to see him off. Go ahead and start without me, Adaira." Briony grabbed Niall's arm, squeezing it painfully, and dragged him to the foyer.

"What are you doing?" Niall asked once they were alone.

"How dare you talk to Adaira like that! She's na the same person who hurt you all those years ago. Yer staying in her family's inn, yet you had the gall to call her a witch. What is wrong with you?"

Niall crossed his arms, his voice as firm as granite as he said, "From what I've seen, people never truly change. You were a hero back then, so I'm certain yer still that same good person. She was cruel back then, so that cruelty must still reside within her. She may veil it well, but 'tis there. Be glad that now you know the truth."

Briony clenched her fists to keep from slapping the man. "You know *nothing* about who she is now, so dinna pretend that you do."

Niall blinked in surprise. He opened his mouth but thought better of it and closed it again. He stood silently for a moment and then replied, "If yer so certain she's changed, then perhaps I . . . misjudged her. With time, she can prove her true character to me."

Briony jerked back in shock at the sudden change. *Is he being sincere? I can' tell one way or the other.*

He dazzled her with a strangely white smile. It was so beautiful that Briony just gaped at him. But then she remembered herself and realized they were standing closer than she liked.

"Hmm, well, good. I'm glad yer seeing reason now. However, before you go back in there, you need to think up a really good apology fer how you acted. That will give you a chance to prove yer character to me as well."

Niall frowned as if he'd expected her to forgive and forget

more easily, but then he nodded. "As you wish. I can see this is important to you and that you need some time. I suppose I can get some food down at the tavern fer now. Just know that getting forgiveness from the two o' you shall be my highest priority until 'tis attained. After that, I have more interesting things in mind."

For reasons unfathomable to her, Briony felt a blush rise to her cheeks. *What's wrong with me? I know almost nothing about this man except that he has a fearsome temper.*

Niall grabbed her hand and kissed it, drawing a slight gasp. He smirked and stepped away. "Until later, then, lovely Briony."

Briony stood in a daze as she watched him stride out of Everton Inn, only managing to recompose herself once he was no longer in view.

When she returned to the dining room, everyone was in a much merrier state. Adaira was flitting about like a butterfly as she served her guests, Santiago was telling lively tales, William was stuffing himself with food, Lucia was flirting with Mr. Burgess, and Mr. Burgess was—

Briony stifled a laugh as she sat down next to Santiago. Mr. Burgess looked far too uncomfortable as Lucia tried to feed him from a spoon. He leaned away and—

CRASH!

Mr. Burgess had tilted back so far that he'd collided with Adaira and they'd both ended up on the floor with mashed potatoes all over them.

"Are you all right, mistress?" Mr. Burgess asked, gripping Adaira's hand as the two of them rose to their feet.

Adaira cleared her throat. "Aye, o' course. How clumsy o' me. I—"

"You? Nay, I was the clumsy one. 'Tis my fault since I'm the one who . . ."

Briony stopped listening to their words and realized something their body language was screaming loud and clear. *They fancy each other!*

O' course they do. How could I na have seen it sooner?

She chuckled at how oblivious she'd been, unintentionally catching Santiago's attention. He gave her a questioning look.

Briony leaned over. "I never noticed how perfect they are fer each other."

Santiago smiled and looked back at the couple. "Are they?"

"Aye. I've never seen Adaira act like this before. Mr. Burgess is a good man, and she deserves someone who will treat her well. I'm happy fer them both."

"Yer a good friend, Briony. I'm sure Senhorita Stubbins would say you deserve the same."

Briony turned away shyly. "If you knew me better, you would na say such things."

"I doubt that," he mumbled, almost as if he hadn't meant for her to hear.

Briony looked back at him. *There's something else behind his words, something below the surface. But what?*

The man continued, "I'm glad we decided to give our friendship another chance. If the way you care about Adaira is any indication of how you treat your friends, I'd say I'm quite fortunate."

She didn't have anything to say to that, so she returned her attention to Mr. Burgess and Adaira as they continued to awkwardly and adorably speak to each other.

"'Twas a mighty fine dinner you prepared, Mistress Stubbins."

"I'm glad you enjoyed it, Mr. Burgess. Are you certain the stew could na have used a wee bit more salt though?"

"Nay, 'twas wonderful, mistress. I'm sure everyone else thought so, too."

"Mine was rather watery," complained William.

John's eyes homed in on William like a hawk watching a mouse, and the room grew so quiet that Briony could hear the crickets outside.

"The boy must have gotten the only bit like that, fer mine was *excellent*." He gave William a look that dared him to say otherwise.

William stared down at his bowl, cheeks reddening in embarrassment. "Sorry, Mistress Stubbins."

"Well, if Briony can be a dear and bring out my pie while I finish cleaning this up, perhaps I'll be able to redeem myself."

Adaira grinned, not bothered by William's comment in the slightest.

Mr. Burgess, on the other hand, nudged his son's shoulder before bending down to help Adaira with the mess.

"I'm sure 'twill be delicious!" William blurted with overwhelming enthusiasm.

Everyone laughed at that, and immediately the cheerful mood was restored. The group spent the remainder of the evening in good spirits, though Briony couldn't help but notice that Lucia didn't seem thrilled about Mr. Burgess and Adaira's friendliness.

Sorry, dear, it just did na work out. Yer na destined to be more than friends with him.

Briony felt Santiago's eyes on her. *Is that what's destined fer Santiago and me as well? Why can I na help wishing fer something more?*

She almost gasped at the unexpected thought and moved her gaze to the floor. She groaned inwardly. *Adaira was right—I do have feelings fer him. But can they lead anywhere?*

Truth and Deception

Briony woke much too early the next day after having a mostly restless night. Her realization of her feelings had left her mind too frazzled to sleep. Questions had been roiling within her, questions building upon questions.

What does this mean? Should I tell him how I feel? What do I even feel? What if he does na feel the same way? Why would he feel the same way toward someone like me? But if he does na know I'm illegitimate, could he be interested in me? What will he say when he finds out? Should I tell him?

They all left Briony with a colossal headache that reminded her of the time she'd snuck down to the tavern as a fourteen-year-old and bought some ale, just to spite her mother for telling her to stay away from it.

It was one of many things her mother had forbidden her to do, and in a moment of rebellion, Briony had stolen a bottle of Irish liquor from the tavern and drunk the entire thing.

Briony shuddered at the memory of how awful she'd felt afterward. After vomiting up her lunch, Briony had staggered home and gone directly to bed. She hadn't woken until the following morning, and when she finally had, her head had felt like someone was beating it with a hammer. The worst of it was that her mother hadn't even said a word and just acted like everything was normal.

Looking back on it, Briony was sure her mother knew what she'd done, but Bethany must have figured that the consequences of Briony's rash decision were punishment enough. And she was right—Briony had learned to trust her mother's words much more readily, and she had stayed away from alcohol in all forms until her mother deemed it appropriate for her to have a small amount when she reached eighteen winters.

Briony checked the time after getting ready for the day: nine o'clock. It was early to see Santiago, not that she wanted to right then. She was still too shaken up to know how to behave around the man.

Then she remembered she was due to see Dr. Sherwin anyway. *I might as well go see him early and get my mind off o' my tangled feelings fer a few minutes.*

She raised her hand to the doctor's door when she arrived at his house, but she had only barely touched the wood when the door opened. She stumbled backward in alarm.

"Oh, hello, lass. Good to see you," chirped Vincent McLaren. He stood leisurely in the doorway, not looking the least bit guilty for startling her yet again.

"Mr. McLaren, I did na see you."

A small grin trickled onto the man's face. "Aye, and I imagine na many people see you either."

Briony sighed in exasperation at his many riddles. "What are you talking about? Everyone here always sees me, even if I wish otherwise. And I know they also wish na to see me."

Vincent winked. "Ah, but most o' the people in this village are nearly blind."

Briony frowned and was about to go around him, but then she remembered their previous conversation. "I'd like to speak with you about what you said the other day."

Vincent's only response was a vacant expression, so she added, "About my mum?"

"Have you na figured it out yet, lass? Now, I can' be giving you all the answers without you even trying. That would be far too easy. Nay, you must find the truth fer yerself. You would na believe me even if I told you." Vincent McLaren slid around her and began walking away.

"How can you know that if you dinna even give me a chance?" Briony called.

He didn't bother turning around, but he shouted back,

"You never have believed in fairy tales!"

Briony ran her fingers through her dark hair. "Humph! What a loon. . . . And here I thought I could get a sensible answer out o' him. Perhaps I'm as mad as he is."

She stood pondering the fisherman's words, for something was pricking at the back of her consciousness, something important.

But then she spotted Lady Oliver coming up the road. Three female servants scuttled behind her, doing their best to keep up despite the heavy bundles they carried.

The horrid woman hadn't noticed Briony yet, so the young midwife ducked into Dr. Sherwin's house before that changed.

The doctor was his usual terse self when she entered, though he did seem a little surprised to see her so early. Still, he didn't comment on it and merely sipped his tea without even greeting her.

"How much longer do you think 'twill be before Sa—Mr. Mendes can do any walking on his own?" Briony asked once she had written her note about his status.

Dr. Sherwin made eye contact with her over his teacup for a flash of a second before looking away. He grabbed her notes and checked over them.

Just when Briony was starting to think he wouldn't answer her, he said, "From what you've written, he seems to be ready now. Only fer a few minutes at first, mind you, to see how he does. If there are any issues, let me know immediately. Otherwise, report back to me two days hence. Now, I have to be going; Mr. Levins thinks he must be dying because he's had a cough fer three whole days. I better na keep him waiting."

Briony chuckled. "If 'tis na that, he's surely dying from the pain in his knee, you know. You may have to check that, too."

A ghost of a smile played at Dr. Sherwin's mouth as he looked at the young midwife. As quickly as it appeared, though, it vanished without a trace, and the man's stony visage reemerged. "You better get going, then, too so I can lock up. I won' let myself fall behind because you got in the way."

Briony was so shocked by the tiny hint of amity that she just nodded and shuffled out. She watched the doctor march off, not quite believing that the man had almost smiled at her.

In all my life, he has never shown me anything but contempt.

Maybe his opinion has changed because I've been helping him. She shrugged at the thought and decided to go chat with Adaira a bit before she braved her walk with Santiago.

When she arrived at the inn, she spotted a raven atop the roof. While Mr. McLaren had been right that Briony wasn't superstitious, his words today had rattled her. She couldn't help but think back to the raven she had seen just before she lost her mother. This raven was much larger than that one, and noisier too, as it called out in its signature "kraa" several times.

As it turned its beady eyes on her, Briony's stomach dropped. People said fairy women called banshees could take the forms of ravens and that their cries were harbingers of death. At that moment, the raven's gaze made Briony start to wonder if there could be some truth behind the tale. She found herself entranced by its stare, too terrified to look away.

Movement at the inn's entrance drew Briony's attention, breaking the spell. Unfortunately, she was already so shaken up by seeing the raven that she didn't notice the stick near her foot until she had slipped and fallen forward onto her face.

"Mistress Briony," yelled a high voice. Soon, Fergus appeared at her side. His tiny hands tugged at her arm in an attempt to help her up.

Briony smiled as she stood, conscious of loud flapping as the raven flew off. "Thank you, Fergus. I'm so glad to have someone as strong as you to help me. Yer going to make a fine husband someday."

The praise was like magic on Fergus, and the boy started practically bursting with pride.

"Fergus? Where are you?"

"Here I am, Mum. Mistress Briony fell and needed someone s-strong like me to help her up," he boasted. He still stumbled over his words sometimes, which only made him all the more endearing to Briony.

Penelope McGuff emerged from Everton Inn with her typical frown in place. She took a quick look at Briony and then set her eyes on her son.

"Well, she's obviously up now, so you need to start heading back to the house this minute, or there'll be no dessert after supper tonight," she threatened.

Fergus gasped and sprinted up the hill with all his might.

Penelope shifted her attention back to the midwife. "I shall have you know, Briony, I've always wondered about you. Yer mother was very secretive about yer family. On many occasions, I tried to get her to tell me who yer father was, but she would never admit to anything. Now, I'm na going to say that you can' be around my Fergus at all, but he's a wee bit too familiar with you. He's na old enough to realize whose company is best to keep. Until that happens, dinna be so friendly with him."

The older woman didn't even wait for a reply before walking back toward her house. She wouldn't have gotten one anyway, since Briony was too caught off guard by the announcement to react at first.

Once she took it in, though, Briony kicked at the dirt in frustration. *Why do I feel surprised? This is the way things have always been. 'Twas stupid o' me to think Dr. Sherwin was warming up to me. Mrs. McGuff's words were the wake-up call I needed; no matter how hard I try, I'm never going to be accepted. I'm na meant fer anything more than a lonely and disgraceful existence.*

And that's why I can never tell Santiago how I truly feel. Aye, we're friends, but that's as far as it can go. Anything beyond that will only lead to heartbreak.

Soon, Briony arrived at Santiago's room and lifted a trembling hand. She could hear a muffled conversation inside the room, but it halted as soon as she knocked. The door jerked open, Captain Costa on the other side.

"Ah, senhorita! What a pleasure to see you again." His dark eyes were friendly, and a smile graced his face.

"Greetings, sir."

The man nodded to say he was leaving and started moving past her. *What was he discussing with Santiago? Was it that same topic as before: morta?*

Suddenly, Briony's curiosity became too much to bear. *I have to know what 'twas.*

"Sir!"

Captain Costa turned to her. "Yes, senhorita?"

"I have a question fer you. I came across some o' the

99

sailors talking about something the other day. They used the word *morta*, and I wondered if you could tell me what it means."

The man's eyes narrowed infinitesimally as though he was deeply considering something. He drew in a breath—

The door opened behind her. "Briony, you're here. I was hoping you'd arrive soon. I've been wanting to talk to you."

Santiago leaned against the doorframe, trying his best to smile even though Briony could see that it took some effort. Somehow he had made it across the room on his own, so quickly that she hadn't even heard his footsteps until he was already opening the door.

Santiago gave his captain a pointed look as Briony tried to respond. Unfortunately, she just stood there gaping like a fish. Not only had she almost been caught talking about *morta*, but seeing Santiago again was making her stomach do flips.

The man continued waiting for her reply, but his body was still angled toward Costa.

After a few seconds, the captain broke the silence by saying, "My apologies, senhorita. I'm needed down at my ship. I'll be happy to answer your question later if you come by to see me."

"Briony doesn't need to do that. *I'll* take care of any questions she has."

Briony's eyes widened at the sudden shift in mood. *I thought they were friends, but Santiago's tone reminds me o' when he was talking to Niall.*

Briony's mind swirled with emotions as Mr. Moreland returned to her thoughts. *Part o' me would like to never speak to him again after what he said to Adaira, but . . . another part o' me wants— nay, longs—to see him again. Surely he can' be all bad. He does na know how much Adaira has changed; once he does, I hope he'll understand why I'm such good friends with her.*

He was quite rude to Santiago, though, too, and 'tis na like I know much about him—

"Briony?" Santiago prompted.

Briony looked up, noticing that his gaze was now fixed on her. Her eyes shifted over to Costa, but the man wasn't there.

"I'm sorry, Santiago. I guess I got sidetracked fer a

moment. Are you ready to start our walk?"

***

"Everyone seemed a lot busier today. I've never seen so many people out and about at once. Is something special going on?" Santiago asked. They had just finished their stroll and were in the sitting room, alone but for Adaira's cat, who lurked behind a chair in the corner. Santiago's walking was much better today, and he'd even gone several steps with just his cane.

"'Tis a busy time fer us, with Johnsmas being only a few days away."

He gave her a blank look, which surprised her.

"How could you na know what Johnsmas is? Norway recognizes it as well, from what I hear. Surely yer business partners told you."

Santiago frowned in confusion and shook his head. "My business with Norway is only a recent development. I don't normally go this far east in June."

There was a quiver in the man's voice as he spoke. Briony almost didn't notice it, and had it been someone she was less familiar with, she wouldn't have thought it strange at all. But something about it tugged at her awareness. She looked at him closely, noting his clenched fingers and the way his gaze had shifted away from her.

He's hiding something.

"Are you *positive* you've never heard o' it?"

Annoyance sprang onto Santiago's face, and he snapped, "Yes, that's what I said."

Briony drew back in her chair at the outburst. *I know we sometimes get under each other's skin, but I dinna think I said anything to warrant that.*

Unless he's lying to me.

Santiago sighed and returned his eyes to hers. "I apologize. My sister has been a nuisance lately, and she's the one I'm truly upset with, not you. I shouldn't have lashed out at you."

Briony gave him a sympathetic smile. "I understand having a temper that flares up at the wrong people sometimes. I've been trying to be more controlled in that area myself."

101

His lips twitched as if he wanted to smile. "And are you having much success?"

"What do you think?"

A full-on grin spread over Santiago's face at that, laughter dancing in his eyes. "Now, don't think you can trick me into getting myself in trouble."

Briony smiled back, feeling herself fall into his green eyes. Her heart began to throb, and she was suddenly aware of the fact that they were *very* alone, sitting *very* close to each other. Santiago's knee was practically brushing against hers, and her hand was only inches away from his arm.

How did I na notice that before? Sweat broke out on Briony's palms, and she brought her wayward hand into her lap.

Something dimmed in Santiago's expression, though it was difficult to tell if it was because of Briony's subtle withdrawal or something else.

Briony drew in a shaky breath. "A-Anyway, Johnsmas is a holiday to celebrate Midsummer. We light a bonfire on Everton's highest hill, sing ballads, and dance. 'Tis one o' the happiest nights o' the year. Out o' all the times to come to Orkney, this has to be the best one. You do have to be careful about the naughtier lads though. They like to snatch the burning heather from the flames and light the grass on fire. Their parents usually stop them before that happens, though, and if anything does catch on fire, the men are quick to put it out. Some o' the boys even try to prove their bravery by jumping through the flames. We've had a few complaints o' burned bottoms, but whether they're from the fire or their parents' beatings, I could na tell you."

Santiago laughed heartily before gripping the cane beside him with a more somber look. "I'm glad I'll get to attend the festivities, then. I only wish I could be on my feet without this cane long enough to dance with you."

"Oh, that is sad to think about. Are you a good dancer?"

"Tolerably good. I wouldn't say I have any great talent."

"I must admit I do love to dance. The world melts away fer a moment, and I feel as free as a bird."

"In that case, I hope to dance with you as soon as I recover. Then when the world melts away from you, I can come along."

Briony searched Santiago's face, but there was nothing pretentious, nothing humorous in his countenance.

Instead, there was an intensity in his eyes that soon proved too much for Briony to take, and she turned her attention to the floor. "You must na say things like that. People will start indecent rumors if they hear you."

"What will they say? Surely they can't think you're an immodest woman," Santiago said confidently.

This is it. I've been keeping this from him long enough. He deserves the truth, even if that means he wants nothing more to do with me. I'm illegitimate. I have to say it!

She took a few deep breaths and opened her mouth. "I . . . appreciate how certain you are o' my modesty. You dinna know my family history like everyone else does though. If you did, you would na treat me as well as you do."

"Briony," Santiago whispered. The earnestness in his voice drew her eyes to his. Within their green expanse, she saw nothing but kindness and honesty. "Nothing you tell me will change the way I see you."

His words gave her the courage she needed, and she said, "I was born out o' wedlock, just as my mother and grandmother were. The town looks down on me fer it. Everyone expects I will follow the same path and end up with a 'natural' child."

There was silence. Briony groaned inwardly, for it seemed like confirmation of her worst fears. She felt moisture spring up in her eyes as she mentally said goodbye to their friendship.

A few moments later, she heard something she never imagined he would say. "I'm sorry this has been going on, but you're not your mother or your grandmother. The rest of Everton should be able to see that, too."

Briony almost jumped from her seat. "What? You can' mean that. I'm illegitimate, so 'tis normal fer my neighbors to act as they do. 'Tis the way o' the world, and 'tis the way *you* should be reacting right now."

Santiago gave her a look of disbelief. "How can you say that? Do you truly think me that shallow? Do I think it was right of your family to have children out of wedlock? No, I believe my mother would turn over in her grave if I did. But, Briony, you had nothing to do with how you were born. How can anyone judge you for others' choices? I believe in judging a person based on their character alone."

An incredulous smile made its way over Briony's face. It started small, but soon her happiness grew so strong that her entire being seemed to glow. "Do you mean that?"

Santiago placed his hand on her shoulder. "Yes, Briony. I do."

"You can' know how nice 'tis to hear those words." Briony felt like her tongue had loosened, and before she could stop herself, more words began to spill out. "Santiago, there's something else I need to tell you."

Morta

"Daniel! You must get Briony Fairborn now!" Freda screamed from her bed.

Daniel Calhoun, who could no longer enjoy his lunch, meager as it was, yelled back, "Stop being dramatic, woman. I'm too busy to go find the midwife, so get over it."

Freda waddled out of the bedroom to her husband with such a hateful countenance that it would terrify anyone stupid enough to earn it. She was in her eighth month, practically bursting, and she refused to let *anyone* yell at her.

"Daniel Calhoun, if you dinna get Briony Fairborn right this minute, I'm going to kill you!"

Mr. Calhoun looked up from his bread angrily, but when he saw Freda's face, he knew he had gone too far.

He replied, "I'm already on my way," leaping from the table and rushing out like a scared dog.

When he didn't find Mistress Fairborn at her house, Daniel asked Penelope McGuff where she might be. Penelope wasn't in a good mood and practically ran him off, but she did say that Briony had been spending a lot of time with that Mr. Mendes at Everton Inn. Daniel hurried that way, and when he entered the inn's sitting room, he was relieved to discover Mrs. McGuff had been right.

He came up to Briony, so desperate to get her help that he didn't even bother to wait until she and Mr. Mendes noticed him.

He heard her say, "—something else I need to tell you,"

and interrupted:

"Mistress Fairborn, I'm so glad to see you."

"Mr. Calhoun, what's the matter?" Briony asked. She hoped he hadn't overheard them—she knew for a fact that Daniel didn't share Santiago's opinion on her illegitimacy.

"'Tis Freda. . . . ," Daniel panted. "She says she needs you right now, and I think she means it this time. I ran all the way to yer house, but you weren' there. I was lucky Mistress McGuff pointed me in the right direction."

Briony bolted to her feet. "Let's go right now. Is she in labor? Is she hurting?"

Daniel, wide-eyed at the thought that his wife might truly be in labor, raised his hands to show he had no idea.

Briony turned to Santiago with an apologetic look. "Please excuse me."

"Of course. Good luck!"

Briony lifted her skirts and hustled toward the Calhouns' house. "So? Tell me what's wrong with her."

"Well, I dinna rightly know. She just said she needed you right away," Daniel admitted with a hand on the back of his neck.

Briony stopped in her tracks and sighed. *Is this another false alarm?*

Freda Calhoun had always been notorious for her melodramatics, and pregnancy had only worsened that personality trait. "Did she seem unsteady on her feet to you?"

"I did na notice, but I was out burning kelp this morneen. She was in the bed when I got home."

Briony nodded in understanding. Daniel had been working much more in the past few months, supposedly to make up for the fact that his wife could no longer help him turn the seaweed into ash. *The real reason, though, is probably to escape his wife's orneriness.*

"I just brought on a new fellow to help me. He says he recently arrived here and plans on staying a while—Niall Moreland. Have you met him yet? He seems mighty peculiar. . . ." Daniel trailed off.

Briony's breath caught at the man's name. "Aye, I met him. I'm na sure what to make o' him."

I wonder why he's planning to stay fer a while. I hope that means he came up with a good apology fer Adaira.

Daniel opened his mouth to say something else, but then he seemed to recall whom he was speaking with and clammed up. Silence spread over them like a thick fog that didn't let up until they reached the Calhouns' house.

A low groan sounded as Daniel opened the door, and the two of them hurried to Freda's side.

"'Tis about time you showed up, Briony Fairborn. It hurts so much. I'm sure the bairn is almost here already with how long it took you," the woman screamed from the bed. Her hair was matted with sweat, and her face was red.

Briony bit her tongue to keep from retaliating and began checking to see if everything was all right.

The woman's pain turned out to be a false alarm, just as Briony had expected it would be. Freda was just nearing the end of her first pregnancy and didn't seem to realize that what she was feeling was pretty common.

What rotten luck. 'Twould have been much better to spend more time with Santiago than take care o' a woman who does na need it.

Briony considered walking back to the inn, but then she thought about the moment right before Mr. Calhoun had shown up. She wasn't sure exactly what she'd been about to say, but now that she wasn't directly in front of Santiago and could think straight again, she was glad Mr. Calhoun had stopped her.

She was still in shock over the way Santiago had reacted when she'd told him about her parentage, but there were other things about him that didn't sit right with her, no matter how he made her feel.

Briony needed answers. She had to know what he was hiding from her. *Even if that means breaking my word.*

***

Several crew members were making their way off the *São Nicolau* as Briony arrived. Most of them were very rugged, with dark hair and beards, though a couple had light hair like Santiago's. She waited politely as they disembarked, trying not to make eye contact with anyone.

"Senhorita!" called one sailor when he noticed her. He was a short man with greasy black hair and an ugly mustache. Briony guessed he was about thirty-five years old, judging from the number of wrinkles etched into his sun-weathered complexion.

She pinched her face into a polite grin before looking away, assuming he would get the message that she didn't want to talk. She wasn't that lucky, though, and before long, he and three of his friends were standing directly in front of her, far too close for comfort.

The sailor held out his hand to her, and she shook it for courtesy's sake. It was sweaty to the touch, and Briony was all too ready to release it. The others around the man leered and spoke among themselves in Portuguese. Part of Briony was glad she couldn't understand them, for she feared she would only be more uncomfortable.

"I'm looking fer Captain Costa," she said, unable to prevent a slight quiver in her voice.

"No Costa here," the man replied in broken English. "We help you." He smiled, revealing several gaps between the few teeth he had. It was a lascivious smile, and Briony had little doubt what sort of "help" he had in mind.

"Nay, 'tis quite all right. I shall seek him elsewhere," she said before stepping back to leave.

The man grabbed her wrist and tugged her forward. "We love help senhoritas."

The other men cackled and moved to encircle her. Briony tried to wrench her wrist away, but the brute was too strong. She winced, making the man sneer even more.

Another man slid his hand down her left arm before grasping her shoulder.

"Stop!" Briony shouted, trying to sound less scared than she was.

"We stop when we want," replied the sailor holding her wrist. He squeezed even harder, and Briony expected he wanted her to cry out from the pain.

She gritted her teeth to keep it in, though, as red-hot anger swept through her veins. *These men are about to have a fight on their hands.*

The man holding her suddenly released her wrist. "Aaah!" Then he screamed something in Portuguese, and though Briony didn't know the meaning exactly, she could tell that he was insulting her.

She clenched her right hand into a fist and was just about to hit him in the face when—

"Senhorita Fairborn!"

The four sailors turned their heads, and when they did, their faces paled.

A series of loud Portuguese words came from that same voice, words that made the sailors immediately step back.

The leader of the group flexed his hand and stared at Briony strangely. She looked down and gasped; his entire palm and the undersides of his fingers were a pale pink.

What in the world? It looks like something burned him.

The greasy-haired sailor mumbled something to his comrades, and they all darted off into town like they'd just seen a ghost.

Briony sighed in relief and rubbed her wrist, noticing the start of a bruise. She looked up to see who her rescuer was and spotted the same young sailor she had seen coming out of Santiago's room with the captain.

Briony wasn't sure if she could trust him, but he had just saved her from the other sailors, so she smiled in gratitude.

His mouth was set in a stern line, but his eyes were full of concern as he hurried down to join her. "Senhorita Fairborn, did they hurt you?"

"'Tis nothing," she said, hiding her wrist behind her back.

"Capitão[18] Costa. Come." He held out a hand.

She took it, noting how gentle he was as he led her up the now empty gangplank. Everyone else had scattered during their conversation, intent on pretending they'd neither heard nor seen anything amiss in the last few minutes.

Briony and the young sailor made their way to the room she'd been to before, which she now assumed to be the captain's quarters. The man rapped on the door shortly before

---

[18] Captain.

a sharp voice told them to enter.

The two of them went inside and found Costa sitting at his desk. Briony stepped forward purposefully, while the other man stayed behind her.

The captain's features brightened once he realized who his guest was. "Senhorita Fairborn, what a surprise. Welcome."

He rose from his seat and shook hands with her but pulled back when she winced in pain. "Are you injured, senhorita?"

"'Tis only a slight bruise," she answered.

"And how did you come by it?" he queried.

Briony opened her mouth to respond, but the young sailor quickly shouted something in Portuguese.

Costa's expression darkened. "Senhorita, did one of my men hurt your wrist?"

Briony nodded, which made the captain's face turn even grimmer. He growled in Portuguese to the other sailor, who replied with something else before exiting the room. Briony wasn't sure what it all meant, but she could tell the captain was furious. He said nothing for a couple of minutes and ran his hands over his face.

Just when she was starting to feel like she should leave and return later, he looked over to Briony and said, "I'm deeply sorry for what happened to you today. Adriano Rodriguez is seeing to it that the ones behind your mistreatment will be here shortly to receive discipline. I know that's only a small consolation, and I cannot help but feel responsible for what happened. Senhorita, please accept my sincerest apologies."

"Thank you. It did take me by surprise. I hope that none o' the other women in town have had a similar experience," she said, unable to keep a bit of resentment from her voice.

"I assure you I'll make it very clear to the crew that this sort of behavior is unacceptable. This shall never happen again as long as I'm captain," he promised. He appeared very firm in his resolve, so firm that it would have been easy to believe him.

Then why do I still feel so suspicious?

Bah, I'm being ridiculous. Just because he's the captain does na mean I should blame him fer everything the crew does, right? A man's character is na as easy to read as the pages o' a book.

"Senhorita Fairborn?" Costa asked, drawing her attention

back. "Is there anything else I can do to put your mind at ease? Perhaps it would be better to distract you from what happened; what was it that you originally came aboard for?"

She gazed at him blankly for a moment before she remembered. After checking to make sure they were alone, she said, "I'll be fine, sir. I appreciate yer concern fer my well-being. I actually came here to continue our conversation from this morneen . . ."

"Ah, you came to learn what 'morta' means. Even though Senhor Mendes does not want you to."

Briony's stomach tensed with guilt, but she wasn't going to let that stop her from finding the truth. "Aye, you said *you* would tell me."

"That I did. But I must wonder where you heard such a word. It isn't something people say in typical conversation." He leaned back in his chair, and he almost seemed relaxed if not for the doubt twinkling in his hard eyes.

"I dinna see why 'tis any concern o' yers. I simply wish to know its meaning," she snapped.

"Now, now, senhorita. You came to me. The least you can do is be honest if you want honesty in return." The man's sardonic smile made Briony's jaw clench.

She furrowed her brow as though considering where she might have heard it. *There's no way I'm going to tell him the truth.*

"I fear I can' recall. I must have overheard one o' the sailors say it."

Captain Costa's smile widened, making Briony suppress a shiver. "Well, that truly is too bad. I would have wanted to speak with the person you heard it from since *morta* means 'dead.'"

Briony's blood ran cold. *I'd thought 'twas something unpleasant, but I did na realize 'twould be this. . . .*

I can' jump to conclusions. Maybe they were just talking about Santiago's parents or the fact they almost died during the storm.

But why did Santiago react like that when I asked him what the word meant?

And Santiago and the captain dinna seem to be on good terms. . . .

Surely they can' be involved in something dangerous. Santiago is a good man. At least, he seems to be. How well do I truly know him? Has

111

my attraction to him been clouding my judgment?

"Senhorita?"

"Hmm?" Briony looked up at Costa and realized she'd been silent for several seconds.

"Where was it you said you heard that word?"

Briony's eyes narrowed. "I already told you I dinna remember."

She looked pointedly at the clock on his desk. "Ah, is that the time? I better get going—I promised Adaira I'd help her at the inn. Thank you so much fer yer time, sir. I'll just let myself out."

The captain rose as Briony did, his ominous smile making it clear he knew she was lying. "Farewell, senhorita. I'm sure we'll see each other again soon."

A Long Way to Go

"Adaira, I need yer help," Briony said. She'd gotten a good night's sleep after her conversation with Captain Costa, but rather than feeling better now that it was morning, she was even more shaken up than before.

The innkeeper's daughter immediately put down her mixing bowl and pulled up a chair. "What do you need?"

"I-I—" Briony stammered as she tried to think of how to voice her worries. *I dinna want to say I was eavesdropping and overheard something that may or may na be bad—*

"—am struggling because o' the young Mr. Mendes," Adaira finished.

"Aye, I'm so confused right now that I dinna know what to think. I—How did you know 'twas about Mr. Mendes?"

"Just keep going. Tell me what's troubling you."

"I just, I dinna know if I can trust him. Most o' the time, he seems completely honest and funny and charming and . . ." Briony trailed off with a blush.

A knowing smile appeared on Adaira's face, but she didn't say anything.

"But I feel like he may be keeping something from me. Something important."

Adaira's eyebrows furrowed in deep thought. "You mean like how yer keeping yer feelings from him?"

Briony's eyes widened. "Nay! That's na—Nay, that's na it!"

Adaira's smile turned playful. "Then you dinna have feelings fer him?"

"Nay, 'tis na that, I do, but I—" Briony broke off with a gasp. "Adaira, you did that on purpose."

Adaira leaped from her seat and pointed at her friend. "That's a confession! I knew you were interested in him."

"Na so loud, Adaira. I dinna want all o' Everton to hear."

"So has he shown interest in you, too?"

I should have known I'd have to talk to her about this eventually.

Briony sighed. "'Tis hard to say. Sometimes he gives me these looks and I think he feels the same way. He never declares it openly, so maybe I'm just seeing what I want to see. How can I know fer sure?"

"'Tis all in the wee things he does. If you watch couples when they first start courting, they say more with their actions than they do with their words. Their eyes light up when the other person enters the room. They laugh and smile more easily. Their hands move toward each other without even meaning to. 'Tis heartwarming to see."

Adaira stared into the distance as if her mind had wandered elsewhere.

Could she be thinking o' a special someone right now? I'd bet money that Mr. Burgess does those things around Adaira. I hope he does na make her wait much longer before he declares his affections.

Does Santiago behave that way around me?

Briony grabbed Adaira's shoulders. "Wait, wait, wait. That's na why I came here. Before Mr. Mendes and I could ever be more than friends, I have to know if I can trust him. What should I do?"

Adaira rolled her eyes and chuckled. "Silly goose, what do you think? Talk to him. Yer a smart, sensible woman, but when it comes to love, yer as foolish as the rest o' us. Tell him what's troubling you and *tell him how you feel*. See where that takes you. From what I've seen, Mr. Mendes is a good man. He'll give you an honest answer."

Briony opened her mouth to protest her friend's use of *love*, but Adaira shushed her.

"Ah, before I forget, that man from before, Mr. Moreland—he brought me a bunch o' flowers yesterday and gave me a heartfelt apology fer his behavior. He did na make any excuses, and he said that he wished to make it up to me by treating me better from here on out. Something about how the past was all but forgotten and if you trusted me, then he did, too. He said he wanted to talk to you, too. Who knows? If Mr. Mendes does na work out, perhaps Mr. Moreland might na be so bad, after all."

Briony frowned in surprise, but then a small smile worked its way onto her face. *I knew Niall was na all bad.*

"But anyway, get to it, lass." She spun Briony around toward the kitchen exit. And Santiago's room.

Briony groaned, but she did as she was told. When she reached the merchant's door, she gave it one soft knock.

She waited for his customary invitation, but within two seconds, the door was opening and she was face-to-face with the man himself.

All coherent thought left her as she stared at Santiago with an open mouth.

"Good morning, Briony. Are you all right?" His eyes were etched with curiosity and concern.

Briony cleared her throat. "Nay, I'm quite fine. Quite fine. Aye, nothing wrong at all."

Santiago raised his eyebrows. "Right."

"Right. So are you ready to go? I think today is a great day to take you to Drulea Cottage. If you'd like to go, that is."

"Ah, delightful. I've wanted to see it ever since you told me how nice it is." He grasped her arm in his, setting her heart aflutter and stealing her breath at the same time.

Should I tell him the truth about what I overheard? And that I need to know if I can trust him? And worst o' all, that I fancy him? Briony shook her head and marched onward, trying to ignore her anxious thoughts.

Soon, the two of them were making their way up the hill and Drulea Cottage was coming into view. Large patches of thrift and honeysuckle dotted the landscape, bringing fragrant scents to their nostrils as they approached. The recent rain made the plants more vibrant than usual, and even after living here for all her life, Briony was struck by her home's natural beauty.

"Now I understand why you like Everton so much," Santiago said as he, too, stood entranced.

Briony smiled and led him inside. It was a fairly simple layout with the kitchen area on the left side, a dining area with a good-sized table and chairs in the center, and a fireplace on the right side. Her bed was in a little nook in the back corner, not readily visible when people first walked in. A second door led outside to a nice vista of the ocean where two more chairs sat waiting for occupants.

"Has your family always lived here?" Santiago asked as she led him to one of the indoor chairs. He propped his cane against the table and eased into his seat.

"Nay, but I'm the fourth generation to call it home. The person who first owned Drulea Cottage died before he finished putting it all together, and 'twas abandoned fer many years before my great-grandmother claimed it. I dinna know how she did it, but somehow she managed to complete what he started," she said with a hint of pride. "Why the first owner named it Drulea Cottage, though, I could na tell you."

She sat down in the chair opposite him, fidgeting with her dress.

"Your childhood must have been a very blessed one," he said, making her look up with a quizzical frown. "I mean, not many people have the chance to grow up in a place as beautiful as this."

"Ah, I suppose that's true. I may na have traveled before, but I dare say 'twould be difficult to find a town in a lovelier spot. How about I make us some tea, and then I can take you out back to see the view?" she asked, rising and going over to the cupboard.

"That would be wonderful."

An almost comfortable silence settled over the two of them as Santiago surveyed the cottage's interior and Briony got out a kettle.

If I was na stewing with nerves, I'm sure 'twould feel very pleasant having him in my home. Moments like these make me think that maybe 'tis na such a stretch fer him to reciprocate my feelings. Surely he would na seem so happy if he did na enjoy spending time with me. How much o' a push does one need to exchange feelings o' friendship fer feelings o'—

"Briony?"

"Aye?"

116

"I was saying, if you'd like, I could take you down to my ship today or tomorrow."

Briony dropped the teacup in her hand as her face turned white. The cup shattered into several pieces on the floor, making Briony draw back in surprise. She knelt to retrieve the broken bits, but her mind was absorbed with guilt.

Santiago rose from his chair and stumbled forward to help.

"Stop!" she barked. "I'll get it."

He froze as soon as she spoke, leaning heavily on his cane.

"Um . . . about what you said . . . I actually already went down there—"

"You what?" Santiago's countenance instantly transformed from concern to outrage.

Briony had never seen him so angry, and she took a few steps back in fear of what he might do. "'Tis just that—"

"Just what? Doesn't your word mean anything to you? You promised not to go there without me, and now I find out that you went anyway?" Santiago's voice lowered to a whisper as he said, "*Does a promise to me mean nothing?*"

Briony's eyes widened, and she reached for his arm. "Santiago, I—"

He held up a hand. "Don't. I don't think I could believe whatever you say right now. Maybe I never should have trusted you anyway."

He turned away slowly and made his way out the door, teetering as he went. Briony knew it was irresponsible of her to let him go alone, but she found herself unable to move.

Once he was out of sight, she dropped to the floor beside her shattered teacup. She sat there for a few minutes, trying to sort out her twisted thoughts.

Whatever that conversation was between Santiago and the captain, I dinna care anymore. Maybe I can convince him I'm sorry, that I was wrong to go on my own.

Briony rushed to the doorway and spotted him a ways off down the hill, standing right at the cliff's edge. He was peering out at the turbulent blue expanse, with his hands on his hips and his cane on the ground beside him. He didn't look very stable on his feet, but his frustration seemed to be holding him in place.

What if he refuses to listen? He already stopped me when I tried to explain. . . . But I can' just leave things as they are. I have to try again.

Briony went down to him, tears flooding her eyes. He seemed to hear her approach and turned toward her.

That was when the unthinkable happened.

Santiago's foot stumbled over a stone, making his entire leg give out. Rather than just collapsing onto the ground, though, his body tilted backward until he slipped off the cliff.

He fell quickly, hitting the water with a loud splash.

As soon as he dropped, Briony reacted on instinct. She knew that with his ankle still healing, there was no way he could stay afloat in the choppy waves.

I have to get him out o' there. She sprinted to the edge of the cliff and dove in after him, not caring about the sharp rocks waiting below.

Unspoken Words

The water slammed into Briony, weighing down her already heavy dress. An exhilarating thrill charged through her body, making her want to cry with joy. Something was calling to her, calling her deeper into the water. Something she'd felt her entire life, whispering at the edges of her consciousness. Something wonderful—

Briony shook her head a few times. *I have to stay focused on what's important right now—rescuing Santiago.*

Underneath the water, she opened her eyes, searching for him. *He was just here. Where could he have drifted? I can' lose him!*

Briony panicked as pressure built up in her chest and her throat began to throb. Her eyes stung as she looked right and left, but he was nowhere near the surface. Her gaze went deeper into the dark, briny water.

There!

Santiago was descending quickly—*Why is he na struggling? Is he already—*

Briony pressed her legs together and moved them up and down like a dolphin, propelling herself toward him. In almost no time, she reached Santiago and closed her hand around his arm. His eyes were closed, and he didn't respond when she grabbed him.

Wake up! I'm na losing you today! She pulled him upward, fighting against the surging water and the siren song in her heart.

After an eternity, they broke through to the surface.

Sunlight streamed down on them, making it easier for Briony to think clearly again. She tugged Santiago toward the shore, praying it wasn't too late.

She felt sand beneath her feet; soon they would be out of the ocean entirely. And that was when its tempting call returned.

Come, it seemed to say. *Come and sink beneath the waves. This is where you belong. Where you've always belonged. Leave behind your lonely half-life on the land and see what a full life looks like here below. Come. . . .*

Santiago gasped in a breath of air. *He's alive!*

The realization gave Briony the strength to draw her gaze from the sea, even though it pained her to do so. She helped Santiago the rest of the way out before the two of them collapsed onto the sand.

Briony said nothing as the man muttered under his breath in Portuguese. She simply gripped his shirtsleeve to reassure herself he was truly there. *He's safe. He was so close to being gone forever.*

Santiago must have felt her trembling, for he lifted his face to hers. His eyes sparkled with gratitude, relief, and something else she couldn't identify.

"I-I feared I would na get to you in time," she whispered.

Without warning, Santiago launched himself at her, bringing her into an embrace. Briony stiffened under his touch, taken off guard by its intimacy.

"Thank you," he panted. He stroked her head gently, easing away the tremors in her body and igniting sparks in their place. They skittered across her skin, making her warm all over. *If only I could stay in this moment—*

But then Santiago pulled back and rested his hands on her arms. "Your eyes are all red. Were you crying?"

She nodded, unable to speak, for her mind was so caught up in his touch. Santiago lifted a hand toward her cheek, making her heart skip a beat. She dared not breathe as it drew nearer.

But just when she started to feel the heat of his hand, Santiago seemed to realize what he was doing and dropped it to his side. He opened his mouth as though he wanted to speak, but then he paused and looked away.

He hadn't let go of her other arm. His hand felt so nice against her skin, despite the sand under his fingers. *Does he know he's still touching me?*

After a few seconds, Santiago's eyes returned to hers, determination furrowing his brow. "Briony, there's something I must tell you. I—"

"Santiago!" a far-off voice interrupted. They both turned to see where the sound had come from and spotted Adaira, Lucia, and John Burgess racing toward them on the beach.

Much to Briony's disappointment, Santiago released her arm. There was a slight flush to his face, probably from the force of hitting the water so hard. He rubbed his hands against each other to rid them of the sand.

Once the trio reached the soaked swimmers, Lucia sank to her knees and put an arm around Santiago's shoulders. "Are you two hurt? What happened?"

The merchant shook his head and smiled a little. "No, I fell from the ledge up there," he explained, "but Briony came in after me and saved me."

Everyone's attention slid to the young midwife. Their gazes held both respect and confusion. Something else flashed in Adaira's eyes, though, and an understanding passed between the two friends.

Adaira caught the fact that Santiago used my first name.

Mr. Burgess said, "Mistress Fairborn, that's amazing. How did you do that?"

Briony shrugged, just as bewildered as everyone else. *I can' very well admit I've never swum before. It just came instinctively.*

"Well, whatever it was, I'm eternally in your debt," Lucia said. "We better still take you to Dr. Sherwin now, Brother, to make sure nothing is amiss."

Santiago nodded and allowed his sister to help him stand. She placed his arm around her neck to give him support. Mr. Burgess quickly went around to his other side and did the same.

Adaira looked at Briony with concern, so the midwife smiled and rose to her feet to show that all was well.

Physically, at least. Emotionally . . . She stared at Santiago's back as Lucia and Mr. Burgess led him down the beach. *He seems so close and yet so far away. I miss the feel o' his touch. If only his arms were around me instead.*

Unexpectedly, he moved his head back, and their eyes met for the briefest of seconds. Something important lay hidden within those green orbs—

But the moment was over as quickly as it started, and Santiago turned his head as he continued forward.

What could he have wanted to tell me?

After she convinced Adaira she was well enough to be left alone, Briony tried to process what had just happened. She stared out at the waves that she'd always avoided, wondering what she should do next. Eagerness rippled through her heart, spreading down to the tips of her toes. *I have to swim again.*

Briony stepped forward and bent down to remove her wet shoes, but then a noise startled her. Her hands lurched back, and she spun around.

Niall Moreland stood a few feet away, both hands behind his back, positively beaming at her. He looked just as dangerously handsome as last time, his hair slightly windswept and his cheeks ruddy. "Briony! What an enchanting sight you are."

Conflicting emotions skittered through her, the main one being nervousness, thanks to their last encounter. Strangely, though, she also felt something akin to excitement at seeing him again.

She lifted a hand to her messy hair. "I'm completely drenched, and my lower half is covered in sand. I'm na sure what's so 'enchanting' about that."

"You'll just have to trust me." He took a step closer. "I'm so glad I ran into you. I would have come to see you sooner, except I just got a job helping Mr. Calhoun burn kelp down at the beach. I hope you dinna think I forgot about you. Or yer apology."

Briony shook her head. "I spoke rashly before. I heard from Adaira that you already made up fer what you did, and she was the only one you needed to apologize to."

"Nay, you were right. You were introducing yer friend to me and I behaved like a rogue. Allow me to show you how sorry I am." He removed one hand from behind his back and revealed a string of sea trout.

"This was my first day off, so I thought I'd catch some fish and try to convince you to give me another chance. But now I've gone and found you without even trying, so perhaps 'tis a sign." His smile turned charming and a little shy at the same time.

Briony pursed her lips as she considered the offer. "Sea trout is my favorite, you know. How did you catch so many?"

"'Tis in my blood—fishing, that is. So what do you say? Would you have dinner with me tonight?" He winked as if he already knew her answer.

She tried to suppress it, but a real smile edged its way onto her face. "That sounds like a great idea."

"Splendid. Then I'll see you at the inn at six o'clock." Niall turned and sauntered away with a spring in his step. As he turned from her, Briony glimpsed what looked like some sort of gray material in his other hand, but she couldn't get a good look before it was out of sight again. *'Tis almost as if he was trying to hide it from me.*

Wait a moment. How did Niall catch all those fish without a fishing rod?

***

When Briony strolled into Everton Inn that evening, she was surprised to hear shouts coming from the dining room. She wandered back and found the Mendes siblings, Adaira, the Burgesses, and Adaira's father seated at the table.

"And I say a man should be able to drink as much as he wants, whenever he wants, regardless o' what day o' the week 'tis!" Terrence Stubbins bellowed. His ire was directed at John Burgess, and Adaira was gripping her father's hand.

"Da', dinna get so upset. Mr. Burgess was only—"

"I know what he was saying. Dinna try to cover fer him just because he's been making eyes at you since dinner started."

Lucia choked on her water as Adaira's mouth dropped open like a fish's. Mr. Burgess didn't say anything, but his face was quickly turning as red as his hair.

It appears I've arrived just when things are getting interesting. How sad that I'm previously engaged.

Briony cleared her throat. "I'm so sorry to interrupt—"

She stepped completely into the room, feeling awkward now that all eyes were on her, especially a certain pair of green ones. "Has anyone seen Niall? I'm supposed to be meeting him here."

Adaira, looking incredibly grateful for the distraction, practically leaped to her feet. "Ah, o' course! Briony, Mr. Moreland said you'd be coming. He's waiting fer you out in the back. He said he has something *special* in mind."

Briony didn't miss her friend's suggestive tone, nor could she bring herself to look in Santiago's direction.

Adaira grabbed her friend's arm. "Here, let me take you."

Once they were out of the room, Briony whispered, "Adaira, that was so embarrassing. Why did you have to say it like that?"

"Oh, no reason. You just should have seen *someone's* face when I said it." She wiggled her eyebrows.

Briony pushed her away playfully. "Adaira! Yer the worst."

"What can I say? 'Twas too good o' an opportunity to let it pass by. After all, 'tis na every day that my dearest friend has two men after her. Enjoy it, love."

"Will you just—Never mind. 'Tis no use trying to get you to stop."

"It took you long enough to realize that."

Briony rolled her eyes and chuckled. "Now what is this special thing he had in . . .?"

Upon the grass, there was the perfect setup for a romantic evening: food, drinks, and a bouquet of wildflowers set atop a large quilt in a spot that afforded a lovely view of the ocean. Niall sat with a large grin as he waited for Briony to join him.

Butterflies danced about her stomach as she took a seat across from him. Her mouth was suddenly as dry as dust, and she looked to Adaira for help, but the woman was already almost back inside.

"You came. I was na sure you would." His voice flowed to Briony's ears like warm honey, drawing her back to his dark, mysterious eyes. They were hopeful, that much was certain, and she wondered what he was thinking.

If that hope is fer more than friendship, then he's going to be sorely disappointed. I've already set my heart on Santiago, stupid as 'tis. Surely Adaira was wrong that he's interested in me, right?

"I-I wanted to come. Now I have the chance to get to know you a wee bit more."

She mentally kicked herself. *What's wrong with me? This is Niall. Why am I acting like such a flirt?*

Niall flashed a brilliant smile and quickly blessed the food. As soon as he did, though, he tore into his trout with strange abandon. It wasn't at all like he'd behaved when they were at the tavern together. Briony was never much for ceremony, but it was almost obnoxious how he took new bites out of the fish before he'd finished swallowing the previous ones.

Briony frowned, unsure how to respond.

After a few moments, Niall noticed her discomfort and wiped his chin with a napkin. He had the decency to look sheepish and ducked his head away from hers as he tried to clean himself up.

"So what would you like to know about me?" Niall asked.

"How many questions can I ask?"

Niall laughed. "As many as you'd like, as long as you dinna overwhelm me with several at once."

Briony pondered for a moment. "Why did you come back *now?*"

Niall pressed his fingers together with a slight frown. "I meant to return much earlier to thank you fer what you did, but as a bairn, I was always forbidden from doing so. My mother could na forgive the other bairns' treatment o' me, and yer heroism was na enough to convince her. She . . . She and my sister passed away recently—"

"I'm so sorry, Niall. Yer mum *and* sister? What happened?"

Niall didn't say anything for a moment, and Briony wondered if the memories were still too painful. "They both came down with an illness and died within a few weeks o' each other."

Briony grabbed his hand. "I lost my mum almost a year ago to influenza, so I completely understand."

Niall brightened at her touch and rubbed his thumb along the back of her hand. Goose bumps erupted along her arms, startling her so much that she pulled her hand away with a gasp.

"I beg yer pardon. I did na mean to go too fast fer you."

Briony cocked her head in confusion. "Too fast? What do you mean?"

Niall huffed as if frustrated. "Dinna play coy with me, Briony. You called *me*, after all."

"I dinna understand. How could I 'call' you? What does that even mean?" A tremor of dread shot through her.

He stared hard at Briony, his black eyes meeting her amber ones. They stayed like this for several seconds until Niall broke eye contact with an awkward laugh. "I suppose you truly dinna know. How disappointing. I guess I'll have to work a wee bit harder, then. That's all right though."

He quickly changed the subject to the Johnsmas celebration, much to Briony's relief. They conversed easily about the new topic before sliding smoothly into many other things. The rest of the meal passed so pleasantly that Briony nearly believed she'd imagined the tension before. Niall's demeanor was full of charm and kindness, and the affectionate smiles he threw her way dispelled her previous anxiety about the evening.

Then Briony heard the clock inside strike nine and looked around with wide eyes. *Is that truly the time? I've been enjoying myself so much that I did na realize how late 'twas. We must have been in such deep conversation that we did na even hear the seven and eight o'clock chimes.*

"What's that?" Niall asked.

"'Tis the clock inside, telling us time has run away from us."

Niall cocked his head in confusion. "Clock? What's that?"

"You dinna know what a clock is?"

"Oh, nay, o' course I do. I meant to ask *where* the clock is."

"On the wall? In the kitchen?"

"Ah, that's right." He chuckled in self-deprecation, but something felt off about his tone.

"Aye. Well, I better get going. Thank you so much fer the

lovely time, Niall," she said as she rose to her feet.

Niall also stood, his face tinged with sadness. "I only wish it could have been longer."

He flashed another smile, which she reflected all too effortlessly. Energy crackled between them, and she was surprised by her sudden reluctance to leave. She pushed the feeling aside and stepped back.

"Thank you again. Good night, Niall."

"Good night."

Briony walked backward a few feet until she tripped over a pebble on the path. "Oh, silly me!"

She inclined her head to Niall before scurrying away as quickly as she could without looking like a complete idiot.

She had almost reached Drulea Cottage before her cheeks lost their rosy hue. Once she let go of the embarrassment, though, her mind went back to something Niall had said.

Or rather, did na say. What did he mean by—

A rustle caught her attention. It seemed to be coming from the woods beyond the cottage. She glanced over and gasped in fright.

Two glowing eyes were looming between the trees, looking directly at her.

Briony jumped back before her wits kicked in and she realized it was probably just a woodland animal. Still, those eyes were fairly high up, and they reflected the fading sunlight that hadn't yet retreated into the Simmer Dim of summer. *Maybe 'tis a deer. Could it be a bear?*

The eyes, unblinking, began to slide closer. They were staring at her strangely, almost as if they recognized her. She froze. *What do I do? Should I run?*

But then, just as abruptly as they'd appeared, the eyes shifted to the right and vanished behind a tree.

Briony let out a breath she hadn't realized she'd been holding. *What was that thing? Most animals run away as soon as they see me, but why na this one?*

A shiver coursed through her, and she hurried the rest of the way home. Once she arrived, Briony bolted the door and shut all the windows. Terror overwhelmed her at the possibility that the animal was still nearby.

In moments like these, I hate living alone. If Mum were here, I could easily chalk all this fear up to foolishness, but without her, I have nothing to anchor me back to reality.

Briony placed a tremulous palm on her chest and found that her heart was racing.

Get a grip, Briony. 'Twas just an animal out in the woods. No need to get emotional. She rubbed her hands against her dress, trying to be braver than she felt.

Even so, it would be hours before sleep finally found her.

A Day of Mourning and Magic

When Briony woke, the glowing eyes were still on her mind. They had haunted her dreams all night long, leaving her jittery and tired. She quickly dressed and made herself a cup of tea.

Mum always said tea was one o' life's greatest blessings, and right now, I believe she was right. After a few sips, she was already starting to feel her nerves uncoil.

Something seems different about today, but I can' quite pinpoint—

She let out a short, pained gasp, oblivious of the tea slipping from her mouth onto the table.

'Tis today. One year since she passed. The thought bubbled in Briony's mind like boiling lava, spreading through her being and leaving devastation in its wake.

She'd known the day was coming, but the newcomers had offered her a welcome distraction from that truth. *Now that the anniversary o' her death is finally here, though, it almost feels like I'm losing Mum all over again.*

Bethany's final words rang in her ears. *"You must stay away from the water. . . ."* Briony could still see Bethany's beatific expression when she'd heard her daughter's answer, a promise that was now broken.

What would she say if she were here? Would she be angry or frightened?

Briony swept her hand across the table, knocking her cup

and saucer onto the floor. She slammed a fist down, not noticing the pain it caused. Then she turned her attention to the horizon far beyond her cottage, cursing the waves that had stolen so much from her.

When they stole my father, they also stole my only chance at a normal life. The sea left me an outcast. Mum tried her best, but ultimately, she was just as broken as that china.

Briony wandered over to the cup and saucer's remains, gathering them in her hands in the same manner as the tears gathering in her eyes. "Mum, why did you have to leave me like this? I'm so alone. . . ."

She sat on the floor for several minutes, unwilling to move and face a reality that left her aching for comfort and belonging. It was so much easier just to sit in her grief, so much easier to let it billow over her and knock her down like those dreadful waves below her home.

Suddenly, the toll of the mantel clock roused her from her grief-stricken state only for her to find long, shallow cuts across her palms where she held the broken china.

Briony dropped the pieces, wincing at the pain that was all too noticeable now. She didn't mind it though; the pain reminded her of all she'd lost in the past year. *'Tis gratifying in a way. A suitable punishment fer forgetting what today is.*

I doubt anyone else will see it that way though. She hurried to the well just past Drulea Cottage to wash the blood from her hands. She didn't worry that someone else would be there, for no one else dared use it.

People claimed the well was a gateway to the fairy realm and that a group of trows[19] liked to frequent it. Most bairns believed they might get snatched away if they got too close, but Briony had always known it was just nonsense. Now the stories served as a good way to make sure she wasn't bothered whenever she went there.

The water stung as it flowed over her marred skin, but its cool temperature was refreshing on the already hot day. Briony inspected her hands to make sure they were no longer bleeding. Even though the cuts weren't very deep, they would

---

[19] An Orcadian form of troll.

130

still need to be wrapped. Briony did this quickly, wondering if there was any way to hide the injuries from curious eyes.

What a scolding I'll hear if Adaira learns I've hurt myself. Just as I would have heard from my mum if she were still here. More tears threatened to fall from her eyes at that thought. Now that her mother was gone, she wished with everything in her to hear Bethany's voice again even if it was only to reprimand her for being so careless.

She took a few unsteady steps, then a few more, doing her best to recall precisely how her mother had sounded—

"Dearie, what are you doing here?"

Briony started. Her heart had been so overwhelmed by grief that she hadn't even noticed how far she'd wandered down the hill.

Adaira stood at the inn's entrance, broom in hand, as she gave Briony a hard stare.

"Adaira, g-good morneen," the midwife choked, trying to force a smile onto her face.

Adaira put down her broom and placed her hands on her hips. "Nay, 'tis na a 'good morneen,' Briony, so dinna pretend otherwise. Did you think I would forget what today is?"

"Dinna worry about me, Adaira. I'll be fi—"

"Dinna you dare say 'fine.'" Her eyes flashed. "You know I know you better than that. Yer na to walk Santiago today, and yer na to report to Dr. Sherwin. I'll take care o' it. You need to take a day to yerself. Visit yer mum's grave, and let yerself feel everything that needs to be felt. You did na let yerself truly mourn her passing when it happened. You closed yerself off so much that fer a while, I feared I'd never get my old friend back. Go to the churchyard and be with yer mum."

Adaira's tone and body language left no room for argument, so Briony simply embraced her friend. No more words were said as they stood there, for none were needed.

I thank You, Lord, fer a friend such as this.

When Briony pulled back, the sad tears on her cheeks now mingled with joyous ones. She nodded a silent goodbye and went on her way, still hurting but feeling far less alone.

***

Bethany Fairborn had always been a strange woman. She had been so concerned with people's opinions of her that she had taken many precautions in raising Briony, precautions that proved futile. Briony knew all about manners and keeping a pristine house and arranging her hair just so—

Briony sighed. *Did Mum truly think any o' that would change the way the neighbors looked at us? These people have trouble turning a blind eye to even the slightest flaw.*

And an illegitimate child is no slight flaw.

What's even worse is I'm at least the third in a line o' illegitimate daughters. That makes it a cycle o' wantonness, one I can never hope to escape from.

Mum should have moved away to get a fresh start in a town where no one knew the name Fairborn, but that stubborn woman refused to give up the family home, no matter how difficult it made our lives.

And yet . . . what o' the other home she spoke o'? What made her abandon it?

With Mum gone, 'twill be difficult to find an answer to that. Maybe I never will. . . .

After about an hour musing on thoughts and memories such as these, Briony slipped away from Bethany's grave and headed home. Her soul felt lighter, and the weight of grief had lessened enough that she could smile again. Just a little bit.

When she returned to Drulea Cottage, her eyes caught sight of the ocean. *'Tis so still today. Almost like it knows what day 'tis.*

Briony sat in one of her chairs outside and watched the soft waves. An old tune came to her mind, one her mother had taught her as a child. Bethany had said it was part of her Fairborn heritage, as old as Drulea Cottage itself.

The words sprang from Briony's throat effortlessly, giving homage not only to her mother but to all the Fairborn women of old:

"Now, youthful daughter, beware o' the sea,
O' the things it can squander and steal from ye.
Beware o' promises spoken in haste,
And always keep yer heart, always keep yer heart.

High up on the rocks above the seashore,
A woman sits weeping fer memories o' yore,
O' a handsome young stranger whose strange eyes bore,
A fire so strong it made her heart soar.
Where is this stranger whom she did love?
He's gone to the sea while she weeps above.
Gone to the sea, gone to the sea,
And so she sits weeping fer her lost love."

A sudden footstep caught Briony's attention, and she jumped up only to find Santiago a few feet behind her. Somehow he had climbed up the whole hill with only his cane to assist him.

Briony waited a few seconds for him to speak, but the man's countenance was unfocused as if he couldn't see her even though he was looking straight at her.

"Santiago, I did na realize—"

Briony cut off mid-sentence as Santiago closed the distance between them and swept her up in one of his arms. Before she realized what was happening, Santiago leaned in and kissed her.

Almost immediately, Briony's lips responded, moving against his instinctively. She melted into his embrace as butterflies fluttered to life in her stomach. Santiago's hands grasped her shoulders, drawing her deeper into the kiss, making it impossible to think.

She wrapped her arms around him, placing her hands on his strong back. Euphoria flowed through her body, filling her with the urge to press closer and let the moment stretch on forever.

It wasn't at all what she'd thought it would be to kiss him—in those scarce moments when she'd allowed herself to think such things—it was far better than that. Her soul was ablaze, burning brighter and hotter than any bonfire the town had ever seen.

I knew it! I knew he felt the same way! The thought exploded across her mind. *He l—*

But I have to know fer sure. I have to hear him declare his feelings fer myself. Does he care as deeply as I do? She pulled back to ask, opening her eyes—

But he was loosening his arms, letting her go, stepping away.

"Santiago?"

Pure shock shone from the man's face. He slipped his free hand behind his back as if he feared what it might do next. "Br-Briony, I apologize. I don't know why I just did that. I—" He cut off, his voice full of regret as he avoided her gaze.

". . . What?" Her question was the smallest whisper, the bare minimum to be audible, but that was as much sound as she could get out.

"There's no excuse for my behavior. Please don't think I'm someone who would take advantage of a woman. I can only pray you'll come to forgive me. I promise it won't happen again."

A lump formed in Briony's throat, one that killed any attempt at responding. All she could do was gawk at him as she felt her hope, which only moments before had been soaring like a bird, suddenly plummet to its death.

Is that pain on his face? 'Tis hard to tell when he won' meet my eyes.

"I must depart. I'll see you tomorrow." He had barely uttered the words before he was moving away from her, down the hill, out of sight.

Rising Temperatures

As Briony sat in her chair with her fingers over her tingling lips, she tried to get a handle on what had just happened. *Something I wish with all my soul that I could forget about.*

Well, most o' my soul, at least. The part o' me that's reasonable. The part that can' stop thinking about the fact that Santiago promised never to kiss me again.

But there's a tiny part o' me that can' shake the joy that it happened in the first place. I know some o' the villagers exchange a kiss or two fer a spot o' fun, but Santiago does na seem like the sort to do that; he's much too sincere o' a person.

Something drew him to me and led him to reciprocate my feelings, even if 'twas just fer a moment.

Except now he regrets it. Briony tapped her lip as she mulled it over. *Why would he regret it? I dinna think I did anything to make it seem like I disliked it.*

Did he dislike it? He's the one who initiated it, after all, na me. But afterward . . . his reaction was so strong. Almost like he kissed me against his will.

What a ridiculous thought.

Briony kicked at a nearby stone to vent her frustration. *I have no experience with matters o' the heart. They're more difficult than anything I've dealt with before.*

Mum did na gave me much to go on either. All she ever said was "Stay away from the lot o' them. They'll cause naught but ill fer you."

Thanks, Mum. Does that mean I'm naught but ill fer you, since I'm the result o' yer time with Da'?

And now that yer gone, I'm left with nothing. No father, no mother, and no idea what I'm doing with my life.

That lump Briony had felt earlier was still in her throat, but she shoved it back. She shoved back all the sadness, all the heartache, all the longing. She was tired of being a weeping wreck.

Ever since Santiago arrived in town, all I ever do is cry. I cried because Adaira thought Santiago and I had a chance, I cried when he and I argued, and now I'm on the verge o' crying again.

The time fer tears is done.

Briony felt the heat first. It appeared in her fingertips, wrapping them in an angry, powerful warmth before spreading through her palms.

Within a second of her noticing this, a loud noise sounded overhead. Briony peered up only to see lightning rip the suddenly black sky in two and strike about thirty feet away from her.

Briony held out a hand, waiting for droplets to fall, but nothing came. The clouds just continued to roil and crackle like a volcano about to burst.

CRACK! Another bolt touched down, this time only fifteen feet away. A section of dirt was left charred and smoking in its wake.

Briony hurried into the safety of her home, praying that no one would be injured in the freak storm. She gripped her table just to have something to hold on to. There were a few more peals of thunder, this time farther away. She stayed completely still, too afraid to even breathe.

But then, just as abruptly as the storm had arrived, all the noise stopped.

No wind.

No lightning.

No thunder.

Nothing.

After a few minutes of eerie silence, Briony peeked out the door. Her eyes widened at the clear blue sky that looked just the same as it had only ten minutes before, no tempest in sight.

As if it never happened.

But it did happen. I did na imagine it. Briony walked out and caught sight of the blackened dirt where one of the lightning strikes had hit. She touched the place gingerly and gasped at the residual heat.

Heat . . .

Briony looked down at her hands in bewilderment. *They seem perfectly normal now.*

But heat like that can' be normal, can it?

Now that I think about it, that was the same sort o' heat I felt when that sailor grabbed me. . . . And then he got those red marks on his hand. That can' be a coincidence, but how could I be responsible fer it? This does na make any sense!

Briony gripped her head as she tried to figure out what was going on. *Human beings can' burn people just by touching them. 'Tis impossible.*

And yet . . .

I have to go see Dr. Sherwin. If anyone can remind me o' what's rational, 'tis him.

Briony hurried into town, skirting around everyone with more care than usual. She didn't care how odd it looked that she was putting ten or more feet between herself and everyone else.

No one seems to have noticed anyway. They're probably too focused on the fact that Johnsmas will be here morn.

"Dr. Sherwin!" Briony knocked frantically against the door as soon as she arrived.

"What is it?" The doctor wrenched the door open with a growl. "Oh, 'tis only you. Hurry up, then. The sooner you get yer notes down, the faster yer gone."

"Um, but, Doctor . . . ," Briony started, but the man had already turned and gone back inside.

She followed him into the office, unsure of how to explain her problem.

Dr. Sherwin was going through a trunk in the back, completely oblivious that Briony wasn't already at the desk writing notes.

"Dr. Sherwin, I'm na here fer that. . . ."

He turned to her with a frown. "You realize yer behind, right? I have na gotten any updates on Mr. Mendes's condition in almost a week. I was just about to go check on him myself

137

when you got here."

Briony wrung her hands nervously. "Aye, I know I've been irresponsible, but I have something else to discuss with you. 'Tis about me."

The man's eyes narrowed. "Was it one o' the foreigners?"

"What? What are you talking abou—" Briony cut off as understanding dawned on her. "How dare you! How could you assume I would do something like that? I know I have a family history o' it, but I've never done anything promiscuous. I'm na that kind o' person, no matter what this town thinks."

Briony clenched her hands into fists, feeling her temper flare up as it had earlier at Santiago. She glared at this arrogant, insensitive, prejudiced man, feeling like he represented all the pain and hardship she had borne over the years.

And, just like earlier, a familiar heat appeared in her fingertips. It began to spread into her palms—

Fear washed over her as she lifted her hands.

"This is why I came to you." Briony's voice was a tiny whisper.

Dr. Sherwin looked at her in confusion.

"My hands. Please help me." She reached out a hand to the doctor's arm, almost grabbing it, but she stopped herself a few inches away.

"You can feel how warm 'tis, right?"

"What in the world—'Tis burning up! How is that possible?" He extended a finger and tapped her palm, but as soon as he did, he drew back with a yelp.

"Does it hurt?"

"Nay, there's no pain. It happened earlier this morneen, just before a storm rolled in."

Dr. Sherwin raised his eyebrows. "Storm? There has na been a storm today."

"You did na see it? 'Twas gone within a few minutes, but I could na figure out what was wrong with my hands. Can you help me?"

"Let's just see how hot 'tis, shall we?" Dr. Sherwin shuffled around her and rifled through his desk until he found a strange tube.

"What is *that*?"

A proud expression came over the man's face as he held it out to her. "This is something every doctor in the world needs. I heard the famed Dr. George Martine[20] used a device like this, and I was lucky enough to get my hands on one. It calculates internal body temperature. Now, hold this under your arm."

After a few minutes, the doctor retrieved the peculiar device and examined it.

Briony's stomach dropped when she saw the shock in his eyes. "What? Nay, that can' be." He shook the thermometer several times, blinked, wiped his glasses against his shirt, and checked again.

"Well? What does it say?"

Dr. Sherwin turned to Briony with a look of horror. "I— Surely there must be a mistake—"

"What does it say?"

"One hundred and fifteen degrees. But you should na be standing here if that's the case. You should be . . ."

Briony nodded to get him to continue.

"Well, you should be dead, mistress."

His words seemed to suck all the air from the room. Briony inhaled several times, attempting to get a good breath, but she couldn't. Dr. Sherwin's office was suddenly far too small. *I have to get out o' here.*

Briony fled as quickly as she could, desperate for wide, open spaces where the air came easily and no one stared at her as though she shouldn't exist. She gripped her chest, trying to relax her breathing and slow her heartbeat. *How can this be? What's going on with me?*

"Mistress Fairborn!" called the doctor, appearing behind her. "You can' be out and about in yer condition. You must drink some water and get rest immediately."

"But—"

"Dinna argue with me, Mistress Fairborn. You may be a midwife, but yer na an expert on this. Let's get you home."

He extended his hand to her, but Briony pulled away. "You just told me I should be dead right now. Why should I trust yer judgment any more than my own? *You* certainly dinna

---

[20] A Scottish physician in the eighteenth century who used an early form of thermometer.

know why this is happening."

Dr. Sherwin huffed, unused to someone doubting his professional opinion. "Are you sure you feel fine? Na faint in the slightest?"

Briony shook her head adamantly.

The doctor pursed his lips. "Well, let me get you some water. *Please.*"

She was determined to deny him, but there was something about the way he said "please" that made her pause. She studied the man, trying to determine his agenda. *It can' be that he genuinely cares about me, can it?*

"All right, I'll drink some water and go home after this."

"Good. And I'll be by in about two hours to see how—"

"Dr. Sherwin, that's unnecessary—"

"Mistress Fairborn, we must be cautious. We dinna know what's causing this."

Briony paused, considering his words. "I'll come down to see you early morn on my way to Everton Inn."

The doctor rolled his eyes. "I'll come to *you* at about ten o'clock to check on you."

"But I need to walk with Mr. Mendes—"

"That is out o' the question. You can' risk getting anyone else sick if what you have can be spread. Besides, morn is Johnsmas, so I'm sure Mr. Mendes will wish to see the festivities. He'll get plenty o' time to walk then. You need to stay home."

Briony put her hands on her hips. "Na attend Johnsmas? How can you suggest something like that? I feel fine. What if yer device is broken and there's nothing wrong with me?"

He scrutinized her with hard eyes.

He's wrong. He has to be. It must be the machine. My temperature can' be that high. Na so high I should be . . . dead.

After a moment, Dr. Sherwin sighed in resignation, seeming to realize he was no match for Briony's stubbornness.

"I'll come to you at about ten o'clock. If all is well, then you may resume yer normal activities and do as you wish. *Including attend the Johnsmas celebration.*"

"Thank you," Briony said, her voice full of sincerity.

The doctor spluttered a bit before catching himself. "Well,

get going, then. I've plenty o' other things to do before Johnsmas arrives."

Intentions

Dr. Sherwin came just as he'd said, right at ten o'clock. Briony was eager for him to arrive and finish so she could go down to Everton Inn. She fidgeted as the man sat in the chair opposite hers.

"How do you feel this morneen?" His eyes were full of that same emotion from yesterday, the one that looked far too much like concern.

"I feel great. I'm ready to get started fer the day, and I'm sure Adaira will need my help, so if you could just hurry along with—"

"Mistress Fairborn, stop," Dr. Sherwin cut her off as he checked her pulse. After a minute, he nodded to himself. Then he pulled out that bizarre instrument from earlier and stuck it under Briony's arm.

Briony wanted to snarl at him, but that might make the visit take longer, so she kept her mouth shut.

Five excruciatingly long minutes passed, and the doctor looked at the results from the tube. His face suddenly relaxed, and he said, "Ah, much better. You appear to be back to normal."

"But, Doctor, that instrument must have been having issu—" She closed her mouth again.

"What was that?"

Briony shook her head and said nothing. *I can' risk him forcing me to stay home.*

"Well, in that case, feel free to go down and see Mistress

Stubbins. I won' stand fer any shortage o' pie tonight, so you best do whatever she tells you, you hear?"

"Aye, Doctor!" She grinned.

Dr. Sherwin rose slowly from his seat. "Excellent. I'll see you tonight, then." He turned to leave.

"Hey, Doctor?"

"What is it?"

Briony pointed at him with a wicked smirk. "Best na let the others see you smiling. 'Twill ruin yer reputation."

There truly was a smile on the man's face, but as soon as he heard Briony's words, he hurried out the door.

Briony chuckled at the man's brusque departure before turning pensive. She glanced at the place where her mother's bed used to sit. *I may na be as alone as I thought, Mum.*

With that thought in mind, Briony checked her hair and put on her headscarf before she, too, dashed outside.

***

Briony had just walked into Everton Inn when her ears caught a voice speaking in Portuguese.

She ducked behind the door even though she recognized the voice as Lucia's. She wouldn't have hidden from her except that there was something urgent in the other woman's tone.

She almost sounds desperate. Whatever she's talking about, 'tis na something I'm meant to hear. I wonder what it could be about—

When a second voice whispered something back, Briony blushed. *Santiago.*

She could hear the siblings strolling down the hallway, getting nearer to the front door. "Para a Briony?"

She couldn't stifle a soft gasp. *They're talking about me.*

The conversation instantly ceased. There were no footsteps for several seconds.

They must have heard me! Briony swept her eyes around, wondering how she could get out of this situation without making it obvious she'd been listening in. Her gaze homed in on Adaira's broom, and she sprang toward it.

It was only just in time too, for as soon as she did, Lucia and Santiago stepped into view.

"Briony." Lucia beamed, though her cheerfulness seemed forced.

Briony glanced up from sweeping as if she'd only just noticed them, too. "Oh, hello. I was trying to clean up a wee bit since Adaira is so busy. . . ." She looked between them, noting how Santiago avoided her eyes.

"How thoughtful of you. Truly, Adaira is lucky to have a friend such as you. I only wish I had the chance to know you as well as she does. Unfortunately, I was just talking to my brother about how we'll be leaving soon."

Something sharp pierced Briony's chest at those words. Phantom pain snaked its way through her, making her drop the broom.

Why am I so surprised? I knew this was going to happen. I've known it from the first day I walked with Santiago.

"How soon?" She looked directly at Santiago as she asked.

The man's eyes shot to hers. They were full of unspoken questions and longing, combined with a healthy dose of shame. *But maybe I'm only imagining the longing.*

"Well, we didn't want to miss the party tonight, and the ship's crew has to restock a few more things, but the repairs are all finished, and my brother is fit to travel again. We should be leaving within the week," Lucia replied. She didn't comment on the abandoned broom, though her eyebrows rose questioningly. "As long as nothing *unexpected* happens."

Briony's eyes returned to Lucia, but the blond woman was staring pointedly at her brother.

"There you are, Briony. Thank goodness! I did na know how I was going to get everything ready in time," exclaimed Adaira as she appeared behind Lucia and Santiago.

Everyone jumped at the interruption and turned to Adaira, who stood there with twitching hands.

"Is something wrong?" Briony asked.

"Aye, there's simply too much to do. Every year, people want more and more o' my food. I fear my popularity as a cook shall be my undoing," Adaira said dramatically, but Briony could tell there was genuine worry behind her smile.

"Perhaps we can help, then," suggested Santiago.

Briony sent him a grateful smile, and when he returned it,

she had to look away to keep herself from getting lost in his gaze.

"Please, what can we do?" Lucia asked.

Hope sparked in Adaira's eyes at the sight of new volunteers, and she eagerly began assigning tasks. All of them got to work preparing ingredients, stirring mixtures, and doing everything else Adaira could think of to make sure the celebration was perfect.

Adaira must have recruited Niall as well because he soon appeared with some baskets in his hands. He winked when he spotted Briony, but he didn't have a chance to speak to her before Adaira was pushing him down the hallway.

Briony noted that Niall and Santiago never stayed in the same place very long, and when they did have to work together on something, they did so with hardly a word spoken between them. Briony wasn't sure if this was progress or not, but at least they weren't practically getting into a fistfight this time.

"Briony," Santiago said, catching hold of her arm as she walked by with some linens. Adaira had tasked her with putting fresh towels in all the guest rooms.

"Aye?" Briony asked, still smiling from a joke Adaira had made a minute before in the sitting room.

"Can we talk? *Alone?*"

Briony's face fell. "That may be difficult right now."

Santiago rubbed the back of his neck and turned his eyes to the floor before shifting them back to her. "Then later tonight? Once the celebration ends?"

"Aye, that would be fine." He was so somber that she couldn't help but feel uneasy. This wasn't going to be a light conversation, no matter the topic.

Santiago smiled slightly before leaning in and whispering, "Thank you."

Briony bit her lip anxiously, drawing Santiago's gaze to her mouth. Her heart rate sped up, as much from the man's proximity as from his request.

But suddenly, Santiago stepped back and strolled into the kitchen, leaving Briony standing there trying to calm herself down.

"Dearie, what are you doing? Does yer chest hurt?" Adaira

146

asked as she came around the corner.

Briony looked down at where Adaira was staring and discovered her own hand pressed against her heart. She flushed in embarrassment and dropped her hand. "N-Nay! Everything is perfect."

"Well, good. I'm glad I found you alone. There's something I must tell you. I just heard from Matthew Levins that Mr. McGuff said that—"

"Please, Adaira, just get to the point."

Adaira rolled her eyes. "Fine. So basically, everyone is saying that yer being indecent with na just one man, but two. Mr. Moreland has made it no secret to Daniel Calhoun that he fancies you, and Laird Oliver received a pretty penny from Mr. Mendes the other day to make up fer some slight that you *supposedly* gave him."

Briony was silent as she processed this information. She'd told Santiago she would handle Oliver, but she'd completely forgotten about the incident until now.

He should na have given that oaf any money. 'Tis my issue to deal with, na his. And why would he anyway? What am I to him?

The kiss replayed in her mind, followed by his request to talk to her alone.

What could he want to say? Is it just to say goodbye? Or is Lucia wrong? It seems idiotic to hope he could wish to . . . stay here with me. But could he?

And what about Niall? He does fancy me after all. That must be what he was trying to say at dinner. What can I tell him?

"I'm sorry people are spreading rumors about you. I'll do what I can to stop them. I already told Matthew Levins that he could forget about getting any pie fer a long time if I heard him talking like that again."

Briony nodded, still so focused on Santiago that she barely heard Adaira's words.

"Anyway, fer now, let's just get back to work. We'll deal with that when we can, so try na to think about it, aye?"

"O' course, love," Briony said. *She's right. I have more important things to do than think about the town's constant disapproval o' me.*

By the time midday arrived, Briony was all too ready to

stop for lunch. *This is the most I've worked since . . . probably two years ago when Adaira last recruited me.*

She sighed, glancing over at her friend as she zipped from room to room. Adaira always got so stressed about the celebration, worried she wouldn't have enough food or that something would be overcooked or undercooked. *Basically, she worries that something will be less than perfect.*

This year, though, Adaira seemed even more frantic than usual. She was ordering everyone about with the domineering attitude of a military general, to the point that Briony wondered if she should tell her friend to back off some.

'Tis almost as if she's trying to impress someone. . . . Then realization dawned on her, and Briony smacked her head for not thinking of it sooner. *That's what this is! The whole town has been talking o' the grand food Adaira makes on Johnsmas, so 'tis no wonder she's so eager to make sure everything is just right in front o' Mr. Burgess.*

Briony frowned and looked around. *But where is he?*

She hadn't seen the man all morning; neither he nor his son had been in their room when she replaced the linens.

They must have left shortly after breakfast. I wonder if their hostess sent them on an errand.

Briony entered the kitchen and found the woman in question muttering to herself about all the tasks she still needed to do. Briony stifled a chuckle before clearing her throat several feet behind the innkeeper's daughter.

Adaira jerked and nearly spilled the bowl of batter in her hands. "Briony! Dinna do that."

"I was na trying to frighten you this time. Truly! I just was wondering, where are the Burgesses?"

The unmistakable blush that appeared on Adaira's face was all too heartwarming, and Briony had to smile.

"They went to the market fer me, and then they were going to go fishing fer our dinner. 'Twas too thoughtful o' them. I did na wish fer them to trouble themselves, but John insisted on getting more ingredients fer me since I'd be cooking so much today."

"Aye . . . that was so thoughtful o' *John*." She drew out the man's name, all while smirking at her friend.

Adaira gasped, no doubt just realizing her slip of the tongue. "Now, Briony, dinna be coming to any conclusions—"

"What sort o' conclusions are you talking about? I merely agreed with you that *John* was being so *thoughtful*. What's there to conclude? He must just be a thoughtful person. I'm sure he would have done that fer just *anyone*."

"Briony, stop it. Yer imagining things." Adaira turned her back on her and resumed stirring.

Briony hummed in agreement. "O' course. I must be. Then I suppose it does na matter to you that a certain young, *beautiful* blond happens to be speaking to him right now?"

"What?" Adaira spun around and almost dropped her bowl.

Briony gestured to the foyer, where Lucia was in the process of conveniently slipping right toward Mr. Burgess's arms. The only problem was that Mr. Burgess's arms were already full of bags—

"Lucia!" Briony called in a vain attempt to stop her.

"Mistress!" Mr. Burgess shouted at the same time as he tried to catch her.

Both Lucia and Mr. Burgess landed on the floor in a heap of sugar, salt, and flour.

Santiago and Niall must have heard the noise, for they soon appeared and hurried over from the other room.

"Lucia, are you all right?" Santiago extended a hand to his frazzled sister. She had managed to fall onto Mr. Burgess, who had received the brunt of the mess. His clothes were stained all over, and his hair was as white as Nathaniel Levins's. Lucia, not nearly as dirty, had several speckles along her neck and arms, but her dress appeared unsullied.

Lucia trembled as she gripped her brother's helpful hand and stood. "I-I . . ." She looked from one concerned gaze to another, her eyes landing on Mr. Burgess last.

Then she burst into tears and ran off down the corridor before shutting herself up in her room. Santiago hurried after her, and the others heard him knock at his sister's door several times before finally being let in.

Adaira held out her hand to Mr. Burgess. "Here, let me help you."

149

"Da', I just dinna see why—What happened?" William asked as he stumbled inside with far too many bags to carry safely. He set them down and gripped his father's other hand as Adaira pulled the man up.

"Just an accident, son. Dinna worry. *I'm fine.*" Mr. Burgess gazed at Adaira as he said the last part, and a sweet smile came over his face.

"But what about all the food?" William stared down in dismay. Everything John had been carrying was now on the floor, and very little of it looked salvageable.

"'Twill be all right, William. I do believe I'll have enough fer tonight, and I can buy some more morn." Adaira rubbed William's shoulder soothingly.

"What an awful morneen!" The boy scraped his foot against some of the sugar, creating a small white cloud.

Briony touched Adaira's arm. "I've got some extra things at home. 'Twill be enough fer morn's breakfast, at least."

Adaira gave her a grateful smile. "Thank you, dearie. I'd be most grateful fer them."

"I'll go get them now, then." She turned to leave.

A hand suddenly grabbed hers. "And I'll help you."

Briony jumped at Niall's voice as well as the strange tingling sensation in her fingers. It was not unlike the heat she'd felt the day before when that freak lightning appeared.

She stared up into his dark eyes. They swirled like violent waves in a storm. They were full of energy and passion. *And danger.*

But what sort o' danger? Does it mean I should stay away?

"A-All right," she found herself saying, almost without even meaning to. "Come on."

Briony marched up the path, ignoring the upright hairs on the back of her neck. She tried to subtly pull her hand from Niall's, but he held firm.

She gulped as fear made her chest tighten and her heart quicken. *Or is it something besides fear?*

"How are you, Briony? I missed you yesterday. I looked fer you around town, but I could na find you."

Briony stopped walking and turned to Niall. There was no threat in his expression, nothing sinister in his tone. *But I dinna like feeling trapped.*

"If you wish me to respond, then kindly remove yer hand."

Niall frowned a bit, but he did as she wanted.

"Thank you. Yesterday was the anniversary o' my mum's passing, so I spent some time by myself."

Niall's eyes widened. "Ah, Briony, I'm sorry. I did na realize—"

"Dinna worry about it. 'Twas just a hard day."

In more ways than one.

Niall looked like he wanted to say more, but before he could, Briony asked, "How long do you think you'll stay in town?"

The man cleared his throat, seeming relieved to change subjects. "Well, I've been enjoying Everton much more than I thought I would. The atmosphere, the scenery, the *people* . . ." He looked at her pointedly. "I may end up staying fer a long time."

Briony didn't know what to say, so she began walking again, this time being careful to keep her hands far from his.

"Are you still helping Mr. Mendes go fer walks?"

Briony noted the edge that appeared in Niall's voice. "Aye, I am."

"Is that necessary? I thought you were just the town midwife?"

"There aren' that many expectant mothers right now. Dr. Sherwin requested my help."

"Ah, so 'tis an extra source o' income. . . . You must be struggling to provide fer yerself all on yer own."

How dare he! Briony swung around angrily.

"That's na what I—"

"You need na worry about that anymore now that I'm here."

"What are you saying, Niall?"

Niall flew forward and gripped her waist. With an earnest grin, he drew her close and leaned in. At that moment, all the danger within his eyes seemed to melt away. In its place, a fierce love burst forth, wrapping Briony in its intensity and warmth.

A nervous excitement erupted in her stomach even as Santiago's face danced through her mind. *Is he about to*—

"Must I spell it out fer you, Briony? I mean to make you mine, plain and simple."

Lost?

Briony gaped, taking a few seconds to process what she'd just heard. *'Tis much harder to think with his arms wrapped around me. And his eyes staring deeply into mine. And his mouth inching closer—*

She gasped and jumped away, trying to ignore the hurt on Niall's face as she did so. "Th-That's very sweet o' you, but we barely know each other. We may have met when we were bairns, but I have na seen you in years. . . ."

And you have na even asked to court me! She would have said this aloud, but her mouth was suddenly too dry to form the words.

"Surely you feel the connection between us," he purred, his mouth returning to its former grin.

Briony opened her mouth to deny it, but she paused when she felt a shiver down her spine. She looked into the man's eyes; within them, she saw hints of acceptance, passion, and a wild freedom that made her chest constrict with longing.

But is there love?

She drew her gaze away, angry at her thoughts. *I should na be stupid. This man wants to marry me, and he's telling me directly, which is far better than what Santiago has done. Despite my feelings fer Santiago, I know they can' go anywhere. He will be going home soon; Lucia said it herself.*

Why na give Niall a chance? Once my heart recovers from Santiago, perhaps what I feel fer Niall will turn into love.

Briony gave the man a shy smile. "I dinna deny that there's *something* here."

Niall stepped closer again. His lips were only a few inches away, starting their descent toward hers. He gingerly clasped her shoulder, making Briony's pulse accelerate.

But Santiago . . . He wants to tell me something after the celebration. Dinna I need to hear him out first?

Briony blinked a few times, feeling an odd shudder pass through her as she fully realized what she was doing. What she was about to do.

"We better get going before the others start wondering why we're na back yet." Briony pulled away and hurried up the path, not waiting to see if Niall followed. She darted into her cottage and grabbed what she needed so fast that she was already back at the entrance before Niall had even gotten to the top of the hill.

"Take this, please." She gave him a bag, staring at his hands rather than his eyes. She was sure her face was aflame with embarrassment.

"O' course, my lady." Niall bowed jovially as if there was nothing bizarre about Briony's behavior.

Briony gulped and practically fled back to the inn without giving Niall the chance to say more.

"Ah, finally! That took longer than I thought 'twould. What were you two doing up there?" Adaira said as they arrived. Briony didn't miss the suspicious gleam in her friend's eyes, nor the way Adaira's gaze cut over to Santiago to make sure he was listening.

Briony glared at her before casting nervous glances at Niall and Santiago. The first was practically beaming at Adaira's innuendo, but the second was scowling.

Briony coughed and said, "Adaira, may I speak to you fer a moment?"

Adaira, who was only too happy to oblige, took Briony upstairs to her room. She plopped onto the bed and sat Briony down next to her. "Am I right, dearie? Did something happen?"

"Shh! This is more complicated than you realize."

"Why? Something did happen, I knew it!"

"Aye, yer right. Niall, he—" Briony sighed and took the plunge. "He told me he wants to marry me."

Adaira squealed.

"Pipe down over there! Some o' us are trying to get some sleep," shouted Mr. Stubbins from the next room.

Adaira covered her mouth, but a flurry of giggles still escaped. "I knew it. I knew it. What did you say?"

"I have na given him an answer yet."

Adaira clapped her hands, but then she frowned. "But what about Mr. Mendes?"

Briony sighed. "Here's where it gets complicated: the other day, he kissed me."

Adaira's eyes bulged. "He did *what?*"

"You good fer nothin' daughter! If I hear you again, I'm about to—"

"Oh, be quiet! Otherwise, you'll never go back to sleep," Adaira yelled at the wall.

The two friends heard Mr. Stubbins grumble for a few seconds, but then everything got quiet.

Adaira leaned closer to Briony and whispered, "I'm sorry. Did he truly kiss you?"

"Aye, he did. Yesterday, when I was sitting outside, he marched over and kissed me with nary a word o' greeting. And then afterward, he apologized fer it and said 'twould never happen again. 'Twas so bizarre I dinna know what to think."

"Did he na explain why he did it?"

"Truly, he acted as surprised as I. As though he had na meant to do it. He asked to talk to me after Johnsmas tonight, but then Niall proposed! And just to add to the mess, Lucia said she and Santiago will be leaving within a week. I just dinna know what to do." Briony held her face in her hands, rubbing her temples to stop the headache that was beginning to form.

Adaira placed a consoling hand upon her friend's shoulder. "It sounds like you need to hear Mr. Mendes out before you tell Mr. Moreland anything. But first, answer this: What was the kiss like?"

"Adaira!" Briony exclaimed, a little louder than she meant to. She caught herself and said more quietly, "Did you forget that he promised na to do it again?"

"People say all kinds o' things in the heat o' the moment. Maybe he wants to talk to you because he realized he was being stupid."

Briony groaned. "This is the most excitement I've had in all my life."

"Ah, but that's part o' the fun." Adaira elbowed her with a grin. "But 'tis past lunchtime. How about you and I have a picnic at Cramer's Field? The weather is too lovely to eat indoors, anyway."

"Aye, that sounds—"

KNOCK!

Without waiting for a response, William Burgess pushed his way inside and glanced around the room. He scampered over to Adaira with a smile, one hand behind his back. "Mistress Stubbins, we got the fish!"

Adaira chuckled as she turned to the boy. "You did? How wonderful. How many did you catch?"

William shifted the hand behind his back and revealed several small fish dangling from a string. He proudly displayed them to the women, oblivious to the puddle he was forming on the floor.

"Oh, what a feast we shall have. That's more than enough fer dinner tonight." Adaira patted the boy on the shoulder. "Well done."

Briony smirked as she watched the exchange. *'Tis as if he's already her own.*

"Aye, we got so many that we figured we could eat some fer lunch, too. Da' already invited the others downstairs to join us."

Briony paled. *There go my chances at a peaceful lunch. Now I'll be lucky if I'm calm enough to eat anything at all.*

"I'll go tell Da' I told you." William spun around and scampered off, leaving a watery trail behind him.

Briony sighed as soon as the door closed. "I'm na sure I can handle both Mr. Moreland *and* Mr. Mendes right now. I dinna even know my own feelings."

"What better way to figure out which o' them you love than by spending more time with them?"

"'Tis na that simple. . . ."

Adaira raised an eyebrow and put her hand on her hip. "Briony, listen to me. You may na be sure you can handle so much fuss, but frankly, I've na seen so much life in you in years. Yer mother, God rest her soul, was so determined to keep you safe from the world that you never got to just be yerself. Ever since—" She cut off with a shaky breath and bit her lip.

Adaira cleared her throat and tried again. "Well, you know. And after her death, you were so heartbroken. But then these people showed up, and now look at you. Yer the fiery, fun-loving, passionate woman you always should have been. And I, fer one, am grateful to those men fer the part they've played. Stop being frightened o' yerself. Sit beside me at lunch and think about what you truly want. Then see what Mr. Mendes has to say tonight and go from there. Make yer choice and stand confidently in it because I *know* 'twill be the right one."

***

Before long, the group sat on a couple of blue blankets, surrounded by the beautifully lush grass and flowers. Briony had sat down beside Adaira, but somehow, Niall had ended up on the other side, with Santiago directly across from her. They had brought along tea, biscuits, and Adaira's delicious porridge to go with the fish. All in all, it would have been an idyllic picnic, were it not for the tension running through Briony's body.

To make matters worse, Niall kept watching her. She had avoided eye contact the entire walk outside, trying to distract herself by talking to William about his fishing trip, but that didn't keep her from feeling the heat of the man's gaze.

Lucia pinched her lips into a grin as she steeped her tea. "What lovely weather this is."

"Aye, 'tis much cooler than yesterday," Mr. Burgess agreed.

A rumble came from Santiago's throat, much deeper than his normal speech. "Indeed."

Briony, who happened to be sipping her porridge, accidentally made a loud slurp. *He does na sound pleased at all.*

When she peeked over, she realized that he and Niall were locked in a staring match, both looking like they'd just swallowed a jar of lemons.

Suddenly, Santiago's gaze shifted to hers, wherein all the animosity vanished. He seemed to be trying to tell her something with his eyes. *What could he—*

"Briony?"

Briony jumped and turned to Adaira. "Aye?"

"Lucia was wondering how long you've been a midwife fer."

Lucia nodded, giving Briony a smile that would have seemed sincere if not for a slight twitch at the corner of her mouth.

She almost looks like she's in pain. Did she notice the look her brother was giving me? I better be more careful; otherwise, everyone will know something's going on.

Briony reflected the false smile the best she could and said, "Oh, I apologize. I'm far too easily distracted. To answer yer question, my mother shared her skills as a midwife with me over the years. I helped her more and more as I grew older. 'Twas only after her passing last year that I began doing it by myself."

"What about yer da'?" William asked as he munched on a biscuit.

Mr. Burgess elbowed his son and cleared his throat.

"What? What did I do?" William looked from his father to Briony to Adaira, completely confused.

"'Tis all right, Mr. Burgess. 'Tis an innocent question. William, I . . ." Briony expected Lucia probably knew this already, and Niall surely had heard about it from Daniel Calhoun.

Even so, 'tis hard to say it out loud.

"I never knew him. Na even his name. Just that he was lost to the sea—"

Niall huffed, cutting her off. "Lost? That's an interesting way o' putting it—"

Briony's attention whipped around to the dark-haired man. "What do you mean? Do you know something about my father?"

Niall blushed and looked down at his plate. "Uh . . . Nay, I just had na heard it put that way before?"

158

Briony grabbed the man's chin and jerked him her way, forcing him to meet her eyes. "Listen to me. If you know something about my father—"

Adaira tapped her friend's shoulder and leaned close to her ear. "Briony, this may na be a good place fer *that kind o' conversation.*"

Briony looked around at everyone, only then remembering they weren't alone. Adaira's big brown eyes were full of sympathy, John Burgess was visibly uncomfortable as he kept his attention on his food, William was staring blatantly at Briony and Niall, Lucia appeared scandalized by the whole affair, and Santiago was—

She couldn't tell; there were far too many emotions swirling in those green eyes, each one swallowing up the next so quickly that she couldn't identify it before it was gone.

"We'll talk more later," Briony whispered to Niall. The man nodded and sent her a small grin.

William opened his mouth. "So did you—"

"*Lucia*, would you tell us about yer home in Portugal?" Adaira interrupted.

"Certainly," Lucia said a little too cheerily. "It's in the city of Aveiro, right on the coast. It's one of the loveliest places you could ever go. There are so many colors and interesting people. We travel a lot in boats called barcos moliceiros since canals run through the whole city. Merchants are always out selling their wares, and the ladies wear such fine dresses. It's so diverting. You'd probably be overwhelmed at first by all the sights and sounds, but once you got past that, you'd love it as much as I do."

"Have you two always lived there?" Mr. Burgess asked.

"Yes. Our parents met in Aveiro and fell in love, both with each other and with the city itself. It's so full of energy that I cannot imagine living anywhere else."

"It sounds amazing. I should like to visit it someday. I hope you dinna find our village too dull fer yer tastes," Adaira said.

"Quite the contrary. I'm liking it very well. Everyone has been so kind and helpful that I can see why my brother's so taken with it."

Briony nearly choked on her tea, but she managed to conceal it with a cough.

Santiago, on the other hand, seemed unfazed, except for a brief tremble in his left hand. "What makes you say that?"

Lucia patted his shoulder. "You may deny this, Brother, but I've noticed a change in you since coming here. When our parents died, you closed yourself off. . . ." She looked hard at him before whispering something too soft for Briony to discern.

Santiago smiled and nodded to his sister. Something beyond words passed between them, making Briony's heart seize up. *Santiago loves Lucia so dearly. Is it fair to ask him to stay with me?*

As she was ruminating on this, a hand grasped her arm. She turned to Niall, who was looking at her with an odd expression. "What is it, Niall?"

His eyes slipped to Santiago and back to her. "N-Nothing, nothing. I just wanted to tell you how much I'm looking forward to tonight. I think 'tis time to tell you everything."

An Evening to Remember

The moment had finally arrived. The sun was low in the sky, the bonfires were ready to be lit, and all of Everton was gathered at Mary's Hill, abuzz with excitement. Briony stood with Adaira and the Burgesses as they watched Laird Oliver approach the largest woodpile.

"Let the celebration begin!" the laird cried with a pompous grin. He dramatically raised his pieces of flint and steel before striking them together to produce a few sparks. The sparks fell upon the sticks in the woodpile, and before long, the first fire blazed into existence.

Fergus McGuff, William Burgess, and two other small boys ran up with twigs, held them in the flames until they caught fire, and then scurried off to light the other woodpiles nearby. A group of girls near Briony giggled at the boys' antics but refused to join them for fear of getting dirty.

Dr. Sherwin, Donal McGuff, and Nathaniel Levins picked up their fiddles and began playing a merry tune. The young men grasped their sweethearts' hands and drew them into a dance. Briony laughed at the older men as they scoffed at the festivities, for their smiles revealed they were enjoying themselves as much as the rest—no Orcadian could resist the magic of Johnsmas.

The sailors seemed to be having fun as well. Briony watched them dance heartily with every woman who would join them, though they spent the most time with the pretty ones.

161

Briony smiled as her neighbors frolicked without care on this one night when all woes were forgotten. *Fer one night, it does na matter who I am or what my parents did. This is my one night o' freedom from all that.*

"May I dance with you, senhorita?" asked a familiar voice behind her.

Briony jumped a bit and turned to the young sailor who had helped her at the dock. She almost didn't recognize him, for he was dressed in his finest attire and had a fresh shave. *He looks very handsome with his hair tied back like that.*

"I would be honored," Briony declared and took the man's hand. He led her over to where the others stood waiting for the next dance. A few sailors glared at him with overt jealousy, but he didn't seem to care.

"Yer name is Mr. Rodriguez?"

The man nodded. "Yes, but call me Adriano, senhorita."

Briony felt her lips curl up in response. "All right, Adriano 'tis. Are you enjoying yer time in Everton?" Briony asked as the fiddlers started a jig.

"Yes. Very beautiful place. A good place for Senhor Mendes to fix his ankle."

Briony frowned as something tugged at her memory. *Something about Santiago . . .*

All the faces blurred as they twirled and leaped among the other dancers. She looked for Santiago, trying to compel the memory to fully appear.

There he is. He was sitting in a chair beside his sister with some food. *What memory do I have o' Adriano and Santiago in the same place?*

She gasped as it dawned on her. *Adriano was there with Santiago and the captain that day when they were talking about morta.*

Briony had put that conversation at the back of her mind when she decided she was going to trust Santiago, but now something struck her that she hadn't connected before.

Santiago got so upset with me that day when he fell in the water. He was angry that I'd gone down to the ship by myself. What if he was trying to keep me from being alone with the captain? Costa seemed very suspicious when he told me what "morta" meant. I need to know what they were talking about. Whose death was it?

162

"Adriano, do the captain and Mr. Mendes get along?"

The man's brow furrowed in confusion at first, but then something hardened in his eyes. "They are friends, senhorita. It was an accident."

"What? What are you talking about? What accident?"

Adriano clapped a hand over his mouth as he realized what he'd said and shook his head.

Briony grabbed the man's arms. "Adriano, tell me."

"I-I—"

A hand appeared on Adriano's shoulder. "May I cut in?"

Briony and Adriano turned to see Niall standing there. He looked even more mysterious in the light of the fire, and his dark eyes seemed to glow with flames of their own.

"Certainly," Adriano replied, stepping back. The grin on his face was so tight it looked painful, and his eyes begged Briony not to say anything as he bade her goodbye.

Briony nodded at the young man and watched him wander over to a group of sailors who elbowed him in the ribs and threw their arms around his shoulders. They seemed to either be teasing him or congratulating him on his short dance with Briony.

Niall drew her attention back to him when he held out his hand. Briony hesitated for a moment before taking it. She tried to conceal her annoyance at his interruption, but it didn't seem to work, for Niall's first comment was "I hope I'm na too much o' a disappointment as a dance partner."

Briony coughed a little, embarrassed he'd noticed her lack of enthusiasm. "Nay, 'tis na that at all. I'm sorry, my mind was elsewhere."

I have to find out what Adriano was talking about. Surely Costa did na have something to do with Santiago's injury, right?

"Well, I hope it does na take too long to bring yer mind back to the present. The next song is about to start, and I've been looking forward to dancing with you."

The man's words wove a strange spell over her, and what Adriano had said suddenly seemed far less important. All that mattered was this instant right now with Niall. "Do you dance often?"

A brilliant smile lit up Niall's face. "'Tis one o' my favorite pastimes. I saw how beautifully you danced earlier, so I would guess 'tis one o' yer favorites as well."

"Aye, you could say that."

"In that case, let's give the others something worth talking about, shall we?" Niall offered with a gleam in his eyes. He pulled her closer just as the music picked up, drawing Briony into the most exhilarating dance of her life. He moved them in time to the music, forward, side to side, and backward. Briony twirled around and around, reveling in Niall's company as much as in the dance itself. The flames beside them leaped, almost as if they were keeping in time with the music as well.

Others near the couple laughed and clapped their hands. Everyone seemed to be having a wonderful time—

Except for one person. Briony's gaze fell upon someone who didn't seem nearly as happy: Santiago. He looked out at the dancers with a troubling grimace, pausing when his eyes met Briony's.

"Have you been thinking o' what I said?" Niall asked, glancing in the direction Briony was looking. He scowled for a brief second at the merchant, but then he smoothed his brow as he turned back to her.

"Maybe. Are you ready to tell me the truth?" Briony countered.

"Aye, but you won' like it."

Briony sulked, tired of him skirting around the issue. "Just tell me, Niall. I dinna want any more games."

Niall sighed and pulled her away from the other dancers until they were out of earshot. "Very well. When we first met, I was na entirely honest with you. I did na come to Everton to thank you fer what you did all those years ago. I came here to save you."

"Save me? From what?"

"Do you truly na remember what happened that day?"

"You mean the day we met? I only remember bits and pieces. I remember finding you and telling you to run. I remember punching Adaira in the face and my mother wanting me to apologize when she found out. But then Adaira apologized instead, so we started to become friends. . . . The rest o' that day is hazy."

"I suppose it makes sense fer you to forget. 'Twas a terrible day—"

"But if you ran away, how do you know more than I do?"

Niall turned away awkwardly. "I did go fer help as I told you before, but I lied about returning too late. My parents and I did find you, and we weren' the only ones. *Yer father was there, too.*"

"My father? But he'd been gone fer years already. That does na make any sense, Niall."

"Yer father was part o' the same . . . *clan* that I am. He was with my parents when I found them. The three o' them went to rescue you, and . . ." Niall's voice broke off.

Briony put a hand on his shoulder and spun him around to face her. There were tears in the man's eyes. "What happened then, Niall?"

"They killed him."

All the breath left Briony's lungs. She stood frozen for several seconds before she could force herself to inhale. "What? Wh-Who did?"

"*They did.*" He gestured toward the crowd. "The people o' Everton murdered yer father."

Briony's eyes widened. "N-Nay, that can' be—"

Niall wrapped his hands around hers. "And when yer tears called me, I knew you needed me to save you from them. To make up fer my failure before."

Briony opened and closed her mouth several times, but she was too dumbfounded to speak. *He knew my father? Mum said Da' was lost to the sea. How could he have been murdered?*

"Briony, how can you na know what I am? 'Tis what yer father was. 'Tis what *you* are! Why does yer blood sing when yer near me? Why does the sea call to you? I saw you swim when you saved that merchant the other day. You were glorious. But still, it must have felt incomplete."

A tremor coursed through Briony's body at his words. Something inside her knew he was telling the truth, but fear made her step back. *This man knows far too much about me.*

"Yer na meant fer the human world, Briony. Yer meant fer mine. Come away from these people, these murderers. They'll do the same to you as they did to yer father once they know

165

what you are."

Heat began to spread from Briony's fingers, down her arms, and into her core. Despite her fear, she had to know, once and for all. "What am I?"

"Yer a selkie."

Briony took a deep breath.

Then another.

Finally, after the third one, she was able to meet Niall's gaze. Hope danced within his eyes, as dark as a starless night. *He wants me to believe him. To swallow everything just like that. To turn my back on this entire town.*

"Yer mad."

The man's mouth dropped open before he shook his head in disbelief. "After everything I've said, *that's* yer response? To deny everything you know is true? What o' the connection between us? You yerself said 'twas there."

"I know what I said! But that does na mean I have to believe everything you tell me. If what you say is true, then why did you leave me behind that day?"

Niall jammed his fingers into his pockets. "Because yer mother denied us. She did na want you to have anything to do with yer selkie blood. She wanted to raise you as a human."

"She knew my father was a selkie? And she did na bother telling me?"

This story is getting more and more difficult to believe. Whatever I thought I felt fer this man must have been a delusion. He has clearly lost his mind.

"O' course she knew. She—"

Briony held up a hand. "Enough. I'm done with these lies." She looked back at her neighbors, just now noticing how far she and Niall had strayed in the midst of their conversation.

Niall suddenly lashed out, grabbing Briony's shoulders. His nails dug painfully into her skin as he pressed himself to her. He placed his lips at the curve of her ear.

"Niall, let me go!"

"We belong together, and I'm going to make you see why. You may na believe me, but maybe you'll believe this." Then he released her and looked up.

Briony followed his line of sight and gasped at what she

166

saw: black clouds had appeared out of nowhere above the town. Thunder rolled within their depths, and sparks of lightning bounced between them. A strong wind swirled through Briony's locks, tugging them free from the pins that had held them prisoner.

Just like the storm yesterday . . .

The other villagers soon became aware of the strange weather, and when droplets began falling on their heads, anxious chatters replaced all traces of music and gaiety.

Briony looked to Niall, not convinced he had anything to do with this. He raised a knowing finger, waiting. There was a savage gleam in his eye that frightened her more than she cared to admit.

What is he waiting for?

CRACK!

A bolt of lightning zapped the ground beside the bonfire, mere inches from Laird Oliver. The man sprung straight into the air before uttering a slew of curses. Everyone started screaming and running toward town.

But then Briony glimpsed another bolt just a few feet away. This one singed Daniel Calhoun's clothes, and—

Briony's nose wrinkled at the smell of burned flesh. Daniel howled in pain as he cradled his right arm. His pregnant wife tugged on him desperately, but Dr. Sherwin had to grab the man by the shoulder before he came to his senses enough to get moving.

Lightning bolts struck all over Mary's Hill, hitting the tables and chairs—

One of the nearby trees caught fire. The flames spread slowly across the wet bark, sending up a thick plume of smoke.

Adrenaline surged through Briony's veins, urging her to get to safety.

"Niall, did you—"

Briony turned to the man, but in all the chaos, he had vanished. She scanned her surroundings and spotted Adaira with the Burgesses, hurrying through the sea of people. Adaira waved to her, but Briony gestured for the younger woman to keep going.

I have to find Santiago first. He can' have gotten far with that ankle.

167

"Santiago!"

A hand seized her arm. Briony started and tried to pull away—

"Briony, it's me."

Briony relaxed—it was just Lucia. She was drenched and trembling, but she appeared unhurt. "We have to go!"

"But what about—"

"I'm here."

Briony spun around, and when she saw the green-eyed merchant, she let out a shaky breath. *He's fine.*

Santiago stood there, cane in hand, like a beacon in the darkness. His eyes were full of relief as he looked at her. "I was trying to find you. . . ."

"Santiago, I—"

Another bolt of lightning cut her off. *This is no time fer a conversation.*

She took hold of Santiago with one hand and Lucia with the other. "Let's go!"

Briony led the Mendes siblings down the path to Drulea Cottage and ushered them inside. She heaved the door closed, praying that lightning wouldn't strike her home.

She stumbled into the kitchen and lit a candle. She took a few deep breaths, trying to staunch the fear gripping her heart. "We should be fine now. Let me make some tea to calm everyone's nerves. Feel free to have a seat while I do that."

Santiago nodded in gratitude, though his smile was tight as he helped his shaking sister into a chair. Briony went about her task mechanically, just barely remembering to get out three teacups rather than one as she tried not to glance out the windows. *If I focus too much on the storm, I'll be as out o' sorts as Lucia is. I'm na even sure she could carry on a conversation right now with how distressed she is.*

When the tea was ready, she turned back and almost leaped out of her skin when she saw Santiago standing a foot away.

"Thank you for providing us with shelter." He gave her a heartwarming smile that made Briony's hands jitter.

He grabbed her hands in his. "Are you all right?"

"I-I'm just a wee bit shaken up still," she squeaked, glad

the candlelight hid her blush.

Santiago nodded, but he said nothing before walking away with a cup of tea.

Briony frowned at the rude gesture, but within seconds, he had given his sister the cup and returned to Briony's side.

"Briony, I wanted to ask you—"

"Aye?" She gazed up into his eyes, and the rest of the world disappeared for a moment. She forgot about the tempest and what Niall had said; she even forgot that Lucia was just on the other side of the room.

Santiago put a hand on his neck and looked away, breaking the trance she was under. He grabbed a teacup for himself and stared at it as if it was incredibly interesting. "What was Mr. Moreland talking to you about at the party? Before the storm arrived, I mean."

"Oh." Briony couldn't keep the disappointment out of her voice. "He . . ."

He's insane. He thinks he's a selkie. And worse, he thinks I'm one, too.

Briony shook her head. She wasn't about to tell him *that*. She settled on something easier that wasn't too far from the truth. "He wishes to marry me."

Shock flashed through Santiago's eyes before he veiled it behind a neutral expression. "And how did you reply?"

Briony peered at the man, eager to find something that would tell her what he was thinking. *How much does he care about my response? Is he hoping I said nay?*

But trying to read him right then was like trying to read a book in another language: useless and frustrating.

She gave up with a small sigh. "I made it very clear that I dinna want him. Even though now I've lost my only chance o' getting married."

Santiago coughed and said in a raspy voice, "Nonsense. Any man would be lucky to call you his wife. Has no one ever asked you before?"

"Why would they when I'm illegitimate? You may na come from a home where that's a stigma, but here 'tis like the kiss o' death. Rejecting Niall means I've doomed myself to spinsterhood fer the rest o' my life."

Unless you prove me wrong . . .

She looked back at her companion, who was grimacing as though in pain. "Did you get hurt out there? Do you need anything?"

"No, I'm fine," he snapped, "but you speak as though you regret your choice. Do you?"

"I . . ." Briony's cheeks heated again, but this time with shame. "Yer right. I suppose I should na complain about my situation when I'm the one who put myself here. And to answer yer question, nay. I'd rather be an old maid forever than marry . . . *him*."

Santiago's face softened, and the low light made his eyes twinkle like dew on summer grass.

"I've never seen such a light green in someone's eyes before. . . ." Briony flinched when she realized she'd spoken aloud. *That was meant to stay in my head forever!*

She couldn't bear to look at him after saying something so humiliating, so she focused her attention on sipping her tea. It seemed like an eternity before he spoke again.

"In my country, it's said that green signifies hope, but they must have gotten it wrong. The lovely gold of your eyes holds more hope than any color I've ever seen."

Briony's heart lurched, and her mouth dried at his words.

"As your friend, would you promise me something?"

Briony looked up, locking gazes with him even as her heart withered at the word *friend*. *I was wrong. He does na love me, after all.*

"Promise me you'll never let that hope burn out." Santiago smiled like it wasn't a big deal, but a slight quiver in his voice told her he was anxious for her to agree.

And she knew with all her being that she didn't want to let him down. *Na now. Na ever.*

"I promise."

"What is it that you hope for?" he asked.

Fer you to care fer me as I do fer you. Fer you to hold me in yer arms and kiss me as you did before. . . .

Briony cleared her throat. "I hope fer peace with my mother. Na to feel pain when I think o' her, but also . . . She was such a secretive woman, even with me. I have so many unanswered questions."

And after Niall's mad claims, I wish now more than ever that I could speak to her.

"Why do you ask?" Briony looked at him curiously.

Santiago's expression became a bit sheepish. "It's just that you've helped me so much. I wish there was something I could do for you."

A small, sad smile came onto Briony's face. *He may na love me, but how can I possibly stop loving him when he's so thoughtful?*

"You've already given me more than most o' Everton has: acceptance, regardless o' my background. I can' ask fer more than that."

"Still, there must be something I can do to make your burdens a little lighter," he insisted. "It could be with anything. Besides helping with the birthing process, are there any other responsibilities you have as a midwife?"

"I check in with expectant mothers to make sure they're eating well and that everything is progressing as it should be. I also make sure they're aware o' what 'twill be like when their time comes. And I help with newborns fer the first couple o' months. When I dinna have any midwife duties, I do what I can fer Adaira at the inn."

"I know Senhora Calhoun is with child, but are there any other women you have to check on right now?"

"There might be, but before you ask, know that I would na be able to tell you. I'm sworn to secrecy in all matters related to that since the people here are very superstitious. Were I to tell before it becomes obvious, the poor mother and unborn babe might be kidnapped by trows," Briony said with a playful grin.

"And what, pray tell, is a trow?" Santiago raised his eyebrows at her.

"Do they na have trows in Portugal?" Briony laughed. "Supposedly, they're evil creatures that like to come out at night. Their bodies are small and ugly, and they love to steal human bairns. Sometimes they'll take a bairn and trade it fer one o' their own that they dinna want. When that happens, the babe is called a changeling—"

The word slipped out before Briony remembered why she hated it so much. Her face darkened instantly, and she turned

171

away from Santiago. An intense itch gathered in her toes, urging her to take off her dreadful shoes.

"Briony?" Santiago asked, his voice dripping with concern.

"You-You should check on yer sister." She tried to slow down her breathing, tried to keep herself calm. But after everything with Niall and the weather outside, she feared her mental walls were about to cave in.

"Did I say something wrong?"

"Nay, 'tis . . . Just leave me be fer a moment." She stepped away and placed her hands on the wall, fighting with all her strength not to remember the rest of that day. The day Niall had come to her. The day she would have died if not for—

"Argh!" Briony screamed as the memory washed over her like a furious wave, pulling her into the depths.

A Terrible Day

Twelve years earlier

"Remember, bairn, you must keep yer shoes on anytime you go outside."

"But why, Mum? None o' the other bairns have to do that," asked eight-year-old Briony.

Her mother gave her a thin smile before putting down her dishcloth. "Have you ever looked closely at the others' feet? Did you notice anything different about theirs from yers?"

Briony cocked her head to the side and tried to picture Ewan Sherwin's stinky feet, but all she could remember was that they were stinky. "What's different?"

Bethany bent down and placed a gentle finger on the skin between Briony's toes. "The others dinna have ridges on their feet like yers. Yer special."

Briony frowned. "But you have skin between yer toes, too. Are we both special?"

Bethany looked up at her with a rueful smile. "Aye, I suppose that makes both o' us special. Our feet are just a wee bit different from other people's, but I want you to remember that there's *nothing* wrong with them. They work just as well as everybody else's. Maybe even better. The problem, though, is that some folks dinna like it when people look different from them. And I dinna want you to have more trouble making friends just because o' that, so you have to keep this a secret. Do you understand?"

173

Briony thought long and hard about what her mother had said. At least, as long and hard as an eight-year-old could. *What do my feet have to do with making friends?* She shook her head.

Bethany sighed. "'Tis complicated, my peedie freck, but you'll understand more when yer older. Fer now, can you just trust me?"

Briony nodded only because she knew it was what her mother wanted. *I still dinna get it. . . .*

"That's my good lass. Now, run down to the market and pick up a loaf o' bread fer us. Here, take this. It should be enough." Bethany handed her the money and ushered her out the door.

Briony skipped down the hill, stopping every once in a while to peer at her shoes. She had never been very good at keeping secrets. *I wonder if I could tell someone about my feet once we're friends—*

"Aaah!"

Briony froze. The last time she'd heard such an agonizing cry was when Mum made her bring clean cloths for Mistress Milligan while she was in labor.

Briony wrinkled her nose at the memory.

"Stop, please!"

'Tis coming from the beach!

She scurried down to the shore to see what was happening and was horrified at what she found: a wee lad crouched against the rocks, naked but for a gray piece of clothing wrapped around his waist. Half a dozen bairns stood taunting and throwing rocks at him as he wailed. Briony recognized them all—Alastair Oliver, St. John and Gareth Peterson, Elspet Milligan, Adaira Stubbins, and Ewan Sherwin.

"Stop! Stop!" she shouted, but they couldn't hear her over the boy's cries.

Briony darted her eyes about, hoping she would see an adult who could fix this, but no one was there. She garnered up her courage and dashed toward the group.

Just as she reached them, though, a foot shot out in front of her, causing her face to collide with the hard sand.

More laughter ensued, but this time, it was directed at her. Briony pushed herself up from the ground and scowled at the other children. "Leave him alone!"

"Make us," bellowed Alastair Oliver, the one she was sure had tripped her.

She glared up at him. *He has always been rude to me, but now he's picking on a stranger? That's just too far.*

Briony shoved him, knocking the taller boy to the ground. Then she stumbled closer to the wee lad, who was trembling in fear. She grabbed his arm and ran a few steps, but the other children chased them.

There's no way to outrun them. Unless . . .

Briony stopped in front of some rocks and spun around, positioning the boy behind her body.

She watched as the others drew nearer, a plan forming in her mind, but then she realized something. *My shoes are gone! Did I lose them on the sand?*

Briony took a wobbly step back, hoping no one would see her toes, but then she glanced back at the boy. He was roughly her age, but he seemed younger because of his terror.

He needs me. I have to do what I can to help him. She stuck out her chin with as much determination as she could.

"Can you make a run fer it while I distract them?"

The boy raised his eyes, black as night, to hers for a moment and nodded. "Aye, thank you." His voice sounded hoarse, as though he hadn't spoken in a long time.

"Stop it, all o' you! This is wrong!" Briony exclaimed as she turned back to the bullies.

She felt the boy slipping away behind her, but she didn't dare look. She had to make sure the other children kept their attention on her long enough for him to escape.

"He's a trow. He deserves it," Alastair shouted. The laird's thirteen-year-old son loved to intimidate and belittle others whenever possible, a character trait he had in common with his parents.

"He's no trow. He's just as human as I am!"

"What do you know? You dinna even have a da'," Elspet sneered.

"And she's na human, anyway. Just look at her feet," Adaira Stubbins added, pointing at Briony's webbed toes.

The others all gasped and stared; even Alastair stumbled

back as fear set in over the group.

Briony narrowed her eyes to slits, trying not to let the words get to her. "O' course I'm human. My feet are just a wee bit different. They're special—"

Adaira scoffed. "They're na special—they're *ugly*. There's something wrong with you, and I know what 'tis. Yer a changeling!"

Briony drew in a sharp breath. Mum was right. *How could she call me that?*

To call someone a changeling was to say that person was not only inhuman but also unwanted. Abandoned by the fairies to live out a lonely existence among humans.

But Mum's feet look like mine, so I know that's na true.

Tears sprang to Briony's eyes, but she held them back. Instead, she channeled her rage and swung a fist at the girl who had just spoken.

The punch landed right on the girl's chin, knocking her to the ground with its force.

"She hit me," Adaira whined as she put a hand on her face.

Her complaint seemed to jar the other bairns from their shock, and soon they were all pelting Briony with the same rocks they'd used on the dark-eyed boy.

Briony flinched and tried to get away, but at some point, while she'd been focusing on Adaira, Alastair had snuck around behind her. He laughed at her surprise and slapped her across the face.

Briony fell back as blood spattered from her nose onto the beach. She tried to catch herself, but her wrist landed the wrong way and crunched under her weight.

More rocks slammed into her, bruising her arms and stomach. The children came nearer and enclosed her in a dreadful circle as they kicked at her mercilessly. Briony cried out for help, but her voice couldn't be heard over their chants of "Changeling! Changeling! Briony the changeling!"

Briony shifted to her side and held her hands over her head. The moment felt as though it would never end.

Then a noise resounded over the taunts. Something feral and angry. Briony opened her eyes and peered between Alastair's legs, just barely getting a glimpse of the source.

About twenty feet away, three large grey seals were growling and snarling, their gazes fixed on the children.

The largest seal shuffled a few feet closer to the group, which made most of the bairns scream and drop their rocks.

Briony sat up, wincing in pain at first, but she soon began scooting back, not taking her eyes off the seals. There was something strange about them, something almost familiar, though Briony couldn't figure out what.

Then the large seal barked and locked eyes with her.

Briony's breath caught. Those black orbs were so full of emotion that they looked—

They look like human eyes. And they're na scary anymore. Nay, they seem almost friendly.

Suddenly, sand flew into her face. "Are you talking to it, Fairborn? Does it understand you since neither o' you is human?"

The others tittered at Alastair's joke, but no one else was bold enough to actually speak. Instead, they began taking slow steps backward, all while keeping a close watch on the seals.

"Let's go, Alastair. I dinna like the looks they're giving us," Ewan said.

The laird's son rolled his eyes. "If yer too much o' a coward, go on ahead." He looked at each of them in turn. "And the same goes fer the rest o' you. I'll just catch up with you later."

The girls immediately fled, but the other boys hesitated.

I guess they can' stand being called cowards. But what else do you call six people picking on one wee lad?

Briony's eyes swept over the four boys. *I hope one o' them gets bitten, preferably Alastair.*

Gareth peeked at the big seal, who promptly bared its teeth. "I'm leaving."

St. John and Ewan looked at each other before running after Gareth. Soon it was just Briony, Alastair, and the seals.

Briony coughed and looked up at the boy's hateful face. "Just leave me alone."

"Ha! You need to figure out where you belong, changeling. In the dirt!" He grabbed Briony by the back of the head and slammed her facedown into the sand.

Briony tried to resist, tried to claw at the hands making it impossible for her to breathe. *I have to get him off!*

But he's so much bigger and stronger than me. What if I can' stop him—

But then he was gone, and all the pressure and pain started lifting. Briony tilted her face to the side and coughed up the sand in her throat.

What happened? Why did he let me go? Briony opened her eyes just as she heard the shrieks.

Several village men were racing across the beach, yelling and waving knives at the seals. Briony's vision was hazy, but she recognized Mr. Stubbins, Mr. Levins, Mr. McGuff, and Laird Oliver among the group.

But the shrieks weren't coming from them. They were coming from—

"Alastair," Briony cried. The boy's left leg was in the large seal's mouth, and one of the other seals held his right leg. They were shaking him and dragging him toward the sea. Blood darkened the sand as Alastair got farther and farther away, all the while screaming for help.

It was only then that she noticed how dark the sky had gotten. It looked like it was about to rain buckets of water on everyone, and the clouds were sparking with lightning.

The villagers reached the seals just before Alastair's head was submerged in the water. They wasted no time in attacking the seals, stabbing at them in a wild fury. The animals released Alastair immediately and bit at their assailants a few times before trying to escape. The two smaller ones were successful, but the large one got stuck between Laird Oliver and Mr. Stubbins.

"Briony!" The pounding of feet hit Briony's ears, and she turned from the horrific scene before her.

The voice belonged to her mother, who was charging across the beach. "Get away from them!"

Briony tried to obey, but a burst of pain in her leg made her slip and end up on her side again. The alpha seal yelped, drawing her attention to it.

The beast was staring straight at her, its deep eyes full of distress.

178

"Briony," Bethany called again. The woman reached her daughter and stood in front of her, blocking Briony's view of the seal.

But not her view of the third man's back. Someone new had joined Laird Oliver and Mr. Stubbins in the water, knife high in the air. He slammed it down into the seal's body, and a deafening howl came from the animal's throat.

Briony could hardly process what had just happened; all she knew was that it was the saddest sound she'd ever heard in her life. Tears flooded her eyes until she could see nothing but blurs. "Mum, wha—"

"Dinna talk, dearest. We must leave." Bethany sounded choked too as she lifted Briony and held her close.

"But what about the boy? Is he safe?"

"Who? Alastair? The men got him and are taking him to the doctor."

"Nay, na him . . . *The boy!* Did he get away?" she moaned weakly.

"There's no other boy here, Briony. . . ." The voice trailed off as Briony fell into unconsciousness.

***

As Briony came to, the first thing she noticed was pressure on her hand. Then she heard someone speaking.

"Briony?" The voice sounded funny in her ears, almost as if she was underwater.

She slowly opened her eyes, blinking a few times until her vision cleared. She was lying in her bed, and someone was standing over her. "Doctor? What are you doing here? What happened?"

Dr. Ewan Sherwin released her wrist. "According to Mr. Mendes, you fainted about two hours ago. Yer pulse seems normal, though, and you dinna look ill. Do you feel well? Do you remember what happened?"

Briony placed her hand on her head. *Everything's fuzzy. The last thing I remember is the party. I was dancing with Niall, and—*

Briony gasped as the rest of the night came back to her: Niall's claim about their shared heritage, his accusations of the town, the freak thunderstorm.

And the dream.

Nay, na a dream. A memory. All o' that really happened. Those were the things I've never been able to remember. The things I did na wish to remember.

The seal that day . . . Was he my father? Am I truly a selkie? Briony shook her head in disbelief.

Dr. Sherwin held out a glass of water, which she readily drank. Right then she would have gladly taken something much stronger, anything to numb the feelings and slow the thoughts rattling in her brain.

"I remember—"

"You're awake!" Santiago barged in and knelt next to her. His smile brightened the room as he squeezed her hand, paying no mind to the doctor's disapproving gaze. "I was so worried. I didn't know what to do, so I got Dr. Sherwin."

"You went out in the storm?"

"He searched for over an hour, going from house to house," Lucia added, popping up behind the two men. "I've never seen him so frantic."

Briony gave Santiago a grateful look. "You did na need to do that fer me. You went to so much trouble—"

He waved her words away. "Please don't. I had to do something. When you fell and wouldn't wake, I thought . . ." He choked up a bit before he continued. "Truly, it was no trouble."

Dr. Sherwin cleared his throat, plainly irritated. "I suppose you dinna care too much what *my* conclusions are, then? Na even after what happened the other day?"

Briony's eyes widened. *What if that happened because I'm a . . . Nay, I dinna know fer sure. Perhaps there's another explanation fer all this.*

But this is definitely na something I'm ready to share with anyone. Na until I've talked to Niall.

She shook her head. "N-Nothing happened the other—"

"What are you talking about? What happened?" Santiago's hand left hers as he rose and turned to the doctor.

Briony silently begged Dr. Sherwin not to say anything. *Please, please, please. Just keep yer big mouth shut fer once.*

The doctor coughed and turned away. When he looked back, he almost seemed embarrassed. *If such a thing is possible.*

"Since yer na family, I can' discuss such details with you," he said with a sharp look at the merchant.

Santiago's eyes narrowed. "I care about her well-being, so if this is something serious, then I need to know."

All traces of embarrassment faded from the doctor's visage, and a threatening scowl appeared in its place. "And *why* do you need to know? What ties do you have to Mistress Fairborn?"

"None as of ye—"

"Santiago," Lucia interrupted, grabbing her brother's hand. "I must speak with you immediately."

Santiago looked down at Lucia's hand in surprise. He raised his eyebrows in confusion. "*Now?*"

"Yes, right now. Please excuse us, Briony, Doctor." She pulled Santiago away and into the kitchen. Briony couldn't help but stare at them, her curiosity overriding her manners.

They spoke in quick whispers, but it was clear that neither of them was happy. Santiago was facing away from his sister but appeared troubled. Lucia seemed to be trying to convince him of something important, and her body language was so adamant that it bordered on panicked. Santiago raised his voice at one point, but his speech was in Portuguese, so there was no hope of understanding him.

A hand on Briony's shoulder jerked her attention away from the siblings. "Mistress Fairborn, are you all right? Do you feel safe with them?" Dr. Sherwin drew his hand back awkwardly when he realized what he was doing.

Briony gave the man a small smile. She'd never expected yet another of her childhood tormentors to become something close to a friend. "Aye, I'm fine. But, Dr. Sherwin, how is everyone else? Is Adaira well? Did anyone . . ."

She couldn't bring herself to say the words.

"Mistress Stubbins and her intended, along with his son, are in perfect health. As fer everyone else, they're all living, if that's what you wanted to ask. Mr. Calhoun has a nasty burn, but that's the worst o' it."

Briony was so relieved that it took her a moment to

comprehend everything the doctor had just said. When she did, though, she had to hold back a juvenile squeal. "Intended? Mr. Burgess proposed to her?"

"Aye, Mistress Fairborn, he did."

She chuckled, feeling much lighter than she had before. *Something good came o' tonight, despite Niall's storm.*

"You can call me Briony, you know. We've known each other long enough fer that."

Dr. Sherwin blinked a few times, and a flush spread across his face. "I would never presume to be so informal with you."

Briony chuckled. "Well, that's what I would prefer."

The doctor's mouth opened and closed a few times, but no sound came out. He was entirely perplexed, a sight that was all too funny, and a great guffaw escaped Briony's lips.

"Please dinna be offended," she said when he drew back with a grimace. "I know we have na always gotten along—"

Dr. Sherwin raised his eyebrows as if to say, *Oh, really?*

"But recently, I've felt like that has been changing. That you've changed. And I'm willing to forgive you fer what happened in the past—"

"If yer referring to what happened years ago on the beach, then dinna expect an apology. I was only trying to—"

Briony rolled her eyes. "Dr. Sherwin, please. I'm trying to say something *nice* about you. Dinna ruin it by making me angry."

Dr. Sherwin huffed. "Well, you have an awfully backhanded way o' saying it."

"*As I was saying*, I misjudged you, and fer that, I'm sorry. I hope that you might call me Briony, na as a way o' saying I'm na respectable enough to be called 'mistress,' but as a way o' saying we're . . ."

Dr. Sherwin hadn't met her eyes since she'd transitioned into this topic, and now he looked like he would rather be anywhere else but there. "Out with it, already. You know I've got places to be."

"We're friends," Briony sputtered, though it came out sharply because he had such a great talent for getting under her skin.

Dr. Sherwin was so surprised that he tripped forward and

almost fell over. His flush came back full force until he was as red as a tomato. He gripped his glasses to adjust them, but his hand was shaking so much that they fell on the floor. "I-I would na say . . . 'Tis really na . . ."

Briony said nothing as she watched the flustered man retrieve his glasses. It was all she could do not to giggle in amusement.

"I—" He broke off with a snarl. "Fine. You win, Briony. I'll say it just this once. Aye, we're *friends*."

"Really, I should na have been surprised that you have *some* kind bones in yer body. After all, Adaira changed, so why na you? Does that mean I can call you Ewan, then?"

The man glared, finally making eye contact with her. "Nay, it does na. I'll na answer to anything but Dr. Sherwin. Is that clear?"

Briony sighed. "O' course. As fer what you asked before, I'm na sick. And I do feel safe with Mr. Mendes and his sister. They're good people."

Dr. Sherwin glanced over at the two in question, but he didn't look convinced. "There's something about that Mr. Mendes in how he looks at you. I dinna know what his intentions are, but he does na look at you like a friend would. Be careful."

"I appreciate yer concern." Briony pulled the blanket off and slowly stood. "Now, have you seen Mr. Moreland? I need to talk to him."

"Nay, nay, dinna even think o' going outside right now. 'Tis still raining, though na as hard, and 'tis far too late fer that. You need to rest to make sure yer truly all right. I'll take Mr. and Mistress Mendes to the inn." Dr. Sherwin pushed her back by the shoulders and forced her to sit.

"But—"

"No arguments. You can see him morn." He turned toward Santiago and Lucia. "Let me take you back to Everton Inn. I'm sure you both must be exhausted."

Santiago and Lucia stopped arguing and looked over. Lucia smiled at the suggestion and immediately went to the doctor's side. Santiago, on the other hand, slipped over to Briony and leaned close.

With a determined set to his jaw, he whispered, "We've been interrupted far too many times, amorzinho. There's still something I need to tell you. Tomorrow, just after midday, may I meet you here?"

He was so close that Briony felt his breath against her ear. She suppressed a shiver and nodded, all too aware of how rapidly her heart was now beating.

I dinna know if I'm excited or terrified. This time, will I truly hear what he wants to tell me?

A Dangerous Ally

The morning arrived so slowly that Briony feared it wouldn't come at all. She'd slept fitfully, her mind a mess of thoughts and feelings. She was still trying to come to terms with what Niall had told her, along with what her long-buried memory could mean.

If only there was someone else to talk to about this besides Niall. . . . Someone who would na think I'm mad.

Mad . . . The mad fisherman's face came to her mind. She thought about the things he had said, the little comments that hinted at something more:

". . . I imagine na many people see you either."

"You should be more careful."

"If the others could only see the signs . . ."

"You never have believed in fairy tales!"

Briony gasped. *Maybe I am a selkie and Mr. McLaren knows it. Was he trying to tell me all along?*

If he knew all this time and never told anyone, then perhaps he can be trusted.

Briony got ready as quickly as she could and tore out the door. *Surely I'll have enough time before Santiago comes to see me.*

There weren't many people on the street that morning, but Briony figured they were sleeping off their drunken stupors from Johnsmas. She didn't spot any Portuguese sailors either, but then, they had been just as excited to indulge in the alcohol as the locals.

And no Niall. Even though part of her wanted to talk to

185

him, another part of her was petrified at the thought of facing him again. *To possess that much power . . .*

She shuddered, glad she was almost to Vincent McLaren's stall already.

Unfortunately, she wasn't the only one there. The Olivers were in the midst of an argument with the mad fisherman as Briony walked up.

"What do you mean, 'you dinna have any fish'? I can' survive without my trout," Lady Oliver whined. She wrung her hands as her husband stood beside her, both glaring at Mr. McLaren.

The mad fisherman, on the other hand, was shrugging his shoulders with his hands open. "There's nothing I can do about it, Lady Oliver. I asked around, and none o' the other fishermen caught a thing either. And I *always* get at least a couple o' fish. I dinna mean to brag, but I doubt anyone here or on the Mainland could match my skills. Except fer maybe *you*, Mistress Fairborn."

Briony blushed. She'd thought the man hadn't noticed her yet.

"Yer simply after more o' my money, aren' you?" Laird Oliver jabbed the man in the chest with his finger.

Mr. McLaren dropped his hands and shook his head vehemently. "Nay, sir. Ask any o' the other fishermen, and they shall tell you the same."

Laird Oliver smirked. "Oh, I shall. And if I find out you've been less than truthful with me, let's just say that things won' go well fer you. Come along, wife."

Laird Oliver snatched his wife's hand and spun around, almost walking straight into Briony in the process.

Lady Oliver snarled at the younger woman. "Good morneen, Fairborn wench. Or should I say, witch? Did you come to see yer handiwork?"

"I have no idea what yer talking about," Briony said, trying to skirt around the couple. *I have more important things to do right now than listen to this.*

Lady Oliver blocked Briony's path as she continued, "If this is some sort o' fish shortage, then 'twould na be hard to figure out who's behind it. 'Twould be just like you to do this out o' spite. Do you na think we've suffered enough just by having you in town? And then with that storm last night? Must you make it worse? Yer presence here is a curse on all o' us."

"I—"

"Mistress Fairborn, I need to speak with you. 'Tis most urgent," Vincent McLaren exclaimed as he stepped out from behind his stall.

He grabbed Briony's wrist. "Please excuse us."

Lady Oliver frowned. "Wait—"

"Sorry, sorry! No time, I fear," Mr. McLaren said in a singsong voice and pulled Briony down the street, not stopping until they'd left the market square and were in an out-of-sight spot between two houses.

"Mr. McLaren, what are you doing?"

The fisherman released her wrist and took a step back. "Now you can tell me why you came to see me. 'Tis na yer usual day to buy fish."

Briony's brow furrowed. "Then were you lying when you said you needed to talk to me?"

Mr. McLaren smiled, displaying the gaps between his teeth without shame. It was a crazy sort of smile, one that would have made most people cringe, but Briony only felt affection upon seeing it. "Well, I could na just let them attack you like that. Na when you've done nothing to deserve it."

Briony smiled at the man's kindness. "Thank you, Mr. McLaren. And yer right, I do need to talk to you."

"Thought you might after what happened last night."

"You know what happened last night?"

"O' course. I'm so glad you finally figured out the truth about yerself, lass. 'Twas na something fer me to just tell you, you know. You needed to discover it on yer own; otherwise, you never would have believed me."

"Then I am a selkie?" Briony whispered. She searched his eyes, looking for any shred of doubt within them.

But there was none.

The fisherman put a hand on her shoulder. "Aye, lass. That you are. I just wish you'd kept a handle on yerself a wee bit better. Someone must have really upset you."

"What? Mr. McLaren, I did na cause the storm last night."

187

"What are you talking about? It must have been you. I've seen plenty o' storms in my life, and I know an unnatural one when I see it."

Briony shook her head. "Nay, 'twas na me. 'Twas another selkie. He's the one who told me what I am."

Mr. McLaren's eyes widened, and his hand dropped to his side. "That can' be."

She didn't say anything and just let him sort out her words. Raw fear spread across the man's face, and Briony could tell he was trying desperately not to believe her.

"They left years ago. . . . There's na been any sign o' them since—"

Something changed on Mr. McLaren's face. A strong resolve pushed back his fear until all that was left of it was a tiny tremor in his hands. "You should have come to me sooner. Then we would have had more time."

"Time? Niall did na say anything about time."

"So, *he's* the one who told you, then? I should have known. He did seem a wee bit off. Can' do anything about that now though. Can only plan fer the future. And if a selkie has returned, then he's out fer blood."

"What? Why?"

It was then that Mr. McLaren's expression turned regretful.

"Because I killed one o' them."

At that moment, it was as if time stood completely still. Everything else faded from Briony's mind, faded from reality itself.

"Y-You . . . what?"

"'Twas many years ago now. You may na even remember that day on the beach when the seal attacked Alastair—"

"Oh, I remember," Briony growled. *I definitely remember. And I will never forget again.*

Vincent McLaren killed my father.

Briony stared at the fisherman with new eyes. *Where is the mad but harmless man I've known all my life? The man who wove fantastic and unbelievable tales to me as a bairn? The man who never disdained me fer who I am? And fer what I am.*

She couldn't reconcile her image of Mr. McLaren with his

words. *How could he be the man who . . . murdered my father? Was Niall right to judge Everton so harshly?*

She went back to that day in her mind, trying not to let the painful memories overwhelm her again. *I want to believe Mr. McLaren is a good person and that he did na intend to kill the seal—*

But all I can think o' is that awful cry as his knife drove into my father's skin. The father I never got the chance to know.

The other men were no better, fer they encouraged the slaughter. They wanted to make sure my father was dead.

How much did he suffer that day at Everton's hands?

Briony narrowed her eyes. "How could you do it?"

Mr. McLaren's face lost all its color. He took a step away from her and raised his hands defensively. "I was trying to save the boy. He attacked Alastair. . . ."

"*To protect me.* 'Twas all to protect me. Alastair would have killed me otherwise," Briony murmured, tears springing to her eyes. "But you . . ."

She stepped forward, a surge of power sweeping through her veins. She felt the heat begin in her fingertips, this time knowing exactly what it was. She closed her eyes, not trying to stop it. On the contrary, it was just the opposite: she craved the power that had lain dormant just below the surface for far too long. And as she let it overtake her, her rage only escalated.

Make them pay, it sang. *Make them all pay fer the selkie blood spilled.*

Briony nodded, fully surrendered to the siren call. *I will get justice.*

She opened her eyes to the first person who would feel her wrath. "You murdered my father. Niall was right about you. About all o' you."

A roll of thunder sounded above them. Mr. McLaren's attention jerked upward to what Briony knew would be a dark sky. Dark like a certain pair of black eyes that didn't seem nearly as frightening anymore.

Fear and concern mingled on the fisherman's face when he looked back at her. "Lass, control yerself."

A smile came over Briony's features, animalistic and sinister. "I am very much in control. And I demand justice fer my father's death."

189

Lightning crackled ominously, just on the verge of touching down from above.

Vincent McLaren shook his head. "Nay, yer na in control. You've let yer emotions get the best o' you, and yer about to do something you'll regret."

Briony raised an eyebrow. "Oh, am I? Tell me, what could possibly make me change my mind about you? About this horrid town?"

The fisherman sighed as sorrow washed over his face. "I can' say anything about the rest o' Everton, but as fer me, there's another reason I killed yer father. One I hoped to spare you from finding out."

She reached out her hand toward the man's arm, almost touching him with burning-hot fingers. Mr. McLaren winced, but he didn't move away.

"You better hurry up with that reason. I'm tired o' all the secrets."

"I did it because *she* told me to . . . *Yer mother.*"

All the breath rushed out of Briony's lungs, and the tears that had been suspended in her eyes fell to the ground. She felt her selkie power rush out at the same time, and it took all her strength not to fall over in exhaustion.

"She knew he was a selkie? And she told you to kill him? Nay, that can' be true. He was my father. She would never . . . *never* want that."

Mr. McLaren tugged on his ear and gave her such a pitiful look that Briony had to turn away.

She squeezed her eyes shut. Her voice was just a whisper as she said, "I dinna believe you."

"I thought you might na. You've always had a hard time believing in people. Na that I blame you, after all that you've endured. All yer mother endured."

Briony sniffled. "How am I to know what's real anymore? Everything I thought I knew is a lie. I'm starting to think Niall may be the only one I *can* trust."

Mr. McLaren huffed. "Before you do that, I have something to give you. Something I've been carrying with me since the day yer mother died."

"Something fer me? From my mum?"

The man reached into his ratty pocket and drew out a small piece of folded paper. "Aye. Here, she wrote this fer you. Though she wanted you to have a normal life and never find out what you really are, she told me to hold on to this just in case."

Briony snatched it with trembling fingers. *Will this finally give me answers?*

"Why would she give this to you?"

"Because I accidentally found out something she did na want me to know, and I never told another soul. The Fairborn women, they've always been special. Always been different from the rest o' the town. The others think 'tis because o' being unwed mothers, but I know better.

"When yer mum and I were bairns, I went up to Drulea Cottage to see her one day, and I stumbled upon a secret. She and her mother were standing before a fire. They were arguing, but I was too far away to hear what 'twas about. I snuck closer and watched as yer grandmother threw something into the fire. Bethany screamed so loudly. It was an awful, awful sound. When I heard it, I felt like I was listening to someone die. Yer grandmother left her standing there and went inside. I went over to yer mum, hoping to comfort her, but she was wailing so loudly that she could na hear me speak. When I stepped in front o' her and she saw me, she fell into my arms and just kept crying. I did na know if she would ever stop. . . ."

Mr. McLaren broke off and cleared his throat. When he continued, Briony noted the shimmer in his own eyes. "But she did stop. And when she did, I asked her what yer grandmother had done, what had made her so sad."

"And? What was it?"

"Yer grandmother had burned up yer mother's sealskin."

"Wait. . . . My mother had a sealskin? But that would mean . . ." Briony couldn't finish.

"She was na a full selkie, but aye, she was one, too."

A Mother's Love

Briony tried to stop the shaking in her hands, but it was useless. Nothing made sense anymore. Nothing was as she had thought. She looked away from Mr. McLaren and focused her attention on the letter.

She slowly unfolded it, surprised to see multiple pages when she'd thought it just one, and read.

My dearest Briony,

I hope that after you read this, you can find it in your heart to forgive me. I also hope, though it may be foolish, that you find happiness here in Everton. Happiness has not come easily for our family, but if anyone can grab hold of it, I know 'tis you.

By now, you must have realized you're more different than I led you to believe. I suppose I always knew you would eventually figure it out, but I wanted to give you as close to a normal life as I could, if only to spare you from the heartache I went through.

You could say the Fairborn family truly began when your great-grandmother Edith Fairborn fled to Everton from Rousay to escape an unwanted marriage to a man nearly twenty years her senior. The others in town were wary of Edith, but she made a good name for herself as a respectable member of the community. Even so, it was not easy for her when she began to desire a husband; no one knew her background, for she had kept all of it a secret. Edith found herself very alone, and one day, she became desperate enough to try something a little mad.

Legend claims if a woman cries seven tears into the ocean, a selkie will come for her and love her as his own. While Edith didn't place much faith in this tale, she thought it would not hurt to give it a try. How wrong she was.

Indeed, a selkie did appear, but as soon as he got what he wanted from her, he returned to the ocean, and Edith was left with child. The scandal of it all afforded her one small blessing: when she gave birth to the child alone, no one discovered what her daughter was.

Edith saw the sea in the selkie child's eyes, so she named her Greta, meaning "pearl." Edith told Greta the truth of her heritage, and Greta grew up as an outcast who had to keep her secret well guarded. She finally did catch a young man's eye, but, being naïve and in love, Greta gave him something precious that she should have saved. So in love was she that Greta then did something far more stupid: she showed him her sealskin.

Once he knew she was not human, he ran from her in terror and disappeared from Everton like a ghost. Greta was so hurt that she destroyed her own sealskin and cursed her father's heritage.

But by then, I was already growing within her. And when I was born and my mother realized that the selkie blood had passed on to me, she locked my sealskin away in the hopes I would never find it.

For many years, I had no idea what I was. When the other bairns began to mock me for my webbed toes and obsession with the ocean, my mother told me the truth. Well, part of the truth. She told me my grandfather had been a selkie, but she also said my sealskin had been lost.

There was a chest my mother kept behind the bed. She always told me not to open it, that it held my grandmother's old things and that I would have no interest in its contents. I was eleven winters when my curiosity got the better of me. What I found in that chest brought tears to my eyes: 'twas my sealskin. All those years, I had thought it lost, yet here it had been the entire time. I was so enraptured that I immediately took it to the beach and put it on. I had never felt so alive as I did that day. By the time I returned home that evening, my heart was full.

But my mother discovered what I had done. She hit me and took the sealskin, saying I would soon leave her, just as my father had, just as my selkie grandfather had. I begged her to return the skin, told her I would never leave her, that she was all I had.

She would hear none of it. She built a fire and threw my sealskin into it, not caring how hurt I was. To this day, I don't know why she kept the pelt only to destroy it as soon as I found it.

On that day, Vincent McLaren became my dearest friend. I was so distraught over what had happened that I, like a fool, told him the family secret. And yet . . . he did not run away. Instead, he kept my secret and told me he would always be there for me. If there is anyone in this world you can trust, 'tis him.

I always strove to keep you from knowing of the tension between your grandmother and me. I wanted you to have only happy memories of her, despite the great rift that lay between us. It nearly killed her when she found out who your father was, but I can honestly say she loved you from the moment you came into the world.

That brings me to the rest of what you need to know. You've always been curious about your father, so let me finally tell you what you've been seeking all these years. His name was Einar, or at least that was the name he told me. Aye, bairn, he was a selkie, too. And I knew it from the moment I laid eyes on him. I also knew he was no good for me, but I wanted to spite my mother for the horrible thing she had done all those years ago.

Einar came to Everton with the sole purpose of producing an heir. He was handsome and charming, as all selkie males are. I never had a chance.

Your father kept his true purposes to himself until after I was with child. Once I told him I was going to have you, though, he revealed his true self. He told me of his selkie nature, thinking he would frighten me into submitting to his whims. He wished to take the bairn to the sea, never to see me again. What he did not realize, though, was that I'd known what he was all along and I did not fear him.

I refused to give you up, and so it became a battle of wills. He threatened to reveal my secret, so I threatened to reveal his. He threatened to destroy Everton, so I threatened to have the seals hunted down. He threatened to steal you in the night, so I threatened to burn your sealskin.

Eventually, he said it was not worth the trouble and left shortly before you were born. But I feared that was not the end; I told Vincent everything and made him swear that if your father ever returned to take you away, he would stop Einar by any means necessary.

Perhaps you also know that has already happened. I'm so sorry, dearest one. I never meant for it to turn out like it did, but I hope you'll one day realize that everything I did was out of love. Please do not blame Vincent for his part in it. He was only trying to keep you from harm.

If your father had taken you away, you would have lived such a dangerous life as a selkie. Every time one of the fishermen brought back dead seals for meat and oil, I thanked the Lord that it was not you.

Selkies are very alluring; 'tis almost impossible for an unwed human to resist when one comes to claim a mate. This is why I've always kept you from sharing your lovely singing voice. If a man were to hear it, he would become enthralled with you for a short time.

You, my daughter, have the blood of the sea from both your parents. This shall give you the ability to make your own choices, should a selkie male ever try to claim you. Be better than I was, than Edith was. Don't rush into anything; don't give your heart away too easily.

You're an adult now, and I know that you're fully capable of making your own choices. There's one more thing I wish to tell you, one more secret of Drulea Cottage: hidden beneath the boards that your bed rests on, your sealskin awaits you. Take it and decide what kind of life you truly want.

All my love,
Mum

Little rivers appeared on Briony's cheeks as she sat with the letter clenched in her hand. She said nothing for several minutes, even when Mr. McLaren gently urged her up the road and to his home so that she could absorb everything without prying eyes. The letter had, indeed, given her answers, but they weren't what she'd been expecting.

All the lies throughout the years. All those times when I felt so different and Mum just assured me I was special. . . . Now I know the truth. My other home is the sea. 'Twas always the sea!

It was so much to take in, but despite how overwhelming it was, Briony felt a strange peace. She could finally make sense of her origins as well as everything that had transpired in the last few weeks.

Well, everything to do with my past and Niall. Everything related to Santiago is still a mystery.

"Here," Mr. McLaren offered.

Briony silently took the glass and swallowed the water within, only then noticing how thirsty she was. She took a few moments to truly observe her surroundings; she'd never been in the man's home before.

It was really more of a shack than a house. What wasn't falling apart was still covered in dust and spiderwebs to the point that the cleanliness of Briony's glass seemed out of place. Many of the townsfolk had tried to get Mr. McLaren to fix it up several times because the outside was such an eyesore, but the fisherman seemed fully content with everything just as it was.

Mr. McLaren said nothing, but she could tell he was fully aware of her scrutiny.

She coughed in embarrassment. "Did you ever meet *him*, my—"

"Yer father? Aye, I did." Mr. McLaren's voice was still remorseful as he pulled up a chair and sat down.

"What was he like?"

"He was . . ." Vincent McLaren looked away for a moment before turning back with a firm expression. "Look, lass, do you want the truth or do you want something kind?"

"I thought I made it clear the truth is what I want. *No matter what it may be.*"

The fisherman sighed with resignation. "All right. The truth is, yer father was never good enough fer yer mum. He played the part o' the lovesick fool quite well, but I could see 'twas all an act. I tried to tell yer mother the same, that something was na right about him, but at that point, she would na listen. The selkie charm was too strong. 'Twas only after she was pregnant and he threatened to take you away that she realized he'd never truly loved her. After he left, she told me what he was and that she needed my help to protect you. I . . . I'm so sorry fer what I did."

Briony's heart swelled with sympathy as she took in the filthy, big-eared, almost toothless fisherman. *This man was a true friend to my mum. And na only that, but he also kept me from being stolen away as a bairn.*

"I owe you an apology too," Briony said as she gave Vincent McLaren a sad smile.

The fisherman shook his head, brushing aside her words. "Nay, I should have given you the letter sooner. You deserved to know. I just . . ." He looked away, a hand on his neck.

"'Twas the only thing left that I could do fer yer mother. She wished that somehow you'd never have to find out." The man's Adam's apple bobbed with a thick swallow.

And that was when Briony realized something else. "You were in love with her."

197

Mr. McLaren's head spun back to her so quickly it looked painful. A blush erupted across his cheeks, but his eyes were steady as they met hers. "Aye, that I was. Always will be, too. She never felt the same, so I never told her. She had enough things to worry about."

A touch of mirth appeared in Briony's eyes. "And I know something else, too."

"What's that?"

"Yer na mad."

As if to contest her statement, a huge, almost disturbing smile took over the man's face. "Hmm, perhaps. I'll never tell though."

The smile dropped suddenly, only to be replaced by a strong frown. "So what now, lass? I take it you know you can trust me now. That Niall Moreland, I dinna believe he has good intentions. Has he said anything about why he came to Everton? Did he mention the past?"

"Aye, he did. He was there the day my da' died with his parents. They must have been the other two seals on the beach. The ones that got away."

"Then he seeks revenge fer what happened. But why would he show up now?"

Briony pondered for a moment, her mind running through everything that had happened in the past few weeks. She searched for something, anything that might have been the trigger.

When did he show up? What happened right beforehand?

Briony gasped. "'Tis my fault. . . . I brought him here."

"Yer fault? What are you talking about?"

"I did na know it at the time. I did na know the danger. . . . That silly legend about the selkies. I'd completely forgotten it until Mum mentioned it in her letter. Seven tears in the ocean . . ."

I was so upset that day when Santiago and I argued. Then I sat on the cliff, and I watched my tears hitting the water. . . . If only I'd known what they would lead to.

"And with my mum gone, her threat to hunt the seals was gone too, so there was nothing to stop him from coming here."

Mr. McLaren rose and began pacing back and forth. "Has he talked about taking you away? About going back to his home?"

"He said he was going to save me."

"Then that means he wants to make you his bride. Fer you to shed yer humanity forever. And you could do it, now that you know where yer sealskin is."

Briony said nothing as she let the words sink in. From Niall's perspective, she was sure it made perfect sense. *Why would I stay with the people who murdered my father? Why na run to the ocean's arms instead?*

And yet Briony felt something tugging on her soul at the thought of leaving, a strange tether she had never known existed until now.

She slowly shook her head as she made up her mind. "Nay, I can' do that. I . . . Even though life is hard here, how could I leave everything and everyone I know behind? Drulea Cottage, Adaira, Fergus . . ." She trailed off as another name almost crossed her lips.

The day he kissed me. . . . He'd heard me singing that day! That was why he kissed me. 'Twas an enchantment from hearing me sing. 'Twas na from any real desire to do so.

A question zipped through Briony's mind as quick and sharp as an arrow, an arrow that soon found its mark as it pierced her heart. *Does that mean the connection I thought was between us is just a lie?*

"If yer determined to stay, lass, then you must be very careful going forward. Have you told Niall that you dinna wish to be with him?"

Briony jumped in surprise. She'd forgotten that Mr. McLaren was standing there. She steeled herself and refocused on the matter at hand.

"Aye, I told him. But that was before I knew what he was, what I am. When he told me the truth, I did na believe him, so he started the storm to convince me. I have na seen him since then."

The fisherman pressed his fingers to his temples. "Then this is na over. He will return fer you. 'Tis only a matter o' time. And when he does, I fear what else may happen."

Briony frowned. "What do you mean? Just because I know the truth now does na mean my feelings fer him have changed. I'll reject him just the same."

Mr. McLaren shook his head and let out a pained groan. "Nay, dinna you see? If Everton is keeping you from being with him, what's to stop him from just getting rid o' it?"

"Getting rid o' it? Mr. McLaren, I understand he's powerful, but do you really think he could . . ."

"All the time he spent here, all those days working fer Daniel Calhoun, why do you think he did that?"

"I guess he did it to maintain the illusion that he was human while he was here?"

Where is he going with this?

"Dinna be naïve, lass! He was studying us. Now he knows we're in no position to defend ourselves from the likes o' him and his kind. You and I are the only ones who even know selkies exist. If he attacks the town, 'twill be a slaughter. He already hates us because o' what happened to yer father, and if you reject him again, it might give him all the push he needs to bathe Everton in its own blood."

Eu Te Amo

Briony trudged home, her heart sinking like a stone, for neither she nor Mr. McLaren had thought of a good solution to her predicament.

When will Niall return? A day? A week? What if I have na thought o' what to do by then? I—

"Santiago!" Briony jumped backward. She had been staring at the ground for such a long time that she hadn't even noticed the merchant at the cottage entrance.

"I hope I'm not too early. I simply couldn't wait any longer," Santiago stated. There was a nervous excitement in his tone, one that tugged her drowning heart back up to the surface.

She peered at him for a moment, noting his clenched fists, stiff jaw, and resolute gaze. *Whatever he's about to say, 'tis dreadfully important.*

Briony swallowed and put on her most convincing smile. "Please come inside."

Santiago silently walked in behind her, though his footfalls made her all too aware of his presence. She stood in the kitchen, her back to the merchant, awaiting his words with bated breath. She tried to ignore the creak of the door closing, the slickness of her own sweat on her palms, the masculine scent lingering in the air.

As soon as the door was fully shut, Briony turned, and a slew of nonsense burst from her mouth. "I should get that door fixed. 'Tis such a troublesome noise. Adaira had that

201

same problem with some o' the rooms at the inn, but she talked to Mr. Burgess, who is very good with that sort o' thing, and he said—"

"Briony."

Briony's tongue stuck to the roof of her mouth, preventing her from saying more. Though her eyes had been on his when she began talking, now they drifted down to his lips.

His lips . . .

They had only uttered one word, yet shivers were running through her body. She recalled those lips all too well, for she'd thought of them many times. She knew they tasted of faraway places and secret hopes, of salty air and warm days in the sun.

She longed to taste them again.

She heard Santiago's sharp intake of breath and returned her attention to his eyes. The man's voice was soft but steady as he said, "I know what your response was the last time someone declared himself to you, but I cannot hold back anymore. I *must* say what's on my heart."

Briony didn't speak as her brain and heart warred over which one would overload first from anticipation. *Could this be what I think 'tis? Surely I'm just imagining—*

Santiago stepped forward until they were only inches apart. She saw his eyes darken as he leaned forward. "Briony, eu te amo. I love you."

He said it.

He actually said it.

The confession I thought I would never hear.

Briony smiled then and not just with her mouth; it was as if her joy lit up her entire body.

He was so close. All she had to do was move her head slightly for their lips to touch. Her brain began giving orders to do just that, but then—

What if this is na real? Briony paused and searched Santiago's eyes, those beautiful green eyes, just as she had the first time he'd shown interest in her.

It seems like a lifetime has passed since then. And yet I still feel uncertain.

Briony bit down on her lip hard enough to break out of the reverie she'd been in. She stepped back.

It was just one step, one tiny movement, but it was enough.

Enough for Santiago to know something was wrong. Enough to cause him pain.

"Briony?" The man's voice was quiet and fearful.

And that fear made Briony's heart scream in protest. *How can I do this? How can I hurt him like this?*

That same voice in her head from before—the voice of reason or paranoia, Briony couldn't tell—said, *But if he's still affected by yer song, you can' take advantage o' him now. No matter how much you wish it.* Briony shook her head, trying to whisk the voice away, but she couldn't.

Na when what 'tis saying makes sense.

"What's wrong? Do you not feel the same way?" Santiago stretched out a hesitant hand.

She extended her hand in return, but then she withdrew before their fingers met. "How do I know this is real?"

Santiago's eyes widened, and he lowered his hand. "Of course it's real. I've never been so sure of anything in my life. Don't doubt that. Not even for a second."

Briony put a hand over her mouth, ignoring the moisture threatening to overtake her eyes. She shook her head again, firmly this time. "Nay, I can' be sure. Unless . . ."

"Unless what?"

"Wait here." She spun around and hurried to the bedroom. She pushed on her bed as hard as she could, not caring that it must have looked very bizarre.

Once the bed was out of the way, her hands slid across the wooden planks below, seeking the loose boards she knew she would find.

There! She yanked one free, and her eyes drank in the sight before them: a dusty, folded bit of gray material, large enough to cover a person. Exactly Briony's size.

My sealskin.

A flood of emotions swept through her when her fingers brushed it. This was a part of her identity that she'd never known before, yet her soul had been missing it all the while. She wanted to laugh and cry and scream, but she held all of it inside.

Her fingers clasped the pelt tightly, tenderly, knowing that what she was about to do could change everything.

Briony carefully removed the shoes from her feet, praying her fears wouldn't keep her from being brave.

She came out of the bedroom, sealskin in one hand and shoes in the other. Santiago stood in the kitchen, leaning against his cane with a nervous, impatient expression. When he saw her, his eyes locked onto what she held, confusion seeping into his features.

"Briony, what—"

"There's something I need to show you, though I fear you won' believe me. And even if you do, you won' look at me the same way."

Santiago's brow furrowed. "Briony, I told you before that nothing you tell me will change how I see you. I meant it then, and I mean it now."

Briony turned away and stared out the window, wishing she could believe him. "Nay, once you find out . . ." She swallowed a thick lump in her throat.

She felt his hand on her shoulder, rubbing it softly. "Please don't cry. Amorzinho, I can't bear to see it."

"What is 'amorzinho'?"

"In English, I believe you would call it 'sweetheart.' And that's what you are: the kindest, sweetest heart I've ever known. How many people would still be so kind after all the suffering you've endured? When we first met, I didn't know why you were so guarded, but when we encountered Laird Oliver in the market, I started to realize you had good reason for it. When he came to my room later for money, he was so adamant about how horrible of a person you were. . . . I knew then that you were being mistreated. And since then, I've seen how your neighbors act toward you. Only a few show you any compassion and yet . . . How could anyone good enough to help a prejudiced fool like myself be worthy of such hatred?"

Briony let out a humorless laugh. "Be careful o' what you say. You may wish to take it back soon."

"Briony, just tell me what's bothering you."

She sighed, but she didn't turn from the window. She couldn't bear to look him in the eye, couldn't bear to see his face once he knew the truth.

Instead, she chose to focus on the cool waves, undulating softly in the breeze. Briony wished with all her being that she could freeze this moment in time. *Then I could hold on to the love shining in Santiago's eyes, the warmth o' his hand upon my shoulder, the tenderness o' his voice.*

But like glass when it drops, she knew the moment was about to shatter.

"Santiago, I'm more different from you than you realize. I'm different from everyone in this town. I'm na even hum—"

Santiago gasped, making Briony lose her train of thought and, with it, the truth she was about to utter.

"Santiago?" She spun toward him. The man's visage bore sheer panic, so much so that she grabbed his arm. "What's wrong? Are you ill?"

Has he figured out what I am?

And yet he didn't flinch from her grasp. He didn't even seem to have heard her; his gaze was on something else entirely.

"What are you looking a—"

But as she turned, she saw the answer to her question: a large ship on the horizon, one bearing white flags with red crests.

Santiago released a series of short, angry whispers in Portuguese, making Briony all the more curious.

"Santiago, please. Who are those people?"

Finally, Santiago seemed to hear her. He looked her deeply in the eyes and said, "Do you trust me?"

"O-O' course I do. But, Santiago, yer frightening me."

The man's mouth tightened, and he grabbed hold of her hand. "We have to leave. *Now.*"

And then they were tearing out of the house, racing down the hill as quickly as Santiago's ankle could handle. Briony didn't know where they were going, but a small part of her was glad she'd been interrupted from what she'd been about to say. *I dinna know who those people are, but perhaps 'tis better na to tell Santiago the truth right now.*

But Santiago's gaze kept sliding back to the ship until Briony's anxiety became almost unbearable. All the things he wasn't saying with his words were loud and clear through his body language: the way he held her hand so tightly as though she would slip away, the way his brow held a deep line of worry, the way his feet pounded against the ground as they moved.

I dinna know how 'twould be possible, but I almost feel like what we're trying to avoid might be worse than Santiago's rejection.

The two of them skidded to a stop in front of Everton Inn, and Santiago turned to her. "Briony, stay here while I get my sister."

"But, Santiago, I dinna know what's going on. What are we doing? Why do you have to get Lucia?"

Santiago huffed. "You said you trust me. Just wait here, and I'll explain afterward. There's no time."

"I—All right." Briony nodded.

Santiago nodded back and rushed inside, not bothering to shut the door in his haste.

Briony watched the entrance and tapped her foot for a few minutes until she heard shoes hitting the ground. Lots of shoes.

She turned to the noise and gaped at the sight of ten uniformed men marching up the path. Their eyes possessed no warmth, and they carried guns against their shoulders.

Briony's first instinct was to flee, but when she stepped backward, one of the men shouted, "Stop!"

Briony halted at the intimidating voice. The men all stopped at attention about thirty feet from her, save for the one who had spoken. This man looked to be in his early fifties with graying hair and a stocky frame. The commanding air about him told her instantly that he was the one in charge.

"Senhorita, I'm Comodoro Cardoso. I'm seeking Senhor Mendes on behalf of the Portuguese government. Do you know where he is?"

Briony tried to speak, but she found her tongue paralyzed. These men looked like they would shoot her without any restraint. There was a hardness about them that was almost inhuman. *As if I know what it means to be human.*

"Senhorita, this is a matter of grave urgency. Do you know Senhor Mendes?" The man's voice was colder than the dead of winter. His brown eyes sized her up, spending an uncomfortable amount of time on her womanly features.

Briony looked away, shocked at the man's shameless indecency. Soon, though, that shock gave way to indignation, and she replied, "Sir, you've given me no good reason to help you."

"What was that? Are you saying you know but you're not going to tell me? Do you have any idea what I could have done to you for withholding information? I'll ask you one last time, and I hope you're smart enough to answer. *Where is Santiago Mendes?*" Briony looked back at the man just as the veins on both sides of his neck grew more pronounced.

Briony gulped, but she held her ground and focused on her own anger instead. This man's arrogance demanded rebellion, and she would gladly give it.

When it became clear she wasn't going to say more, Cardoso turned to one of the other men. "Alves!"

The man in question stepped up to Briony and gripped her wrist. Hard.

Cardoso smirked when Briony winced in pain. "Now, senhorita, let's try again. Where is Senhor Mendes?"

"*Right here.* And why does that matter?" Santiago shouted, appearing behind Briony at the inn's entrance. Lucia stepped out from behind him, as skittish as a rabbit caught in a trapper's snare.

"Ah, just the man I was looking for."

"What is this all about?"

Santiago sounds as if he does na have any idea why these men are here, yet he did na seem that way a few minutes ago when he went to get his sister.

Other people inside Everton Inn trickled out to see what all the commotion was about. Briony could see Adaira, Mr. Burgess and his son, and some of the other sailors from Santiago's ship.

"Don't try to pretend you don't know why we've come. You know *precisely* why," Cardoso sneered.

"Unhand Senhorita Fairborn and tell me, then." Santiago glared at Alves with eyes like daggers until the man let go of Briony's wrist.

Cardoso sent Alves a disapproving glance before returning his attention to Santiago. "Very well. Santiago Mendes, I am Comodoro Cardoso of the king's navy, and on behalf of His Majesty, King Joseph,[21] and the Royal Navy, I hereby arrest you for high treason."

Contradictions

Briony waited. She waited for the outrage that would pour from Santiago's mouth, the disbelief that would appear on his face, and the glance that he would give her as a sign that everything would be all right.

She waited with complete faith that that was what was about to happen.

And yet . . .

Santiago's eyes flickered over to his sister, whose look of terror had increased tenfold. Beside Lucia, Captain Costa stood solemnly, his hand squeezing the woman's shoulder in a gesture of comfort. A look passed between the siblings, and Lucia gave an almost imperceptible shake of her head.

Briony turned to the commodore as he stared at Santiago with a hungry expression. This man was clearly used to being a predator, and right now Santiago was his prey.

Na if I can help it.

"What are you talking about? That's the most ridiculous thing I've ever heard," Briony blurted, moving between Santiago and the commodore.

Cardoso scowled, glaring at her as if she was a measly fly to bat out of the way. "Is it? Then you must not know Senhor Mendes very well, senhorita. *I* happen to know that Senhor Mendes was one of the conspirators in an assassination attempt last year."

"Nay, yer lying."

Cardoso laughed, grating on Briony's nerves. "Oh, how

noble of you, trying to defend him. What are you, his lover?"

Briony's face heated up. She was so embarrassed by his words that she couldn't think of anything to say.

"And not just any assassination attempt either. Senhor Mendes was part of a group trying to murder His Majesty the King."[22]

Briony let out a quiet gasp, at which the commodore smirked triumphantly.

He peeked around Briony and asked, "Do you deny your involvement in the affair, Senhor Mendes?"

Briony spun around, raising her eyebrows at Santiago expectantly. But what she saw in the man's eyes wasn't the strength and determination she'd thought she would find. What she saw in them was sorrow, hurt, and—

Santiago broke eye contact and stared at the dirt. "No, I do not deny it."

"What?" Briony whispered, her voice so low that no one could hear it.

Except fer him. And while Santiago didn't acknowledge her openly, Briony couldn't help but notice how he winced as if her question physically pained him.

This is the man who just declared his love fer me, the man I was about to share my deepest secret with. . . .

Santiago held out his wrists as Alves placed handcuffs upon them and the other officers aimed their rifles in his direction.

"Senhorita Mendes and Captain Costa, I will also need to speak with you. Join me on my ship *at once.*" Comodoro Cardoso cast one last smile at Briony before he and his men started heading back to the ship, prisoner in tow.

Briony didn't even notice the horrible man's glance, for she was too much in shock to be aware of anyone except the bound man limping down the hill. Her eyes bore into him, silently begging him to look her way. *Please let me know this is na happening right now or that there's some kind o' mistake.*

But her wish never came. Santiago didn't turn back even once as he made his way down to the large ship at the end of

---

[22] A political scandal known as the Távora Affair that began in 1758.

210

the dock.

Lucia and Costa followed closely behind the officers, the first weeping quietly and the second consoling her with gentle words.

As Santiago shuffled onto the ship and disappeared into its interior, Briony whispered his name, unable to comprehend what was happening. She tried to push forward, to reach him, but she found that her legs had lost their strength. She wobbled a few times, trying to regain her balance, but it was no use.

Briony collapsed, and all went black.

**

"Briony? . . . Briony?" Adaira's voice drifted in and out of Briony's ears. There were other voices too, but she wasn't aware enough to identify them. She didn't want to be aware enough to do so anyway. She didn't want to be aware of anything.

'Tis so much easier to sleep. Then I dinna have to remember. . . . But just as she was about to fade back into oblivion, Santiago's face flashed through her mind.

Moisture appeared on her cheeks, and all the realities of what she was trying to avoid came back to her. She swiped a hand across her face, but the tears had already formed tiny rivulets that wouldn't stop flowing.

She clenched her hands, needing to touch something real, something unaffected by feelings. Her fingers grasped something soft—a seat cushion.

She opened her eyes and found herself in one of the sitting room chairs at Everton Inn. Adaira was whispering nearby with Dr. Sherwin while John and William Burgess stood a few feet away.

"Oh, yer awake!" Adaira rushed over and wrapped her in a bone-crushing hug.

Briony offered her friend a tight-lipped smile, though she could still feel the water running down her face. "A-Adaira, thank you. I—"

But that was as much as she could get out; she was just too

raw everywhere.

"Bless you, dearie. I'm so sorry about this." Adaira rubbed her back for a few moments as Briony sobbed.

She knew she looked pathetic, but she simply couldn't make herself stop.

But not everyone was as sympathetic as Adaira.

"Mistress Briony, did he really do it? Did he try to kill the king?" blurted a voice, drawing Briony back from her pit of self-pity.

She blinked away her tears to look at the owner of the voice, jumping when she realized William Burgess was mere inches from her face.

John Burgess yanked his son backward and snapped, "William! You can' just say things like that."

William frowned, confusion swirling in his eyes. "But why na? That's what everybody wants to know, right? I'm just helping out by asking."

Adaira let out a small cough that sounded suspiciously like a laugh. "Aye, William, yer very helpful. Except there's one thing you did na think about."

"What's that?"

Adaira put a kind hand on William's shoulder and looked him dead in the eye. "Briony is very sad right now, so she may na be able to talk about it just yet. We have to be thoughtful about things like this."

William glanced from Adaira to Briony, and it was like a spark ignited in his eyes. "Oh, I see. I'd be upset too if I was in love with a murderer. Do you want me to go beat him up fer you, Mistress Briony?"

John Burgess gritted his teeth so hard that it looked uncomfortable. He gripped his son's arm and pulled the boy behind him. "I'm deeply sorry, mistress. Please excuse us."

The man turned to William and gave him such a dangerous look that his son clamped his jaw shut and dashed down the hallway. John marched after him, and soon enough they both disappeared into their room.

"Well?" Dr. Sherwin said.

Briony turned to see whom the doctor was talking to and was surprised to see that she was the object of his gaze. "Well, what?"

"Now that young Burgess has already asked, we're all waiting on yer answer. Did he truly do it?"

"Dr. Sherwin, please. Have a heart," Adaira complained.

The doctor rolled his eyes. "Mistress Stubbins, firstly, as a doctor, I'm well aware o' the organs I possess, and secondly, 'tis something we have a right to know. After all, we've been treating him and housing him fer weeks, and now we find out he may have been a criminal all this time."

Briony took a deep breath. Her mind was starting to piece itself back together and analyze the situation, but certain things weren't adding up. "I know as much about this as you do. He never told me anything to suggest he was involved in . . . something like this."

"Mr. Mendes is such a kind soul. He would never try to murder someone, much less a king," Adaira said.

"I would na be so certain," Dr. Sherwin argued. "How much do we really know about the man after all? He could have been playing us fer fools, gaining our trust, just to—"

"Just to what? Kill us all when he got the chance? Dr. Sherwin, you may na have gotten to know him very well while he's been here, but I have. And everything I've learned about Santiago Mendes contradicts that." Briony sat up straighter in her chair, feeling herself become more and more certain of the merchant's innocence.

Dr. Sherwin narrowed his eyes. "But when the commodore told him the charges, Mr. Mendes did na deny them."

"And that's the part I can' figure out. The man I know would never do something like that, yet he did na defend himself when given the chance. There must be more to this than we realize. Something is preventing him from speaking the truth."

"Or yer love is blinding you from the truth." Dr. Sherwin winced right after he spoke, and regret shone from his eyes as he looked down at her.

Briony bit her lip, restraining herself from saying something rash. "Perhaps yer right. Maybe I am blinded by love. But because o' that very love, I can' give up hope. Na yet."

"What are you going to do?" Adaira asked.

"I have to hear it from Santiago himself. If he's responsible fer what the commodore said, he's going to have to say it to my face. If I'm right, though, he won' be able to do that." Briony stood and faced the door.

But Dr. Sherwin touched her shoulder before she could take a step. "Briony."

She turned to him, and he instantly looked away, dropping his hand and holding it behind his back. "I . . . I'm sorry. Fer yer sake, I hope yer right. Just be careful."

Briony grinned. "Trust me, Doctor. I can handle myself better than you think."

Briony tramped out the door to Cardoso's ship. The farther she walked, though, the more her bravado wore off, and by the time she'd stepped onto the gangplank, she was practically shaking.

Remember that yer doing this fer the man you love. And what's more, he told you he loves you, too. That thought gave her the strength to cross the threshold into the commodore's quarters.

But will it be enough to get me through everything else?

"Ah, Senhorita . . . Fairborn, was it? What brings you to my ship? Come to check on your lover?" The commodore sneered as Briony entered, waving his hand for her to take a seat. He didn't bother to rise from his desk, either due to a lack of courtesy toward all women or maybe just her.

Briony clenched her jaw even as a telltale blush stole across her cheeks. She told herself she wouldn't be intimidated by this man, no matter who he was. *After all, I'm na just anyone, right? I'm a selkie, fer goodness' sake! This man can' stop me from getting what I want.*

"I need to speak to him. 'Tis very important."

"And why should I care about your needs? What's in it for me?" A lustful smile spread over his lips as he raised his eyebrows at her.

Briony scowled, making it very clear how she felt about his implication. "Are you na worried you might have arrested an innocent man?"

The commodore rolled his eyes and leaned away.

"Senhorita, don't waste my time."

"Why are you so convinced he's guilty?"

"Hmm, how about the fact he didn't even deny the charges? That seems like a clear indicator of the man's guilt. Besides, even if Senhor Mendes had denied them, I already have enough evidence to ensure his execution once we return to Portugal."

All the blood drained from Briony's face, and what she'd been about to say got stuck in the back of her throat.

"What's wrong, senhorita?" Cardoso's eyes lit up at her discomfort. "Many of the other conspirators have already been tried and executed, so it's safe to say that shall be his fate as well."

"What kind o' evidence?" Briony whispered.

Cardoso growled in frustration. "This is government business that doesn't concern a common Scottish senhorita. In fact, I don't know why you're still here. Leave now before I make you leave."

"But I—"

"Alves!" The commodore looked to the door as the officer he'd called entered the room. "Escort the senhorita out of here, and don't allow her back on the ship."

Alves nodded once and shoved Briony out the open door.

Briony spun around to tell the officer not to touch her again, but he simply grabbed her wrists and continued to force her down the hallway toward the deck. Briony dug in her heels as hard as she could, determined not to go down without a fight.

When that did no good, she decided it was time to resort to extreme measures. *I refuse to let Santiago leave here without speaking to him. Even if it means revealing my secret.*

Briony closed her eyes and tried to sense the heat that had come upon her so suddenly before. If she could just control it, she could—

There! Briony willed the heat to spread across her skin, down her arms, and into her hands.

Alves gasped and let go of Briony's wrists, gaping at her in shock. He lifted his hands only to see that his fingers had turned bright red.

"What's the problem, Alves?" Cardoso called from inside.

The man replied with a startled shout in Portuguese.

"Nonsense! Skin can't burn someone."

Briony heard the commodore rising from his chair and rolled her eyes. *Am I finally worth standing up fer?*

When the man appeared in the doorway, he placed his hands on his hips and stared Briony down as if he was scolding a child. "Now what's the real problem here? Did you not understand that you need to leave?"

Briony's eyes narrowed at his condescension. *Maybe 'tis time fer something worse than a simple burn.*

She turned her attention upward to the brilliantly blue sky, which she could just barely see beyond the stairs. She set her mind upon creating a—

"Senhorita Fairborn! Senhorita Fairborn!" The unexpected voice hit Briony's ears, distracting her from her task before she could truly begin. She blinked and saw Adriano Rodriguez scrambling down the staircase toward her, urgency written all over his face.

When he reached her, he leaned close to her ear and whispered, "I must speak with you, senhorita, about Senhor Mendes."

As he pulled away, Briony gave him a sharp nod. She turned back to the navy men with a grimace. "Be glad Mr. Rodriguez arrived when he did."

"That sounds dangerously like a threat, senhorita." Cardoso crossed his arms and took a step toward her. Alves, on the other hand, was still just gaping at her as if he was looking at a ghost.

"O' course na, Commodore," Briony purred, her voice dripping with sarcasm. "Come along, Mr. Rodriguez. I'm na wanted here after all."

Briony gripped Adriano's arm and spun the confused sailor around. Adriano looked back and forth between her and the enraged commodore several times, but he said nothing as she gestured for him to get going.

The two of them climbed up the stairs to the deck outside. A drizzle had started, so Briony adjusted her headscarf and moved a little faster. Adriano didn't look back at her once as he crossed the gangplank and then took her through the market area.

When they came across some of Cardoso's sailors at the bottom of the hill, Adriano stood a little straighter, and Briony tried to do the same. The men only briefly glanced at them, so she hoped that meant they didn't look suspicious.

Once the sailors were out of earshot, Briony stopped and checked to make sure no one else was nearby. "What was it you wanted to tell me?"

Adriano eyed her strangely. "What happened just now on the ship?"

Briony shook her head. "It does na matter right now. Tell me why you were looking fer me. Do you know something about the charges against Mr. Mendes?"

"Yes. It is hard to say in English, but I will try. Last year, two men tried to kill him. To kill the king. We weren't supposed to know, but people hear things. He was going home at night, and they tried to kill him. Their names were Antonio Alvarez Ferreira and Joseph Policarpio.[23] They got caught, but Policarpio got away. People saw the Mendes . . . *carruagem* . . . ," he trailed off with a look of frustration. "What's the word? You sit, and there are horses to pull you?"

"A carriage?"

"Yes, a carriage. People saw the Mendes carriage the night Policarpio got away. The Mendes family does not live there, so why would the carriage be there? Then Capitão Costa tells us we have to leave soon, but it was not time to leave. We—"

Briony's lungs tightened in dread. "Are you trying to tell me Mr. Mendes *was* part o' all this? That he wanted to kill the king after all?"

Adriano's eyes widened, and he waved his hands in front of him. "No, there's more you need to know."

The man's volume had risen to a shout, and he looked about wildly to make sure no one else was listening.

The street was still deserted, save for Gareth Peterson sitting on the ground outside the tavern in a drunken stupor. Briony doubted he even knew what day it was, so she wasn't

---

[23] The two men arrested for attempting to murder King Joseph I.

worried about him overhearing. "Continue."

"I didn't know why we had to leave. I asked the crew, and they thought Senhor Mendes did something bad. They thought he helped Policarpio. I didn't think so. Senhor Mendes is too good to do that.

"Then I heard shouting. They were so mad. I couldn't hear what they were saying. Then Senhor Mendes came out. But there was the storm. We had to save the ship. I had to do my job or we would die. The mast was . . . What's the word? I knew it would fall. I saw that it would fall. He pushed him, and Senhor Mendes fell under it. The mast was on his ankle, and he couldn't move.

"I saw the gun, and it would kill Senhor Mendes, but the water pushed him down. I thought we would all die. But graças a Deus[24] we saw Everton, and we got here. We lived." Adriano smiled, proud that he had managed to tell the whole story.

Briony frowned. "But, Adriano, who was it?"

Adriano cocked his head to the side. "What?"

"*Who* tried to kill Santiago?"

Adriano took one final glance around, and when satisfied that it was still safe to speak, he mumbled, "Capitão Costa."

"What . . . ," Briony trailed off.

Is that why Santiago insisted I avoid the ship? He always behaves so strangely around the captain. . . . And Adriano's suspicious words at the Johnsmas gathering . . . Talking about an "accident." If Costa tried to kill Santiago before, then he's certainly capable o' being behind this whole conspiracy.

I wonder what he and Santiago were arguing about before they hit that storm.

"Adriano, could you help me—"

"No, senhorita." Adriano shook his head. "This is as much as I can do fer Senhor Mendes. I . . . I know I'm a coward, but I just can't. You have to go on without me."

Briony bristled at the man's lack of loyalty, but then she thought of something in her mother's letter. *My voice holds sway over the likes o' men, so would I be able to get him to do my wishes?*

She opened her mouth to find out, but then she paused,

---

[24] Thank God.

ashamed at herself. *He's barely more than a boy. How can I force him to be further involved in something that could get him killed? Nay, 'tis best to keep him from as much o' this as I can.*

She nodded and said, "You've already helped me when you did na have to. Fer that, I'm very grateful."

Adriano released the breath he'd been holding and took a step back. "I wish you well, senhorita."

Briony nodded and held back a small sigh as the man walked off in the direction of the tavern. *How am I going to get Santiago out o' this? This feels much too big to do by myself. . . .*

Ah, Lucia! Surely she knows her brother is innocent. And once she learns o' the captain's treachery, maybe she'll have an idea o' how to prove he's the one behind this.

Lucia and Costa had gone with Cardoso when he arrested Santiago, but Briony hadn't seen them at the commodore's ship or run into them in town. *Maybe they went back to their own ship.*

The last time she'd been on the *São Nicolau* had been an unpleasant experience, to say the least. After the latest incident with the commodore and Alves, Briony was fed up with men viewing her as an object to control. *'Tis na just the Portuguese men either; Niall has been doing the same thing by trying to force me to be with him.*

If I manage to get Santiago out o' all this, will he eventually be the same way? Even my own father used my mother fer his wishes and did na care fer her own. What makes Santiago any different?

The green-eyed merchant's face ran through her mind, along with all the moments they'd spent together. She thought back to his confession, trying not to get caught up in the emotions tied to it and instead focusing on what had happened directly after.

When I stepped away from him because I could na believe his words, there was something he did—When he said my name, he sounded so heartbroken, but there was also something else in his voice. What was it?

But the answer soon became apparent. *'Twas fear. Santiago thought he was going to lose me.*

Because he would have let me go. He was na going to force me into something I did na want. Briony held back a tear at the revelation, surer than ever that she was going to rescue Santiago, no matter what.

The *São Nicolau* seemed deserted as she crept aboard. *Maybe Lucia went back to the inn while I was talking to Cardoso.* She was just about to deem the trip a waste of time when she heard low voices coming from the captain's quarters.

Briony snuck up, quiet as a mouse, and leaned her ear against the door.

She jerked back in surprise. It wasn't fully shut.

She peeked around the door, careful not to put any weight on it again in case it made noise this time. Inside, Lucia and the captain stood at arm's length from each other. They were engaged in a heated debate over something. *Yet again, this would be so much easier if I understood Portuguese. If only I'd convinced Adriano to give me a wee bit more help.*

Still, she tried to listen for anything that sounded familiar. She heard Santiago's name a few times as Lucia wrung her hands. She also caught the word *morta* again and shivered.

Is Lucia trying to get Costa to help her free Santiago? She's going to be sorely disappointed if that's the case.

Briony lost her visual of Lucia when Costa leaned in close to whisper something—

Briony gasped. She'd been wrong; Costa wasn't whispering to Lucia. He was kissing her.

But Briony's gasp had been too loud. Lucia and the captain broke apart at the sound and looked toward the door.

Briony drew back, her heart galloping like horses. She didn't think they'd seen her, but they'd definitely heard her. Her eyes darted about for a place to hide—

But there was nothing on deck that was large enough, and soon, she heard footsteps. If she didn't think of something fast, Lucia and Costa would find her. *I dinna even want to think about what would happen then.*

With no time to run back to town or down to the sailors' quarters, there was only one thing she could do. Briony raced over to the edge of the deck and dove into the sea.

Playing with Fire

Briony zoomed through the water like a bullet, trying to stay out of sight for as long as possible before returning to the surface. She went past fish and dolphins, even some sharks, all of which scattered in different directions upon noticing her. Only once her lungs began burning with need did she return to the surface and only then by peeking her eyes and nose above the water.

She sank back slowly, grateful that no one seemed to be following her. *But then, how could they? They're na selkies, so the only chance they'd have o' keeping up with me would be to bring the entire ship. I'm sure I'm faster than any rowboat, no matter the strength o' its oarsmen.*

With these thoughts in mind, Briony felt the claws of panic lose their hold over her heart. She lifted her entire head into the air and did a more thorough scan of her surroundings.

The shore was a good distance away, but she could easily reach it within a few minutes if she tried. She was glad to be far enough from the Portuguese ships that no one would have been able to identify her as human; at best, someone might think she was a seal poking its head from the water.

She chuckled at how ironically accurate that assumption would be, but her laughter quickly turned bitter. *I have na even had the chance to wear my sealskin yet with all the madness since the commodore's arrival.* Her soul longed for the wholeness that had begun calling to her from the moment she had laid her hands on the pelt.

But now she had another issue to deal with: determining what she'd just witnessed on the *São Nicolau*.

Does Lucia have feelings fer the captain? He did na look like he was forcing himself on her. Did Costa tell her he would help save Santiago? Is she just pretending to like him to get his help?

Or is it something worse? Could she have been a part o' the attempt on Santiago's life?

Nay, she loves her brother. I've seen how she is with him. Surely 'tis na just a lie, right?

Briony shook her head to clear her dark thoughts. *Until I know the truth, I can' depend on Lucia fer help.*

She smacked the water with her hand. *My life never used to be this complicated. Would it have been like this if I'd grown up with my da' instead o' my mum? I certainly would have lived a freer life, but then I would na have known Mum.*

Maybe 'twould be better just to go back in time to when she was still alive, back to when everything made sense.

Except everything did na make sense even then, did it? There were so many things I did na know, things about my parents and myself.

And back then Adaira was the only friend I had. . . . Well, Fergus, too, I suppose. Now I can also say that about Santiago, Mr. McLaren, Dr. Sherwin, and even Mr. Burgess to an extent.

But I will lose one o' them soon unless I figure out how to help him.

Briony deliberated the situation with Santiago for a long time, meandering toward the shore as she did so. So engaged was she in her thoughts that she didn't notice a solitary figure watching her from the beach.

The breeze was cold against her back as she plodded through the wet sand. It whistled through the nearby trees like the gentle voice of a lover. The sea, too, whispered sweet promises in Briony's ear, begging her to return to its embrace. But Briony was too distracted to hear either of them.

Only once she had placed her feet on the dry ground did Briony sense something strange. And by that point, it was too late. She looked up from her feet, gasping when she realized she wasn't alone.

"Hello, my dear. I've been waiting fer you." Niall stood before her with an ominous countenance. Trails of saltwater dripped from his hair onto his smooth chest. Briony tried to look anywhere but at the muscular physique before her, her eyes settling instead on a particularly interesting blade of grass. She was very thankful he had at least taken the time to cover his lower half with his sealskin.

I guess he's na bothering with human propriety any longer.

"I-I did na see you there," Briony sputtered, trying to sound casual even though her heart was pounding within her.

He's here to take me away. What do I do? I've been so caught up in what's happening with Santiago that I never thought o' a plan fer when Niall returned.

"That's because yer watching the ground when I'm right in front o' you."

Briony's lips twitched. *Is he trying to make a joke?*

"More humans have arrived since I was last here. *Why?*" His severe tone sent a tremor through Briony's body.

When she didn't immediately answer, Niall grabbed her chin and forced her to look him in the eye. Their faces were almost touching, and Briony had to suppress the urge to draw back.

"They came to . . ." Suddenly, an idea struck Briony, clear as a lightning bolt. It was a mad, terrible idea, one she never should have thought of. *But it also might be my best chance.*

She leaned in toward Niall's face until their noses met and stared deeply into his eyes. If she tried very hard, she could almost imagine they were green rather than black. She could almost replace his angular, aquiline face with a sturdy jaw and a short blond beard.

Santiago, forgive me.

"'Tis some trivial human issue. I've barely paid attention to it since it won' affect us in the slightest," she purred, looking back and forth from Niall's eyes to his mouth.

A tiny softening passed over the selkie's face but only for a moment before it vanished behind a veil of cynicism. He took a step away from her and shook his head as if to clear his mind.

Briony held back a sigh of relief. *The effect I have on him might be just strong enough to work.*

"'Trivial human issue'? Do you mean to tell me that since you've learned yer heritage, you've lost all interest in the goings-on o' this town? I'm na naïve enough to believe that."

Briony added a low hum to her voice, hoping it would bolster her selkie allure. "Why do you retreat from me? I thought you wanted me to accept my true nature and forsake this place. To accept *you*."

Niall ran a hand through his hair, conflict all over his face. "And how am I to know yer sincere? The last time we spoke—"

Briony slammed her mouth against his, effectively shutting the man up. She was surprised at how pleasant his mouth felt against hers, softer and warmer than she'd thought it would be. Still, it didn't compare to Santiago's, and doing this felt like the greatest sin of her life.

But it can' be helped. 'Tis the only way.

After a few minutes, Briony moved away to catch her breath. She giggled at Niall's slack-jawed expression. "Does that tell you anything?"

Briony's guilt increased tenfold at the blazing smile that spread across the man's face, but her resolve held firm.

Niall grabbed her right hand and interlaced their fingers. "You can' know how happy it makes me. I can' wait to show you all o' what you've been missing out on. Life is so much more beautiful than you've ever dreamed, Briony. And now you'll get the chance to see that."

Briony squeezed his hand, still doing her best to conjure up Santiago's image in his place. "And I'm so happy you'll be the one to show me."

"Then let's na waste any more time. Let's get yer sealskin and be rid o' this wretched place." Niall started leading her inland, toward the town, but Briony stopped.

"Niall, you can' be seen like this." She gestured to his bare torso. "I know where the skin is; stay here and let me get it."

Niall frowned. "I thought you no longer cared about this town. Surely yer na worried about yer neighbors' opinions?"

Briony shook her head vehemently. "O' course na. I just dinna want anyone to slow us down. Or fer anyone to discover what you are. What *we* are."

Her words seemed to placate him some, but a trace of suspicion still lingered in his eyes. "In that case, come with me." He tugged her back toward the beach, not stopping until they'd reached a large group of boulders. "Wait here."

Niall ducked out of sight only to reappear a couple of minutes later, fully clothed. "We'll come back here afterward to retrieve my skin. Then we can disappear forever into the sea."

Briony masked her disappointment with a grin. Niall still didn't fully trust her, which meant he wasn't as enthralled as she'd hoped. *If my plans are going to succeed, I'll have to be very cautious.*

She gripped his hand in hers, dreading the gossip that would come from being seen like this. *Again, it can' be helped. Na when the stakes are so high.*

"Niall, there is one other thing we need to do before we leave," Briony mumbled as they walked.

"Hmm? What would that be? Would you like me to cause a wee bit more chaos? I could burn everything down if you'd like. You and I both know this village could na do anything to stop me," Niall said in an offhanded manner as if it was of little consequence.

But Briony knew that deep down that was precisely what he wished to do. *He's testing me to see if I've truly forsaken my human life.*

"Actually, I'd like it if you taught *me* how to do it. Then I can destroy it all myself."

"I'd be happy to," Niall said with a sinister smile, "but there are a few things you need to know before I do that. First, most selkie powers can only be used in our human forms, like summoning a storm, burning things with a touch, and enchanting others with our singing. You may have already discovered some o' these on yer own, but I'll make sure you learn how to control them. We're also nigh irresistible to humans when we wish to be. We can even affect other selkies if we try hard enough and they're na on guard.

"When we're in seal form, we're much more limited. While we're faster than normal seals, we can' access any o' those other abilities I just mentioned. That's why 'twas so easy fer the villagers to kill yer father. If he'd been able to return to human form, they would na have stood a chance.

"Let's see, what else do you need to know?" Niall tapped

his lip. "Ah! Regardless o' the form we're in, we can usually sense each other's presence. If we're near each other, we can even sense another selkie's death. The only exception would be when someone is na a pureblood, like you or yer mum. Yer father was a pureblood, like me."

"What was he like?"

"Yer father? We called him Einar when we were in human form. He was . . . very powerful. The most powerful selkie I've ever met. I told you before that he was in the same clan as me, but *clan* is a human term. Among ourselves, we call it a herd, just like a normal group o' seals. We dinna have royalty or nobility or anything close to that in the selkie world. We live simply, just enjoying life under the waves, and the strongest among us is our alpha. That was yer father. I always admired him—"

"Did he ever mention me or my mum?" Briony jumped in.

Niall grimaced. "He never spoke much o' his time on the land, but that's the way 'tis when yer a selkie. 'Tis easy fer everything to become like a dream once you return to the sea. My parents told me he had a bairn somewhere, but I never knew who or where you were until the day we met.

"You may na have felt the connection between us then, but I suspected you were one o' us. And when I told my parents and yer father what happened, Einar instantly knew I was talking about you. He did na even wait long enough to transform before he was hurrying to yer side. I've never seen him so frightened before. . . ." Niall's voice faded away, and Briony thought she spotted a tear in one of his eyes.

Even though my da' left me, it sounds as if he truly loved me. In his own way. Briony sniffed as she, too, got choked up.

Suddenly, Niall cleared his throat. "Anyway, let's see what you can do. Regardless o' yer form, you should always be able to sense the sea when 'tis nearby. Shut yer eyes. Listen to the world around you. Can you feel the sea, just beyond yer reach? As a selkie, yer part o' it, a creature o' water. Embrace that truth, and then try to call the water in the air."

Briony closed her eyes and focused as hard as she could. She thought of the ground beneath her feet, hard and compacted with rocks. She thought of the grass and trees just behind her, swaying in the wind. She thought of her neighbors in the village, oblivious to how powerful she was.

And she was only just discovering that power for herself. Even she didn't know how far it extended—

There! There's the ocean. Briony tried to imagine herself as a mere extension of it, like a puzzle piece within a larger picture.

Yet there was a part of her that rebelled against this thought with all its strength. It refused to give up her individuality, refused to believe she was anything more than just Briony Fairborn.

My human side, she realized. *Born o' the sea and shore, what does that make me? Belonging to neither yet longing fer both.*

Briony clenched her teeth. *Whatever these differences are, I can' let them hinder my plans. If Santiago returns to Portugal, he will almost certainly die. I have to make this work.*

Briony reached upward with her mind, seeking something to grab hold of. Something she knew was there even though she felt nothing. *Why? Why can I na feel the water in the sky as I feel the sea? Does it recognize my mixed blood? Is that why it won' submit?*

Briony opened her eyes and turned to Niall for help, but his only response was a slight upturning of his mouth. Something very akin to a smirk.

He does na believe I can do this. Did he expect this would happen? That I would fail simply because I'm na a full selkie?

All my life, I've been considered inferior to everyone else. First fer being female, second fer being illegitimate, and now fer na being a pureblood.

Then she remembered what Santiago had told her when she'd revealed she was born out of wedlock. *"Briony, you had nothing to do with how you were born. How can anyone judge you for others' choices?"*

Briony glared upward at the sky. *I'm na giving up on this so easily. I'm tired o' being inferior fer things I can' control.*

Briony stretched her mouth wide and began to sing the Fairborns' song. She put her whole heart into it, belting out the words in a fierce command for the sky to do her bidding.

"Now, youthful daughter, beware o' the sea,
O' the things it can squander and steal from ye.

227

Beware o' promises spoken in haste,
And always keep yer heart—"

A rush of power pressed against Briony's consciousness, and she almost fell over from the force of it. But she wasn't frightened, for the power came eagerly like a dog when it hears its master's voice. She grabbed hold of it with her mind, rejoicing at its touch. The water felt soft and malleable, keen to please her. The sky quickly turned as dark as night, full of swirling, sparking clouds, waiting to do as she willed. No more was she inferior and ignored, and with this newfound power inside her, Briony felt invincible.

She turned to Niall triumphantly, giving him a smirk of her own that she made no effort to conceal. *If that surprises you, Niall, let's see what you think o' this.*

Briony spun away from him and shifted her attention to the docks. She pulled the invisible strings connecting her to the storm, and lightning spilled forth. Over and over, bolts sliced through the air, their thunderous booms echoing in Briony's ears as they struck the water around the Portuguese ships.

Soon Briony saw the commodore emerge from his quarters to see what was going on, but he quickly scuttled back below deck. The other sailors on the ship crawled out of the woodwork shortly after that, running about to make sure everything on deck was secure before creeping back to their hiding places. *Like roaches.*

Briony couldn't control the exact spots where the lightning hit, but she could confine the storm's energy to one small area. And with enough time, one of the bolts was bound to hit the commodore's ship.

The only problem was that she didn't wish to harm Santiago. *Once a bolt strikes the ship, I'll just release the energy. That way, the ship will be too damaged to take him back, but Santiago will still be safe.*

But do I truly wish to release it? When have I ever been this strong before? Why should I let it go? I could finally repay the damage everyone has done to me. How lovely to see the commodore's pride go up in smoke . . . And why na turn my attention to the laird's house after that? 'Tis about time someone knocked him and his wife down to where they belong—

But then she felt a cold hand on her arm, one that seemed to suck the power straight out of her.

"Briony, let go o' the storm." Niall's voice was calm and collected, but sweat was trickling down his forehead.

He fears me. Good.

"Stay out o' my way," Briony shrieked and shoved him to the ground. She turned her back on him and tried to regain the energy that had started seeping away.

"Briony!" Niall took hold of her again, this time pulling her away from the docks. "Release the power before it consumes you," he screamed in her face, his hands squeezing her arms so tightly that it hurt.

But the pain was like a wake-up call, and Briony felt a haze leave her mind as the rest of the storm's energy fell away. It sprinkled the ground around them as tiny raindrops, a poor reflection of the beautiful, destructive power it once had been.

Briony took a deep breath and sank to the ground. She raised her hand to catch the droplets as they fell, trying to come to terms with what she had just done. And almost done.

If it had na been fer Niall . . . I might have lost myself. Such power . . . I was nowhere near prepared fer it. That power could have overwhelmed me, maybe even killed me. Did Niall just save my life?

"Yer clearly na ready to do this on yer own." Niall rubbed the back of his neck and turned away with a sigh. He was silent for a long time as he looked out at the churning waves.

"You have more power than I expected fer na being a pureblood, so part o' this is my fault. I should have warned you o' the water's love fer destruction. Nature always has a balance between help and harm, but when we harness its power fer our own means, we come into contact with both sides.

"Aye, the ocean is full o' life and beauty, but 'tis also deadly when it wishes to be. If you let it, that hunger fer violence will spill over. And if you hold on to it fer too long, that power could consume you."

Briony clasped her trembling hands together as she tried not to burst into tears. It had been her first taste of power, her first taste of having agency over her own life. *And how did I handle it? By almost losing my mind to the ocean and killing someone . . .*

But then another thought came to her, one she hated to admit. *Na all o' those vengeful thoughts were because o' the ocean. There's more bitterness sealed up in my heart than I realized. And if I'm na careful, even without the ocean's influence, it shall swallow me up until I'm just a shell o' who I want to be.*

A lot o' good I turned out to be fer Santiago. . . .

The man's face came to her mind. She imagined what he must be thinking, feeling. *I'm sure the commodore is na treating him well—who would when Santiago's suspected o' conspiracy to murder? And o' a king no less!*

"So, what happens now?" Briony asked.

Niall pursed his lips. "The way I see it, there are two options: you let me take charge o' this and you can still watch the town burn or we leave now and return when, and if, you can handle doing it on yer own. There's no way o' knowing how long that might take though. I'll leave it up to you."

Briony stared at him in surprise. *He's letting me make this decision even though vengeance was one o' his main reasons fer being in Everton in the first place?*

But neither o' those choices gives me what I want. Neither o' them will save Santiago, and both o' them mean I have to leave Everton. Forever.

She didn't say anything at first, and the longer she waited, the bigger Niall's scowl grew. She turned away so that she didn't have to look at his face, but she knew she would have to say something soon; otherwise, Niall would decide for her.

A voice whispered in her mind, *If you go with Niall, maybe life would na be so bad. Surely you can see how much he cares fer you. He may even love you. Santiago won' be able to do that once he learns what you are. Even if you save him, what then? He'll just leave you and you'll be left with a broken heart.*

Briony shook her head. *But maybe Santiago won' reject me. Maybe he can still love me anyway?*

That same voice returned. *Who are you trying to convince? You dinna believe that. You know yer a monster. At least Niall understands that and accepts you as you are.*

Misery settled around Briony's shoulders like a blanket, but rather than warming her up, it just left her feeling colder than before.

But then she caught sight of a lone fisherman out on the waves, and a third option came to her. It wouldn't solve all her problems, but it might buy her some time.

She smiled at Niall and added a low musical tone to her voice, "All right, Niall. Let's do this yer way. . . ."

***

"And where does that path lead, senhor?" The man's accent was distracting, but Laird Oliver did his best to ignore it and appear welcoming. It took a great deal of effort, though, since these men had overstayed their welcome as far as he was concerned.

Oliver glanced in the direction the man was pointing and bristled. "Up there? That goes to Drulea Cottage, the Fairborn wench's house. Why do you ask?"

The man said nothing in response. He simply smiled, but the expression only made him appear more menacing.

The laird shuffled back a few steps and cleared his throat. "I have several things to get to, you know, being the laird and all."

Laird Oliver hurried away, his gait like a waddling penguin's as his great stomach teetered from side to side. He only hoped the other man wouldn't follow, for there was no way he would be able to outrun the foreigner.

But the second man didn't turn, didn't speak, and didn't even notice the bumbling oaf's departure. Now that it was clear who was responsible for the freak storm, he had far more important things to think about.

He walked back toward the ship, nearly bumping into a clumsy fisherman on his way.

"Ah, sorry there, sir. Got so carried away with my latest catch that I did na even see you. 'Twas right lucky I did na drop them all over the dock, especially since—"

"Do better next time!" He didn't have time to deal with this, not when he had just discovered something so remarkable. He climbed aboard the waiting ship, already thinking of the new possibilities within his grasp.

Plans and Counterplans

Briony dashed through town like a squirrel, narrowly missing Vicar Peterson in her haste. She shouted apologies as she ran off to the sound of his irritated grumbling. Time was of the essence right then, and she couldn't stop for mere courtesy.

Briony had convinced Niall to wait for her at Drulea Cottage that evening while she retrieved her sealskin. At least, that was what she'd told him. In reality, the sealskin lay hidden beneath Briony's clothes, and she was actually on her way to the mad fisherman's house.

"Mr. McLaren!" She banged her fist against the door over and over when she arrived at his shack.

A few seconds later, she heard footsteps, and the fisherman opened the door. Mr. McLaren's hair was all in disarray, making it clear he'd been asleep. As soon as he recognized her, though, he seemed to come alive with energy. "Come in, lass. Quickly!"

Several fish lay in a tidy pile upon the table with knives and fishing gear laid out for cleaning. Briony shut the door and turned to the fisherman. "Mr. McLaren, you were right about everything. Niall wants to burn Everton tonight."

"He's back already? Where is he?" Mr. McLaren was picking up the closest knife and raising it above his head.

"That won' do any good, Mr. McLaren. He's far too powerful." Briony gently pried the knife from the man's hand and set it back down.

"Then you mean to just let him do this? I thought there

was more fight in you than that, lass."

Briony shook her head. "Nay, you misunderstand. There is a way to stop him, but na with violence—"

"Then yer going to leave with him? I won' let that happen." Vincent tried to grab the knife again, but Briony stepped between him and the table.

"Mr. McLaren, please just wait and let me explain. He's at my house right now. In human form. *Without his sealskin.*"

Vincent's eyes widened. "And you know where 'tis."

She nodded. "Aye, I do. And once you get it, we can use it as leverage."

The mad fisherman smirked, showing off the many gaps in his teeth. "'Tis about time someone had the advantage over him. Where do I need to go?"

***

Briony made her way back toward Drulea Cottage, her feet pattering against the dirt. She could see her home from here, standing alone at the crest of the hill, brilliant stars all around it. The candlelight shining within told her that Niall was still waiting for her. And with Mr. McLaren on his way to get the pelt, all Briony had to do now was stall long enough for the fisherman to reach the cottage.

If I'm right, Niall will give up this plan for vengeance once he realizes Mr. McLaren has the skin.

Sudden footfalls nearby made her turn in surprise. *Who would be out at this hour?*

"Senhorita Fairborn!" All the blood left Briony's face when she realized Captain Costa was approaching her. His body language didn't appear threatening, but she knew he was a threat all the same. She tried not to look alarmed as he stopped a few feet from her.

"Captain, 'tis late to be out. I'm on my way home right now." She pointed at the cottage and moved to leave, but the man's next words made her stop cold.

"Earlier today, when that storm came up over the ships . . . I saw you on the cliffs up there. I know you were the one who caused it."

"Wh-What are you talking about? Th-That does na make any sense, sir. How could I have done something like that? Yer mistaken."

Captain Costa scoffed and shook his head. He took a step closer. "*How* you did it is a mystery, but I know what I saw."

Briony backed up a few feet. *Can I make a run fer it? Would he catch me before I got to the cottage?*

She glanced up the hill again, but it seemed too risky. *'Tis better to talk my way out o' this and then leave casually.*

"Nay, that's na possible," she said.

"And last night at the Johnsmas gathering—"

Briony gasped. "That was N—" But then she caught herself and clamped her mouth shut before she could say more. *I should na mention Niall. 'Twould just complicate things further.*

The captain raised an eyebrow. "Hmm? That was *what?*"

"'Twas na me."

He sighed in frustration. "Deny it all you wish, but still listen to my proposition."

Briony said nothing and waited for him to continue.

"You want to save Senhor Mendes. I want to save Senhor Mendes. You have the ability—somehow—to create storms. If we work together, we can both achieve our goal."

"How?"

"Work your magic. Create chaos. While everyone is distracted, I can sneak onto the ship and free Senhor Mendes. I'll make sure my men and Senhorita Mendes are aboard the *São Nicolau*, and we'll leave before the commodore can stop us. We'll disappear forever, and Senhor Mendes will be safe."

'Tis a good plan, she admitted to herself, *better than any o' my ideas, except fer the "disappear forever" part.*

"*If* I can create storms as you claim, then why would I want yer help? Why na just rescue him myself?"

The captain rolled his eyes with a snort. "Don't try that on me. Why you need my help doesn't matter. All that matters is you do. If you could do it on your own, then you would have already. The man's life is in your hands. You can either help me, or you can let him return to Portugal for a mockery of a trial that will undoubtedly result in his execution."

Briony pursed her lips, not wanting to seem too desperate.

235

He needs me much more than I need him, but he's acting like he has the advantage. He may think he has some hold over me because he knows my secret, but I know a secret o' my own.

She gave Costa a hard look. "There's still something I dinna understand: Why do you want to help Mr. Mendes now when you tried to kill him before?"

The captain's face hardened until he resembled chiseled stone. All life fled from his eyes only to be replaced by something terrifying. And despite her powers, fear rose to the forefront of Briony's mind. *My stupid, impulsive mouth is about to cost me more than I want to give.*

Briony was just about to sing the man into submission, but then Costa gripped her throat. "My reasons for helping Senhor Mendes are none of your concern. I wanted to do this the nice way, but apparently that's not an option. Now, I don't know what kind of witchcraft you possess, but it's only thanks to my *generosity* that you're still alive right now. I can end that at any point I wish. Do you understand?"

Briony couldn't speak, couldn't breathe, could barely—

"*Do you understand?*"

She nodded even though she couldn't remember what he was talking about. The edges of her vision started to blur, and her eyes began to get heavier—

But then Briony was gasping on the ground. She took giant gulps of air and touched a hand to her burning throat. She looked up into the captain's baleful eyes and had to resist the urge to cower.

"If you tell anyone what you *think* you know, I'll make you regret it. You better get going now, and I'll get my men ready to leave. I expect to see that storm in three hours' time. Don't disappoint me, or you'll have missed your only opportunity to save Senhor Mendes."

Briony rose to her feet without another word, giving the captain one final glance before stumbling back to Drulea Cottage's door. Before she could open it, though, a voice grumbled, "I did na expect you to make me wait fer so long."

She spun toward the voice with a gasp and found Niall leaning against the cool stone wall outside. "Niall? Why are you out here?"

The selkie pushed himself up and strode over. His steps were heavy against the dirt, pounding like Briony's nervous heart. "Where have you been?"

His tone told her she better be truthful or else. *I dinna want to know what that "or else" might be, but there's no way I can tell him the truth. Na when I've been plotting to stop him with the very man who killed my father.*

"I told you I had to get my sealskin. 'Twas in a place where no one would look fer it." She went inside the cottage and ducked behind the door. "Wait a moment."

When she was certain Niall wasn't going to enter, she removed the sealskin from under her skirts and stepped back into the doorway. "Here 'tis."

But the joy she'd thought she would see on his face wasn't there; instead, all that shone forth was disappointment.

She pasted a smile on her face. "You dinna seem pleased, but I dinna understand why. Now we can leave this place and only return once I can control my powers."

Niall said nothing for a long time, neither entering the cottage nor moving to depart. Briony was about to speak again when his mouth suddenly twisted into a scowl and he shouted, "Do you think me daft? Stop pretending yer going anywhere with me. I know you dinna plan to leave. I saw where you went when you left."

"What are you—Did you follow me?" Briony checked behind him as surreptitiously as she could, but Mr. McLaren hadn't arrived yet. *Now would be a great time fer you to get here!*

Niall, who was so angry he hadn't noticed her looking past him, made short work of the space between them and stopped only when their faces were mere inches apart. Briony could feel the heat radiating off him just as her own body temperature seemed to drop ten degrees.

"Aye, I followed you. Right to that whalp's[25] house. There's no way yer skin would be there, na in a thousand years. Yer planning something with him, aren' you? What are you up to?"

Niall's hands were clenched into fists, and Briony felt sure

---

[25] Devil's.

that at any moment he would take a swing at her.

He knows where I went, but he must na have heard our conversation; otherwise, he'd be at the beach getting his sealskin already.

"Choose yer next words wisely. Dinna try any charms on me. 'Tis much harder to use them on another selkie unless there's already some trust between the two o' them, and right now I dinna have a grain[26] o' trust in you."

Briony's breath came in short bursts as her lungs struggled to take in enough air. *Niall is unpredictable, and if he directs his violence toward me . . . I dinna know how far away Mr. McLaren is either. Maybe Niall can still be reasoned with if I'm honest with him.*

"I—Yer right, I lied to you. It may na make sense, but the truth is, I dinna want to destroy the town. 'Tis still my home, and I've no wish to leave it."

A gleam of vicious triumph glimmered in the man's eyes at her confession, but just as quickly, sorrow flooded his face. He took a few steps back until he was outside again. "I suppose I already knew that deep down. My hopes and wishes were just clouding my eyes and stopping up my ears. 'Twas obvious when I saw how you looked at *him*. The way yer eyes followed him every time he was near . . . ," Niall trailed off with a huff.

"Niall, who are you—"

He shook his head. "A being so far beneath us, so weak and pathetic . . . How could you ever care fer someone like *Mr. Mendes?* But I should have expected it, with you growing up surrounded by these *humans* all the time. And with a mother who would have done anything to be one, too. That's even worse than being human vermin. She knew real power, yet she hid yer heritage from you, kept you from yer birthright so the two o' you could pretend to be something you weren'.

"But 'tis na like she's the first selkie to do that. I told you before that my mum and sister died from illness, but that's na what really happened. My stupid, naïve sister made the mistake o' falling fer a human and running away to be with him. Then, when we finally found her and my mum tried to get her to come home, they both ended up dying. All because Elene thought she could throw away who she truly was.

---

[26] A small amount.

238

"And now you've turned out the same way." Niall was practically spitting as his rage continued to escalate.

Briony could hear the lightning crackling outside as power welled up within Niall, power like what she'd experienced when she'd attacked the commodore's ship. But this was far stronger than what she'd held in her fingertips. She'd come close to losing all control, close to succumbing to the ocean's darkest urges, but this was beyond that.

"Niall, dinna do this."

But Niall didn't seem to hear her. The black swirls of his eyes were darker than ever, filled with a malice she'd never seen before.

"Please stop this!" Despite her fear, she forced her legs to propel her body forward until she stood right before him, toward the danger all her instincts told her to flee from. She grabbed his arm and shook it, trying to wake him from the trance he seemed to have fallen under.

Niall grasped her shoulder and shoved her away from the cottage, pushing her several feet down the hill, where she landed face-first in the dirt.

"The ocean gives life, and the ocean takes it away. And this town has taken advantage o' the ocean's generosity fer far too long."

Lightning was striking all around Niall now, over and over with fearsome heat. Briony flipped over and stood with shaky legs.

The monster before her still looked human, but Briony didn't know if he could even be reached now. She might be too late to stop him from achieving his horrendous purpose. *What have I done?*

He smiled. "Everton's day o' reckoning has arrived."

Over the Edge

Screams drew Briony from her state of shock. They pierced the darkness as terribly as the lightning hitting the ground.

Except 'tis na just hitting the ground anymore! She gasped at the sight of flames rising from the town below. Her neighbors were flying through the streets in a panic, and Briony could see why: the tailor shop and the McGuffs' house were alight.

Fergus! Briony forgot about Niall and charged down the hill with nary a care for her own well-being. All she could focus on was the thought of the little boy potentially trapped and scared. She reached the burning house and stepped inside. "Hello! Fergus? Is anyone in here?"

Most of the fire was above her, hungrily swallowing the thatched roof. The smoke was so thick within the confined space that Briony struggled to breathe. Only a few licks of flame had reached the floor, and they were quickly spreading toward the McGuffs' table.

"H-Here," came a voice. Whoever it belonged to was too hoarse to identify. Briony covered her mouth with her hand and made her way forward, edging around the table.

Briony hastened into the back bedroom, her eyes flicking between the open window and two beds before landing on their target, Penelope McGuff. The woman was on the ground, facedown. The rest of the family was nowhere in sight.

"Mistress McGuff!" Briony dropped to her knees and took the woman's hand, but Penelope didn't stir.

CRASH!

Briony turned—The roof had collapsed, and the fire was stretching its fingers into the rest of the house. She clasped both of Mrs. McGuff's wrists and dragged her into the main room. Briony's muscles strained and protested from the effort, but she refused to give up. She only had to make it a few more feet to reach the doorway. *Just a wee bit farther!*

The room blazed hotter as the flames found more material to devour. Briony cried out with her mind for rain, but the clouds above the town ignored her; they had a different master now, and they wouldn't easily switch allegiances.

"Help!" Briony didn't know if she could make it the rest of the way. She could barely handle Penelope's dead weight, and with the smoke in Briony's lungs, her body could give out at any time.

Briony couldn't tell if she was even going the right way anymore, but she knew she had to trust her gut and keep moving; otherwise, both of them were going to die.

With a strength she hadn't known she possessed, Briony plunged through the smoke, her feet going one step at a time until, suddenly, she saw it: outside. She almost cried in relief as she brought Penelope over the threshold and onto the dirt path. Briony pulled the unconscious woman a few more feet before falling to the ground next to her. She breathed in great lungfuls of clean air, grateful to be alive.

But is Mistress McGuff all right? Briony turned to the woman and checked her wrist. She smiled in relief when she felt a strong pulse.

But then more screams stole away her momentary happiness. Briony may have saved one woman, but the storm was still raging, and people were still in danger. She spotted Matthew Levins putting out the fire at the tailor shop with Daniel Calhoun, but no one had even tried to save the McGuffs' house yet.

And where are Mr. McGuff and the bairns?

I'm na sure I can go back in there and make it out again. I need to put out this fire before the entire house burns down.

She turned her eyes up to the sparking sky with determination. All she had to do was wrestle away a wee bit of Niall's control.

Briony glanced toward the selkie on the hill and was glad to see his attention aimed at the market. *This is my chance.*

She remembered the water's weakness for her voice and called out as loudly as she could:

"I heard a mother lull her bairn,
And aye she rocked, and aye she sang.
She took so hard upon the verse,
that the heart within her body rang."

A tremor of power shot through her, a tiny echo of what she'd felt last time. It was working.

"O, cradle row, and cradle go,
and aye sleep well, my bairn within;
I ken not who thy father is,
nor yet the land that he dwells in."[27]

Briony urged the clouds to exchange their angry bolts for a calm rain, a gentle but consistent flow that would douse the fire ravaging the McGuffs' home. The clouds directly above the cottage obeyed, though most of the sky was still following Niall's lead.

"Wh-Where am I? Are the bairns safe?"

Briony turned to Mrs. McGuff, glad to see the woman had woken. "Mistress McGuff, 'tis Briony Fairborn. We're safe, but I did na see Fergus or Hannah in the house."

"I got them out the window and told them to run as fast as they could toward the tavern. Donal was meeting up with some friends there. I tried to follow them, but I—Briony Fairborn?" The woman's eyes widened as she realized whom she was talking to. "Did you . . . save me?"

The woman's disbelief was almost humorous, though it hurt Briony's heart at the same time. She set her mouth in a firm line and said to the older woman, "I know 'tis hard to believe someone like me would do that, but aye, I did. And I would do it again fer anyone in this town, even if only a few

---

[27] An Orcadian ballad called "The Great Selkie o' Sule Skerry."

243

would do it fer me."

Briony rose to her feet, confident that Mrs. McGuff and her home would both be all right now. She turned to leave when she felt a hand on her arm.

She looked back into Penelope's big brown eyes, shocked at the softness within them. "Briony, I-I'm sorry."

Briony didn't need to be told what the woman was referring to; Mrs. McGuff's tone and countenance made it clear she was apologizing for much more than just this moment.

Many spiteful words threatened to spew from Briony's mouth, but she held her tongue. She knew Mrs. McGuff was hoping for forgiveness, but silence was all Briony could give.

Now is na the time fer words anyway. Na when the rest o' the town still needs me.

Briony proceeded down the hill, hoping against hope that Fergus and Hannah were safe with their father. She wanted to go to the tavern, but the inn was nearer and she had to check on Adaira. *If anything has happened to her, I'm going to kill Niall myself, sealskin or no sealskin.*

When Briony got to Everton Inn, she was glad to find Adaira and William huddled at the entrance, shaken up but unharmed. Adaira shouted when she spotted her friend, "Briony! Come inside, quickly. 'Tis too dangerous out there."

She grasped Briony's hands and pulled her under cover, nearly wrenching Briony's arm from the socket. Adaira drew her into an embrace and sobbed upon her shoulder. At first, Briony thought the woman was just relieved to see her, but the way Adaira clung to her made Briony wonder—

"Adaira, where's Mr. Burgess?"

But the innkeeper's daughter was too hysterical to say anything; she just continued to blubber and lean on Briony as if she lacked the strength to stand on her own. The midwife looked instead to William to see how he was faring and was glad the boy didn't appear nearly as upset.

"He's down at the tailor shop, trying to put out the fire," William explained.

"Then why . . ." Briony grabbed Adaira's shoulders and leaned her back far enough to look her in the eye. "Adaira, *what happened?*"

Adaira tried to pull herself together, but it was only between sniffles that she was able to say, "M-My . . . father. He's gone. He's just gone."

"What? How?"

Adaira shook her head, too distressed to say more. She fell back into Briony's arms and began to moan.

A sudden tap on her arm drew Briony's focus back to young William. "I saw what happened, Mistress Briony. 'Twas the scariest thing I've ever seen. Mr. Stubbins was coming up to the inn, and this giant bolt o' lightning just fell right on him. Da' and I got him to his bed, but he was already dead by the time we put him down. I did na realize how powerful someo—*something* could be."

Adaira wailed louder at the child's words, making William clam up as he realized how insensitive he sounded. At least Briony hoped he realized it after she glared at him with a look sour enough to curdle milk.

Briony slowly pushed Adaira back into a normal standing position and stepped out of her friend's embrace. "I'm so glad yer both all right. I'm really sorry about yer father, Adaira, and I know you'll hate me fer this, but I can' stay."

Adaira looked at Briony as if the words weren't registering in her brain. "What?"

Briony sighed before turning to William and patting the boy's shoulder. "Look after her until yer father gets back, aye?"

William puffed out his chest and frowned indignantly. "That's what I was doing. Da' told me na to let her out o' my sight. Right before he kissed her . . . blech!"

William's disgust amid such dire circumstances made Briony chuckle. "Yer doing a splendid job, William. Just keep at it, then."

William grinned at her and nodded. He clasped Adaira's hand with all the love of a boy looking after his mother, and Briony saw Adaira's face brighten a little. *If we get out o' this alive, 'twill na be long before they're truly family.*

Briony was just about to run back out into the rain when Adaira came to her senses and grabbed Briony with her free hand. "Briony Fairborn, you better na be thinking o' going back out there in this. There's something unnatural about this storm. If you leave now, I may never see you again."

Briony stared at her sweet longtime friend, fully aware of how accurate those words were. "Yer absolutely right. This storm is as far from natural as it could get, but if I dinna go, more people are going to get hurt."

Adaira opened her mouth, and Briony could already see the question in the woman's eyes, but Briony spoke again. "I'll explain more later, but I have to go *now*."

Adaira still seemed confused, but trust won out over her fear, so she nodded and released her friend's hand.

Briony turned and hurried out before she could change her mind. *'Twould be far too easy to just stay at the inn, where things feel safe, but the truth is nowhere is safe right now. I can' know if Niall will stop anytime soon. If he keeps getting angrier, he might kill everyone before he's satisfied.*

The only way to end this is to find Mr. McLaren and get that sealskin.

The Wounds That Never Heal

Briony was passing the Calhouns' house when she heard, "Briony! I could use yer assistance over here!"

She stopped in her tracks and turned to find Dr. Sherwin and Steven McLaren standing at the church entrance. She gasped at the sight of the old man's face, for it was covered in bright-red burns.

Briony deliberated between going over and continuing down to the beach, but then she saw the panicked look in the doctor's eyes.

Steven McLaren grumbled under his breath as she approached, but she ignored him and asked, "What can I do?"

"Finish bandaging up Mr. McLaren here while I see to the others. Take this," Dr. Sherwin ordered, handing her some wrappings. He picked up his bag and went deeper into the church, toward Matthew Levins, who was sporting similar burns along his arms.

Many other fire victims were sitting within, either crying or praying as lightning continued to strike outside. The commodore and many of his men were there too, filling the space with their enormous numbers. Briony even spotted Laird Oliver with his wife. Neither appeared injured, but the pompous looks that usually graced their faces were absent. In fact, everyone's face wore the same expression of terror, and

Briony's part in all this made her guilt all the more intense.

Steven McLaren grimaced when Briony began covering his wounds, but he didn't speak to her; even when she adjusted a bandage and she was certain it must have hurt, the only sound that came from his lips was a faint hiss.

"Mr. McLaren, do you know where yer son is?" Briony asked as she finished.

"*Why* do you want to know?" The man's voice was so acerbic that Briony didn't pity him when he fell into a coughing fit shortly afterward.

Briony put her hands on her hips. "He was supposed to meet me a while ago, but I have na seen him. Is he in the market or down at his boat? 'Tis very important that I find him. *Fast*. If you know where he is, tell me."

The old man raised his eyebrows in surprise at her tone, but then he winced in pain. "Tam was with me when the tailor shop caught on fire and went running to help put it out, same as the other men."

Briony rolled her eyes. "Na him. I've no reason to see Tam. I meant Vincent."

"Why would I know where that madman is, you witch?"

Briony clenched her fists and opened her mouth to shout insults of her own, but then she heard, "She's no witch, you old fool, and she deserves better than you calling her one."

Briony's mouth dropped open as Dr. Sherwin marched forward and looked Steven McLaren in the eye. "Briony Fairborn has done more fer this town than you ever have, and she has put up with far more than she should have. If you think talking to her like that is the best way to repay her, then you best start looking fer another doctor. I hear the one in Hollandstoun is decent. And that goes fer all the rest o' you, too."

Dr. Sherwin's eyes swept over the crowd, many of whom had been listening in. The villagers were so surprised that they didn't dare speak and looked away as if they hadn't been staring. Briony smirked at the bewildered faces of the Olivers as they, too, pretended they hadn't heard the doctor's words.

Steven McLaren was in such shock that when he tried to reply, all that came out of his mouth was gibberish. The doctor turned back and resumed glaring at the old man until Steven scuttled off to his friends, no doubt to gossip about what had just happened.

Dr. Sherwin turned to Briony, who was still gaping and trying to think of how to express her gratitude. "Briony, are you leaving? I still need you. Almost everyone is too frightened to be o' any use. Besides the commodore's surgeon, yer the only levelheaded person here."

She shook her head sadly. "I-I'm sorry, Doctor, but I have to find Vincent McLaren. He's the only one who can help me fix this."

"Vincent McLaren? I can' say I've seen him, and even if I had, I dinna see how he could help you—Fix this? What are you talking about? 'Tis a frightful storm, aye, but 'tis na something you can fix. . . ." Dr. Sherwin trailed off as he spoke, and a curious look came onto his face. "Does this have something to do with why yer temperature was so high the day before Johnsmas?"

Briony let out a humorless chuckle. *Ewan Sherwin may be the sharpest man in all o' Everton.*

"It almost sounds like yer implying something beyond science is behind this," Briony said with a raised brow.

The doctor narrowed his eyes. "Dinna evade the question, Briony."

She sighed. "To tell you the truth, 'tis my fault fer all this. If I'd been certain o' my feelings sooner, maybe this would na be happening now."

"You do realize I have no idea what yer talking about, aye?"

"Just trust me. I'm o' far better use to you out there than I am in here."

The doctor looked like he wanted to ask more, but he held back and replied, "Then I wish you all the luck in the world. Be careful."

Briony smiled and—

"Briony, is that him out there?" Dr. Sherwin pointed with a look of alarm. "What's he holding?"

Briony followed the doctor's finger and almost wept with relief at the sight of the mad fisherman racing through the street. *He has the skin! We're saved!*

"Mr. McLaren, over here!" Briony waved her arms in the air.

Vincent turned toward her voice, and when he saw who it was, he grinned and held up the pelt triumphantly.

Briony stepped out into the rain to meet him, Dr. Sherwin on her heels, but then—

CRACK!

The sound was so loud it was deafening. At the same time, a flash of light flew across Briony's vision just for an instant before it was gone. And yet, despite its evanescence, there was no way it could have gone unnoticed.

For what it left behind could not be undone.

Briony and Vincent locked eyes—*Did he get struck?* But then Briony heard the sound of a fall from behind. She spun around and gasped, the truth hitting her as painfully as a real lightning bolt. There, at her feet, lay Dr. Sherwin.

The man was facedown, his clothes scorched in several places as steam rose from his body. Briony knelt and turned him over, praying against all odds that he was somehow all right.

"Dr. Sherwin? *Ewan?* Wake up!" The man's eyes were closed as though he was sleeping, but Briony knew better. A red leaf-like pattern had appeared on the doctor's skin, starting at the right side of his neck and snaking under his clothes until it reemerged at the base of his elbow. The lightning had gone directly through him.

Briony shook Dr. Sherwin's shoulders as hard as she could, screaming all the while. "*Ewan Sherwin, wake up!* Yer the town doctor. We need you too much fer you to leave like this."

She felt a gentle hand on her shoulder, but she jerked her head toward the intruder with a snarl. Vincent McLaren flinched back, letting his hand drop to his side.

"*What?* Why aren' you helping me wake him? He has to wake up. He has to. . . ." But she looked back down at the immobile form before her, a mere shell of the man she'd grown so fond of in recent weeks. "He can' be gone. . . ."

Briony dissolved into great, heaving sobs that carried over the booming storm. A flood of rain descended on her head, and the lightning bolts started fading around her. The sky seemed to weep with her as she mourned this loss, one that hurt more deeply than she would have expected. Ewan Sherwin had always been very reserved, and there was much about him he'd never shared with her, but Briony had learned enough to know she would miss him dearly. Others in the village would grieve the death of a great doctor, but she cried for a lost friend.

She remembered what he had just declared inside the church, and at that moment, she made a promise, a promise to Dr. Sherwin and a promise to herself.

No matter what, I will no longer let myself be mistreated. I'm na going to just accept the taunts and judgment in silence anymore. As Dr. Sherwin stood up fer me, now I'm going to stand up fer myself.

Again, Mr. McLaren's hand found its way to her shoulder, but this time, Briony accepted it gratefully. It helped her recognize that even in the wake of such tragedy, she wasn't alone. *Aye, there are still others who support me and will help me get through this. That is, if I live long enough to do so.*

She looked up through her tears at the cause of her heartache, but he was so far up the hill that she could barely see him. A mess of black hair and rage, Niall's silhouette reminded Briony of the nightmares she'd been plagued with since her mother's death. All of them had included the ocean, but many had also contained a mysterious shadowy figure that brought about Bethany's death. Briony had often thought it was just a manifestation of her fears, but the strong similarities between Niall and the nightmare man were unmistakable.

Briony shook her head at her thoughts. *This is no nightmare. This is real life, and Niall is na invulnerable. He may na be human, but he has a weakness. One that could save the lives o' everyone else here.*

With a surge of renewed determination, Briony looked to the sealskin still clutched in Mr. McLaren's fingers. "You got it."

"Aye, I did. Had to get around those awful foreigners. They wanted to know what I was holding and nearly forced me onto their ship. But then one o' them got . . . ," he trailed off and looked pointedly at the doctor. "It gave me enough time to run before they'd noticed I'd gone. But I was na fast enough. If

251

I'd just gotten here sooner—"

Briony noticed the sadness in his voice and took the man's hand from her shoulder before giving it a gentle squeeze. "This is na yer doing."

Mr. McLaren frowned. "I hope yer na implying 'tis yers."

Briony said nothing for a long moment and just stared at the still-warm corpse in front of her. "Regardless o' who's to blame, one thing is certain: *this ends now.*"

She focused her energy on the storm above her, calling to it with her mind. Using all her willpower, she pushed the darkness and rain away from her in all directions, creating a small circle of blue sky that extended from the church up to Everton Inn. She tried to push it farther, but Niall's power was too great. *This is as far as I can go. Fer now.*

Mr. McLaren gazed up in amazement. "What are you doing?"

Briony smiled. "Bringing attention to myself." She grabbed the sealskin from the fisherman's hand before he could react and dashed toward the hill. Toward Drulea Cottage, the only home she'd ever known, and toward Niall Moreland, the man who'd told her who she really was.

Except he's na a man at all. He's a selkie. A selkie I summoned here and even considered marrying. And one who may very well kill me if I dinna stop him.

A Killer

Just before she crested the hill, Briony hesitated. She looked at the sealskin in her hand as she considered what she was about to do with it. *I can'. I can' use something so precious to manipulate someone, na even when that someone is Niall.*

Briony slipped the pelt beneath her clothes, right next to her own, as she decided she would only use it if absolutely necessary. *Maybe he can still be saved.*

She took those last few steps purposefully, mentally preparing herself for whatever Niall might do—

"Ah, there you are. Back fer more fun?" Niall had spotted her instantly, though he made no move to approach her from his position a few feet away. His hands were still raised, funneling tremendous amounts of energy into the clouds above.

Briony tried to make her voice as even and calm as possible as she said, "Niall, yer killing people. I can' let that continue."

Niall snorted. "And you think you can stop me? I noticed yer attempts to get rid o' my storm. I knew you'd try something like that, but did you honestly think yer tainted blood could compete with mine? The water may hear yer call, but it shall always obey mine first."

She'd been tormented for her lineage all her life, but for some reason, Niall's words still stung. *I thought knowing my selkie nature would finally make me feel like I belonged somewhere, but now the only selkie I know is throwing those hopes back in my face.*

253

Briony felt that very blood he'd been mocking begin to boil as hurt and anger swirled within her. Heat pulsed beneath her fingertips, and power beckoned from the sky above. *Would the water truly obey Niall first? Or would my own rage be enough to take control?*

Briony reached upward with her mind, reached out to touch the storm—

But then her mother's face appeared among her thoughts. All those moments when Bethany had smiled as she held a newborn babe. All those moments when she'd encouraged Briony to keep moving forward, to do everything she could to foster better relationships. All those moments when she'd urged Briony to forgive, even when it didn't make any sense.

The memories brought a sense of peace to Briony's heart, reminding her of what was truly important in that moment— not her anger, not even justice for all the offenses against her.

Nay, 'tis the people. And now I'm the only one who can save them. Even if most o' them would na bother to save me, I can make the better choice. I can choose to do what's right.

'Tis what Mum would have wanted. 'Tis what Dr. Sherwin would have wanted. And despite all my neighbors' failings, 'tis what I want, too.

Briony lifted her chin and glowered at the man. "I know what yer trying to do, Niall, but this time, I'm na going to lose control. Na with all these people's lives at stake."

Niall raised a surprised eyebrow, lowering his arms as he took in her words. The storm didn't dissipate, but now that he wasn't adding more fuel, the lightning started to die down.

Niall pointed to the houses below them. "Those worthless worms deserve far worse than anything I've done so far. This storm is only the start."

"I *know* there's good in you. You dinna have to do this."

"Dinna be so naïve, Briony. Do you think this is the first time I've taken a life?"

Briony's eyes widened. "What do you mean?"

Niall smiled, stretching his lips back from his perfectly white teeth. "We selkies learn how to harness our powers from an early age. Why do you think Everton has so many storms? Did you think it mere chance how yer beloved merchant's ship arrived here?"

All the color left Briony's cheeks, and a gasp filled the air. "Are you saying *you* made the storm that night?"

Niall scoffed. "Nay, if it had been me, that ship would never have made it to the dock. You can be sure o' that. But after hearing the captain talk about how the storm came out o' nowhere, I knew 'twas the work o' a selkie. We're all around, after all. Maybe even closer than you think. And killing humans can be so . . . *entertaining*."

Briony shook her head, not believing the words coming out of the man's mouth.

"Dinna look at me like that. If I had na stopped you before, you would have already wreaked havoc upon the very people yer trying to save. You have the same desires in yer heart as I do, and fer good reason. After all, that boy almost killed you, and if I had na stopped him, he might have tried again."

"What are you—Alastair Oliver? *You killed Alastair?* Nay, that can't be right. He died eleven years ago. He . . ."

"Drowned? Ah, I take it back, Briony. Yer na naïve. Yer just stupid." Niall threw back his head with a laugh.

"But you would have still been a bairn. . . . ," Briony whispered.

"'Twas na so hard. The boy thought himself invincible. I simply pretended to be a poor wounded seal lying on the sand. He must have thought I was an easy target, fer he wasted no time in coming at me with a stick.

"But I was na nearly as helpless as he thought, and though I was a bairn, my wish fer revenge gave me all the strength I needed. When I flopped into the water, he chased after me as I knew he would. And once he was waist-deep, I simply took him fer a ride. After all, 'tis na everyone who gets to see just how deep the ocean truly is."

Briony felt her eyes get misty. *If this is what Niall was capable o' as a child . . .*

Niall growled. "Dinna tell me yer crying over him. It almost takes the fun out o' killing you. *Almost.*"

He raised his right hand again and summoned more lightning, so quickly that Briony barely had enough time to lift her own hands to protect herself. She shut her eyes out of reflex, crying out with her mind for the storm to spare her.

Light flashed behind her eyelids, and thunder crashed in her ears as her body started to heat up. *This is the end.*

Santiago's face came to her mind—*I hope Costa got him out safely. I never even told him how I feel. And now I'll never get another chance.*

But a few seconds passed.

And then a few more.

Briony could still feel her heart beating in her chest. *What in the world—*

A great snarl made her open her eyes. Niall loomed over her, his expression equal parts wrath and confusion. "How are you still breathing? *Why will you na die?*"

Again, Niall summoned the lightning, bringing forth several bolts that scorched the earth around her, but none of them touched her.

Briony looked up at her hands as she, too, tried to figure out what was happening. And then, as another strike came, she watched it descend from the clouds and bend away just as it was about to reach her, right before landing a few inches from her feet.

The storm obeyed me. Even after Niall told it to destroy me, it still preserved my life.

Niall hissed, "I suppose yer a wee bit stronger than I thought. No matter. You may be able to stop a few bolts, but can you handle the full extent o' my abilities?"

Suddenly, the lightning's intensity doubled. Bolts rained down from the heavens, and she could feel the heat as they singed her clothes. Such raw power was almost more than she could bear.

Briony continued to cry out to the clouds, begging them not to harm her, but she could feel her influence starting to wane. *I can' keep this up.*

"N-Niall, please."

But Niall said nothing. He just continued his assault, forcing Briony to keep her hands above her head. She could feel her arms starting to tremble beneath the strain.

"Hey! Over here, selkie," a new voice shouted over the roaring thunder.

Briony and Niall both turned in shock to see who would dare to get involved in this, someone who knew what Niall was yet still had the gall to provoke him.

A mad, middle-aged, almost toothless fisherman stood twenty feet from them. He smiled at Niall as if he hadn't a care in the world. "Selkie, I thought you wanted revenge fer what happened twelve years ago. Why do you attack one o' yer own . . . when the real killer is here before you?"

Farewell, Aveiro

The sound of water roused Santiago from his dozing, bringing him back to cold, hard reality. He glanced around the brig with a sigh. He'd been dreaming of better times, of green fields and white beaches next to a beautiful midwife he'd wished to call his own.

But the pain throughout his body made true rest nearly impossible; the commodore's interrogation techniques had made sure of that. Santiago suspected he had a broken rib or two, and every time he turned his head, the bruises along his neck screamed in protest.

It was all the worse because he couldn't give Cardoso the answers he sought. *It would be so much simpler if I really had been the one who took the carriage that night. If I'd been the one who tried to murder the king and put the duke on the throne.*

But it wasn't me.

It was . . . someone else. Someone who was very clear about what will happen if I don't pretend to be guilty. And I can't let Lucia pay that price.

Has it truly only been a few months?

He longed for the simplicity of the previous year. Everything about his life in Aveiro seemed so far away that it was almost as if his memories belonged to someone else. *If I'd known what was going to happen that night when Lucia came to me, perhaps things would be different now.*

***

"Brother, I need your help," Lucia cried as she hurried to his side.

Santiago rolled his eyes, maintaining his position on the balcony rather than turning. *I wonder what "urgent" request I get to hear about this time. It's probably for money to buy some trifle that all her friends have. Her weakness for fashion trends is going to empty my pockets at this rate.*

Lucia nudged her shoulder against his. "Well?"

"Well, *what?*" Santiago couldn't keep the bite out of his voice. He'd only just returned from his latest trip and was about to leave again in the morning. *This is my one opportunity to relax. I don't want to spend the evening listening to silly whims.*

Lucia pursed her lips into a pout and twirled a strand of blond hair between her fingers. "Don't you care what I need help with?"

Santiago groaned. "Just tell me already so I know how much money you need. I'm tired; I'm not in the mood for games."

Lucia gasped, and Santiago could already see wetness forming in her eyes, but he couldn't bring himself to care.

"You've been gone for months. If that's the kind of response I get when I ask for help, then forget I asked." She turned and strutted back toward the ballroom.

But after a few seconds, when it had become apparent Santiago wasn't going to react, Lucia spun around and shouted, "I'll just get someone else to help me!"

Santiago sighed as Lucia marched back to the party. *She's right. Lucia is the only family I have left, and we barely see each other anymore. The least I can do is make her happy while we're together.*

But lately, all he seemed capable of doing was pushing her farther away. No matter how much he tried to be the loving brother she deserved, he just felt so despondent every time he came home.

Truth be told, the word *home* no longer sounded right to his ears now that his parents were gone. The Mendes house, so big and empty despite Lucia's frequent parties, felt more like a mausoleum than a home anymore, and ever since his parents' accident three years before, Santiago spent as little time there as possible.

Lucia had dealt with her grief by surrounding herself with the city's numerous diversions, while Santiago had simply run away from everything that might make him remember the past.

I'm sure Mamãe[28] and Pai[29] would be scandalized if they knew I was a merchant now. They always wanted me to accept my birthright, and now that they're gone, I'm further from that than ever before.

I hope Andreas is having a more enjoyable evening. Santiago glanced into the ballroom and was glad to see his friend smiling and laughing with his sister as they danced.

Lucia has grown very close with him since our parents died. I wonder if there might be something more between them soon. Andreas may be a commoner, but he's one of the best men I know.

Perhaps, just perhaps, I can find happiness again, too. The joyous atmosphere of the room and the smile on his sister's face made Santiago consider the possibility.

Maybe I can meet someone—

"Open the door! By order of His Majesty the King!" The harsh shout from the street below wrenched Santiago out of his reverie.

The sounds of merriment abruptly ended within the house, and nervous whispers took their place. Santiago peered down from the balcony at the ten quadrilheiros[30] standing right outside the door. He'd never seen that many gathered in one place since they typically stayed in Lisbon near the king. *What could be so important for them to show up here?*

"Santiago!"

The man turned to find his sister standing before him, a nervous Andreas at her side. Her entire body was trembling as though she would fall apart at a moment's notice, and Santiago observed the way she gripped Andreas's arm with such intensity that her knuckles had turned white.

"Are they going to arrest us? Why are the quadrilheiros here?" Lucia whimpered in a low voice, her breaths so shallow she could barely get the words out.

Santiago reached out and patted her shoulder. "Calm

---

[28] Mom.
[29] Dad.
[30] Portuguese police officers of the day.

down, sister. We've done nothing wrong. I'm sure they just need information for something—"

The door creaked open below them, and Santiago motioned for Lucia to be silent.

"What's the meaning of this?" Tomas Cabral, head servant for the Mendes family, demanded. Santiago smirked at the older gentleman's steady voice; it was difficult for anyone to intimidate Tomas.

"Are Senhor and Senhorita Mendes in?"

Rather than answering, the man said, "Why have you come?"

The leading officer growled and said, "Senhor Mendes is to be taken into custody and his sister brought in for questioning."

Lucia gasped. "What?"

"Shh," Santiago insisted.

"You're arresting Senhor Mendes? On what grounds?" Tomas didn't sound nearly as confident anymore, but Santiago was proud of the man for not allowing the quadrilheiros into the house yet.

"Treason. Now, stand aside!" A sudden slam indicated that Tomas had been shoved into the door, and the quadrilheiros' stomping feet told Santiago they'd forced their way inside.

Andreas gripped his friend's arm. "Let's get out of here!"

Santiago frowned. "But I've done nothing wrong. Let's just talk to them. If we run away, that will just make us look guilty."

The other man shook his head sadly. "You put too much faith in the courts. They want you for treason. Remember what happened to Ferreira and Policarpio? They were tortured. You may be all right with that, but they want your sister, too. Do you think she'll be spared simply because she's a woman?"

Santiago glanced at his sister, whose face was paler than he'd ever seen, and before he knew it, his protective instincts kicked in. He pointed to the street below—a jump from there would hurt, but it was their best chance of escape. "Andreas, take her to the *São Nicolau* and get as far from here as you can. The men are already aboard, so you won't need to wait for morning—"

"I'm not leaving without you," Lucia shouted, her voice strong despite her fear. "We've already lost our parents. We can't lose each other now, too."

She stared hard at him until Santiago couldn't bear to look anymore. He turned away and nodded his assent. "Fine. Let's get going, then."

The footsteps were getting closer now. Andreas wasted no time in lunging off the side of the balcony. One loud thump later and he was encouraging Lucia to do the same.

She climbed over the side and looked down. "I can't do it!"

But then the quadrilheiros were entering the ballroom—it wouldn't be long before they were spotted.

"Sister, you have to. It's the only way." Santiago threw his leg over the side of the balcony and positioned himself next to her.

"Hey! Stop!"

Santiago turned and saw all ten quadrilheiros sprinting toward them.

"On three, Lucia. One. Two. *Three!*" Santiago leaped, praying his sister would do the same. He rolled to break his fall, but the landing still made his bones ache.

"Lucia? Are you all righ—" Santiago broke off when he spotted Lucia on the ground with Andreas squished beneath her. She'd had a much softer landing than he had. The poor man must have tried to catch her.

Santiago grabbed Lucia and pulled her to her feet. "Come on, you two. There's no time to lose."

Andreas, looking a little dazed, accepted Santiago's hand and also rose to his feet.

"Stop! By order of the king!"

It looked like the quadrilheiros were about to jump down after them, so Santiago ushered Andreas and Lucia toward the docks. He had no idea where they'd go once they boarded the *São Nicolau*, but anywhere seemed safer than here.

The lateness of the hour, together with the moonless sky, made it easy for the trio to sneak to the *São Nicolau*, completely unnoticed. Santiago boarded the ship with a troubled mind and a heavy heart, reluctant to depart under such dire circumstances.

Fleeing now will lead to disaster, I'm certain of it. I'm all but declaring my own guilt when I don't even know why I'm being charged.

Santiago stewed over the possible reasons anyone would suspect him of treason. *I've always been a loyal subject to the crown, and despite my . . . distaste for the prime minister,[31] I've always done my best to uphold the law.*

Then he remembered what Andreas had said about the men accused of treason. Santiago knew well whom he had been referring to since everyone in Portugal knew some version of what had happened to Antonio Alvarez Ferreira and Joseph Policarpio. Everyone knew what they had done for the Távora family, and everyone knew it had ultimately cost them everything.

The Távoras had been one of the most powerful noble families in all of Portugal, but that was before the prime minister accused them of treason. Even the children were imprisoned and would have suffered a cruel fate if Her Majesty the Queen hadn't intervened. Santiago had been astounded to hear of the prime minister's merciless intentions. *Then again, drastic measures were needed. After all, someone had tried to kill the king.*

Through word of mouth, Santiago had learned that His Majesty's life had almost been taken the September before on his way home from a rendezvous with one of his mistresses.

No one should have known where he was, due to the nature of the visit and the fact that he was riding in an unmarked carriage. Yet somehow someone did, and armed men shot at His Majesty and his driver. Some people said two men, while others said three were involved in the attack. The would-be assassins only managed to shoot His Majesty in the arm, and once the king returned to his residence in Ajuda, the prime minister wasted no time in starting an investigation.

Shortly thereafter, Ferreira and Policarpio were found and hanged for attacking His Majesty's carriage. But rumors slithered from ear to ear that one of the men had only been hanged in effigy, that he'd somehow escaped the night before he was to die.

---

[31] Sebastião José de Carvalho e Melo, 1st Marquis of Pombal, was the prime minister at the time.

In the weeks following, the Távora family was arrested, supposedly for being behind the whole affair. The assassins had confessed that they were following the family's orders, with the goal of putting the Duke of Aveiro on the throne.

And on January 12, the prime minister had had the Távora family executed.

Whether the Távoras really did it or not, though, I can't be sure. The prime minister has always hated them, so it would be easy to blame an assassination attempt on them to get them out of the way.

There's nothing to openly connect me or Lucia to the family. Reminding himself of this provided a little comfort, but he couldn't quite quell the nervous jump of his pulse. Accusations of treason were few and far between.

If the quadrilheiros think I'm part of the conspiracy, there's no way I'll get a fair trial; my fate will be decided from the moment I'm arrested.

"Where are we going?" Lucia asked in Santiago's ear, piercing through the man's concentration as skillfully as an assassin attacking a target.

Santiago jerked back in surprise, his calm facade slipping away for a moment to reveal the anxiety lying beneath. "We were scheduled to leave for England, but I doubt that would be safe now. We'll have to think of an alternative. . . . Andreas, do you have any ideas?"

His friend nodded, solemn and confident. *If he's only pretending to be composed like me, he's doing a much better job of it.*

"Norway."

Santiago looked at the man curiously. *The São Nicolau has never been to Norway before, and as far as I know, neither has Andreas.*

"What could *possibly* be there? Isn't it absolutely frigid?" he asked the captain.

"In the winter, yes, but by the time we arrive, summer will have already started. I have a friend there who can help us. We'll find a place to stay, somewhere far from the reach of His Majesty and the prime minister."

"And we'll come back when it's safe, right? We will come back home?" Lucia asked, touching Andreas's arm.

The simple action reminded him of how young his sister still was, just shy of seventeen.

"Of course we'll return. We'll need to give you a proper

birthday celebration with all your friends, won't we?" Santiago gave Lucia his most encouraging smile, hoping he could put her mind at ease.

"I don't mind being away on my birthday, so long as I'm with people I care about." Lucia's eyes flickered between Santiago and Andreas, making Andreas blush.

Santiago coughed to dispel the awkward feeling that had settled over the group. "Well, let's get the sailors up, then, so we can leave."

"Y-Yes, let me do that," Andreas said and hurried off to rouse the crew.

Santiago took one last look at Aveiro, a beautiful city of canals and boats, wondering when—if he would see it again. *I've left the city so many times, but it never felt like this before.*

"What's going on?" a voice asked. Santiago spun around and watched as the crew made its way onto the deck. Several of them appeared to have just woken up.

"Mr. Mendes, we weren't expecting you until the morning. Is something going on?" the same voice spoke again, though this time, Santiago recognized the speaker as the ship's newest recruit. He racked his brain for the man's name, but nothing came to him.

Andreas shuffled over to Santiago. After a few seconds, he realized why Santiago wasn't answering, so he leaned over and whispered, "Adriano Rodriguez."

Santiago cleared his throat and nodded his thanks. "There has been a change in plans, Rodriguez. We've learned of a more lucrative venture in Norway, so we'll be traveling there instead. My sister shall be joining us as well. I expect there will be no trouble, or you'll have to answer to both the captain and myself." Santiago's pointed expression left no doubt of what he meant by his last statement.

A few whispers passed between the sailors before Rodriguez spoke up again. "Norway is much farther away. Are there enough provisions for us to make it?"

Santiago grinned. Most of the sailors kept their opinions to themselves, especially if it could look like they were questioning Mr. Mendes's judgment. *This Rodriguez fellow is still almost a boy, yet he's bold enough to ask what must be on everyone's minds.*

"No need to worry about that. We always bring more than enough, so we'll be fine."

Before any further questions could be asked, Andreas shouted, "Well, you heard Mr. Mendes! Let's get going!"

"But, Capitão," First Mate Silva said, "some of the men went into town for a drink and haven't returned."

Santiago frowned. The longer it took them to leave, the more likely they'd be caught by the quadrilheiros. *The officers might already be on their way to the docks now.*

"It's important that we leave as soon as possible. If the men aren't back before the ship is ready, then we leave without them. Understood?" Andreas barked.

The men jumped to attention with shouts of "Aye!"

"Good. Then get to your positions. I want to see those sails out!"

The sailors were quick on their feet as they followed Andreas's orders.

Once the king and prime minister find out we're gone, we'll have more to worry about than quadrilheiros; we'll have the navy to deal with. And the São Nicolau may be fast, but she's no match for Portugal's finest ships. These next few minutes could mean the difference between freedom and . . . execution.

"Of all the times to go out for a drink," Andreas grumbled, slamming a fist against the mainmast.

"Is there any way we can help?" Lucia asked, but she didn't realize she was blocking one of the sailors from moving past her.

Santiago gently grasped his sister's shoulders and shifted her out of the way.

"Brother, why—" Lucia asked, completely clueless that she was being a hindrance instead of a help.

"I think the best way to help would be for you two to go to my quarters," Andreas interrupted. "Look over the maps and find the fastest route to Norway from here." The man's voice was kind, though Santiago could tell he was trying to get Lucia off the deck.

Santiago nodded. "Good idea. Lucia, let's go."

"But . . ."

Santiago didn't wait to hear what Lucia had to say and simply began steering his ditzy sister to the captain's quarters.

"Ah, there they are, the scoundrels," Silva shouted.

Santiago turned to see four drunken sailors staggering down the dock. They were so intoxicated that they could barely keep themselves from falling flat on their faces, yet somehow they were still carrying a tune.

"Hurry up, or you'll be left behind," Costa called.

"You'll never guess what we just heard," one of them sang out, as though he was continuing the next line of their song.

"What? What did we hear?" another drunken sailor asked.

"Get on the ship already! Can't you see we're about to leave?" Silva ran down the gangplank and grabbed one of the men by the arm. "Get up here, then."

The man Silva was holding on to, an unpleasant fellow by the name of Claudio, looked him hard in the eye. "They're coming, you know."

Silva rolled his eyes. "Who's coming, you old fool?"

"Them!" Claudio turned and pointed back toward the streets. Within seconds, men with torches appeared from around the buildings.

Santiago's stomach dropped. The quadrilheiros were here.

Everything seemed to go in slow motion for a few seconds. Santiago raced down the gangplank, took hold of another drunk crew member, and dragged the man onto the *São Nicolau*. Silva brought Claudio up and dumped him on the deck before returning to get the next man. The last fellow made his way up on his own before plopping onto the floor and vomiting right next to Lucia's feet.

"Stop! The more you run, the worse the consequences will be." The lead quadrilheiro and his men charged forward—they were almost to the ship.

"Help me get the gangplank," Silva shouted. He and Santiago pulled the board up just as the officers reached the end of the dock.

"After them, men!" The quadrilheiros began jumping into the water and swimming toward the ship.

Andreas appeared next to Santiago, holding a flintlock pistol. He cocked it, aimed at one of the officers, and—

"What are you doing?" Santiago shoved the gun upward, making the bullet soar high in the air.

Andreas's eyes narrowed, and he moved to reload. "What's necessary. Unless you'd rather I wait for them to board and *then kill them?*"

Santiago shook his head frantically, sliding his hand back onto the pistol. "This isn't right! If you kill them, there's no way we can return!"

"*Don't. Touch. That.*" Andreas's voice was so cold, so alien, that Santiago backed up in shock.

"What are you—"

But Andreas was already recocking the pistol and aiming downward.

BANG!

Santiago's heart stilled. He didn't look, but somehow he knew that the shot had reached its target.

He gawked at the captain, someone he'd called a friend for years now, wondering if he truly knew the man at all. Santiago stood there in a daze for a few seconds, not noticing that Silva had taken hold of the ship's wheel, and they were starting to move away from the harbor.

Andreas didn't show any signs of regret or even disturbance at his actions. He simply reloaded the pistol and said, "Just leave this to me. Get Lucia below deck. *Now.*"

Santiago, not knowing how else to respond, turned to find his sister. He came back to his senses when he saw her crouched beside the mainmast, sobbing.

"Lucia, let's go." Santiago clutched her shoulders and pulled her up.

She was shaking uncontrollably, and the only sound coming from her mouth was a quiet whimper.

"It's going to be all right. Come with me," Santiago said.

He helped her reach the doors to the captain's quarters before glancing back at Andreas once more. The man was shooting bullet after bullet at the quadrilheiros, officers who carried only spears and knives, his face completely emotionless.

Lucia sniffled again, and Santiago repeated his words from before, "It's going to be all right."

But as the two of them went inside, Santiago's stomach

269

churned. Lucia may have believed him, but he knew his words were a lie.

Behind the Mask

"What do you mean, 'it could take a month to arrive'? When Lucia and I calculated the course, it was only going to be a few weeks at the most," Santiago argued, pointing to Norway on the map.

Andreas folded his hands together calmly from his seat across the table, a perfect contrast to his friend's volatile demeanor. It had been a week since that night in Aveiro, and things between the two friends had been tenser than ever.

"Yes, that would be true in normal circumstances. But we're running from the law. It's of the utmost importance that we avoid detection. If we go by the shortest route, the one *you* plotted out, we'll pass several other trade ships. Curious eyes lead to wagging tongues, and word of our presence could reach the navy before we get to our destination. We must be rational about this."

Santiago's eyes widened, and he jumped to his feet. "Rational? Since when has any of this been *rational?* What's rational about running away when we've done nothing wrong? What's rational about going to Norway, of all places?"

Andreas sighed and shook his head as though Santiago was too ignorant to understand. "What are you really angry about? And I know it's not about the ship changing course."

Santiago slammed his hand on the table, earning only the slightest wince from Andreas. "Those men back there didn't need to die. That was never what I wanted."

Andreas rolled his eyes. "You're a fugitive now, Santiago.

271

Did you think we could escape without bloodshed? How naïve are you? Killing those men bought us the time we needed, so don't expect me to apologize for it. I'm doing what has to be done. Don't try to make me feel guilty just because you lack the nerve to do the same."

Santiago turned and stomped out, slamming the door. He slid a weary hand down his face, again questioning why he'd agreed to flee in the first place.

***

The next days passed in much the same way for the two friends: colder than a Norwegian winter. They exchanged no words, and as more time passed, the larger the gulf between them became. Lucia noticed the strange atmosphere, but when she asked Santiago about it, he brushed her off and claimed she was imagining things. The future was so uncertain that Santiago didn't wish to add to Lucia's worries. And if she knew about the rift, he feared she would make things worse by trying to force them to reconcile before they were ready.

Santiago looked out at the water one morning, his mind swimming with sorrow. The days had been growing warmer, and summer would soon be upon them. They had celebrated Lucia's birthday the evening before, though Santiago hadn't been able to shake his guilt as they sang to her.

What a miserable situation to be in. The worst of it is that it's at my expense. What else will this end up costing her?

A cough nearby drew Santiago's attention. He turned and spotted two sailors swabbing the deck. They were hunched close together, whispering as they worked.

"There's no way that truly happened," the younger sailor said.

The other sailor nodded, and when he did, Santiago recognized him as Claudio Perreira, one of the riggers. "Would I lie to you? That's what I heard, clear as day. Why else would his carriage be there in the middle of the night? He must have been there to get Policarpio out."

Santiago started at the familiar name. "You, there. What are you jabbering about?"

272

The two sailors froze. Santiago marched over and put his hands on his hips. "Well?"

The younger sailor swallowed hard before looking up. It was Adriano Rodriguez. Claudio, on the other hand, refused to make eye contact.

Adriano shifted from foot to foot. "S-Senhor Mendes, we didn't see you there. We were swabbing the deck, and—"

"Aye, sir! That's what we were doing. Except I just remembered the first mate has another job for me. I better get to it." Claudio scuttled off before Santiago could say anything else.

"As slimy as a worm," Santiago muttered under his breath. "Rodriguez! Where do you think you're going?"

Adriano Rodriguez, who had been trying to slip away too, began mopping the deck as though that had been his intention all along. It was almost believable, except he'd already washed that spot. "Just cleaning up, senhor."

Santiago crossed his arms and looked pointedly at the younger man. "What were you talking about before I came over?"

"Nothing important."

"*Who* helped Policarpio escape?"

All the color drained from the sailor's face, and the mop began to shake in his hands. "You heard that?"

Santiago said nothing as he waited for an answer.

"I . . . I don't really . . ." Adriano shifted his eyes in all directions, searching for an escape. But when he found none, he sighed in defeat. "Claudio said *you* did, senhor."

"What . . ." Santiago shook his head. "Why would he think that?"

"That's what he heard when he was at the tavern the night we left. He heard your family's carriage was in Lisbon last year when Policarpio was about to be executed. The men are saying that you got him out and that's why we had to leave in the middle of the night. . . ." Adriano's voice was just above a whisper as he shared, "And that's why Capitão Costa killed the quadrilheiros."

Santiago thought back to the previous September, wondering how anyone could think his carriage had been in

273

Lisbon. *The only people who use the carriage are Lucia and me.*

. . . and Andreas.

A scowl formed on Santiago's face as the memory came to him. *Yes, Andreas did ask to borrow the family carriage last year. Was it late summer or early autumn? But he wanted to visit relatives in Évora, not Lisbon, so there's no reason anyone would have seen it there.*

Unless he lied to me . . . No, Andreas is still my friend. He wouldn't do something like that. And even if he had, he would never help a wanted man esca—Santiago almost chuckled at the irony. *Andreas may be helping Lucia and me get to safety, but Policarpio tried to murder the king. He wouldn't help someone like that.*

"No, it must be a mistake. I haven't been to Lisbon in over a year. It must have been someone else's carriage," Santiago said confidently.

Adriano cocked his head to the side, puzzled. "Then why—"

"Rodriguez, just forget about it," he said in a stern voice.

The young sailor snapped his mouth shut and nodded.

"You best get back to your swabbing. And if you hear someone talking nonsense like that again, just tell him what I told you. Understood?"

"Aye, senhor!"

"I'll need to find Perreira, then, too." Santiago started to head in the same direction the rigger had gone, but then he paused. He looked toward the door to the captain's quarters. The tiniest doubt lingered within him, slithering through his thoughts, whispering of what could happen if his trust was misplaced.

Santiago clenched his fists, ashamed at his disloyalty but unable to crush his fears. *No, I'm being ridiculous.*

But that little doubt refused to succumb to reason. *I'll just confront him directly, then. Once I ask where he took the carriage, I'll be able to rid myself of these impossible notions.*

Santiago tramped up to the door and threw it open. "Andreas, I need to speak to you—"

"Ah, I was wondering when you'd be at my door," the captain said with a smile. He sat at his desk, hands folded in his lap.

Santiago stopped at the chair on the other side of the desk, but rather than sit, he stood behind it. For some reason, he didn't feel comfortable taking a seat right then. "You were, huh?"

Andreas raised an eyebrow at Santiago's guarded tone. "Of course. I've been wanting to end this inane conflict between us, but you seemed bent on prolonging it. I'm very glad to see you here; now we can put it all behind us."

Santiago pursed his lips, ruminating over his friend's words and trying to determine why they irked him so much. "That's not the reason I came. I'm not quite ready to put everything behind us, despite how *inane* you think it is."

"Why are you here, then?" Andreas's voice was suddenly sharp, hostile, and perhaps even a little wounded as it hit Santiago's ears.

"I need to check something. How was Évora last year?"

"Why do you ask?"

Santiago leaned toward the captain, searching his eyes for truth. "When you borrowed my carriage last year, is that where you went?"

Andreas's face hardened, and all traces of geniality evaporated. "Do you remember what I told you the day your parents died?"

But before Santiago could respond, Andreas was punching him in the face.

Santiago reeled back, cradling his jaw where he'd been hit.

Andreas was on his feet, glowering with hatred. "*Well?* What did I tell you?"

"You're asking this now?"

"*Tell me.*"

Santiago stared at the man in shock. He'd never seen Andreas out of control like this. "You told me that whatever I did with the rest of my life, you would make sure it succeeded."

"That's exactly right. And I have. When you ran away from your birthright to chase this stupid idea of becoming a merchant, did I laugh at you? Did I say it couldn't be done? No, I helped you buy a ship. I even became captain!"

Santiago went around the desk, stopping a few feet from Andreas. "If you thought it was stupid, then why did you help me? Why not just tell me what you really thought?"

"Because you still had a part to play, and I couldn't very well lose your friendship just yet."

Santiago looked at the man in disbelief. *Even my worst fears weren't this bad.*

"You mean you were just using me this whole time?"

Andreas threw back his head and laughed. It was a cacophonous, chilling sound. "Of course I was. And once your parents were gone, it was easy to gain your trust. You were so desperate for someone to care . . . just as I'd hoped."

Santiago's eyes widened at the implications. He flew forward and grabbed hold of Andreas's shirt. "*What are you trying to say?*"

The captain didn't look the least bit worried as Santiago tried his best not to suffocate the man. "You ask far too many questions. I knew this day would come, but I guess it came a little sooner than I thought. Oh, well, it's not like I really need you anymore."

Santiago tried not to let the barbs get to him. "Don't avoid the question, Costa. *Did you have something to do with my parents' deaths?* I could end you right now, so answer me."

"How could I? I mean, it's not like the criminal who murdered them just happened to know where they'd be that night. Quite a shame the murderer was never caught." Costa winked.

Santiago raised a fist, about to smash the man's jaw—

"Ah, not so fast." Costa had pulled out a dagger from his clothes so quickly that Santiago hadn't even noticed. Now it was aimed right at his chest.

Santiago stopped, the knife hovering just above his heart.

"As I recall, the police couldn't find motive, weapon, or killer. The only thing they could determine was the type of weapon. A dagger." The captain smirked and glanced at the knife in his hand. "Rather like this one, in fact. Or perhaps *precisely* this one. How fitting, then, for you to leave this world in the same way your parents—"

"*Argh!*" Santiago grabbed Costa's wrist and shoved him away. He looked around for anything he could use as a weapon, his eyes settling on the captain's pistol.

But suddenly, Santiago pitched to the side and fell on the floor. Everything started sliding, falling, hitting the wall—

Santiago pulled himself up using the desk, but then the ship was heaving to the opposite side—

The cabin door flew open, bringing in a torrent of rain as the ship rebalanced and Costa, too, found his footing.

"Capitão, Senhor Mendes, come quick!" A sailor appeared in the doorway, his eyes distraught. "Silva went overboard!"

"Show me!" Santiago followed the sailor out, not bothering to check if Costa was behind him.

A monstrous storm the likes of which Santiago had never seen was swirling directly above the *São Nicolau*. Lightning descended in vicious bolts while giant black clouds blocked out all sunlight. Waves rocked the ship back and forth, making it almost impossible to stay upright. The mainmast started to bend; it wouldn't be long before it collapsed.

Santiago gripped the side of the ship and made his way forward—

But something hit him from behind, propelling him toward the mast—

CRACK!

Santiago was on his back, trying to scramble out of the way, but he couldn't move quite fast enough. The top half of the mast crashed down, landing on his right ankle.

He cried out as pain tore through his body. It was so intense that he felt his mind swimming, drifting in and out of consciousness. He tried to pull his foot out, but it wouldn't budge.

Santiago was trapped. "H-Help. . . ."

All of a sudden, a silhouette appeared directly above him. Santiago's heart leaped—

But then a pistol was in his face. With what was left of his strength, Santiago willed his eyelids to stay open. *If this is to be my final moment, I'm going to make sure I look my killer in the eye.*

Captain Costa stared down at him with a triumphant smirk and cocked his gun. "In regards to your previous question, I have no idea how Évora was last year. I had a previous engagement in Lisbon, and it would hardly have been gentlemanly to betray my associate's trust. I'm sure you understand."

"D-Don't . . ." Santiago reached his hand out toward Andreas, hoping the friend he'd met years ago was in there somewhere.

"Goodbye, Santiago Mendes."

Santiago slumped forward and fell into darkness.

***

When he woke later with Lucia hovering over him, he was in too much pain to tell her what had happened. The sailors had gotten the mast off him and lifted him onto a stretcher before he'd even opened his eyes. Lucia was weeping and asking him if he could hear her, but then Costa was beside her, wrapping an arm around the woman's shoulders.

"Don't cry, Lucia. Santiago will get through this. He's strong, and luck has always favored him. Even more than you realize." The captain made eye contact with Santiago as he said this, smiling as Santiago squirmed with wrath.

But the movement only made Santiago's pain worse, and he soon passed out again.

For the next several hours, Santiago strayed down paths between waking and sleeping. He couldn't tell what was dream and what was reality. He watched his parents die at the hands of his friend in one moment, and he felt the soft touch of a woman's hands in the next. He saw Lucia trembling as Costa loomed in the shadows. Unfamiliar faces morphed into the faces of crew members before shifting back again. Everything was tangled in Santiago's mind like thread, and no matter what he did, he couldn't separate the scenes into individual pieces. Instead, his mind kept sliding among them, faster and faster, with no sign of stopping—

A voice broke through his thoughts, shattering the cascade of images he'd been swept up in. It was a woman's voice, tender and sweet. "Yer going to be all right, you hear? The doctor and I won' let you down."

Santiago felt warm breath at his ear, just for the shortest of moments, and then he was asleep again, though this time, the dreams that filled his mind were peaceful.

Escape

Santiago smashed his fist against the ship's hull, angry with himself for dredging up so many bad memories. *I should be focusing on how to get Lucia away from Costa. I can't trust him to keep his promise. And once we get back to Portugal, how can I keep her safe if I'm locked up?*

But what can I do? Costa has me backed against a wall with a knife practically at my sister's throat—

BOOM!

Santiago jumped a few feet into the air at the unexpected roll of thunder, which was swiftly followed by the sound of heavy rain.

A grin came onto the merchant's face. *A storm. Perfect. If it's strong enough, it could delay our return and give me more time to come up with a plan.*

The ship suddenly rocked to the side a bit before righting itself. More thunder roared, close enough for Santiago to wonder if lightning would strike the ship.

Wet shoes squished nearby, and he turned only to come face-to-face with the last person he would have expected to see.

"What are you doing here?" Santiago crossed his arms and scowled at the intruder on the other side of his cell.

Captain Costa rolled his eyes and shook a set of keys in his hand. "Rescuing you. What does it look like?"

Santiago scoffed and made no move toward the door. "You're the one who wanted me to take the fall for you. Why would you help me escape?"

"You're still asking too many questions." Costa opened the door with a growl. "Just hurry up before I change my mind."

When Santiago hesitated, Costa added, "Unless you'd prefer to go back to Portugal and be executed?"

Santiago narrowed his eyes. "Fine. Lead the way." He forced his body forward, ignoring the pain in his ribs.

Captain Costa marched up the stairs, his pace so brisk that Santiago could barely keep up in his current state. "We have to get to the *São Nicolau* before anyone notices you're missing. Lucia is already aboard, along with the rest of the crew."

"What about Senhorita Fairborn? Is she safe?"

The captain paused at the top of the stairs, considering Santiago's question. He turned back with a look akin to sympathy. "You've got bigger things to worry about than that witch right now. I'm doing you a favor by getting you away from her."

The captain turned to keep going, but Santiago took hold of his shoulder and pulled him back. "What do you mean? How dare you call her that."

Costa sighed. "See for yourself." He opened the door and stepped outside.

"What do you . . ." Santiago's voice trailed off as he followed the captain out into a massive storm. The wind hit him with such force that he had to brace himself to keep from losing his balance. Torrents of rain fell from the sky, pelting his skin like tiny bullets. Meanwhile, lightning sought out anything it could destroy, shooting from the clouds in constant bursts.

"Is that smoke?" Santiago pointed toward the town, where two pillars of darkness were rising into the air.

Costa cast a cursory glance that direction, but his face betrayed no concern. "Yes, the villagers are dealing with the fire. Don't worry about it. This is our chance to get out of here."

"Where's the commodore? And his men?"

"Don't know. Once the storm hit, they ran into town. Probably holed up somewhere until everything's over. They're fools if they think they can be safe from this sorcery. The only way to be safe is to get as far away from here as possible."

Santiago frowned. "There you go again, talking of witches. What are you trying to say?"

Costa waved his hand at the chaos around them. "Do you think this storm is normal? That it just happened to show up now right when you need to escape? All this, it's thanks to her. *She* conjured it. For you."

"What? You're saying Bri—Senhorita Fairborn made the storm happen? Have you lost your mind?"

The captain gave him a withering expression. "Don't believe me if you wish, but just know that twenty minutes ago, these skies were completely clear. I seem to recall the tempest that brought us here was rather like that too, appearing without any warning. But what's more important right now is getting to the ship before we miss our chance."

Santiago watched Costa hurry across the deck and start going down the gangplank. He lifted a foot to follow him, but then—

CRACK!

Santiago fell backward in shock—the lightning had only missed him by a few feet.

Costa spun around and frowned when he saw that Santiago wasn't directly behind him. The man gestured with both hands, and Santiago nervously rose again, taking a wary look at the scorch mark by his shoes.

He shifted his focus from the ship to the burning town. *If I leave now, I can make sure Lucia is all right.*

Suddenly, the storm began to calm down. The flashes of lightning started to become less frequent, and the rain softened—

Santiago's eyes were drawn to several bright flashes at the top of the hill. While the weather in the rest of Everton was dying down, the storm near Drulea Cottage was stronger than ever. And angrier. All the lightning that had been spread across the town had shifted to that one area.

Santiago peered through the rain, trying to get a better look at the bizarre phenomenon. Costa had called it sorcery, and while Santiago didn't believe that, he couldn't explain what was going on. But the longer he stared, the more he could almost imagine someone controlling the storm and calling

281

down the lightning—could almost see someone lifting a hand toward the heavens—

His breath caught. "Impossible . . ." Santiago shook his head, trying to remove the image from his vision, trying to remind himself of what was real.

But the scene before him remained. Someone truly was standing at the top of the hill, his hand raised to the sky, and there was also a second figure standing a few feet away.

Lightning struck all around the second person, lightning that the first person seemed to summon at will. The second person crouched down with arms lifted to protect . . . *herself*—

"It can't be her. It can't be. . . ." But Santiago was already racing across the deck, leaping down the gangplank, and making his way toward the town. He paid no heed to Costa's calls, for his thoughts were only on one thing.

Regardless of what logic told him, he ran. Regardless of the fact there was no way he could recognize someone from that distance, he ran. He ran with everything in him, for his heart told him the truth: Briony Fairborn was under attack.

And if I don't get there soon, it might be too late to save her.

A Soul for a Soul

The lightning instantly stopped as Niall's target shifted from selkie traitor to self-professed killer. He bared his teeth at the fisherman, looking more beast than man, and when he spoke, his voice was pure menace. "What did you say, *human?*"

Mr. McLaren stared back into the selkie's black eyes. Defiantly. Fearlessly. As if there was nothing Niall could do to him unless Mr. McLaren allowed it.

But then his eyes flickered over to Briony's, sending her a silent message: *Make yer choice, lass.*

The woman's mind flew back to her conversation with Mr. McLaren before he went to get Niall's sealskin.

***

"He's at my house right now. In human form. *Without his sealskin.*"

Vincent's eyes widened. "And you know where 'tis."

She nodded. "Aye, I do. And once you get it, we can use it as leverage."

The mad fisherman smirked, showing off the many gaps in his teeth. "'Tis about time someone had the advantage over him. Where do I need to go?"

"Head toward the docks. Then turn left and go out to the beach. Keep going until you can see the McGuffs' house above you and you've almost run out o' land. There are some boulders near there. Look behind them and you'll find the skin."

Mr. McLaren nodded. "I know where that is. But before I go, there's something else we need to discuss."

"Hmm?"

"If we can' get him to leave peacefully or we can' trust that he'll stay away once he does, then we'll have to . . ."

"Have to what?"

The man sighed. "Then we'll have to take away his powers."

"Th-They can be taken away?" Briony glanced down at her hands, thinking about the abilities she had only just discovered. The thought of losing them was so repulsive, so *wrong*. "Nay, 'tis too much. I can' do that to him."

Mr. McLaren grabbed Briony's hands in his own and looked at her tenderly. "I know how serious this is. You wish to save him, and I admire you fer that. But it may come to a point where 'tis a choice between him and the whole town. Can you live with it if everyone here is gone?"

Briony yanked her hands away with a huff, but there were tears in her eyes. "In the past, I might have said I could. But I realize now that I care about these people whether I want to or na. I might even be upset to lose the Olivers."

Mr. McLaren's lips turned up at the corners. "Truly?"

A tiny laugh escaped Briony's lips, and she gestured with her thumb and index finger. "Just a wee bit."

"Then you have a better heart than I do."

"But to take away Niall's powers . . . Would it kill him?"

Vincent shook his head. "Nay, but part o' his soul would be lost, and his connection to the ocean would be severed forever."

"H-How . . ." But before she'd finished her question, the answer came to her.

Mr. McLaren turned and picked up two things from his table. His countenance was somber as he held them out to her. "With that heart o' yers . . . I know you can do the right thing when the time comes. Whatever it might be. That's why I'm trusting you to decide."

Briony looked deeply into Mr. McLaren's eyes. This was a man who'd lived a lonely existence, carrying secrets that most people would never believe. He was both the man who'd loved her mother and the one who'd killed her father. And he was the man who'd saved Briony's life.

She took what he offered and slipped them both into her pocket. "Thank you, Mr. McLaren. Na just fer this but fer everything. You've been protecting me all my life. Na just from my da' but also from anyone finding out my secret. I know 'tis a debt I can never repay."

Mr. McLaren flushed and put a hand on his neck. "There's no debt. After what I did to yer father, you dinna owe me anything. In the beginning, I did it out o' love fer yer mother, but at some point . . . in the back o' my mind . . . I started caring fer you as if you were my own. I know yer mother never felt the same way about me, but—"

Briony cut him off by wrapping her arms around him. Mr. McLaren stiffened in surprise, but then he reciprocated the embrace, and they stayed like that for a long time.

When Briony pulled back, her tears from earlier were sparkling on her cheeks. "You dinna know how much it means to hear you say that."

Mr. McLaren cleared his throat and blinked a few times as though trying to hide tears of his own. "I better get going, lass."

The fisherman moved around her to leave, and Briony called out to him as he did, "Do stop calling me 'lass' though. You've more than earned the right to call me Briony."

**

I know what I have to do. And with Mr. McLaren's life on the line, I can' waste any time.

Niall was so focused on the fisherman that he didn't notice Briony slip away and step over the threshold of Drulea Cottage. He didn't notice her pull the sealskin from under her clothes and drop it onto the dirt floor. And he certainly didn't notice her take the flint and steel from her pocket.

Briony's hands shook as she moved to strike the steel, and before she knew it, she had dropped the flint on the floor. As she bent to retrieve it, she heard Niall say, "Well?"

285

"You heard me, selkie," Mr. McLaren replied.

Niall let out a humorless laugh. "Aye, I did. I just wanted to be sure before I ripped you apart."

Briony picked up the flint and vigorously struck it against the steel.

A spark.

But when Briony held it over the pelt, the light fizzled out. *The sealskin must be too wet from the water that soaked through my clothes.*

She looked up to see if Mr. McLaren was safe. He was holding a small dagger between himself and Niall, but the selkie didn't seem intimidated in the least.

"Ah, you brought a knife. That makes this even easier."

"Come no closer," Mr. McLaren warned, swiping the dagger through the air. "You may be powerful, but yer na invincible."

"That's where yer wrong, murderer," Niall sneered. And then, before Mr. McLaren or Briony realized it, Niall was right in front of the fisherman.

He seized Mr. McLaren's wrists, smiling as he burned them. Mr. McLaren yelped and dropped the knife.

Heat. That's it! Briony grasped the sealskin and forced her body temperature to rise. She felt the pelt begin to warm up and watched as steam lifted off it. Within seconds, it was completely dry. Ready to be set alight.

"Agh!"

Briony looked up at the sudden groan. Her breath caught in her throat at the sight of Niall slowly pulling the dagger from Mr. McLaren's stomach. Blood seeped from the wound, and the fisherman slumped to the ground.

Briony screamed, but she knew she couldn't run to his aid. *Na until I've finished this.*

Again she struck the flint against the steel, but this time, the spark eagerly latched onto the now dry sealskin.

She dropped Niall's pelt before she, too, could get burned and watched as the flames expanded outward until the entire skin was ablaze.

Niall, hovering over Mr. McLaren to stab him a second time, turned. Maybe it was because he heard the crackling of

286

the fire, or perhaps it was because he smelled the odor of burning flesh. Either way, Briony quickly slid to the side to give him a better view.

"What are you . . .?" He trailed off as confusion gave way to acute comprehension. "*M-My . . . s-skin.*"

Niall darted forward and shoved his hand into the flames.

But it was too late. He howled in pain and pulled his hand back. And as he cradled it against his chest, tears began flowing down his face.

Briony tried to get to Mr. McLaren, but Niall's uninjured hand shot out like a snake and wrapped itself around her throat. "*Where do you think yer going?*"

Briony coughed and tried to get a breath of air, but Niall's hand was so tight. She looked at Mr. McLaren, but the fisherman was lying on the ground, unconscious or maybe even worse.

"How could you do this to me? How could you—"

Rapid footsteps drew Niall's attention away, and his grip lessened ever so slightly.

Briony tried to catch a glimpse of who it was, but she was already starting to see spots. *Who would be here now?*

A familiar blond head appeared at the top of the hill.

"S-Santiago?"

"Briony!" Santiago skidded to a halt, his breaths shallow. He surveyed his surroundings, going from Briony and Niall, to the fire near their feet, to the fisherman lying in a pool of blood.

Briony, too, looked toward Mr. McLaren's pale form and prayed that there was still time. *If I can just get to him, maybe I can find a way to stop the bleeding. But how? If Niall squeezes much harder, I'll pass out. Perhaps I can—*

"Niall, don't do this. Whatever the issue is, surely it can be resolved without further harm. Let Briony go," Santiago said calmly, hands raised to show he wasn't a threat.

The dark-haired man's expression became a sneer, amplified by the light of the fire. "Stay out o' this, human. You know *nothing*. You see *nothing* beyond what yer tiny mind can accept. This is a matter between Briony and me. Stop distracting me so I can enjoy this."

Niall smirked at the woman he held captive. "Now, my dear, there's only one thing to be done. I must take something o' equal value from you. And since you've stolen my very soul, I'd say there's quite a lot I could take. The only question is . . . what to choose?"

Briony trembled, but she refused to cower. Her eyes locked onto Santiago's. *I thought I would never see him again. Yet here he stands, risking his life to save mine.*

He looks so frightened.

Briony's arms ached to hold him, to reassure him that she would be fine. But she couldn't force her mouth to form a lie that neither of them would believe.

She had fended off Niall's powers earlier, but it had taken a toll on her. *Whatever Niall is about to do, I doubt I have the strength to stop him.*

Before Niall could make a decision, though, a brilliant light drew everyone's attention to the horizon. Glorious reds and oranges dazzled their eyes, proclaiming the arrival of the sun.[32] All the clouds had withdrawn, and a new day was here. In mere minutes, Everton would be bright again. As if the storm had been no more than an awful dream.

When Briony looked away, another sparkle caught her eye—the knife, It lay on the ground beside Briony's left foot, forgotten.

A weak chuckle escaped her throat as an idea blossomed in her mind. "'Tis over, Niall."

Niall turned back to her with a growl. "'Tis na over! Far from it, fer I have na paid you back yet."

"Aye, but you've no power anymore. 'Tis all burnt up, just like yer skin." She inclined her head toward the now dying flames, hoping he wouldn't notice her also sliding the knife toward Santiago. "Take a good look at it turning to ash, gone forever. In yer quest fer vengeance, you've become the very monster you wished to destroy."

Niall's eyes flashed hotter than the fire, but his fingers loosened, and as he replied, his voice shook. "I've no regrets over the deaths. The humans got what they deserved."

---

[32] The sun rises in the Orkney Islands at about 4:00 a.m. around the summer solstice.

Briony shook her head and coughed. "That's na what I meant by 'monster.' Aye, yer a murderer, but now yer also something else. Something you deem far worse."

Niall's eyebrows raised suspiciously. "What could be worse than that?"

Santiago crept forward and took the dagger, Niall none the wiser. A spring of pity welled up in Briony's heart; try as she might to hate Niall, she couldn't help but wonder how things could have been different.

If he had na come to Everton and I had never met him, would Niall still have hated humans so much? Would his heart have become so bitter that he couldn't see beyond his own prejudice? Would he have been willing to kill the innocent to get revenge?

"Well? What have I become?" Niall scowled, waiting for a reply.

As Santiago raised the knife into the air, Briony whispered a single word, the word Niall hated above all else. "Human."

Niall grunted in surprise as the dagger sank into his right shoulder. His hand dropped from Briony's neck, and he fell to his knees.

Briony staggered backward, her feet just barely getting out of the way as Niall landed on the floor.

"Don't move," Santiago shouted at Niall as he raised the knife again, this time red with blood.

Niall hissed but said nothing. As crimson liquid dripped onto the back of his neck, Briony saw the resolve fade from his face. He knew it was over. And, as more tears fell from Niall's eyes, Briony couldn't help but regret what she'd done.

Santiago appeared at Briony's side, one hand rubbing her shoulder while the other kept the dagger aimed at Niall. "Are you all right?"

Briony nodded, but she couldn't quench the rivulets running down her cheeks. She leaned against Santiago's chest as he embraced her, eager to put all this behind them. Except—

"Mr. McLaren!" Briony pulled away from Santiago and raced to the fisherman's side.

She rolled him over onto his back, trying not to think the worst when she saw his eyes closed. She grabbed his wrist, but

289

there was no pulse.

"Mr. McLaren . . . Mr. McLaren! Please . . ." She pressed her ear against his chest, but again, there was nothing. She opened his mouth and breathed into it as she'd heard Dr. Sherwin say to do for drowning victims. *One, two, three breaths.*

She leaned away, waiting for something to happen, for him to suddenly breathe.

But there was nothing. Vincent McLaren, the mad fisherman, the great storyteller, the keeper of Everton's secrets, was gone.

Another friend gone forever.

After a few minutes of weeping, Briony returned to Santiago's side, her bloodshot eyes glaring down at Niall, the man who'd stolen her friends. Briony sensed the sky above her, waiting to do her bidding. She knew she could bring down the lightning and end him at a moment's notice.

But as she stared at Niall's bent form, her anger subsided. *This is a broken man, and while he certainly deserves death, I dinna think I can bring myself to give it to him.*

Instead, she turned to Santiago and said, "Take him to see the water."

Niall's face tipped up, his mouth hanging open in astonishment.

Santiago looked at Briony as if she'd lost her mind, but she squeezed his hand and said, "Please."

Santiago still seemed unsure, but he gave her a small smile and nodded.

Santiago helped Niall to his feet, dagger still poised to strike. The three of them made their way to the cliff's edge and looked out at the blue waves. They watched the sun continue its ascent into the sky, taking in its majestic beauty. And down below, two ships rose and fell with the crashing waves.

"Can you hear the sea, Briony? Can you hear it calling to you?" Niall asked.

Briony sniffled. "Aye, Niall. I can hear it."

Niall's voice cracked as he said, "Well, I can'. Na anymore. It does na recognize me." Then he looked away from the water and let out a loud sob.

Santiago lowered the knife, his expression full of

confusion. Briony imagined that it must have looked quite strange indeed.

Even if Santiago knew the context, 'twould still be difficult to understand and believe our story. 'Tis the story o' a man who once belonged to the sea and the story o' a selkie who once thought she was only human.

"Thank you fer this, Briony," Niall said. He suddenly stumbled a bit, and Santiago grabbed his arm to steady him. "And I do believe I've chosen what to take."

Then, before Briony or Santiago could register the meaning of Niall's words, Niall made his move.

All the breath that Briony had just gotten into her lungs instantly left her. She tried to speak, but nothing came out. She tried to move, but she found herself paralyzed in shock. All she could do was watch.

Watch as Niall threw Santiago and himself over the side of the cliff.

To Love a Monster

As the splash echoed in her ears, Briony's limbs regained their mobility, and she lurched forward to the edge of the cliff. Santiago and Niall were nowhere to be seen, and fading ripples were the only proof they'd even hit the water. The fall could have easily knocked one or both of them unconscious, and the sharp rocks around the cliff could have done a lot worse.

The sun hadn't fully risen, and the water was still waiting for light to brighten its depths. It would be very difficult for a human to see anything underwater right then.

But na fer a seal.

Briony pulled out her sealskin. There was no time for decorum now, so she stripped off her clothes and lifted the pelt above her head. Before she put it on, though, she hesitated.

I dinna know what will happen once I transform. What if I get so lost in the thrill o' the sea that I forget myself? Will Briony Fairborn no longer exist?

But this is my best chance.

Briony put the pelt on, and as she did so, a warm tingling sensation swam through her body. The second skin melded with the first, and she marveled at how perfectly they fit each other. Her body shifted from human to seal so fast that her mind almost couldn't keep up with the transition. Colors vanished as black-and-white vision took over. The hands and feet she'd always known suddenly became flippers. And the sound of the sea roared in ears that felt like they could hear everything.

Again she looked down at the ocean, but this time, she recognized it for what it was: home.

Briony plunged off the cliff, her body streaming through the air. When her splash of arrival soon followed, it would have seemed insignificant to anyone passing by, but to her, it was one of the most glorious moments of her life. Though she had swum before, that moment was nothing compared to the bliss of sliding through the water as a seal. As she was meant to.

The seal opened her eyes and saw beauty stretching out in all directions. An underwater world ready to be explored and delighted in.

But it was not to be.

For the seal remembered. And though she felt alive and whole and free, she knew she didn't fully belong here.

And someone needed her help. *Santiago, I'm coming for you.*

Briony dove deeper, and it wasn't long before she spotted Santiago and Niall. Locked in a struggle, the two men were oblivious to her presence as she swam up behind them. Santiago tried to escape Niall's grip and return to the surface, while Niall pushed his opponent downward. At this rate, he was going to drown them both.

Realizing this, Santiago changed tactics and stabbed Niall with Mr. McLaren's knife. The dagger went into his chest on the left side, undoubtedly close to his heart. Niall grimaced, but he refused to let go even as Santiago pulled out the blade and jabbed at him again. This time, Niall dodged the attack and slammed his hand into Santiago's wrist, sending the merchant's only weapon to the sea floor.

Before Niall could do anything more, Briony zoomed forward and sank her teeth into his leg. Niall let out a garbled cry of pain, bubbles of precious air gushing from his mouth.

Niall looked down at his attacker, and his eyes widened in recognition. In that moment of eye contact, two pairs of black eyes stared each other down, one full of envy and the other full of shame.

But then Briony reminded herself of all Niall had done. She reminded herself of what he had taken from her. And she reminded herself he had to be stopped.

Briony bit down harder, feeling bone beneath her teeth. Niall again cried out, but this time, he retaliated with a strike to the top of her head. Briony's vision went hazy for a second, and she let go of Niall's leg to reorient herself.

And that was when Niall went after Santiago a second time. The merchant, who had taken advantage of Niall's distraction to make a break for the surface, once again found himself caught. This time, Niall had a grip on Santiago's ankle.

But the humans were running out of air. Soon they would slip into unconsciousness, and death would find them.

There wasn't time to save both of them, not when one of them didn't want to be saved. Briony steeled herself and went after Niall's hand on Santiago's ankle, digging her teeth deep into the flesh.

Niall let out a horrid screech, but he wouldn't loosen his grip, even as blood flowed freely from the wound. Briony pulled at his hand, and with all the strength she had, she managed to wrench it free.

"Nay! Dinna!" Niall's distorted voice reached her ears as she released his hand and watched him slip deeper into the dark water.

Briony didn't wait to see if he would try to swim back up. Instead, she turned her attention to Santiago, hoping there was still enough time. The man's eyes were open, but he wasn't even trying to reach the surface anymore. In fact, he wasn't moving at all, and it was as if all the light had faded from his eyes. *He does na even seem . . .*

Briony couldn't finish the thought. She clutched his arm in her mouth and began to ascend.

Please be all right. Please be all right. Just hold on a wee bit longer.

In about thirty seconds, though it felt like hours, Briony's head burst through the water.

But then a great wave broke over the top of them, sending both seal and man tumbling back below. Briony held on tightly and went careening toward what she hoped was the shore. She waited until they were almost to the beach before coming back up to the open air.

The seal filled her lungs as the sunlight streamed down on

them, but there was no intake of breath from Santiago. She pulled him toward the shore, dragging his body onto the sand as the water became shallower and shallower. Until—

Briony released him and turned to look. The man's eyes were closed, and his chest wasn't moving.

Nay, yer going to be fine!

Briony grabbed her own tail, clawing at the pelt she loved so dearly, desperate to make it separate from her human skin.

Her seal self had done all it could to save Santiago. The only hope he had left would be if she became human once more.

Though it felt like her soul was being ripped in half, Briony continued to pull the two skins apart. Soon she could see her feet pressed together within the skin. As she kept going, she felt the pelt slide away from her body, and with it, her human senses returned. Santiago's blond hair, the blueness of the sea, the pale tone of her skin—black and white had transformed to colors once more.

Briony placed her mouth upon Santiago's and breathed, just as she had done for Mr. McLaren earlier. *One, two, three—*

Water spewed from Santiago's mouth in a sudden cough. He took a deep gasp of air, his chest heaving with the effort.

Briony, too, gasped in incredulous relief. She kissed Santiago's mouth over and over in jubilation. "Yer alive! I thought I lost you. I thought I lost you."

Santiago cracked his eyes open, and when he saw who leaned over him, a brilliant, exhausted smile came over his face.

Briony smiled back at him, reaching for his hand and interlocking their fingers.

"I thought I was gone, too. But you saved me. Again," he wheezed.

Then Santiago's eyes drifted downward, and his expression changed from happiness to shock. Within a second, he pulled his hand away and put it over his eyes, his cheeks redder than Mr. Burgess's hair. "Briony, y-you're . . ." He gestured blindly toward her body.

Briony's eyes widened, and her cheeks flamed up in embarrassment. She picked up her sealskin and wrapped it around herself. "I'm so sorry! I . . . I can explain that. You-You can open yer eyes now."

Santiago slowly removed his hand, though the pinkness in his face remained. Briony helped him up into a sitting position, and he immediately turned his head from side to side, searching. "Where's Niall?"

Briony couldn't say the words, so she simply shook her head.

Santiago sighed and looked away. "I don't understand. Why would he do any of this? Why did he try to kill you? And what happened to that seal in the water? And Mr. McLaren. Is he—"

"He's gone."

Santiago ran both hands down his face. "What is going on, Briony? None of this makes sense. You realize that, right?"

"Aye, I'm well aware o' that. I'll tell you everything. I just dinna know where to start. . . ."

Santiago waited patiently, giving her the chance to explain. His face was full of confusion, but despite that, she could see the trust in his eyes. *Whatever I tell him now, he will believe me.*

Except the problem is na so much whether he believes me or na. The problem is whether he will still want me after he knows everything.

"Before I tell you, there's one thing I want you to know. And that's this: I love you. Please remember that after you've heard all there is to hear."

Santiago's quick intake of breath made her heart pick up its pace. She watched as another smile overtook his face, starting at the corners of his lips and spreading out until he was almost glowing.

Before she knew it, he was leaning forward and lifting his fingers to her cheek. He held them there so tenderly, just barely touching skin to skin. Lightning pulsed through her where they made contact, igniting her entire being with energy and heat.

"You don't know how long I've wanted to hear you say that. I—"

Briony pulled back, shutting her eyes tightly. "Dinna say anything more. Na until you've heard the whole story. Otherwise, I might na be able to tell you."

Santiago didn't speak for a few seconds, and Briony

instantly regretted her words. But she knew she was in danger of losing her nerve. She needed to tell him now while she still could.

"Yes. If that's . . . what you want." The soft response was so sad, so solemn.

Briony opened her eyes, but she couldn't look Santiago's way as she spoke. "Thank you. The truth is, I'm na all you think I am. And Niall—he was . . . he was like me. Where yer from, you may na know the stories or what the word *selkie* means. . . ."

Briony looked up at this point, but there was no recognition in Santiago's eyes. He was still waiting for her to explain it in a way he could understand.

She swallowed thickly before inching her right foot toward him.

"Briony, why are—" His voice broke off as he noticed the webbing between her toes. "What is that?"

"Even in human form, a remnant o' my other nature remains." She pointed to the skin wrapped around herself. "This is my sealskin."

Santiago's brow furrowed. "What do you mean, yours?"

"The seal in the water . . . was me. To be a selkie is to be both human and seal yet also something else entirely."

Santiago froze as he took in her words. And in those beautiful green eyes, Briony saw it, the thing she'd known she would see: fear.

"You can't mean that, Briony. You couldn't be . . . a seal, selkie, whatever it is." His tone was incredulous, but the look on his face belied his words.

Briony sighed and closed her eyes, hating that she was about to make him even more afraid. But it was necessary.

She lifted one hand to the sky, summoning darkness above them. The swirling clouds were heavy with rain, barely containing themselves as they awaited Briony's command.

When she returned her gaze to Santiago, her heart wilted even more at his shocked countenance.

She ordered the clouds to disperse and then reached for Santiago's hand. "'Tis all right. I did na cause the storm earlier. 'Twas Niall. Truly! I'm still me. There's no need to—" Briony broke off when Santiago jerked his hand away.

"I'm sorry, I . . ." Santiago stared down at his fingers as if they had betrayed him, his face red with shame.

Briony shook her head with a tight smile. "Nay, I understand." She rose and turned her face toward the sea, surreptitiously wiping away a stray tear.

Silence followed, and Briony felt a lump form in her throat. Her hopes and wishes for the two of them seemed so far away now. *Just the impossible dreams o' a silly, foolish girl.*

That same cruel voice in her head, the one that always came out when she was feeling sorry for herself, whispered, *You knew this would happen. You knew he would react this way once he found out. Why did you na put a stop to these feelings before it came to this?*

Briony nodded to herself, for she wished these self-deprecating thoughts were wrong, but the evidence was clear.

"I can see now that I made a mistake. I should have told you so much sooner. Perhaps then I could have saved both o' us from heartache. I dinna blame you fer being frightened. All the appalling things Niall did: the storm, the deaths . . . I'm capable o' that, too. I'm so sorry you got caught up in all o' this."

Briony opened her mouth to say more, but then a hand grabbed hers and turned her around. "*Stop.* Stop right there."

Santiago put both his hands on her shoulders and stared at her fiercely. Angrily.

Briony stared back in bewilderment. "Stop what?"

"Stop talking about yourself like that. As if you and Niall have anything in common. I may not know a thing about selkies, but *I do know you.*"

"What . . . What are you saying?"

"I'm saying that Niall was a right canalha,[33] but just because you're both selkies, that doesn't make you one, too. How many times have you saved me now? And after Niall tried to kill you, you *still* showed him mercy. It was far better than he deserved. Far kinder than most humans would have been." Santiago's gaze remained fixed on her, all traces of fear

---

[33] Scoundrel.

replaced by a firm resolve.

Briony's emotions, on the other hand, were all jumbled within her. Part of her was elated to hear him say she and Niall weren't alike, but another part of her couldn't accept his words. "You suffered because o' that decision. 'Tis probably better if you stay away from me. I'm dangerous, Santiago."

"I don't care." He tucked a strand of black hair behind her ear before resting his palm against her jaw.

Briony pulled her face away. "You dinna know what yer saying. But that's my fault. I've bewitched you, and I'm sorry."

Santiago frowned. "Bewitched me? Yes, you could say that. But why is that something to be sorry for? I'm saying *I love you*, whether you're human or not."

"Nay, you only think you do. I. . . I made you believe that. I did na mean to—I did na even know what I was doing. I—"

"You what?"

Briony took a deep breath before confessing, her voice only a whisper. "The day you came to Drulea Cottage and k-kissed me, 'twas na o' yer own will. When I say 'bewitched,' I mean real magic. I dinna understand it, but the song o' a selkie holds sway over humans. When you heard me singing, it enchanted you. It made you think you were in love with me. And I fear you've been confused ever since. Otherwise, you would have surely run away by now."

Santiago's brows furrowed as he recalled the memory. "I do remember feeling like I'd lost myself for a moment. Like I told you then, I'm not the sort of person to do that. I . . ." Suddenly, the man's mouth curled up, and he laughed.

"Yer laughing? I dinna think anything I just said was humorous," Briony snapped.

But Santiago's lips merely widened into a giant grin. "Oh, Briony. You think *that* was when I fell in love with you?"

"'Tw-'Twas na then?"

Santiago shook his head, still beaming. "What do you think I wanted to tell you the first time you saved me? If only my sister and yer friends had shown up a little later."

"You—" But Briony didn't have time to finish, for his mouth was already upon hers. And after that, all thought vanished in the wake of a steadily rising fire in her blood. The kiss was slow, sweet, and so much more than just a kiss. With it, Santiago conveyed not only the sincerity of his affection but also the depth of his trust. He was choosing to trust her character even in the midst of the unknown. Even in the midst of his fear.

And that just made her love him all the more.

The rest of Briony's doubts and anxieties fell away at that moment. *All this time, I thought Santiago could never love a monster like me. But maybe . . . just maybe, I'm na a monster, after all. And if Santiago can still love me after knowing all o' what I am, then I should start loving myself, too.*

When they broke apart, Briony found herself smiling from ear to ear.

But there was still something that needed to be addressed. "Santiago, about the charges against you . . . I know you could never have tried to kill the king, so why did the commodore say you did? And why did you na deny it?"

Santiago's face fell flat, and he tightened his hand into a fist. He didn't say anything at first, and Briony worried she had upset him. But this was a conversation long overdue.

If we're going to have any sort o' future together, the time fer secrets is over.

"Yes, you're right to ask. All right, I'll tell you everything. No more hiding. No more lies."

Playing the Hero

Briony listened to Santiago's tale, from its chaotic beginning, to the heart-wrenching betrayal, to the difficult position he now found himself in of having to lie to protect his sister. So many questions suddenly found their answers, but as he concluded, Briony realized there was something Santiago didn't know.

And she dreaded having to tell him. "What does Lucia think o' Captain Costa?"

Santiago frowned. "She doesn't know anything of his true nature. She still thinks him an honorable man. If she knew the viper he truly is, it would tear her apart."

He sighed, his face full of sadness. "She's a flirt of the worst sort, but with Costa, it has always seemed like something more. Something real. Why do you ask?"

"Well, after you got arrested, I ran into Adriano, and he told me that Costa tried to shoot you during the storm. I assumed that must be connected to the charges against you. I tried to find Lucia to see if she could help me prove yer innocence, but then . . ." Briony grimaced.

"What happened?"

"He-He kissed her."

"*He what?*" Santiago practically shouted, his protective instincts taking over. "I have to get to her *now*. Who knows what sorts of lies Costa has been filling her head with since I got arrested, but I have to get her away from him so I can talk some sense into her."

"But you just said 'twould hurt her if she knew the truth."

303

"That was before I knew how serious things had become between them. A broken heart is one thing. . . ." Santiago gasped, and his expression changed to panic-stricken. "Briony, what if he—You don't think he—"

Briony clasped Santiago's hand and gave it a gentle squeeze, knowing exactly what he couldn't bring himself to say. "Let's na jump to any conclusions just yet. Do you know where Lucia is?"

Santiago took a deep breath and nodded. "When Costa got me out of the brig, he told me Lucia was already aboard the *São Nicolau*. He was going to use the storm to get out of Cardoso's reach. . . ."

Briony put a hand on Santiago's arm when he trailed off. "What is it?"

Santiago gave her a rueful smile. "I just remembered the next thing he said. It seemed entirely mad at the time, but now I realize he was partially right. And that means I owe you my thanks."

"Fer what?"

"He said you created the storm as a diversion so we could escape."

"Captain Costa did want me to make a storm fer you," Briony said with a scowl, thinking of the unpleasant memory, "but I did na actually get the chance to do it. 'Twas Niall's doing, na mine."

Santiago opened his mouth to speak again, but then Briony realized something.

"Wait. Costa broke you out o' the brig? Why would he do that?" she asked.

"Well, Lucia loves a hero after all," said a new and all too terribly familiar voice.

Santiago and Briony spun around, instantly on the defensive. Briony's hand was already reaching toward the sky when her eyes glimpsed the pistol in the captain's hand.

"Tsk, tsk, I wouldn't do that. Are you quite sure you're faster than this?" Costa waved the gun and smiled.

Santiago positioned himself in front of her. "I should have known you'd show up after Niall was out of the way. A coward through and through."

The captain's eyes narrowed, and he slid forward. He was quiet and controlled, though Briony knew now just how dangerous he truly was. A snake that could strike at any time. "Careful. Remember who has the power here."

Santiago, on the other hand, did nothing to conceal his hatred. "Why are you here, Costa?"

"It's as I said. Your sister loves a hero, and I'm more than happy to play the part."

"You were going to let me take the fall for you. I know there's more behind this than just making her happy."

Costa sighed and nodded with an exaggerated roll of his eyes. "I suppose that's true. The little idiot has proven herself more bothersome than I'd thought possible. Simply refuses to leave without you. Normally, I wouldn't care about that and just dispose of her, but I recently had a beautiful idea."

At this point, the annoyed look on Costa's face shifted to a smirk. "Would you like to hear about it? Would you like to know why I need *dear, sweet Lucia?*"

"*Don't say her name*," Santiago whispered, his body shaking with rage.

Costa smirked, clearly enjoying the exchange. "Why ever not?"

Before Santiago could respond, though, the captain leaned around him to make eye contact with Briony. He lowered his voice and said, "Shall I share the happy news with you, then? It warms my heart too much to keep it to myself."

The man's large smile and flat, dead voice were so frightening that Briony's first instinct was to dive back into the ocean and swim for her life. But there was no way she was going to leave Santiago alone when she'd only just gotten him back.

Instead, she mustered her courage and replied, "I did na think you capable o' such feelings."

Costa's smile widened, but the tightening of his grip on the gun told Briony he was anything but pleased. "Ah, you've seen through me. But don't tell Santiago's sister that. You see, she's to be my wife soon, and I would hate to spoil her dreams of wedded bliss."

Briony instantly reached for Santiago's shoulder to hold

him back, but he was already leaping forward.

"You demônio,"[34] the merchant snarled.

Costa, completely unruffled by the outburst, waited until Santiago was almost upon him before aiming his pistol—

BANG!

Right at Briony's chest.

Before she realized it, she was staring up at the sky, the hard sand beneath her. Excruciating pain racked through her, so potent that everything else seemed a mere haze in its wake. Briony reached out with her hand, desperate to grab hold of something, anything.

Warm skin met hers, long fingers wrapping around her own. "Briony! I'm here. I'm here!"

Briony tried to glance toward the sound of the voice, but the tears flooding her eyes made it impossible to see anything more than a blurry shape.

"She needs help, We have to get her into town now!" Santiago's voice was pure panic.

"She's a witch. She'll be fine. Besides, I know all the worst places to shoot someone, and that one didn't hit anything essential. Now, I suggest you come with me; otherwise, my next shot will be lower."

A strangled cry broke free from Santiago's lips, and he whimpered, "I'm sorry, Briony."

Nay, dinna leave me. Dinna go! Briony screamed in her mind, but all that came out was a moan of pain. She tried to hold on to Santiago's hand, but soon it was slipping from her grasp.

Then he was gone. And Briony had never felt so cold in all her life.

---

[34] Demon.

An Unseen Weapon

Emptiness. That was the only word Briony could think of to describe her existence. There was no sound. No light. No warmth.

Where am I? What happened? She tried to speak her thoughts aloud, tried to shout, scream, or even whisper them.

But only silence rang in her ears.

She was utterly alone, and she couldn't even find comfort in the sound of her own voice.

Santiago, where are you? How could you leave me?

She felt it then, sliding down her cheek: moisture. It was the first evidence that she was still alive.

But how is that possible? She'd been certain she'd never wake after she'd fallen on the beach. Certain that was the final time she would close her eyes.

Before she could think about it any further, though, fiery pain again overtook her. The flames licked at her flesh like dogs, spreading from her chest in all directions until they threatened to consume her.

Without her realizing it, Briony's eyes shot open, instinctively searching for relief.

The sun was only a little higher now. She hadn't been out long, maybe half an hour, but with Santiago gone, there was no guarantee that someone else would come upon her.

Her eyes went down to the source of her suffering, fearful of what she would find.

Surprisingly, there was very little blood on her skin, though the hole in her chest proved that the bullet had, indeed, gone into her. Briony tried to push up from the ground to check if it had gone all the way through, but when she moved, the pain escalated so much that she fell backward, her shoulder blades slamming into the unforgiving sand.

"Agh!" She felt the tiny granules digging beneath the skin, making her eyes swim with tears.

I have na bled to death yet, so perhaps Costa was telling the truth about knowing where to place his shot. Even so, there's no way I can move in my current state. He may na have killed me, but he left me completely helpless.

She forced her head to turn so that she could look in the direction of the sea, and when she did, rather than freedom, she saw only danger.

The tide is coming in; if I stay here much longer, I'm going to be swept away.

It was then she heard a sound rising over the crash of the waves, the most beautiful sound she could have hoped for: a voice calling her name.

"Here! *Please.* I'm here!" Briony bellowed with all her strength.

She scanned the cliffs overhead, for she was certain that was where the voice had originated.

And sure enough, a figure soon appeared near the spot where Briony had jumped—it was Adaira.

Adaira's eyes lit up when she noticed her friend on the beach. She waved her hands frantically above her head. "Briony, I see you!"

She then turned in the other direction and shouted, "John, she's here! We have to go down to the beach!"

More tears fell onto Briony's face, but these were nothing like the ones from before. These lacked any bitterness or despair; instead, they were full of gratitude and happiness. *Adaira will look after me.*

She closed her eyes peacefully and let sleep take her.

***

"Briony! I feared you'd never wake!" was the first thing Briony heard when she opened her eyes. She glanced around, happy to find herself in a bed at Everton Inn. Adaira sat at her bedside, looking like she'd just survived a hurricane.

Truth be told, she has. And yet, despite the dark circles under her eyes, the messy hair, and the fidgeting hands, she still looks absolutely gorgeous.

Briony clasped her friend's hand. "Adaira, you can' know how glad I am to see you."

She then glanced around the room. "Santiago, is he . . . Did he leave?"

Adaira nodded. "His ship vanished shortly after the storm. Lucia, the captain, they're all gone. I'm sorry, Briony."

"Nay, I have to get to him. How long was I out? When did the ship leave?" Briony tried to bring her body up into a sitting position, but it was too painful.

"Slow down. Yer in no condition to move, let alone get to the ship. Besides, there's more we need to discuss."

Briony opened her mouth to argue, but an angry look from Adaira made her think better of it.

Adaira took a deep, calming breath. "After the storm passed, John and I went to look fer you. We . . . We found Mr. McLaren. Briony, what happened?"

Briony turned away with a grimace, feeling the guilt rise in her stomach like acid.

After a few seconds of silence, Adaira said, "You told me the storm was na natural and that you had to leave or more people would get hurt. As yer friend fer over half yer life, I think I deserve an explanation."

"I . . ." Briony didn't know how to tell her the truth. She'd planned to, after everything was over, but now she couldn't even bear to look Adaira in the eye.

"Does it have something to do with this?"

Briony looked back and found Adaira holding out a long gray sealskin. Her sealskin. Except—

"Nay, it can' be." Briony gasped and grabbed the pelt, inspecting two gaping holes that hadn't been there before.

When Costa had shot her, she hadn't been thinking about the fact she was wrapped in her sealskin. The bullet had passed right through the stomach and back of her seal form.

309

Briony was no expert on what it meant to be a selkie, but the damage was clear: if she transformed into a seal again, it might kill her.

She looked up at her friend and let out a small sob, unable to wrap her mind around all that this meant.

Adaira sighed, her anger seeming to escape with her breath. Her eyes were kind as she reached out a hand and rubbed Briony's shoulder. "I'm sorry, dearie. I'm so sorry."

Briony frowned, wondering at Adaira's words. She gestured to the pelt. "This is—"

"—yers. I know."

"What? How do you know that?" Briony's mouth dropped open in shock.

Adaira gave her a small, rueful smile. "You've always been a wee bit different, haven' you? After that day on the beach when I saw yer webbed toes and then the seals came . . . I started to wonder if calling you a changeling was na that far off. I thought maybe you'd summoned the seals to rescue you, and if I was mean to you again, you might set them on me." She looked away, her voice low. "That's the real reason I became yer friend. Na because I felt bad fer what I'd done but because I feared what you might do to me."

Briony took in a sharp breath at Adaira's confession. "Are you saying this friendship has been a lie?"

Adaira turned back and raised her hands, panic in her eyes. "Nay! Nay, that's na it at all. Aye, the friendship started under false pretenses, but it did na take long before I realized how good o' a person you are. A far better person than I am."

"Because you thought I would hurt you if we weren' friends."

Adaira's face was as white as a sheet, but she didn't deny Briony's words. Instead, she hung her head in shame.

"Adaira, that does na make sense. Think o' all the times I've been bullied, and I've never hurt anyone fer it."

Adaira wrung her hands, a thought clearly on her mind, though she hesitated to voice it. "What o' Alastair, then?"

Briony shook her head angrily. "You really think I could do something like that? I had nothing to do with his death!"

"We were only bairns then. . . . I would na blame you fer

it. He was horrible to everyone, but he always treated you the worst. If I had that kind o' power and he'd gone after me, I might have done the same thing just to protect myself."

Briony shut her eyes, though she wished she could shut her ears from this nonsense. *How can Adaira believe I'm capable o' such a thing?*

"'Twas na I who killed him. 'Twas Niall."

"What? Niall? Briony, I-I'm sorry. I suppose I should have known 'twas na you. . . ."

"Do you know what helped me get through all the abuse over the years? What kept me from losing my mind? 'Twas having you as my friend." Briony opened her eyes and sent Adaira a withering glare.

The other woman's mouth opened and closed like a fish's for a few seconds, regret all over her face. "I—"

"Leave, Adaira. I . . . I need to be alone."

Adaira rose, her eyes full of tears. She drew in a breath to say more but then thought better of it and fled the room. Briony hated to let her go like that, but this was too much to take in. She needed a little time to work out her feelings; otherwise, she was sure she would say something she would regret.

About an hour later, she heard the door creak open. "Adaira, I told you I needed to be alone."

"Ah, how unfortunate, then, since I need to speak to you," said a heavily accented voice.

Briony's skin prickled in recognition, and her tiny room instantly felt twice as small. She mentally kicked herself for sending Adaira away; facing this man by herself was the last thing she wanted to do right then.

"What could you possibly have to say to me, Comodoro?" Briony said with bluster to hide how vulnerable she felt.

But the commodore seemed all too aware of Briony's fear. He slinked into the room, shutting the door behind himself. He stepped closer and closer until he was right next to her. A smile broke over his weathered face, though its presence brought her no comfort. "Where is he?"

"Where is who?"

"Now, don't pretend. You know exactly who I'm talking

311

about." He stroked Briony's hair, his fingers lingering and rough. "None of the other villagers will tell me anything, but I think you know where he was headed."

"I have no ide—"

Suddenly, the door opened and Adaira stepped inside. Her face was red from crying. "Briony, I know you dinna want to see me, but you need to—"

She gasped when she saw the commodore at Briony's side. "What are you doing?"

In a flash, Cardoso had a knife at Briony's throat. "Ah, a friend. How lucky! Perhaps you can tell me something since Senhorita Fairborn is rather forgetful. *Where is Santiago Mendes?*"

Adaira's eyes flickered from the commodore to Briony. Briony shook her head, but then Cardoso gripped the back of her neck and held it still.

"He said he was going to Norway! Please dinna hurt her," Adaira squealed.

"There's no guarantee he's still going there. That was his plan before you showed up. He could be going anywhere now," Briony blurted.

But Cardoso wasn't fooled; he raised an eyebrow at her and squeezed her neck to make her stop talking. "Norway, hmm?" He chuckled. "Well, we better get going, then."

Adaira cringed. "We?"

The commodore waved the knife at her dismissively. "Not you. *You're* not important. And you're not going to help me make sure Senhor Mendes doesn't run away again."

He looked down at Briony with a devious grin. "Considering the fact it was *my* ship's doctor who saved your life, I'd say you owe me this much. Wouldn't you?"

He's taking me . . . to Santiago? Part of Briony was elated at this turn of events, but she couldn't have asked for a less ideal way to be reunited with her green-eyed merchant.

"But she's recovering from a gunshot. She needs rest and . . . ," Adaira tried to argue, but the commodore gave her a hard look.

"Not to worry about your friend. She'll have my doctor to attend to her, so as long as she *behaves*, she'll recover just fine. Do you think you can do that, senhorita?" Cardoso removed his hand from Briony's neck, but he still held the knife as a reminder that it would be in her best interest to agree to his terms.

Briony held back a growl, hating to feel so powerless. But then a new thought came to her. *I'm na powerless, am I?*

Without warning, a bolt of lightning crackled outside, making everyone but Briony jump and turn to the window. Adaira turned back and frowned at Briony, but Briony just shrugged her shoulders. The commodore, on the other hand, seemed almost petrified at what could be the start of another storm.

Briony cleared her throat to get Cardoso's attention. He twisted around quickly, his hands twitching as he looked down at her.

Briony smiled. "Aye, Comodoro. I think I can do that."

Taking Sides

"We've been at sea for two days, but your wound is healing at an incredible rate. I've never seen anything like it," marveled the naval surgeon.

Well, you've never treated a selkie before, have you? Is it normal to heal this fast? Now that Niall's gone, I dinna have anyone I can ask. . . .

Or maybe 'tis just because Costa was na actually trying to kill me.

She sighed, wondering if the other ship had already reached land. By all rights, the *São Nicolau* should have, but perhaps they'd run into the same nasty fog that was holding up Cardoso's ship.

When they'd first left Everton, Cardoso had pushed the men almost to their breaking point, hoping to get a glimpse of the *São Nicolau*. But sometime during the night, fog had rolled in, veiling their path.

Visible from the window in her room, the fog was so thick it was almost tangible. Briony easily felt it when she reached out with her mind.

I'm confident that I could make it vanish if I wanted to, but part o' me is glad we haven' spotted the São Nicolau *yet. I dinna want Santiago to be caught.*

On the other hand, she also feared what would happen if they didn't catch up to them soon, for Cardoso didn't seem like the sort to take her back home.

And what o' the captain? He said he plans to marry Lucia, but I dinna know what he intends to do with Santiago. Comodoro Cardoso already believes Santiago is guilty o' treason, so I dinna know how Costa

315

plans to take him back into society. . . . Or maybe he does na intend to do that at all?

Briony released a feral snarl. Ruminating on these questions was giving her a colossal headache.

The naval surgeon jumped in surprise. "Senhorita, are you all right? Do you need something to drink?"

Briony groaned and shook her head. "Nay, 'tis na something a doctor can fix. I appreciate yer concern though. And what you've done to help me recover."

If only he were as good at fixing my sealskin.

The pelt lay behind Briony's pillow, its warmth radiating like a comforting hand upon her back. Her soul ached at the thought of never wearing it again, never again riding the currents as a seal. She knew she should have left it safely at home, but after so many years of not knowing it even existed, she couldn't bear to part with it.

Briony smiled a bit to allay the man's concerns, grateful that at least one person on the ship cared about her well-being. Most of the men were suspicious of her, perhaps because it was considered unlucky to have a woman aboard. But she still preferred their company to that of Cardoso, who openly despised her.

She'd tried to explain to him what happened on the beach with Costa, sans the selkie part, but the commodore would hear none of it. Santiago hadn't denied the charges, so Cardoso had no reason to believe the merchant innocent.

The "biased" testimony of a common Orcadian woman was not going to change his mind. To him, she was merely a tool for bringing a criminal to justice. When she'd called Cardoso out for his definition of "justice," the man had barely restrained himself from slapping her across the face. Her ears still stung from his bellows of her stupidity and naïvete.

Unless Santiago changed his plea or Costa freely admitted guilt, the commodore would be returning Santiago to Portugal, where he would stand trial.

A shout came from the crow's nest: "*São Nicolau!*"

Briony frowned at the sound, her emotions a mixture of hope and dread. *If I can get Costa away from Lucia, maybe, just maybe, I can convince Santiago to tell the commodore the truth. Then—*

She blushed.

Let's na get ahead o' ourselves, Briony. Dreams o' the future can wait. If this does na go well, neither o' us may have a future o' any kind.

Briony shivered. She'd woken that morning in a cold sweat, her mind replaying the moment she'd been shot. *Every decision Costa makes is to his own benefit; there's no reason fer him to keep me alive anymore, so I'm sure he'll kill me this time if he gets the chance.*

I'll just have to make sure he never gets that chance.

Briony and the surgeon both rose, but the man instantly ushered Briony back to bed. "I'll return to check on you in a little while. Stay here where it's safe."

As soon as he was gone, Briony slowly stood, bracing herself against the bed. There was no way she would be staying inside, regardless of how safe it was.

Without warning, the cabin shook with the impact of what could only have been a cannonball.

BOOM! The sound rang in Briony's ears for several seconds after the hit, reverberating through her mind and filling her with terror.

What . . . Are they shooting at us? Briony gripped the side of the bed tighter, her knuckles white. *If they're trying to bring the ship down already, how will we get close enough to negotiate anything?*

SPLASH! SPLASH!

Two shots this time, both misses. But one of them sounded farther away, almost as if—

"Nay! They can' do that!" Briony sprang out of the room, ignoring the pain in her chest. If she wasn't mistaken, one of those shots hadn't come from the *São Nicolau*; it had come from the commodore's ship.

When she came out into the open air, her eyes instantly latched onto the *São Nicolau* a few hundred yards away. The fog had vanished, and brilliant beams of sunlight pierced through the mostly overcast skies.

The men around Briony were moving quickly yet methodically, as if they'd done this far too many times. The commodore stood at the helm, barking orders and keeping the wheel steady.

More cannonballs flew toward them, just as their ship

317

returned the favor with some shots of its own. The air rang with the grisly sounds of explosions and screams.

Briony raced up to the helm with reckless abandon and grabbed the commodore's arm. "Comodoro, stop this! There are innocent people on that ship!"

Cardoso's dark eyes turned to her, his gaze radiating with anger. "Senhorita, you have no place here. Get out of the way." He shook her off him, and she fell to the floor in a heap.

Briony pulled herself up onto her elbows and reached a hand toward him. "But, Comodoro, you have—"

The commodore kicked her away, his foot connecting with her stomach. "Shut up before I throw you over the side!" And with that, he turned his attention from her and continued shouting to his subordinates.

Briony groaned, feeling tears prick at her eyes. Again she pulled herself up, though this time, she brought her body all the way into a standing position. She leaned against the railing, trying to think of what to do. Her eyes traveled upward to the crow's nest, now abandoned by its lookout, and then farther toward the heavens.

Maybe I can do something about this on my own.

***

Santiago trudged forward behind Costa, feeling like his heart remained onshore even as his feet stepped onto the *São Nicolau*. No longer did the planks creak in a warm welcome, eager to carry him once more. Instead, the gently rolling ship seemed more foreign than ever before, as if all sense of belonging had departed from it.

I have to get back to Briony!

Santiago didn't know a lot about gun wounds, but he prayed the captain had been telling the truth, and Briony would survive.

He hoped Mistress Stubbins and Mr. Burgess had been able to find her. Santiago had seen them racing up the hill before Costa had shoved him behind the closest house to hide until they passed.

So wrapped up in his thoughts was he that he didn't even

notice when he and Costa arrived at his room. Neither did he notice who was already inside.

"Brother! I'm so glad you're all right!" Lucia barreled into him, nearly knocking Santiago from his feet. Her petite arms wrapped around his frame and held him there as tightly as she could.

Santiago smiled down at his sister, his eyes moist at the sight of her.

"See, dearest? I told you I'd get him out for you," said a smooth, dangerous voice.

Santiago held back a growl as he felt the tender moment crumble. *I should know better than to let my guard down; as long as Costa is here, Lucia is far from safe.*

Lucia pulled back from her brother with a large grin and turned her affectionate gaze to the captain. "Yes, I should never have doubted you, Andreas. You have a way of always coming through, even when it seems impossible." She skipped over and interlocked fingers with the man before leaning toward him.

"Did you tell him yet, love?" The question was meant to be a whisper, but Lucia was much too loud for Santiago not to catch it.

Santiago gritted his teeth at their familiarity with each other. *Lucia, this man won't hesitate to kill you if you become more of a hindrance than a help.*

"I did share it with him, but he didn't seem nearly as excited as I thought he would," Costa said with a raised eyebrow in Santiago's direction.

Santiago glared in return but quickly hid his true feelings once Lucia turned to face him. Her expression was full of confusion and hurt, and seeing it pricked at Santiago's soul.

He looked away, unable to bear the betrayal in his sister's eyes. "It just seemed a little hasty to me. I mean, you barely know each oth—"

"We've known each other for years. Yes, he's been away on business with you during most of that time, but you've always spoken so well of him. I thought you'd be happy for me. . . ." Lucia's face turned red as tears threatened to spill down her cheeks.

319

"You don't understand. . . ." Santiago reached for her shoulder, but Lucia pushed him away.

"What don't I understand? Ah, this is about Briony, isn't it? Just because you can't be with her, you can't stand to see me happy either." Lucia immediately winced at her own words, seeming to know they were untrue. But instead of apologizing, she simply set her jaw and sent Santiago a hateful scowl.

"You and I both know all I want, *all I've ever wanted,* was for you to be happy," he replied, but his voice lacked conviction as he spoke.

He knew he'd been a poor excuse for a brother, and there was no way for him to win this argument, not when he couldn't tell Lucia the whole truth. *If I could just talk to her alone, maybe——*

"If you wanted me to be happy, you wouldn't have left me after Mamãe and Pai died."

Santiago flinched, feeling the pain behind Lucia's words as sharply as the dagger Costa had used to kill their parents. *I never realized how much my absence hurt her.*

And as he looked into her bitter eyes, he realized it didn't matter if he told her the truth about Costa or not.

Because she wouldn't believe me.

"All that time in Aveiro, I was just waiting for you to notice me, waiting to see if you still loved me like you did before they were gone. But I was a fool. It's only now when I'm about to leave you that you pretend to care about me. Well, it's too late, Brother. Andreas and I are getting married whether you like it or not." Lucia turned from Santiago and placed her hand in the crook of the captain's arm. "Andreas, let's go to your quarters. I don't want to spend another moment here."

Costa gladly obliged his fiancée and led her from the room, smiling back at Santiago as they left.

***

"Mr. Mendes, sir?" a hesitant voice asked.

Santiago glanced to his right, still leaning against the ship's railing. He'd been staring at nothing for he didn't know how long, trying to think of a solution to his predicament but finding none. They'd been at sea much longer than expected, thanks to a thick fog that had rolled in the day before, turning the world ghostly white.

"Yes, Rodriguez?"

The sailor looked around nervously before whispering, "Mr. Mendes, I know what happened with the captain before we got to Everton."

The statement shook Santiago from his state of self-pity, and he turned to give the man his full attention. "What do you mean?"

"I saw the captain try to shoot you during the storm. Was it because of what I told you before, about your family's carriage being in Lisbon?" But then Rodriguez's eyes widened in shock. "Was he the one who got Policarpio ou—"

"Quiet!" Santiago grabbed the man's arm before he could say more. "You can't let anyone hear that. Understand?"

Rodriguez nodded, and Santiago stepped back. The young sailor looked away, his face red with embarrassment. "I . . . I want to help, sir. Before we left, before that strange storm, Senhorita Fairborn asked for my help. I believe she wanted to prove your innocence, to find something on the captain, but I . . . I was too much of a coward to do anything. I don't want to be that way anymore."

He locked gazes with Santiago, his eyes full of determination despite his quivering hands. "So tell me what I can do. I don't care if it's dangerous. I can testify for you, try to find proof of the captain's involvement, something. I don't want you to be on the run when you didn't do anything wrong."

Santiago clapped the man on the shoulder, admiring his courage. "I appreciate that, Rodriguez. I didn't tell the commodore the truth when he arrested me because Lucia's life was on the line. Until we can get her away from the captain, our hands are tied."

"Ship! Off the starboard bow!"

Santiago and Rodriguez spun around, their faces paling at the sight of Comodoro Cardoso's ship. At some point during their conversation, the fog had lifted, making it possible to see

321

the sixty-meter naval vessel almost upon them. Suddenly, the *São Nicolau*'s size of forty meters felt tinier than ever before.

The captain appeared from his quarters, gripping his pistol. Once he spotted the ship, his gaze immediately turned to Santiago, conveying an unspoken question: *Are you responsible for this?*

Santiago shook his head vehemently, not wanting to put Lucia at further risk.

But the captain was already slithering toward him, sparks shooting from his eyes. His hand with the pistol twitched, but then he noticed Rodriguez at Santiago's side.

"They've caught up to us. But how?" Rodriguez looked to Santiago rather than Costa, not just for answers but also for comfort. The man might have been trying to be brave, but fear still threatened to swallow him up.

"Anyone in town could have told Cardoso we were going to Norway," Santiago replied, though he kept his attention on Costa as he spoke.

A humorless chuckle burst forth from the captain's lips. "Ah, but what if it wasn't just anyone?"

"What are you talking about? Who?"

"She knew too much already," Costa grumbled before turning away from Santiago, effectively ending their conversation.

Briony? He thinks she told Cardoso where we were going? And maybe even what Costa is capable of . . . Santiago watched the captain race up to the wheel. *What's he doing?*

"Sousa! Tell the men below deck to start loading the cannons. Fernandes, make sure all the cannons up here are ready to fire at my command."

"What? There's no way we can win against that monster. It's almost twice our size," Rodriguez exclaimed, panic lacing his words.

But the other sailors were already following orders, hurrying to man the cannons regardless of their odds of winning.

Santiago was at the captain's side almost instantaneously. "Costa! Stop this madness!"

But Costa just smirked. "Madness? You've made far too

many unwise decisions to get to judge mine. That little snitch surely told Cardoso who shot her and, more importantly, why. That forces my hand."

"But this is suicide. You're going to send us to our graves."

"You don't think I'd start a battle I have no chance of winning, do you? I checked their cannons when I came to rescue you. Guess what I discovered?"

Santiago huffed and shrugged, flabbergasted that they were having this conversation now when they were all about to die. "That they have more than we do?"

"Yes, they have six more than our seventy-four, but theirs are over fifteen years old."

"How do you know that? And why does it matter?"

"Don't you know anything? They're still using linstock instead of gunlocks. They can't even aim at us when they shoot or they'll be hit by their own recoil.[35] We have the advantage if we attack first. Now, if you're not going to help man the cannons, I suggest you get off the deck and stay with Lucia while I deal with this. Fernandes!"

"Aye, Capitão!" Fernandes turned to the captain from his place on deck.

"Tell the men to fire!"

"No! Don't, Fernandes," Santiago shouted, jumping in front of the captain.

The sailor stared at the two men in confusion; never before had Mr. Mendes told someone to disregard the captain's orders.

And Costa wasn't happy about it either. He threw out his hand and pushed Santiago to the side, making the other man stumble a few steps.

"No one gives orders on this ship except me. *No one.*" Costa's face was red with anger, his body poised for an attack.

And for a split second, Santiago was about to give him the fight he wanted. Until another idea came to him.

"Have it your way, Costa. Just don't take us all down with you in your arrogance," Santiago snarled, brushing off his shoulder where the man's hand had touched him.

---

[35] Gunlocks first came into use in 1745, but they were not immediately used by everyone because older cannons had to be replaced with new ones.

Santiago felt the sting of his former friend's gaze as he marched toward the captain's quarters, but he refused to look back. *Better to look like I'm caught up with wounded pride so that Costa doesn't realize my true intentions.*

Because what he intended to do was going to make the captain's day a whole lot worse.

Song of the Selkie

A quick nod to Rodriguez directed the young sailor to discreetly follow behind as Santiago made his way out of the captain's sight. After explaining his plans, his partner in crime didn't exactly call Santiago mad, but the look of incredulity on the man's face was not very encouraging. Even so, Rodriguez agreed to go along with everything Santiago said despite the very high likelihood of them both getting killed.

Perhaps this isn't the best idea. . . . What if—

But then they heard cannon fire, and Santiago knew they could wait no longer. The two of them burst into the captain's quarters, making Lucia jump from her seat in fright. As soon as she realized who it was, though, she rushed to her brother's side and clutched his arm in a death grip.

"What's going on out there?" she asked, seeming to have forgotten she was angry with him.

"Cardoso found us. I have to get you out of here. Rodriguez will take you to one of the rowboats, and I'll lower you down so you can get away from the fighting. Go north and use the *São Nicolau* as a shield to block the other ship's view. We can't be very far from Norway at this point, so there's a good chance a passing ship will see you." Santiago grabbed one of the pistols on the captain's desk as he spoke, tucking it into the back of his pants.

"A passing ship? But what about you? And Andreas? Are you saying you won't come get us?"

The vulnerable look on Lucia's tearstained face was more

than Santiago could bear. He drew her into a tight hug and held her as if his life depended on it. When he pulled back, there were also tears in his eyes. "I don't know what's going to happen. I just know I have to keep you safe. I'm sorry for not being a better brother, but I'm afraid this is all I can do."

Lucia gave him a small smile and gripped his hands in hers. "You've been a better brother than I've given you credit for. Try to forget what I said last time. I love you."

"And I love you. Now, let's go." Without giving her the chance to say more, Santiago pulled her out the door, Rodriguez close behind.

They scurried across the deck toward the rowboats, neither man daring to turn back and risk catching the captain's eye. The world was a cacophony of sound as cannonballs shot through the air and men raced about in every direction. No one paid attention to the three of them since each sailor had his own tasks to worry about.

Suddenly, a cannonball hit the ship's rigging, sending wood and rope flying in all directions. Santiago ducked out of the way just in time as one of the sails fell to the deck. His heart lurched to see his ship falling apart—again—but there was no time to stop and assess the damage.

"You two, hop in!" Santiago all but threw Lucia into the nearest rowboat as they reached it, and Rodriguez jumped in behind her.

Santiago had just set about lowering them with the davit[36] when he heard Lucia ask, "And Andreas wants me to do this?"

"Yes, it was his idea." Santiago forced himself to nod in a manner he hoped was convincing before deploying the small boat into the water with a splash.

He breathed a sigh of relief, though he still felt his chest tighten at the thought that what may have been his final words to his sister had been a lie.

He turned back to the battle, his gaze scanning the horrible aftermath of the captain's foolhardy decision. Santiago's crew, ship, and sister's life were all at risk because of this man's choice to fight rather than surrender.

---

[36] A small crane on board a ship.

No more. Santiago was tired of letting Andreas Costa make the rules. And with Lucia now out of the way, it was time to change things.

His green eyes shifted upward to the captain just as his hand reached back to grab his gun.

CRACK!

Lightning burst forth from the sky, hitting the water between the two ships with such force it almost seemed to make the *São Nicolau* shake.

What in the w—

Everyone's attention was snagged by the unexpected bolt. The fear among his men, hovering just below the surface before, seemed almost palpable now. Even the sailors on the other ship, trained men of war, couldn't conceal the anxiety on their faces.

There was no possible explanation for the sudden shift in weather. Not when the sky had been clear of a single cloud only moments ago. *None except—*

But before Santiago could fully process the thought, a second sound reached his ears. It started as a low hum over the waters, barely audible over the blood pounding in his ears. A soft, sweet sound that rolled like the waves themselves, building in volume as it seemed to spread over his entire being and grab hold of his very soul. It wasn't words per se but a musical cry that moved up and down in a haunting melisma. [37]

A sound that could only be made by a human voice.

No, not entirely human. Briony? And that was Santiago's final thought before all connection to reality fractured into a dozen pieces. Pieces that his dazed mind couldn't bother to pick up when it could instead just fall deeper under Briony's spell.

He didn't even notice that all the people around him had done the exact same thing, all wrapped up in the haze of the enchantment. Young and old, ally and enemy, all forgot the battle around them and merely strained their ears to hear more.

And the sea itself, usually a tumultuous, untamable force, sat quietly as it, too, drank in the beautiful sound of one of its favorite creatures: the song of the selkie.

---

[37] A group of notes sung to one syllable.

327

***

Briony peered down from her spot in the crow's nest, shocked that her song had actually worked. All the commodore's sailors stood still, vacant expressions on their faces as they stared at her. When she glanced over at the *São Nicolau*, the men there were the same, all frozenly looking her way as though waiting for what she would do next.

She drew back from the edge, uncomfortable with so many eyes on her at once. *Now what? I brought the battle to a halt, but I've no idea how long the effects o' the song will last.*

Will they just go back to killing each other? Santiago is the only other human I've used my powers on, and according to him, the effect was only fer a moment. If I'm going to do something, I have to do it fast.

Briony turned her attention to the *São Nicolau*. There, with his hand on the wheel, stood Captain Costa. As soon as she laid eyes on the man, the ache in her chest intensified, reminding her of what he'd done the last time they'd seen each other. And next to him was none other than her lost merchant, looking up at her like she was water in a desert land.

"Captain Costa! Turn yourself in," she shouted.

Within seconds, the captain, his face still blank, began moving toward the edge of the ship. He said nothing as he grabbed a rope from one of the yards attached to the closest mast and swung himself over to the other ship.

Briony climbed down to the deck, anxious to make certain the man followed through with her orders. But as her feet hit the wooden planks, she thought she heard—

"Agh!"

***

Glossy, dreamlike images floated before Santiago. He watched Costa make his way over to the commodore's ship, his mind not aware of the gravity of what was happening. But then a flash of movement caught his eye—a woman was descending from the crow's nest to the deck below.

"Briony!"

328

His lips uttered her name without him even meaning to, his heart recognizing her even before his brain did. She turned instantly toward the sound, her face breaking out into a bright smile.

But then—

Briony yelped and fell forward as Costa's gun hit the side of her head. She landed hard at the man's feet and didn't move again.

"*What is going on here?*" Comodoro Cardoso bellowed, quickly arriving at the midwife's side with his pistol trained on Costa.

Costa's eyes narrowed, and Santiago wondered if he was about to do something rash, but then the captain's gun clattered onto the floor.

"She's a witch, senhor. I was trying to protect you from her spell," Costa said, raising his hands in the air. He gestured with his foot to the woman beside him.

Cardoso raised a suspicious brow. "A witch, you say? And why would you be trying to protect me when you were trying to kill me a few minutes ago?"

The captain shook his head. "That was never my desire, Comodoro. I was merely doing Mr. Mendes's wishes after he threatened to have me keelhauled. [38] I would never willingly attack an officer, senhor."

The commodore turned a hateful glare toward Santiago while Costa smirked victoriously.

But the captain didn't know his only leverage against Santiago was currently rowing away with Adriano Rodriguez.

Santiago smiled back at Costa, making the other man's expression falter.

"Is what your captain said true, Mr. Mendes?" Cardoso barked, moving his pistol toward the merchant.

Santiago dropped his own weapon and took a step forward. "Not a word of it, senhor. I was never part of the attack on you, and I had nothing to do with the attack on the king either. Keep your pistol aimed on your true enemy, and I can explain everything. Just let me make sure Senhorita

---

[38] To be punished by being dragged through the water under the keel of a ship.

Fairborn is all right first."

Cardoso didn't look convinced, but he nodded and gestured for the man to join them on his ship.

Costa's eyes widened in shock. "What are you doing, Mendes?"

"What I should have done a long time ago, *old friend*. Telling the truth." Santiago grabbed a rope and swung himself over. He knelt before Briony and checked her neck for a pulse.

After a few seconds, he sighed in relief. *Just knocked out. With any luck, she'll wake in the next few minutes.*

Costa gritted his teeth, his fury threatening to spill over. "It's your word against mine. It was your carriage in Lisbon that night. Who do you think the commodore will believe?"

Santiago shook his head, almost feeling pity toward his former friend. "But see, it's not just my word against yours. Others know what you're really capable of, and they're willing to testify against you."

"Not if I can help it!" And before anyone knew what was happening, Costa had retrieved his pistol and grabbed the commodore from behind. He shoved the gun against the man's temple, placing the commodore between himself and Santiago.

Cardoso's sailors reached for their weapons, but Costa shouted, "Don't even try it, or the commodore dies!"

He tugged the commodore backward, positioning himself with his back to the ship's railing, a place where sneaking up on him would be impossible.

"You have nowhere to go, Costa," Cardoso growled.

"He's right," Santiago said. "There's no need for further bloodshed. Just give this up."

Cardoso glanced around, searching for a way out of the situation.

He has to know it's hopeless. With my word, Briony's, and Rodriguez's, he can't get out of this.

But a stubborn gleam shone in the captain's eye. One that made Santiago nervous. "I'll never give this up! Not until I get what's owed me!"

Santiago frowned. "What are you talking about?"

"My birthright. My title."

"Why would you think you deserve a title? You're nothing but common scum," Cardoso spat.

Costa laughed bitterly and pressed the gun harder against the man. "Ah, but that's where you're wrong, Comodoro. That's where you're all wrong. If you only knew . . ."

"If we only knew *what*, Costa?" Santiago asked, hardly believing what he was hearing.

A wicked, mad smile broke out over Costa's face. "You want truth? Well, here it is: my name is not Andreas *Costa*. My father was none other than Luis Bernardo de Távora, the 4th Marquis of Távora. And it was thanks to my help that the king was almost assassinated."

There was a collective gasp as everyone took in the unexpected revelation.

"Not that any of that matters now, though, since you're all going to die anyway." And before anyone could react, Costa shoved the commodore forward and leaped from the ship to the waters below.

Loose Ends

One of the officers—Alves, if Santiago remembered correctly—asked, "What did he mean by—"

CRASH!

Santiago looked up to see the crow's nest falling apart above his head, thanks to a cannonball that had just come from the *São Nicolau*.

Santiago lifted Briony and bounded toward the ship's starboard side just as a second cannonball collided with the hull.

"Return fire, men," Cardoso shouted, one hand against the railing to stabilize himself. "Why are they shooting now, Mendes? Don't they realize you're aboard my ship?"

Santiago shook his head in amazement. "You think I know?"

The commodore took a deep breath to say something, but Santiago didn't wait to hear the man's retort; he had far more important things to do than listen to empty words. He rushed forward to get Briony below deck and away from danger. The ship shook as it took yet another hit, making Santiago slip on the last stairstep.

He stumbled downward, gasping when he almost dropped her. Somehow, though, he regained his footing and pushed the first door open—a closet. He groaned and turned to the next door—no luck either.

Muffled voices and the sounds of loading cannons nearby told him the commodore's men were following orders. He feared what the world would look like when he went back outside—

"Finally!" The third door led to an empty room with a bed. He tenderly laid Briony down upon it, noticing the bandages on her shoulder. A painful reminder of how close he'd come to losing her.

Why is she here, anyway? She should be resting at home, not out on the open sea. Why would Cardoso bring her along?

He stared down at her unconscious form, so delicate in sleep . . . and yet he couldn't help but remember her most recent display of incredible power. Santiago's heart quickened its pace, making him realize the answer to his own question. *Because of me. He knew he could use her to get to me.*

Santiago clenched a fist, enraged that the man's ruthlessness had put his beloved's life in danger. *Such an innocent soul should never be put in harm's way.*

Santiago leaned close to her ear. "If we both make it out of this alive, Briony, I promise I'm going to do all I can to protect you. For the rest of my days."

"Uuuugh . . ." Briony began to stir, her eyelids fluttering.

"Amorzinho, I'm here. It's all right." Santiago stroked her forehead, brushing the black locks away from her face.

Briony blinked a few times before her eyes homed in on his. "S-Santiago? What's going on?"

Santiago rose from his place by her side. "I'm so sorry to do this, but I have to leave you here. Someone from my ship started firing again, and I have to try to end this before more people get hurt. Wait here."

"But, Santiago, I can help."

Santiago smiled at the beautiful woman before him, so eager to jump in even when she was injured. *She might not be feeling it yet, but that blow to the head is going to give her a serious headache very soon. And if her gunshot wound has reopened . . .* There was no way he wanted her back out there where she could get hurt even more.

"You already have. In more ways than you know. And once I'm back, I'll explain it all to you. I promise."

"B-But . . ."

"Shh . . . Please, Briony. For my sake. Stay here."

He leaned in, letting his lips linger against hers while wishing he could simply remain there forever. But the sounds from outside pounded in his ears, making him remember just how impossible that wish was. And if he didn't do something soon, *all* his wishes for the future could perish.

***

Once Santiago was gone, Briony immediately regretted letting him go alone. She stood up from the bed, determined to get back out there.

I'm a selkie! Surely I'm powerful enough to stop this on my own. I just have to think o' the right command fer the men to obey. . . . I can do this. I can. . . .

But a sudden throbbing in her head distracted her from her train of thought. The pain roared across her skull like a lion seeking to devour her. Briony pressed her fingers against her temples and lay back upon the bed, but neither action seemed to help the rising anguish.

The ship continued to shake from cannonball after cannonball, and Briony feared that Santiago's efforts had failed. She forced her legs to move, bringing her body up and then out the door. She climbed the stairs and made her way to the ship's stern, where the commodore was again giving orders.

Briony hoped to see Santiago there with him, but luck wasn't on her side. Before the commodore could notice her, she turned and tried to get a good look at the rest of the deck, but then nausea hit her full force. She launched herself at the railing and retched over the side, emptying her stomach of the little it contained.

Once she was done, she turned her gaze up and glimpsed movement a ways out on the water—

She gasped. *Is that*—

Two rowboats sat several yards out from the ships, one with two passengers and the other carrying a single man.

POW!

The sound of the gun was quiet amidst all the cannonballs and shouting, but Briony heard it as clear as day. She watched dumbstruck as Adriano Rodriguez fell out of his rowboat and into the water. Meanwhile, Lucia sat in silent terror, her eyes shifting from the corpse now floating in the water to the man who'd killed him.

Captain Costa then aimed his gun at Lucia and beckoned for her to join him on his boat. Lucia complied without hesitation, and before long, the two of them were off, becoming smaller and smaller in Briony's vision.

"There's no way I'm letting him get away." Briony lifted her hand to summon a storm, and instantly, her desire became reality as dark clouds swirled above Costa's rowboat. She saw the captain turn back toward the ship; they were too far away for her to see him clearly, but she knew he was looking for her. And the gun at Lucia's head told her what would happen if she allowed her storm to continue.

Briony reluctantly released the clouds, unwilling to allow Lucia to get hurt even if it meant catching the captain. *There has to be another way to rescue her. . . .*

And as she watched the rowboat begin to move again, its oars sweeping through the water, the solution came to her. *Maybe a solution. Or maybe 'twill just result in something worse. But I can' allow that monster to take Lucia. Na until I do everything in my power to stop him.*

Briony raced back to her room, avoiding the sailors as they went about their tasks. She grabbed her sealskin and marched to the commodore's quarters with determination. But as soon as she opened the door, her entire body began trembling in fear.

When entering such a room, most people would have been stunned by the grandeur within. And while it had been impressive the first time she'd seen it, now Briony barely noticed the expensive trinkets and fine upholstery, for that was not why she'd come. Her gaze went straight to the room's great window overlooking the open sea, a window from which Costa's rowboat was plainly visible.

If I dinna do something soon, what will happen to Lucia? Costa already killed Adriano—What if she's next? Even if, by some miracle, Santiago gets the fighting to stop, Lucia will still be Costa's hostage, and he could still use her to escape.

She swallowed thickly as all the potential outcomes of her idea came to mind. *What if I can' do it?*

Briony shook her head and turned to leave—*But if I do nothing and Lucia gets hurt, or worse, I'll have to live with that regret fer the rest o' my life. How can I look Santiago in the eye again, knowing I did na do everything in my power to save his beloved sister?*

She stood there motionless for a few moments, but in her heart, Briony knew she'd already made her decision. She took a deep breath and dropped her sealskin on the floor. Then, with all her strength, she lifted the commodore's chair and slammed it against the window. Several spindly lines spread across the glass just before the giant window shattered and dropped into the sea.

She knelt on the floor and retrieved her pelt, running the pads of her thumbs over the softness. But when her fingers reached the two places where the bullet had passed through, she felt something strange. *What? Where's—*

Briony inspected the holes, unable to believe what she felt and saw. They'd shrunk. Significantly. Almost as if they were—

Healing. And well enough that my plan might just work.

Since my human body is alive and recovering, is my sealskin doing that too? So long as it does na get destroyed, will it heal entirely with time?

With a newfound joy and confidence, Briony stripped out of her clothes. It almost felt like stripping away fear itself, for she now believed she could find the strength to do what was needed. "Hold on, Lucia. I'm coming fer you."

Briony pulled the pelt over her body, feeling the two skins meld together as one. Her sight and hearing adjusted as her senses shifted. The ceiling stretched away from her as though it was growing, yet she knew she was the one doing the changing. She groaned at the sudden aches in her stomach and back as the wounds settled into her, but they were tolerable. More tolerable than she'd expected.

And with the transition from human to animal, Briony's thoughts simplified. For when she lifted her black eyes back to the rowboat out on the sea, she no longer saw Lucia and Captain Costa. Instead, she saw merely friend and foe: a friend to be saved at all costs and a foe she would *not* let stand in her way.

She dove into the water with hardly a sound, her body gliding through its natural element. She ducked below the surface and zoomed toward her goal, making sure she was deep enough not to be spotted from above. In order for her plan to succeed, stealth was required. If Costa even suspected she was near, he might dispose of Lucia as he had Adriano.

When she glimpsed the boat's telltale shadow, she slowly ascended until her head just barely crested the water's surface. Costa was facing away from her, moving his arms in a steady, rhythmic motion as he rowed farther and farther from the chaos he'd caused. Lucia, on the other hand, was facing Briony, and if the girl happened to lift her eyes—

Lucia gasped as her gaze met Briony's. Briony immediately ducked below the water and then slipped under the boat to rise on the other side.

"What is it now?" the captain growled.

Lucia, unaware that Briony was now on the port side of the rowboat, pointed to where the seal had been before. "Th- There's something in the water!"

Costa instantly stopped rowing, but before he had the chance to catch sight of her, Briony was already making her move. She dove directly below the boat and then swam upward as fast as she could. The rowboat heaved to the side, dumping both its passengers into the water before rebalancing.

The two humans flailed their arms as they rose to the surface. Briony wasted no time and flew forward to her target. She gripped Lucia's arm with her mouth and started to pull.

But the poor girl had no idea she was actually being rescued and began to panic even more. She jerked away from Briony and inhaled water as she tried to scream. The seal, not to be deterred, simply grabbed her again and turned to swim back toward the ships.

Lucia squirmed and clawed at Briony with all her might, and when her nails caught on one of Briony's injuries, Briony released her with a yelp. Lucia turned and started moving back to the rowboat as Briony fought through the pain and tried not to pass out.

If I lose consciousness, that's it. And after all the trials I've been through, there's no way I'm going to accept defeat now.

Shaking her head to reorient herself, Briony then joined the two humans at the surface just as they took hold of the side of the boat. When her head broke through the water, Briony took in a great gulp of air, her focus on rejuvenating herself rather than on the two people around her.

"Aaah!" Lucia shrieked.

Briony whirled toward the sound, her eyes widening when she caught sight of the gun Costa was pulling out of the boat. She only just managed to slide out of the way as the man fired a shot. She went under him and bit his foot. He aimed to shoot at her again, but she was already pulling him downward, knowing his gun would be useless below the surface.

But just before he was fully under, Costa tossed the pistol back into the boat and drew out a knife. He swung the weapon toward Briony's neck, but she twisted sideways to throw off his aim and then continued to drag him deeper. The man swiped at her again, this time forcing Briony to release her hold on him.

Then, without warning, Costa turned away and started swimming back up. Briony's first thought was that he was trying to get back to the safety of the boat. Lucia had managed to pull herself into it in the meantime, and no doubt she also thought herself safer for it.

But Briony was a selkie, and in a moment of pride, she believed herself unstoppable. *Nowhere is safe fer Costa anymore, be it on land or in the sea. Fer I am the hunter now, and he is the prize.*

She gave him a few seconds to think he was escaping, time to believe he had a chance before she would strike again.

But then she remembered the loathing in the captain's eyes before he'd turned away. It had been much more than just that of a man looking at an animal. It was almost as if he knew who she was and what she was trying to do. *But if that's true—*

Briony sped after him desperately, hoping she was wrong—

But she'd hesitated too long. By the time she reached the captain, he'd already made his move. And when Briony's head broke the surface of the water and she saw what he'd done, he smiled.

"I do believe this win goes to me, Senhorita Fairborn. An

impressive effort, but you should know better by now."

His words fell on deaf ears, and as he heaved himself into the now empty rowboat, Briony couldn't be bothered to care. For he was exactly right. He'd won.

And more than the blood pooling in the water, more than the knife still lodged in Lucia's chest, it was Lucia's eyes that revealed the truth. She was not long for this world.

"Ah, how I hate loose ends," the captain laughed.

Briony turned only to see that Costa had retrieved his gun.

"Adeus,[39] senhorita."

BANG!

---

[39] Goodbye.

Parting

"We have to catch that fiend, Costa, and bring him to justice," Cardoso ordered Santiago.

The merchant nodded, glad to have someone as powerful as the commodore on his side for a change.

"And after that, I'll expect your full cooperation as a key witness when I bring him to trial," Cardoso continued, his tone leaving no room for argument. "Veiga, see if you can spot him from the crow's nest."

One of the sailors, presumably Veiga, scurried away and clambered up the ropes to get a better view.

The sailors on Santiago's ship were already trying to mend the rigging and broken sail as best they could, though somehow the ship still seemed moderately seaworthy.

It had taken a bit of convincing from Santiago to get them to stop fighting, but the fact that Costa had abandoned everyone, something a captain should never do, had been proof enough that the man didn't have their best interests at heart.

And now that the battle was truly over, everyone was eager for revenge on the man responsible for all the destruction.

It hadn't taken long to discover that Claudio Perreira had shot the cannon that started the second attack. He was currently sitting in Cardoso's brig, no doubt regretting his foolish decision.

But it turned out that the weasel had been acting under orders from Captain Costa, and not only had Costa ordered

Perreira to start shooting again, but he'd also told the sailor to let down one of the rowboats. And by the time everything had settled between the two ships, Costa had slipped away. *That man seems to have made a plan for just about every outcome. Where could he have—*

No, he can wait. I need to find Lucia first.

Santiago called to the commodore, "My sister left in one of the rowboats when the fighting started. I need to make sure she's all right—"

"There's no time for that, Mendes. We have to get Costa now before he reaches Norway. If he truly is a Távora, then who knows what kind of connections he has! I need all the resources I can get, and that includes you and your ship."

"But I—"

"Comodoro! Man overboard!" Veiga cried from above.

Santiago dashed in the direction the man indicated. *Who could it be?*

A few of Santiago's men had died amidst the fighting, but he'd thought everyone was accounted for—

He gasped when he recognized the man, or rather body, bobbing in the water next to one of the *São Nicolau*'s rowboats: Adriano Rodriguez.

"But he . . ." Santiago swept his eyes in all directions, searching for his sister. *Rodriguez was supposed to protect her and get as far away as possible. How did he end up here, just yards from the battle? Lucia, where are you?*

Santiago dove overboard and swam toward the corpse. When he flipped the man over, a deep sadness wrapped itself around him. The man was so young, barely more than a boy, and already his life was over. *But how?*

Santiago's eyes widened when he saw the bullet hole in Rodriguez's forehead. *Surely Lucia couldn't have done this. . . .* Santiago doubted she'd ever even held a pistol before. *Whoever did this must have taken her, too. Wh—*

But he knew who. Santiago took a second look around and felt a spark of hope blaze to life in his chest. "Comodoro, look there!"

Though it had gotten a good distance away, it certainly appeared to be a second rowboat. Santiago just prayed that his mind wasn't playing tricks on him and letting him see what he wanted to see.

"Good eye, man! Now get back in here so we can get going," the commodore barked before turning his attention to his own sailors.

Santiago didn't need to be told twice. He paddled through the water and got himself back onto Cardoso's ship. He ordered his men to follow behind in the *São Nicolau* while he traveled on the commodore's faster vessel.

"What's happening, Veiga? Can you see any better from up there?" Santiago asked.

"There's a man and a woman in the boat. They've stopped rowing. There's something—The boat's shaking. They've fallen into the water, and something's in there with them."

"*What's* in the water? Is it sharks?"

"No, I can't—"

Santiago didn't wait to hear more. He was already rushing to the ship's prow, straining his eyes to get a better view. Veiga was right that there was something in the water with the two people, but he couldn't make out—

Then his stomach dropped. A seal.

Briony, you stubborn woman, I thought you were going to stay on the ship! How could you risk your life yet again?

He groaned inwardly, asking himself why he was shocked at the discovery. *After all, she's proven time and time again that she's willing to give everything away to save someone. I just hope Costa isn't too much for her.*

"Well, Mendes? Can you see what it is?" Cardoso yelled.

Santiago turned to the commodore with an innocent look. "No, I've no idea. It's moving too fast to get a good look at it."

BANG!

Santiago felt his blood turn to ice at the sound. The one moment he'd looked away—

He returned his gaze to the front, only feeling warmth in his body again when he realized Costa had missed and Briony was all right. *That was far too close.*

"Comodoro, can't you make this ship go faster!"

Then he saw Briony pull Costa under, and he almost leaped into the water after them. He only managed to hold himself back by reminding his anxious mind that he would still get there faster by ship. His thoughts swirled as every second they didn't resurface felt like a lifetime.

But then Costa reappeared, swimming toward Lucia, who reached out to pull him back into the rowboat. He grabbed her right hand, and then his other hand lifted out of the water with—

Santiago felt all the air escape his lungs as he watched the knife pierce his sister's chest, embedding itself in her heart. Time seemed to slow as he stared at the girl ahead of them, only just seventeen, always so full of life and laughter—now being yanked out of the boat and thrown into the water like she was nothing.

Briony's head broke the surface right after that, but as soon as she saw Lucia, she, too, seemed to freeze in shock.

Costa, on the other hand, said something to the seal that Santiago couldn't quite discern before turning to the boat and getting inside. Tears spilled down Santiago's cheeks as he wished this was somehow all a dream and he'd wake up back in Everton, his sister safe and sound. And then he saw the gun.

No, not again. Regaining his mobility, Santiago drew out his weapon, took aim, and fired, hitting Costa in the wrist. The captain groaned and dropped his pistol into the water, grabbing at his wound.

The seal turned to see where the shot had come from, and when her eyes met Santiago's, the strain on his chest lessened a bit and he found he could breathe again. She quickly vanished below the water as they continued to approach the second boat, and Santiago turned his attention to Lucia.

"Santiago . . . ," Lucia cried, but her voice was so weak, so quiet. She was barely staying afloat, and her eyelids were heavy.

Santiago jumped from the ship and swam to her, faster than he'd ever swum in his life. He grasped hold of her and got her into the boat. He barely even noticed the captain's presence at that point and didn't worry that the snake would try anything else now that Cardoso's men had their own pistols trained on him.

"I'm sorry, Brother. I . . . I should have trusted you. After you sent me away on the boat, I . . . I changed my mind and told Adriano to take us back—"

"Shh, don't talk," Santiago whispered, trying to stop the tears that were still flowing freely from his eyes.

But Lucia shook her head. "What happened? What was that sound earlier? And the seal in the water—why did it attack us?"

"It doesn't matter now. We have to get you to Cardoso's ship so you can get help."

"I'm so sorry," Lucia said again, but this time, her words were so faint Santiago could barely hear them. "I'm . . ."

Santiago watched, helpless, as Lucia's eyes fluttered shut and her chest stilled. He shook her to rouse her, but there was no response. She was gone. All that he held in his arms now was an empty shell.

A guttural cry broke forth from his lips, rising through the air until it pierced the very clouds.

"Agh, calm down! She was such a nuisance, anyway," Costa snarled.

Santiago's eyes narrowed to slits as his vision turned red. "What did you say?" And before anyone realized it, his hands were around the man's throat.

"Mendes, stop! We have to bring him to trial, and we can't do that if you kill him now," Cardoso shouted from one of his own rowboats as his men prepared to drop it into the water.

"I. Don't. Care." Santiago squeezed harder, enjoying how Costa's face started changing color.

"There's so much evidence against him that there's no way for him to get out of this, Mendes. Do this the right way. The way your sister would have wanted."

Santiago paused, looking down at his sister's lifeless body. She seemed so serene now, and if not for the paleness in her cheeks and the wound in her chest, she would almost look like she was merely sleeping. *What I would give to make it so!*

But a small voice in his mind told him that Cardoso was right. *I'm no murderer, and I'm not going to let my hatred turn me into one.*

With a sigh, he released Costa, who promptly dropped to his knees as he attempted to catch his breath.

"Answer this for me, then, Costa. Why did you want to

345

marry my sister in the first place?" Santiago asked.

Costa looked up with overt disgust. "For your title, of course. The one you wanted to pretend didn't exist. After the attempt on the king's life failed and my family was executed, I knew I'd lost all chance of coming into my birthright as a Távora. My only other option was to marry into nobility, and your sister was the most obvious choice. You didn't want to be noble, so I figured I could convince you to give up your rights and hand them over to the two of us once we wed. Or I could just kill you if you didn't agree and the title would transfer over anyway."

Santiago gritted his teeth, part of him regretting having asked the question. *It's not that surprising, but it just sounds so heartless coming out of his mouth. How did I ever mistake him for a friend?*

Santiago turned away, but his gaze happened to land upon Lucia again, which made the lump in his throat return full force. He shut his eyes tightly, unwilling to allow any more tears to fall in front of the man who'd stolen his entire family.

A hand on his shoulder startled him, and he jumped away before realizing it was Cardoso. Santiago had been so entrenched in his grief that he hadn't even registered the sounds of the commodore's boat approaching or even of the commodore joining him in Costa's vessel.

There was pity in Cardoso's eyes as he said, "We'll get your sister aboard the *São Nicolau*. Then you can take her home."

Home. When Santiago heard the word, Briony's face filled his mind. He knew Cardoso had been speaking of Aveiro, but without Lucia there, all his ties to the physical place had snapped like the broken ropes of his ship. Now, more than ever, he knew that Briony, and Briony alone, was his home. His eyes shifted back to the spot where she'd been, but it was just empty sea. The seal was nowhere to be found.

***

Briony slipped away, overwhelmed with guilt at the death of yet another person she'd cared about. And this one was someone Santiago held dear, making it all the worse. She took

346

one last glance at him, unable to cry in this form but still feeling the urge to as she watched Santiago mourn his sister. Briony had no words to comfort him, no solution to ease his pain. *Especially na when I was the cause o' it.*

At least Costa's true self had become known and he was now in custody. After everything he'd done, Comodoro Cardoso would make sure the man came to justice, and that also meant that Santiago's name would soon be cleared. He would be able to live freely again without fear.

So there's no reason fer me to remain any longer.

Perhaps it was a blessing to be in seal form at that moment, for even though she couldn't shed tears, she also didn't have to try to find a way to say goodbye. It was incredibly difficult, but she knew that was what she had to do. After failing to protect Lucia, she didn't have the strength or courage to face Santiago again.

Santiago may think he loves me, but what if he starts to resent me over time? And what if my "otherness" becomes too much fer him? Nay, 'tis far better fer him to forget about me and leave all these bad memories behind.

With a heavy heart, the selkie submerged once more and started her journey back to Everton. Back to a small town that most people wouldn't give a second glance. A town that she'd grown to love more than she'd ever thought she would. A town of stubbornness and pride but also resilience and determination. Briony was sure the village would recover, and she would be right there to help it in every way she could.

Epilogue

Six weeks later

"Are you ready, Mistress Fairborn?"

Briony blinked a few times and turned to Vicar Peterson, who held out the cog[40] expectantly.

"O' course." Briony grabbed it and took a great swallow of ale. She blinked a few times as she tried to recover, unused to such a strong brew.

"Here you go, Mr. Levins." Everyone cheered as she passed the drink to the old man, who chugged it for so long that everyone thought he would pass out.

But then he burped and muttered something about poor-quality ale.

Briony laughed, for once enjoying his cantankerousness. After all, a wedding was too jovial of an occasion to be anything but happy. *Especially one this important.*

Briony's gaze slipped to Adaira and John Burgess, both of whom were glowing with happiness as all of Everton rejoiced in their nuptials. They would no doubt be the talk of the town for several weeks, and for good reason. It wasn't every day that someone in a town this small got married.

Soon Mr. Levins passed the cog along to the next person

---

[40] A large wooden cup containing ale traditionally passed around to guests at Orcadian weddings.

sunwise,[41] which continued until the rest of the town had gotten a swig.

Once that tradition was out of the way, everyone rose to dance by the light of the fire. Other towns would have held their gathering indoors, but here in Everton, people preferred to do their dancing outside, where they could see the sky.

Briony thought back to how worried Adaira had been a few hours before, talking of her dress and hair but mostly about the food. *The poor dear got herself so worked up that I wasn' sure she'd make it through the ceremony without fainting.*

But Adaira's stress had melted away as soon as the vicar had pronounced them husband and wife.

Briony smiled as she watched Adaira twirl in her new husband's arms. *Aye, how could anyone na be happy while watching those two dance?*

But then Briony's mind shot back to the last time she'd danced.

And to the man she'd never gotten the chance to dance with.

Briony suppressed a groan of frustration, annoyed at her own sentimentality. Thinking of Santiago only brought misery, yet she didn't seem able to stop herself.

Why am I still so upset about this? If he was coming back, he would have done it by now. This is what's best fer both o' us.

"Briony? Are you all right?" Adaira appeared out of nowhere with a gentle hand on Briony's arm.

The young midwife opened her mouth to lie, but as she looked at her friend's face, she knew she couldn't do it. Ever since she'd returned to Everton, Briony had relied upon Adaira more than ever. Their argument from before had been easily forgotten, and the two of them had promised not to have any more secrets from each other.

"Nay, I'm na. I just . . . I think I need to be alone fer a while. I'm sorry."

Adaira patted Briony's shoulder. "No need to be sorry, dearie. 'Tis na easy to let go o' someone and move on. It takes time, often much more than we expect. Go on, and I'll see you

---

[41] In the direction of the sun's movement; clockwise.

soon."

Briony smiled gratefully, glad Adaira understood enough that she didn't need to say more.

She nodded and slipped away from the festivities there on Mary's Hill. She debated going to her rocky outcrop to look out over the sea but decided a dip in the water in seal form would be better medicine for her aching soul. She'd been doing it almost daily since she'd returned, though always at night when fewer eyes were around. And even though it never took away all Briony's pain, sinking beneath the waves usually brought her a small measure of comfort.

She'd almost reached home to retrieve her pelt when a flash of movement caught her eye. She stopped dead in her tracks and stared incredulously at the sight before her: a lone ship coming up near the shore below her cottage.

What would a ship be doing coming in at this hour? She glanced behind her at the other villagers, but they were all so caught up in their revelry that no one seemed to have noticed the new arrival.

Briony took a second look at the ship, and her heart almost stopped beating at what she saw. A white flag was flying at the top of it. A white flag with a large red crest.

It can' be. It can'. . . . But what if . . . Then, as if her own lightning had struck her, Briony's heart leaped in her chest and began pounding at top speed. She flew down the path, losing her scarf in the process but not caring in the slightest. Not when there was a chance *he* would be there.

And as her bare feet touched the wooden planks of the dock, a person stepped off the ship's gangplank. A person with pale-green eyes and blond hair.

"Hello, Briony."

Before he had even finished speaking, Briony was sprinting the rest of the way and throwing herself into his arms. Warmth spread through her as Santiago returned the embrace.

But—

"What are you doing here, Santiago?" Briony pulled back as she remembered not only how excruciating these last six weeks had been but also the pain in his eyes when he'd lost his sister. Pain she still blamed herself for.

351

The man looked away, his face full of shame, which made Briony even more confused. He ran a hand through his hair and took a deep breath before speaking. "I know I don't have any right to come here, not after being away for so long. I'm sorry. After Costa's arrest, Cardoso took us straight to Portugal for the trial, and as an important witness, I couldn't leave until everything was out in the open. I wanted to come back sooner, but I had to make sure justice was done. And I had to take care of the . . . funeral arrangements."

He lifted his gaze and tried to lock eyes with her again, but it was her turn to look away in shame.

"Santiago, I . . . I can' tell you how sorry I am. I-I should have done better, moved faster. If I'd just . . ."

Fingers at her lips put a stop to her sputtering. She looked up, afraid of what she would see. But rather than anger, she saw concern. "What are you talking about? You can't possibly think what happened to Lucia is your fault?"

A tear spilled from Briony's eye then, gliding down her cheek until it reached Santiago's fingers. Understanding lit up his face, and he moved his hand to wipe away the trail of moisture.

"Amorzinho, don't believe that a second longer. The only person responsible for Lucia's death has already paid for it with his life. You are *blameless*. Please don't carry a burden that was never meant to be yours."

Briony swallowed hard, trying to control herself, but it was like Santiago's words opened a veritable flood of tears as she felt the weight of guilt lift from her shoulders. Soon she was sobbing into the crook of his neck as he whispered words of solace into her ear.

When she was finally able to calm down, she leaned back and smiled up at him, still having a little trouble believing he was really there in the flesh. But then she frowned as she noticed something. "Santiago, where's your ship? Was it too damaged to be fixed?"

Santiago gave her an embarrassed grin and put a hand on the back of his neck. "Well, to tell you the truth, I sold her. This ship just came to drop me off and will be sailing back to Portugal in the morning."

"You what?"

He chuckled a bit. "Yes, I decided it was time for something new. I've known for a long time that I wasn't cut out for a life in Aveiro, but it wasn't until recently that I realized I'd like to put down some roots somewhere. And the life of a merchant didn't seem like the right fit for that. . . ." He trailed off and looked at her hopefully.

"But what about your title?"

"It's still mine, technically. I haven't decided yet whether I'm going to keep it."

"So . . . you came here?"

He leaned a bit closer. "Yes, I did."

"To put down . . . roots?"

Santiago nodded, leaning ever closer until their noses were almost touching. Briony knew her cheeks were beet red, but she couldn't look away. She also couldn't stop the smile growing upon her face.

"And what sort o' roots did you have in mind?"

Santiago smirked. "Now, Briony Fairborn, I would think you know the answer to that. After all, I've told you before that you can see right through me."

Briony bit her lip and broke eye contact as embarrassment made her face even hotter. "Perhaps I'd just like a wee bit more certainty. So that I know I'm na imagining things."

She braved another look, but then her eyes widened—

Softness overtook her mouth as Santiago closed the distance between them. She returned his kiss immediately, her hands soon pressing against his back to draw him nearer. Fire sparked through her blood, spreading through her veins until she felt like her entire body would be consumed with it—

And that was when Santiago pulled back, though he seemed reluctant as his lips left hers. He smiled down at her, and his voice was rough as he said, "Did that make it more certain? Briony, I could never put down roots anywhere unless it's with you. If you'll have me, that is."

Briony returned the smile, but then she gave him a thoughtful look. "Well, I might be able to be persuaded. Except . . . there's a question I'll need you to answer first."

Santiago raised an eyebrow. "And what's that?"

She leaned in like she was about to share a secret. "Are you good company?"

He laughed, no doubt remembering the last time they'd had this conversation, though their roles had been reversed. They had come a long way since that day when they'd first walked together.

"I'm afraid I can't answer that. You'll have to find out for yourself."

Briony gave him a quick kiss on the lips before jumping away with a laugh. "Hmm, we shall see."

About The Heart of Everton Inn

An innkeeper afraid of love. A widowed farmer desperate to protect his unusual son. Will their shared hurts heal or destroy each other?

Return to Everton for the story hidden in the shadows of *The Secret of Drulea Cottage*. . . .

In a Scottish village where mythical creatures walk amongst humans, the innkeeper's daughter works hard to maintain her neighbors' respect. But between running Everton Inn and protecting her best friend's secret, Adaira's life is filled to the brim, and it's all she can do to keep everything under control.

When Adaira's first love returns to town with mysterious new friends, her orderly life begins to crack. Skeletons from her past start creeping out of the closet, skeletons that threaten much more than just her reputation.

When recently widowed John Burgess arrives in Everton, he doesn't intend to stay long. Relationships are dangerous, and keeping his distance from the village residents is necessary to protect his son.

But the more time he spends there, the more John realizes raising William alone might be more than he can handle. And that Everton Inn holds a magic of its own, one that could keep him there forever if he's not careful.

Only together can Adaira and John prevent William from being lost, but that may require more honesty than either of them is willing to give.

Author's Note

Thank you for taking the time to read my debut novel. It is such a joy to share this labor of love with the world. I hope the story intrigued, excited, entertained, and surprised you as you went through its pages. There are many ways you could have chosen to spend your time, and it's very humbling that your choice was reading my work.

You may be wondering why I chose to write about selkies instead of more popular legendary creatures, like mermaids or fairies. I've always found selkies fascinating, but I wasn't satisfied with the fiction I found on them. Consequently, I decided to create the tale that I would want to read and one that I hope you enjoyed as well.

Now that you've completed *The Secret of Drulea Cottage*, please consider leaving a review to let me know what you thought of it.

And be sure to join my newsletter at www.clairekohlerbooks.com for news on upcoming releases and exclusive *Betwixt the Sea and Shore* content.

Printed in Great Britain
by Amazon

43589181R00209